Wasting Away

FOREVER YOURS SEQUEL

Melissa M. Marlow

MM Marlow

AuthorHouse™
1663 Liberty Drive
Bloomington, IN 47403
www.authorhouse.com
Phone: 1-800-839-8640

© 2011 Melissa M. Marlow. All rights reserved.

No part of this book may be reproduced, stored in a retrieval system, or transmitted by any means without the written permission of the author.

First published by AuthorHouse 05/02/2011

ISBN: 978-1-4520-9314-7 (sc)
ISBN: 978-1-4520-9315-4 (hc)
ISBN: 978-1-4520-9316-1 (e)

Library of Congress Control Number: 2010916427

Printed in the United States of America

This book is printed on acid-free paper.

Certain stock imagery © Thinkstock.

Because of the dynamic nature of the Internet, any Web addresses or links contained in this book may have changed since publication and may no longer be valid. The views expressed in this work are solely those of the author and do not necessarily reflect the views of the publisher, and the publisher hereby disclaims any responsibility for them.

Contents

To Be Alone:	vii
1. The Other One	1
2. What is it?	11
3. Checking In	20
4. Irritated	33
5. Reading Me	44
6. Staying Busy	53
7. Needs	63
8. Frail	73
9. Committed	85
10. It Will Wait	97
11. Heart Aches	110
12. So In Love	123
13. Broken Plan	134
14. Surprise	143
15. How Close	155
16. Last Attempt	169
17. A Good Day	178
18. Sharing Souls	190
19. Cancer	196
20. Girl Talk	207
21. The Guard Dog	218
22. So Tired	230
23. Staying Busy	240
24. No More Goofing Around	247
25. A Day In The Sun	258
26. New Young Hottie	267
27. Easing The Pain	277
28. Over Reacting	289

29. Restrictions Not Restricting	296
30. A Little Temperature	309
31. A Little Magic	316
32. The Commitment	326
33. Doing Better	335
34. A Little Fun	345
35. The Ring	353
36. Doctor Appointment	367
37. Relieving the Stress	376
38. Shorts	384
39. A Little Stubborn	395
40. The Surge	403
41. Holding	415
42. Oh The Pain	422
43. Where Is The Pain	431
44. The Magic of a Dream	441
45. Desperate to Feel Better	452
46. Getting Weaker	460
47. A Little Pain	468
48. The Surprise	477
Characters	485
Upcoming Sequel- Growing Tears	487

To Be Alone:

What does it mean to be alone to you? Does it mean free time to spend alone to do whatever you want? Or does it mean emptiness, a hole in your heart that engulfs you till you have nothing left.

The desire to which I possessed for James was unexplainable. The kissing, wow, the kissing did so many things to me. I could get lost for days just doing that with him, but he was good at bringing me to the dream world of wanting to give him everything. I wanted him to give me pleasure as much as I wanted to give him pleasure.

He gave me so much happiness. Our time playing games, talking about everything, the dancing, and the learning about each other gave me the security of a best friend. We have been making plans for a future because it helped me see what I could do with my life. Everything I did with him felt so good. He always knows how to touch me just right to make my heart race, and he knows how to comfort me in his company. The way he slightly touched my lower back to guide me, the kissing on my hand to show me he adored me, the slight touch to my face, the tracing of his face on mine, the way he placed his nose on my neck and moved to my ear to take in my scent made me feel wanted, and the way he looked at me with that wanting in his eyes. He was my protector when he pulled me behind him to block what was coming my way. It was everything about him that made me feel better about myself.

I had changed over the last nine months. I grew from being completely in my own world, a loner, and sad unnoticed girl to this amazing creature that people loved to be around. My confidence in myself had grown to give me strength, which I did not know I had.

My time without James was going to be the loneliest time I could imagine. Now without him, what would happen to me…?

1. The Other One

I walked slowly back to my car. I needed to make a plan how to get through this time alone. I knew James had his phone, but I would wait till he contacted me, or I would just let him feel me. Now that I know he could block me a little when we're apart, if he didn't reply he was busy. I still didn't understand it all. I wish I could feel him, or maybe not. I didn't know what he was going to be going through.

Shit, I feel sick again. I found a bathroom and threw up again. I hope this isn't the flu, and James would get it. That would be really bad.

I walked out of the stall and someone from the airport staff was in there. She asked me if I was okay. I assured her I was fine now, but I washed my face with cold water and rinsed my mouth. I started for the car. I wasn't thinking about James anymore. I just wanted to get home and go to bed. Maybe all this stress was too much and I needed sleep. I got to my car and I was feeling a little better. I opened James's note:

Sarah,
There is an envelope on the side of your mattress where I was sitting last night. It has instructions inside. I love you more than you will ever know, and Sarah: 1-2-3-Breath.

Melissa M. Marlow

With all my love,
James

    This is amazing. I have made it this long with no tears, and I wasn't going to have a nervous breakdown. I drove home thinking about the envelope. What was he up to? By the time I got home I wasn't feeling great again. I was nervous about what he left me. I am glad that the anticipation of him leaving was over. I was driving myself crazy over it. I think that is why I am not feeling well. I got home and the queasiness was back. I drank a large glass of water. Mom wasn't going to be home for awhile, so I was going to go to bed. I laid down and reached for the envelope, shit! It was the one his mom gave him.

    I opened it. Yep, the money was all there. I pulled the note out and tucked the money back under the mattress.

My sweet Sarah,

This is for our future and I didn't need any of it. Deposit $300 a week in a bank account until it's all in there. It may look suspicious so smile and say 'waitress'. They won't think anything of it that way. As for you, my little girl, I hope you will wear the ring even if it's only around your neck. I am so in love with you. There is another envelope, go ahead and open it. Each letter is marked with a date on it. Don't open each one till the day it says. Please follow the instructions and remember, Sarah, 1-, 2-, 3- Breathe.

Don't forget to put the ring on the necklace. You wouldn't want to explain this one to your mom and dad.

With all my love,
James

    I gazed at the ring. It was too big on the top of my finger. I could hurt someone with it. I pulled it off. My heart was pounding like I was losing him when I did this. I took the necklace off and put the ring on it, tucking it in my shirt. The hole filled a little. I rolled over and hugged my pillow and put the paper to my face with hopes of smelling him. No luck, but I had to sleep now. I set my alarm for 5 p.m. I was working tonight.

I woke in a rush. What was I forgetting? Oh yeah, work. I didn't have time to think of how I was feeling but I didn't have to run to the bathroom. Good, I must have been tired. I went to work and managed to not think about James other than enough to make me smile, touching my chest where the ring laid. I got home at 10 p.m.

Mom was there in her chair, "Did you get James to the airport okay?"

"Yep."

"Are you okay?"

"Surprisingly, I'm doing okay. I was a little sick this morning at his moms place, but I think it was nerves."

"You got *sick*?"

"Yeah, it came on suddenly, but I didn't sleep much and I was a little torn over him leaving. I feel better now."

"You actually were throwing up?"

"Yeah, a few times today, but I took a nap and I feel better."

She looked at me funny, but didn't say anything.

"Well good night."

"You're going to bed already?"

"Yeah, I think I got sick from being so tired. I have to work all day tomorrow and I don't want that to happen again. I really hate throwing up."

"Okay, but let me know how you are feeling in the morning."

"Yep, I feel better already."

I slept almost dreamless. The dream was back, but James just held me. I think I was feeling very happy knowing we were going to be together forever, so I was content on letting it stay there.

Day 1 envelope:

My love is not found, until I lost
You may look, but never see
The love around you
Saying it was meant to be me.
With all my love,
James

Day 2 envelope:

Is it possible, or should I wonder
The thought of you
To forget, not possible
I will not try.
With all my love,
James

Day 3 envelope: I smiled as I opened this one.

You may hold my hand for a while
You may hold my eyes to linger
You may hold my body for a smile
But my heart
Is yours forever.
With all my love,
James

These three days went without feeling an ounce of being sick. Mom kept asking, but I was feeling fine. We were going up north to see dad. What was I going to do without James there? I would hang out with Danelle; she would be happy about this. She was feeling neglected. I remembered to grab days four and five. I hadn't heard from him at all, but I wasn't desperate in my thoughts, and he was busy.

We got up north about 8 p.m. We went to Sherburn's. I found Danelle and we went down to the dock. She wanted to ask me questions, but I think she was afraid I would be sad. I asked her about Tommy.

"So, does he come up here often?"

"Yeah, every weekend; why are you asking me about Tommy?"

"It's nothing."

"What?"

"Danelle, that's how James and I started, completely arguing and disagreeing about everything."

"Really?"

"Yeah, do you like him?"

She giggled, "No, he's like a big brother."

I smiled at her and raised my eyebrows. In a way, that's what I told her about James when she asked.

"No, no way, I don't like boys like that. Sarah?"

I was smiling at her, not believing her.

Danelle was trying to change the subject, "So, James left?"

"Yep."

"And you're okay?"

"Yep, so far."

"You really like him?"

"Yeah, I do." I couldn't say that without smiling.

"Did you have *sex*?"

I couldn't believe she was asking me this. "Yes and no."

"What do you mean?"

"Danelle, I really don't want to talk about it."

"Because it's too juicy or because it will make you sad?"

I tried to grin, but the tears started to well up in my eyes. Shit, I was doing so well.

She let me off the hook, "Let's go play pool, and be around people."

I was relieved, "Sounds good to me."

We headed back to the house part of the resort. She put her arm around my shoulders as best she could, "I kind of do like Tommy. Promise not to rat me out."

I smiled still holding back the tears. "Try to take it really slow, or you will be a puddle like me."

She laughed as we walked in. Brian and Pat were there. They both treated me like I was going to break. I sat down by Pat, "Haven't heard from you in a while, how's it going?"

"Good I guess, I didn't think it was okay to call you anymore."

"Pat, I can still have friends, right Brian?"

As I turned to him I noticed he was staring at me. I tried again, "Brian, I can still have friends, right?"

He smiled and avoided my gaze. "Yep, the best of friends."

I didn't know what his problem was, but I pulled Danelle toward the back to go play pool.

Brian followed us till we were in the kitchen. "The other one is here."

Danelle stopped and pulled me to stop walking. I had no idea he was talking to me, but I turned around to see why Danelle stopped me.

She said, "I don't think we should play pool."

This confused me, but I was up for anything, "What do you want to do then?"

Brian repeated himself, "The other one is here." Then he pulled me in front of him to look at me in the eyes.

"What do you mean the other one?"

He didn't take his eyes off of me as he spoke to Danelle, "Danelle, can I talk to Sarah for a minute?"

"No!"

She turned to me, "Let's go back down by the beach and hang out. Or we could, um… Brian, we could play a game of basketball."

He smiled, "Danelle, that's a good idea."

They were acting really weird, "What is going on with you two?"

Danelle was disgusted, "Fine, but don't be a jerk. If you make her cry, I'll tell mom."

He finally moved his attention to her, "I won't, go get Pat and the ball. We'll be right out."

I crossed my arms and waited impatiently. He walked closer to me but leaned on the stove. "Did something happen with you and Jason again?"

"No!"

"Sarah, are you sure?"

"Positive. Why?" I was a little short because I didn't like what he was implying.

"He is here, sitting with your mom and dad."

"Oh, basketball sounds great."

I took him by the arm and led him outside. Danelle smiled. We played two on two. Danelle and Brian, against Pat and me. I sucked, so I felt bad for Pat. Brian stopped for a minute and I followed his eyes to the road. Jason was leaning against his truck watching. I hip checked Brian and took a shot. It knocked him back into play. That was the first basket I made. I got a high five from Pat. Jason wasn't budging.

I was guarding Brian and he was dribbling, "Do you want me to say anything?"

"Nope, play."

He took a shot and I stopped it. Pat ran over to give me a high five again, but Danelle grabbed the ball and Brian lifted her to get the shot.

Pat was embarrassed, "Sorry about that."

I laughed, but I glanced over to Jason. He smiled and walked back in.

Brian walked over to us, "What was that about?"

My mind was going wild thinking of all the reasons he would show up without Kylie. I smiled at both of them, "I have no idea."

I grabbed the ball and started playing again. We played until it was completely dark. I sat down on a cooler outside. Jason's truck was still there.

Pat walked over, "We could play pool?"

I didn't want this to be about me so I was going to leave it up to Danelle, "It's your day, what do you want to do?"

"Pool sounds good."

We started walking in and Brian pulled my arm. Pat saw this and stopped too. "Sarah, he's still in there."

I evaluated Pat and Brian and realized something. "Kylie is not here to kill me, and he is still friends with James, so I don't think he will push any issues. It will be fine." I put my arms around both their necks, "What are you guys afraid of? You're both bigger than him anyway, and if that fails dad's not going to let anything happen, right?"

I started walking in and Danelle was laughing. We filed out to the game room and played pool till it was time to go. I had a lot of fun, no flirting, but pure innocent fun. I did notice he was watching me all night long.

Mom and Dad asked if I was ready. I was more than ready to go, especially with Jason watching over me all night, "Yep."

Danelle walked with me to my car. Of course, mom was going to ride with dad. Jason was waiting by his truck. I didn't want to know for what, but Brian and Pat were right behind Danelle and me. I turned around, "Pat, did you need a ride?"

"No, I'm staying here tonight."

Danelle got a great big smile on her face. "Sarah, you could stay too."

I could see Jason from behind them. He stood up shook his head no.

"That sounds like fun." I would have liked to stay, but I saw Jason as he held up the ring finger. Was he here to make sure I was being good? "But, I am really *tired* and I would fall asleep anyway. Maybe I will tomorrow."

I got in my car and they were walking away. I was desperate to keep them there with me, "Hey guys talk to me until mom and dad are ready to go. I don't want to leave till I know they will get there the same time as me."

Brian smiled. Pat came back with him.

Danelle inquired, "What do you think he's going to do?"

I smiled at Danelle, "Nothing, I'm being paranoid, night then."

I closed the door and pulled away. Jason didn't get in his truck that I could see. I was relieved. I hate that James was not here to hide behind. This was going to be hard.

I pulled in and went in the trailer. *Okay, where are mom and dad? Why were they taking so long?* I turned on the TV and threw a movie in. I changed to lounge shorts and a t-shirt. I grabbed a really light blanket and curled up on the chair. I heard the truck pull in. *Good, mom and dad are here.* I took a deep breath and closed my eyes. They walked in and Jason followed. Great!

Dad smiled at me, "So, James got to the airport okay?"

"Yep."

"How are you doing?"

"I'm okay dad. I think I'll go to bed now."

"Wait. Tell me about his mother's house."

I was happy he was interested and couldn't wait to tell him how great it was. "It was really great. It had a big pool. She had rooms for each of them. There were three boats and a floating dock. Have you ever seen a floating dock? And it was beautiful all of it.

"I talked to Clarissa."

Oh, this isn't going to be good. "Really?" *Where was he going with this?*

Jason sat on the couch and watched my face as I answered dad's questions.

"So, James has his own apartment in the basement?"

"It's not just for James; it is also Will's apartment." Oh shit, I walked into that one; I was going to try and recover, "From my understanding."

Did I tell mom this? How much did I say and how much did Clarissa say? Shit. Jason, wipe the grin off your face was all I could think. *James, help me, I need you right now, so bad. Please, James, please hear me.* I pulled my phone out to see if he replied, but there was nothing.

Dad continued to ask me questions, "So, was it nice?"

"Yeah the whole house was nice. Clarissa's bathroom was bigger than this trailer."

"You checked out the whole house?" He was being careful how he was talking to me. I was getting irritated by it.

"Yeah, it's in Minnetonka; I couldn't help myself."

He laughed a little, "I heard you had a pool accident?"

I knew that one came from mom and he was getting down to the real questions, "Yeah, a little clumsy of me, but no lights were on and I didn't know there was one there."

Jason was laughing. I was more irritated that he was in on this whole conversation.

I knew dad wasn't pleased, so I tried to comfort him, "I *did* call mom multiple times to keep her updated."

"Yeah, she did say that."

I got up and headed for the door, I wasn't feeling very well. I really think it is the stress. Yep, I am going to be sick.

Dad asked, "Where are you going?"

I could barley answer, "Bathroom."

I ran out the door. I wasn't going to make it to the outhouse. I went to the side of it and threw up. *Great!* At least it was cooler out here than in the trailer. I leaned against the outhouse to gain my composure.

"Are you okay?" It was Jason's voice I was hearing. I really didn't want him here.

"Yeah, I think I might have a touch of the flu or something."

I walked past him to go back to the trailer.

"Sarah?"

I kept walking. I really didn't want him here.

He sped up to catch up with me. "You're not pregnant are you?"

"No."

"Are you sure?"

"Positive."

"How can you be positive?"

He was trying to be nice but it was making my stomach turn.

"Jason, I'm not feeling…" I ran back to the side of the outhouse and got sick again.

He came to stand by me holding my hair back, but not touching me anywhere. I didn't want him here; I wanted James.

I leaned up against the outhouse again. "Thanks, but I'm okay now."

He put his hand on my forehead, "You're kind of warm."

I didn't say anything and walked away from him towards the trailer. I needed to lie down. I went in and curled up in the chair.

Dad was eyeing me, "So, did you see the apartment?"

"Dad, I'm really not feeling good. You can ask me all the questions you want in the morning." I closed my eyes.

"Here you go." I opened my eyes. Jason was holding out a glass of water for me.

"Thanks." I took a drink and put it on the floor next to me and closed my eyes. I was thinking how bad I would feel if James were sick too. I hope I didn't give him whatever I had because this really sucked. *James I need you. Please let me hear your voice.* I covered with the blanket and held the ring in my hand under my shirt and concentrated on him as hard as I could. It didn't take long to drift off.

2. What is it?

I woke to my phone buzzing. My heart was beating so hard. I answered, "James, I am so sorry for bothering you."

"You can never bother me, my sweet Sarah. Are you okay?" His voice was so warm and comforting.

I closed my eyes to picture him there with me, "Now I am." but I sniffled a little because I had been crying in my sleep.

"Please don't do that." He was pleading with me.

"I was doing well 'til now."

"Sarah, I miss you."

That didn't help the crying because I wanted him to be here with me so bad, but remembered why I was desperate to talk to him. "James, have you been sick at all?"

"What?"

"Remember when I got sick the day I was bringing you to the airport?"

"Yeah," his voice sounded nervous.

"I have been getting sick off and on since then. I thought maybe I had the flu and I was worried I gave it to you."

"Do me a favor and go to the Doctor on Monday. I feel fine, maybe a little sore. This is harder than I thought."

"Do you like it?"

"I love it. I feel like I can do anything."

He made me smile, just what I needed. "James, you can. I am *so* proud of you."

"It's only been three days."

"I know, but…I know you're doing this for us."

"You are the best. Are you doing okay now?"

I took a deep breath and smiled, "Yeah, it's really weird. I only get queasy when I am getting a little stressed."

Now he sounded concerned, "What do you mean?"

"Like tonight, dad was drilling me about your mom's house, and you having your own apartment and it just came on. I don't have any control over it. I was really sad when you left and I got sick at the airport too."

"Sarah, how many *times* have you been sick?" He was sounding more concerned than I thought needed to be.

"I don't know. I haven't been counting."

"Do you get sick every day?"

"No, only when I'm stressed out."

"Please, go to the doctor, and keep track of when you're getting sick."

"Why, what are you thinking?"

"It's nothing, but keep track and I will try to call you tomorrow. I've got to go. I have to run five miles in two hours from now."

"I love you, oh wait. I love the notes."

"You are everything to me, Sarah, goodnight."

"Goodnight James."

I hung up the phone and curled back up on the chair and closed my eyes.

Then I heard Jason, not realizing he was still here, "Are you feeling better?"

I opened my eyes to glare at him, "You're still here?"

"Yep." He wasn't being smug. He was more like concerned, so I eased up a little.

I closed my eyes again, "Yeah, doing better now."

"So, are you pregnant?"

Now I was irritated, "No, I'm positive and I need to sleep or you're going to make me sick again."

"How can you be positive?"

I was going to lose my temper, "Because, Jason, we didn't do that! Now please let me sleep."

"Do you mean at all, or just last weekend?"

"Jason, not now; I need to sleep." I closed my eyes and blocked him out of my existence. It wasn't that hard because I fell asleep not knowing if he asked me any more questions.

I woke kind of early. I pulled out Day 4 note:

I have loved you all my life,
So when I found you
I wondered how this could be true
Then I knew you would be my wife.
With all my love,

James

I noticed Jason was sleeping on the couch. I eased off the chair and moved quietly to the kitchen for some breakfast. I felt fine again. This is really weird.

Dad came out and started the coffee. "What are you doing up so early?"

"I was hungry."

"So, you are still eating?"

I was beginning my day on the defense again. "Why is everyone obsessed with my eating? I eat, I exercise, and I eat more."

He smiled and was letting me off the hook, "So, what are your plans today?"

This sounded like he was lecturing me because James and I were planning something. I wondered if I should try my luck. "I was hoping to go see Carl this morning for a little bit and then hanging with Danelle again."

"You still want to see Carl without James?"

"Yes, please."

"You need to get back to normal, Sarah."

I hated my normal life. It was boring and I was nothing without James. How can he want me to go back to that nothingness? "What is *normal*, Dad?"

"Having fun with people your age and who are here. It's not like you and James are going to be together forever."

I glared at him; how dare he, try to put doubt in my head. I knew what I wanted. "Did you think we were kidding when I said we were getting married in two years?" I was trying to stay calm.

Jason sat up and said out loud, "You are not getting married at 18!"

"Okay, no more discussion on what I should or shouldn't do in two years from now! Can I go or not?"

"SARAH!" I irritated dad.

"Fine!" I walked into the first bedroom and got dressed. It was still pretty warm and the nauseous feeling was coming back. It's got be stress. I didn't feel like I was going to throw up, but I did feel a little ill. I put my hair in a ponytail and walked out.

I tried to be more pleasant and nice, "Did you decide if I can go or not?"

"You really want to go?"

"I wouldn't have asked if I didn't want to go, and I did ask. I could have lied."

"Fine, go, but be back by noon."

"Great!" I grabbed my purse and headed out the door.

Jason came after me, "How are you feeling?"

"I feel okay today."

"You ate cereal?"

"Yep, fine."

He was a little more hesitant on asking, "Why were you sick?"

"I honestly don't know, Jason."

"Do you love him?"

I turned to him. I could see the hurt in his face. I did feel bad, "Jason I am so sorry, but I only have till noon. I need to see Carl."

He opened the door to my car and I got in. "Sarah?"

"Jason, please my time is limited."

"This is *not* the end of the discussion." He was very firm.

I wanted to lighten the mood and said playfully, "It is if I have anything to do with it."

He closed my door and I drove off.

I went to the Reservation first. I didn't know how fast Carl would be out of the hospital. I knocked on the door waiting impatiently.

Sam answered it, "Sarah why are you knocking, you're family now." He pulled me into the house.

"I wanted to see if your dad was home yet."

"No, he'll be at the hospital for about three weeks."

I turned to leave without another word. I was on a mission to see Carl.

"Where are you going?"

"I am going to see him."

Sam was right behind me, "Right now?"

"Yep."

"Can I come with? Clarissa already took Tamara and I'm here alone."

I turned on him, "Are you ready? I only have a little time."

"Yeah."

He followed me to the car. "Can I drive?"

I chuckled, "No, you're only 15 years old."

"So, I can drive and you let James all the time."

"He's 19. Just get in the car, Sam."

He got in but started with the questions. "Do you know what car she got me?"

I smiled with satisfaction, "Yeah, but I'm not telling you what it is, but you will be happy."

He was smiling but disappointed, "You are cruel."

I smiled guiltily, "Yep."

"Sarah, are you okay?" His posture changed from playful to serious.

"Sam, you have feelings too, right?"

"Yeah! I am stronger than James." He touched my hand.

"Sam, knock it off." I pulled my hand away from him. "I need you to be really serious for a minute. Why did you ask me if I was okay?"

"I can't put my finger on it, but something isn't right."

"Okay, how can you figure out what it is?"

"Have you been sick?"

"I thought I might have the flu, but it comes and goes, and I thought maybe you could tell me what's wrong with me."

He was cautious, "I don't know; I've never tried to do that before."

"James wants me to go to the doctor, but I thought maybe you could figure it out and tell me."

"Have you been throwing up? You should let me touch your stomach."

I looked at him disapproving.

"Well, then you will have to wait for the doctor's advice."

"Promise me you're not going to do anything creepy."

"I promise, Sarah, but I might not be able to tell you if you're pregnant."

"What?"

"Sarah, you and James did it? Wait, you didn't then why do you think you're pregnant?"

"James and Jason are freaking me out. And can you quit reading my mind?"

"I'll try, but it's hard especially since you know."

I pulled up my shirt a little and stared out the side window away from him. He put his hand on my stomach. He didn't say anything and sat there. He moved backed to his seat, "Nope."

"Nope what?"

"No baby in there."

"Okay, then why am I getting sick?"

"I don't know. It doesn't feel like anything I have ever felt before. James is right; go to the doctor."

"So, you do feel something?"

"No, I can tell you don't feel good, that's all."

That didn't help; okay, maybe a little. So, we headed to the hospital.

When we got there I got out. I stopped and wondered, *was he telling me everything he knew?*

"Yes, I am Sarah. I really don't know that it's anything."

I felt better. Maybe it was just nerves and it was from the stress. I couldn't help myself thinking, *Sam, please quit reading my mind.*

"I'm trying, but sometimes I can't tell the difference from when you are talking and when you are thinking. Sometimes it's so strong."

"*That* was a thought Sam." I laughed and he shook his head.

"Its okay, Sam. James does it all the time to me."

"He does that too. I thought he couldn't do that. I thought I was stronger."

"You are. His are feelings, my feelings to be exact. I'm not sure how much he gets from others; I know he does a little, but how much I don't know."

He smiled. He liked being stronger than James.

We walked into the waiting area. Clarissa came to me wrapping her arms around me. "Oh, Sarah, you came even without James."

I smiled at her, "They couldn't keep me away."

"Did you like my home?"

I smiled and my eyes got wide. "Clarissa, I am so sorry but we snooped through the whole house. It's amazing. We went in every room. The funny part was we couldn't find the stairs to the basement. We didn't realize it was separate door."

"How long did you search?"

"For awhile; it was at least half an hour."

She laughed, "I guess I left that part out. Did James like his car?"

"He loved it, but you shouldn't have gotten the motorcycle."

"He didn't care for it?"

I frowned, "He did, but I didn't. Too many people get hurt on them."

"Honey, he's been doing motocross since he was 3 years old." She sounded relieved that it was my complaint.

"Well, I didn't know that, but it's too dangerous."

She smiled at me. "Would you like to see Carl? He's doing so much better."

"Yes, please."

She walked me back to his room.

His face, oh his face was so much like my James. This was going to be hard. The tears welled up in my eyes. He put his arm out for me to come to him. I rushed to him as he pulled my head to his chest.

"Clarissa, my sweet, may we have a minute? I need to talk to my daughter in law."

He directed his attention to me, "Oh, you do love him, don't you?"

I couldn't say anything. The tears were pouring out. I missed him so much already.

He straightened me up. "Now, let me see it."

I couldn't believe he knew.

"The ring… I know he gave it to you."

I pulled the chain out with it on the end.

His sadness showed in his eyes, "Why child are you not wearing it where it should be?"

"I didn't want to have to explain and then they probably wouldn't let me see him again until I am 30 years old. They're not like you and Clarissa; they don't understand."

"You're right. Our beliefs are a little different and when you find the right one, it doesn't matter how old you are, if you truly know."

"I feel it is right that he really loves me and I love him."

"Oh, I feel it too. I also feel something else. Dear, are you okay?"

"I have been a little sick. I think it's just nerves."

He seemed more concerned, "Why do you think that?"

"I only get sick when I am upset."

I could see I shouldn't have told him this. He was getting more upset the more I said. I didn't want to upset him. He already has enough to worry about, like getting better himself.

"Really, I'm okay. I had Sam check, and he didn't feel it."

"Well, if Sam didn't feel it, then there is no reason to worry."

I smiled at him, "Sam knows best."

"So, is James happy?"

"I talked to him last night. He likes it but he says it's hard."

"Everything you like isn't always easy."

I completely understood this. We talked for a good hour. I felt like I had James there with me. I felt so much better. I gave Carl a great big hug before I left.

"Please, come and see me every time you are up here."

"I wouldn't miss this for anything." I smiled at him and kissed his cheek.

I went out to the waiting room. Sam made a funny face at me, "You might want to follow me."

I followed him, "Why?"

He held open the door to the bathroom and it hit me like that; I ran inside and got sick. I didn't even feel that one coming on. Sam did though. I rinsed my mouth and went out.

Sam was waiting for me, "Better?"

"How did you know?"

"Just did."

"So, what is it?"

"I told you, Sarah, I don't know I have never felt this before. Do what James told you, and go see a doctor."

"Fine, I will. Are you staying or did you want me to take you back to the Reservation?"

"Are you okay now?"

"Yeah, I feel fine."

"I would like to stay then."

"Sam, thanks again."

He smiled.

I thought of James as I asked Sam this, "Please don't say anything to anyone."

"Not *even* James?"

I smiled, "I will tell him, but please let me tell him. I don't know how he's going to take letting you touch my stomach."

"You're the one that asked me to check."

"I know, so let me tell him, please."

"Promise you'll tell him."

"Yes, I promise."

"I'll take you down to your car just in case I feel it come on again."

"Sam, I am fine."

He agreed to let me go on my own. I walked out by myself thinking about James. I felt like I was leaving him. But I wasn't, I would go back as much as dad would let me. Seeing Carl helped with how much I missed my James.

3. Checking In

I drove back to the trailer. Jason's truck was gone. I didn't want any more stress. Maybe a nap would help. Sleep always helped. I still felt fine, but we'll see how it goes with dad. I walked in and mom was getting ready to sit in the sun. She always liked the warmth of the sun. Dad wasn't there, so I took advantage of this.

"Can I go swimming with Danelle at the resort?"

"Sure, dad won't be back till later."

"Thanks."

I went and got my suit on and headed for the resort. I walked in and nobody came out to the store, "Anyone back there."

"Sarah?"

"Yeah."

"Come on back."

I slid the door open and entered the living area. Brian was sitting on one end of the couch and Mykala was on the other end.

I grinned knowing what was going on. "Hi Brian… Hi Mykala." My grin got bigger, "Playing video games?"

Brian replied to me without acknowledging me, "Yep."

Mykala was sort of embarrassed.

I tried to make her feel more comfortable, "I like video games too." I smiled at her.

"She grinned at me.

"Brian, where's Danelle?"

"She's on the roof."

"Okay, how do I get there?"

"Fine, I'll show you." He got up and led the way to the back steps.

I stopped him, "Mykala?" I was smiling at him, but he was confused by my reaction. "So, how is it going?"

He put his face down, "I can hardly get a kiss from her."

"Brian, slow down and enjoy it."

"What do you mean?"

"If she won't let you kiss her lips take her hand and kiss the back of it; if that goes well, kiss the inside."

"You're nuts."

"Fine, do it your way, because that works so well for you."

"Okay, what now."

"If the hand thing goes well, slowly, very slowly work your way to her shoulder. Show her you would love to accept anything she will share with you."

"You're weird."

"Fine, do it on your own."

"Tell me what's next?"

"Do you like the way she smells?"

"Yeah." He gave me attitude like that was a really stupid question.

I had to smile with my reply, "When you get to her shoulder move to her ear not touching her and breathe in."

"And why would I do that?"

I grinned, remembering how that felt to me when James did that. "To show her you would enjoy smelling her scent *without* wanting to jump her bones. You will be able to kiss her if she's not attacking you first."

"Wait, like this?" He got really close and inhaled.

"No, Brian, let me show you." I took a step into him and moved my face by his ear. I breathed in real slow.

He turned and tried to kiss me.

I pushed him away. "Brian!!"

"Oh shit. That worked for me."

"If *you* ever do that again, I won't help you anymore."

"Sarah, I am so sorry. It's …"

"I know it works, but try that with Mykala, not me."

He smiled, kissed my cheek and pointed to the window.

"Good luck and slow down!"

I went out the window, "Danelle, Laura?"

"Over here."

They were lying in a valley on the roof where nobody could see them.

"Sarah, you're here?"

"Yeah, I wanted to see if you would like to go swimming?"

Laura was suspicious, "Where?"

"Here, off the dock."

She smiled and Danelle turned to her for a reply.

She gave in, "Yes go."

Danelle asked, "Can we use the tubes?"

Laura gave us a disapproving smile, "Yes."

We took off so fast. She grabbed a towel out of the dryer as we were going through the kitchen.

Brian yelled from the living room, "Where are you two going?"

"Swimming." We both said at the same time, and then we were out the door. We both grabbed the biggest tubes, and ran for the dock. I felt great with no sickness. I put the tube over top of my head and pulled it down to my waist and jumped in, and Danelle did the same thing. We were floating and hanging out. After awhile the boys came down. We were having a peaceful time without them. Brian, Tommy, and Pat were coming swimming. Only two of them had tubes and jumped in. Pat and Tommy coaxed Danelle into racing. Brian came and hung onto the side of my tube.

I couldn't help myself to ask, "How did it go?"

"Really slow, but it works."

I had to grin, "So, you were kissing?"

"Yeah, but by the time she started she had to go."

"Oh, I'm sorry. Start slower next time and it might go a little better."

He turned me to face him, "Why did you help me with Mykala?"

I smiled at him, "Brian, you like her, right?"

"Yeah, but…" I could tell there was something else he was thinking.

"We're friends, right?"

"Yeah, but…" he defiantly wanted to say something else.

"But… what? If we're friends I want you to be happy."

"Are you sure you're not doing it, so that if I have someone else I won't hit on you?"

I smiled, "That's part of it. The other is when you're not being a jerk, you're kind of sweet."

He was being sweet, "Are you *that* sure you are hooked on him?"

"Yep."

"How hooked are you?"

I felt bad as I told him, "A complete lost cause."

His eyebrows lifted as he asked, "That bad?"

"Yes, but it is also very good."

"Did you see Jason is here again?"

The panic came to my heart again, "What?"

"Jason's here with your dad. I think they're eating lunch."

"Oh, well, I guess that's alright."

I moved my attention up to the resort and wondered what he was doing, but saw a very handsome boy was walking toward us. He was the spitting image of my James, but thinner. "Oh my god, it's Sam. Here take this, Brian. I have to see what he wants." I pushed the tube to him and swam to the dock.

Brian was disgusted, "Great there's *another* one."

I nudged Brian, "Brian, behave. It's James's brother."

I got out and grabbed a towel and walk towards him. "Sam, is everything okay?"

He smiled. Boy, does he look like my James, only a little younger and thinner. Okay, I was really missing James again. When he stopped in front of me he asked me, "Have you been sick since I saw you?"

"Nope, I am okay now. Why?"

"It bothers me that I can't tell what it is. Can I try again?"

"Sam, it will seem really weird to other people that James's little brother is touching my stomach."

He didn't understand, "So?"

"People won't understand."

"So, I don't care." He was not put off by anyone.

"Sam, I do care. I love James and I don't want others to think I am moving on to someone else. I would be asking to get hit on. Sam, I don't want that."

He smiled a little flirty, "I could keep you warm until he gets back."

"Sam, shut up."

He felt like he was rejected. I could tell because his head dropped.

"Sam, do you want to swim with us?"

He skimmed the lake to evaluate everyone. "Who is *that*?"

"Don't even think about it; she's too young for your experience. Where's Amelia?"

"Her dad won't let us have any time alone. He wants her to get an education."

I smiled at him, "You wouldn't be miserable now if you would have waited."

"Sarah, it's not like that. It just kind of happened."

I smiled and thought about how bad I wanted to be with James.

Sam smiled as he read my thoughts, "Yeah, like that."

"Sam, don't do that. My thoughts are private."

"Then don't think about it."

I thought about marring James, saying it in my head. They won't understand, so keep your mouth shut.

He smiled at me mischievous, "Okay. You know she thinks I'm cute."

"Sam, no... stop that. Do you want to swim with us?"

"No, I really wanted to check on you."

"Are you sure?"

"Yeah, by the way Jason's here."

"I heard." I wasn't pleased about it.

"I can read his mind too." Sam was very proud of his abilities.

"I don't think I want to know what he is thinking."

Sam smiled at me and told me anyway, "He's thinking with James gone, he can try to get close to you again."

"Thanks, Sam, I didn't want to know that."

He smiled, "Goodbye, Sarah."

He walked away. Oh my goodness, did I miss James. This really sucks.

Danelle came over to me, "Who's that?"

I didn't want to say. "James's little brother, Sam."

"Do they all come that cute?"

"Yes, actually they do." I smiled at her. "Danelle, leave that one alone. He has too much experience. You'd be asking for trouble."

Her eyes widened, "OH!"

I grimaced.

I dove back in and went to the tube I left with Brian. "Do you mind?"

"No, but you have to take it from me."

I pulled it so it flipped over my head and I climbed inside it. "You're easy."

He smiled and put his head on the side of the inner tube, "Yeah, I am."

I ignored him. As we got bored with swimming everyone went their separate ways. I told Danelle I would be back later. I went to the trailer. Mom was still in the sun.

She was surprised to see me, "Back so soon?"

"Yeah, I'm going to take a nap. The water wore me out."

I went into the first room and moved to the bed facing upward, so I could feel my stomach. I rubbed my stomach and didn't feel anything. I pushed a little here and there, but nothing. I closed my eyes.

I woke up so much better. I wet my hair and tried to fix it a little and got dressed. I walked out to find mom in the kitchen now.

"I'll meet you guys at Sherburn's." I headed for the door.

"Aren't you going to eat?"

"No, I'm not hungry."

I went straight to Toni's and walked in the kitchen.

Tony was completely surprised to see me, "Sarah?"

I hugged him.

"You need food." Tony always felt like he needed to feed me.

"No, I'm good."

"James would shoot me if I didn't feed you."

I smiled at him.

"What are you doing here? Not that I'm not glad to see you."

I gave him a crooked smile, "You know me. I needed to get away."

I smiled at him, pleading with my eyes to let me stay awhile.

"Go turn the music on. I'll bring the food out when it's ready."

"Really?"

"Will it cheer you up?"

"Yes, very much."

I went out and fingered through the music to find the song I wanted. I put something I could line dance to, and I tried some new steps.

A couple of girls, ladies, walked in and sat at the bar, "Hey, where's Tony?"

"He'll be out in a minute; can I get you anything?"

"How about a drink?"

"That, you'll have to wait for Tony."

They were interested in the dance I was doing and asked, "What are you doing there?"

"Line dancing, but I am adding my own steps."

They both walked out to do them with me.

"Hold on, let me start it over."

I restarted the music and put in a second track so it would continue. We were laughing and they were catching on quite quickly.

One of them asked, "Do you have any more?"

"Yeah, kind of; we can add this."

"That's good."

So, we went through the whole thing again adding the extra steps.

Tony came out of the kitchen, "Sarah, foods ready." He noticed what I was up to. He shook his head and laughed. I ran up to the stage and shut off the music. The ladies moaned a little.

I had to let them know that I couldn't keep it going, "Sorry, my time was limited."

The ladies walked to the bar and ordered their drinks. I sat and ate my French fries.

"So, Tony, are you starting something new with a dance instructor."

I said out loud, "No, I'm nothing of the sort. I like to dance and Tony lets me once in awhile."

I could tell he had an idea, "Well, I could let her dance every Saturday from 5 to 8, if she wants to."

I was excited now, "Really?"

"On weekends you come up. You could let me know, and I can open the doors for anyone that wants to come learn with you."

"Oh, Tony, I'm not that good."

He leaned over the bar, "They liked it and I could use the business. It's gone down since James is not working."

I smiled at him, "But I don't come up every weekend."

"Call and tell me."

He addressed the ladies, "You would spread the word, wouldn't you?"

"Yeah, we would love that."

"Okay. That is settled than."

I was nervous as I asked Tony, "Are you sure you don't mind?"

"Sarah, James said you would continue to surprise me."

"Can anyone come?"

"Why, what do you have in mind?"

"Kids my age; no drinking but they get to dance."

"That could work."

I had a great big smile. "Sarah, only till 8 p.m.; so after that you're out."

"You got it."

I finished my burger and Jason walked in. There were a few more people in the bar now and Tony was tending to them.

Jason came and sat by me, "I was wondering where you went."

"Well, you caught me at the right time; I'm leaving." I got up and took my dishes to the kitchen. He was following me, but Tony caught him. I came back out and hugged Tony.

"You didn't have to clean it up, Sarah."

"Thanks, Tony. I will call you about next Saturday." I kissed his cheek and went out through the kitchen.

Jason was already standing by my car. I need James; why was he doing this? It was obvious I wanted to be with James. He didn't say anything but opened the door, so I could get in. He leaned down a little with the door still open. "Running away?"

"No, Jason, I'm not. I was done eating, that's all."

"So, what's next Saturday?"

"I'm doing something for Tony if I come up here, that's all."

He still didn't close my door. "Are you scared of me?"

"No, Jason, I'm not. I need to go."

"Are you afraid you still have feelings for me?"

"No, Jason, I don't have feelings for you. Well, maybe that I feel bad, but I love James and I don't feel right talking to you, especially when James isn't here."

He closed the door; I felt really bad, but I drove away anyway."

I went to Sherburn's and found Danelle watching the store. She asked me, "Where did you go?"

I smiled at her. "Tony's, I get to dance from 5 to 8 p.m., before all the adults get there. He says I can bring friends next time."

"Really, can I go?"

"Yeah, your mom might let you too, because we can only stay till 8."

"I bet I can."

We hung out all night until mom and dad showed up around 10 p.m. Of course, Jason was with them. I think I got my point across because he didn't try to talk to me, and the watching was a lot less.

Pat came and sat by me, "You seem quiet?"

"No, I'm getting tired."

He smiled at me. "Are you sure?"

"Yep."

"Can you give me a ride home when you leave?"

"Sure."

When mom and dad were ready to go I heard dad, "Sarah!!!"

"I'm coming."

I enjoyed my time with Danelle but told her, "I guess it's time to go."

"I thought you were going to stay the night. Brian had our time planned out. He was going to entertain us."

I smiled at her. "I haven't felt very good all week, and I wouldn't be much fun. I'm starting to feel sick again. I think I need to get some sleep. Maybe next time I won't feel so ill."

Brian ran up to us, "Are you ready?"

I noticed Brian. He was so excited to do whatever he was planning, but I was letting him down. It made me feel bad.

Danelle spoke for me, "She doesn't feel good, so she's not staying."

He pleaded, "But I thought you could show me some more stuff."

I shook my head no, "Brian, maybe next time I can stay."

I turned to walk out but stopped to wait for Pat. He was talking to a girl, and he had a smile on his face. I didn't want to push him out the door. I stood there waiting and I heard dad again, "Sarah, NOW!!!!"

"Okay, I'm coming." I changed my comment to Pat, "Hey, Pat, if you want a ride I need to go now."

Jason spoke up, "You're giving him a ride home?"

He was getting on my nerves, "Yes, do you have a problem with that?"

Jason backed down, and dad grinned to show his approval. I think he was hoping for me to like someone my own age.

Dad was totally cool about it, "Sarah, we'll meet you at the trailer. Take your time."

I couldn't believe I could take forever with someone my age, but I couldn't even have five minutes to brush my teeth with James.

Pat finally ended his conversation with the girl, and we walked out to my car.

We both got in and I had to ask, "You're still going to have to give me directions because it's been a while since I was there."

He directed me this way and that until we were there. He opened his door, "You know there are a lot of guys that like you, Sarah."

"Pat, I really don't care to know. I need to go get some sleep."

"Sarah, he's too old and he wants to get in your pants."

"Pat, that's discussing."

"I'm a guy Sarah; I know these things."

"You don't know my James."

"Okay, but you are going to get your heart broken. Guys are jerks."

"Thanks, Pat, but I will be okay."

I wanted to show him the ring so bad, but it might get back to mom and dad and I wasn't ready to deal with that yet. He closed the door and I headed to the trailer.

I walked in and dad started in right away. "That didn't take long?"

"No, I only dropped him off."

"You know you can see other boys. James is going to be gone for awhile."

"Dad, stop right now! I don't want to see anyone else, and you're going to have to get over it!"

Jason was laughing. He was planting the seed in dad's head and I knew it. I was irritated by all of them, "Goodnight." I started walking to the bedroom.

Dad reminded me, "I thought you hated the bed in there?"

"I do, but none of you are going to bed and I am tired."

I walked away.

Mom followed me into the bedroom. "Sarah?"

"What now?"

"You are sleeping a lot lately; are you okay?"

"Yeah, I'm fine. I was in the sun all day, so I am tired." Oh great, I was starting to turn and my mouth was watering. I got up and ran to the outhouse, not making it again. Shit, now I was going to have to explain this. Jason was behind me again.

"Can't you leave me alone? Jason, I don't want *your* help."

"Sarah, are you sure?"

I didn't know if he was asking if I wanted his help or if I was pregnant, but this works for either, "Positive."

He was being more careful as he talked to me, "How can you be sure?"

"I just am. You need to drop this. Maybe I was drinking and had too much."

"You weren't drinking. I know because I was watching."

"Jason, go home. I'm fine." But my body didn't agree with what I was saying. I threw up again.

He grabbed my hair to hold it for me.

"Jason, I don't want your help." I leaned against the outhouse and slowly sat down.

"You're sure?"

"Yes, positive."

"What did James say?"

"About what?"

"When you were telling him you were getting sick?"

"He told me to go to the doctor."

"He couldn't tell you what was wrong?"

I wondered if Jason knew about James's talents.

"Yes, Sarah. I know he feels things too."

I sat with my head in my hands as I replied to him, "I went to see Sam. He's stronger than James. He said I am definitely not pregnant."

"So there was a possibility?" His voice was a little higher, almost a little angry. He didn't have any right to know this about me.

"Jason, I'm not talking to you about this anymore. I'm not and that's all that matters. Now, please go home. I think it's the stress."

"I am making you stressed out?" He was delighted with that.

I gestured my disapproval of his happiness.

He put his hand down, "Do you feel better now?"

"Yeah."

"I'll leave after you go back in."

I took a deep breath of relief as he pulled me up. I didn't say anything as we walked back to the trailer. I walked in avoiding eye contact with mom and dad and went straight to the bedroom.

I heard Jason say to them, "She might have a touch of the flu."

I got out my note for tomorrow and closed my eyes. *What the hell is wrong with me?* I put my lips to the phone with hopes that James would feel my need for him. His voice would calm me if only I could hear him. I drifted off thinking of his caring touch and his calming voice.

I woke to it ringing, and I answered it. I was relieved it was my sweet Cayuse, my love, and my forever.

"James?"

"Yes, my sweet. Do you feel any better?"

"James, I don't know. I got sick twice today. Once at the hospital when I was done talking to your dad and once when my dad was upsetting me."

"So, *not* when you got up or when you were hungry?"

"James, I'm not pregnant if that's what you're thinking. I couldn't be when we didn't even do it."

I could feel the worry in his voice, "Sarah, we were very close sometimes and it could have happened. How do you know anyway?"

"I saw Sam today when I went to see your dad. He read my mind and he said it wasn't that."

"He can't tell you that unless…Sarah?"

"James, I wanted to know what was wrong with me. He touched my stomach, and he said he didn't know what it was. He has never felt whatever this is before, but there's no baby."

"I am not happy."

"James, I need you." I started to cry.

"Please, Sarah, don't do that; this is hard enough."

"I'm sorry. I love you so much."

He was trying to help me here, "So, you went to see my dad?"

"Yes. It gives me a little comfort when I'm missing you."

"How is he?"

"He looks great, James, he knew about the ring."

"He feels things too. He knew and asked me before I left. He's okay with it now."

"I did really well the first few days, but I hate being here without you."

"Try not to think about how long it's going to be."

"I need your touch to take away all the stress."

"Close your eyes. I will come to you tonight."

I didn't know if what I heard was right, "What?"

"Sarah, close your eyes and wait for me. I will be with you tonight."

"James, you can't come home; you have to finish what you are doing."

"Sarah, in your dreams, I will come to you."

"It won't be the same."

"Do you *trust* me?"

"Of course I do." I believed him, but this did not make any sense.

"Then close your eyes, hang up the phone, and wait for me."

"I love you, James."

"My sweet Sarah, I love you too. Now close your eyes. I will call you as soon as I can."

I hung up the phone and closed my eyes. I was waiting, but he wasn't coming to me like he said he would. I did not get this at all.

4. Irritated

I felt his breath in my ear and his arm wrapped around my waist. The nibbling on my ear was making the warmth rise in my body. I woke abruptly, but no one was there. I crawled out of bed and moved to the door to investigate where everyone was. Jason said he would leave, but he was still there sleeping on the couch. Mom and dad were in the back room sleeping. I pulled the door closed. If he was going to make me feel this good in my sleep, I didn't want to be wakened. I crawled back in bed and closed my eyes. It didn't start again. I tried to think about it to bring it back, but nothing. I gave up trying to feel James and drifted back to sleep.

His mouth was tracing my neck and moving slowly down to my chest, and further to my stomach. My heart was racing from how he was making me feel. He moved over top of me hovering. He didn't talk to me, but I felt him silently ask for the approval from me. He lowered himself to me slightly grazing my body with his. I could feel every part of him touching me. The tingling started as he moved against me. His body felt amazing against mine. He was warm and I felt his desire for me as it caressed against me. We always go *further* in my dreams and I felt the pressure of him against me. I pulled him closer; my need to feel him was desperate. I was getting lost in how good he felt against me, and he taunted me until I couldn't stop the pleasure erupting from me and I felt the rush. He pushed hard to me and moved so I would enjoy it more. His kiss was erotic. I had to open my mouth to breath. The movements he did to touch me were amazing and that feeling of complete pleasure was coming again. I wanted to moan to express how good he felt to me, but this was only a dream. I was trembling so badly, but he wasn't here to put pressure on me to hold me to make it stop, "Oh James."

I felt so good, as the incredible rush came again. He pulled me close and just held me, helping me to calm down, trying to slow my heart rate. I was in heaven and felt so much relief from any stress that I was feeling. He held me tightly, so I could fall asleep in his arms. I pulled the pillow in, so I would have something to wrap my arms around, and drifted off to a dreamless sleep feeling completely loved by my James.

I woke up in a panic that he was still here, realizing it was only a dream. Oh shit, he lives my dreams. I am so sorry, James. You didn't have to do that even though I wanted him too. I was ashamed that I needed him to do that, so I could feel better. *I'm sure I've made him miserable again.* I pulled out my note for today.

Day 5:

In my dreams you are there,
A kiss, a touch, a stare.
Your skin so soft and smooth,
The touch so sensitive too.
I long for you when were apart,
The pain in my heart.
I will return for you my love,
And in your arms I shall fall,
You are my dream after all.
With my eternal love
James

I held the note to my chest. He really knew how I felt and made my feelings grow even more. I took a deep breath and got up; I was a complete mess. It was like he was really here. I was confused, but I changed clothes and walked out. Everyone was already awake. I sat down at the table remembering my dream and I smiled. I could handle anything they had for me today.

Dad noticed right away that I was doing better, "Feeling better I see?"

"Yep, I need food."

He handed me a plate of eggs and then the bacon. I took a lot of food. I was starving. I had a really good workout in my dreams. I smiled some more and ate.

Mom, however, was not as satisfied, "You are feeling better?"

"Yep."

"And now you're eating enough to feed an army?"

I noticed the food on my plate and then replied, "I didn't feel much like eating yesterday, so I am making up for it today." I tried to shrug off what she was implying.

Then it hit me. Did she think I was pregnant too? We haven't even done it. This is so stupid. I ate and went to brush my teeth. Jason didn't even hassle me the whole time I was at the table, and I did feel better about that.

When I was finished I walked out and asked, "Do you have a plan for today?"

Mom spoke up, "We're leaving early."

"How early are we going? Do I need to pack now?"

Jason gave me a disapproving glare.

Mom replied, "No, not yet. Around 2 p.m."

"Can I go hang with Danelle?"

Jason finally spoke to me, "You mean Brian?"

"NO, I mean Danelle! Brian has a girlfriend, Mykala. I have James. We're friends." I glared back at him.

"If you had the flu, don't you think you should take it easy?"

"I feel better now. I think the nausea is gone." I ignored Jason and asked mom, "Well, can I go?"

Dad spoke up, "She is asking."

Mom let her guard down, "I suppose, but be back and ready to go by 1:30 p.m."

"Okay."

I took off out the door.

"Sarah!"

I turned around. I was getting irritated with Jason. "What?"

Jason walked up to me. "If you're not pregnant and you have been sick, don't you think you should take it easy today?"

"No, Jason! I feel so much better."

"Yeah, I heard."

"Well, do have to repeat myself?"

"No, you were dreaming."

I was shocked. How much noise did I make? I couldn't say anything.

"You should be more careful; I could have been your mom and dad, and they would have known you have done it with him."

"Jason, you don't know what you're talking about."

"Sarah!"

I moved closer to him, "We haven't gone all the way, but when the time comes, he will be the one."

I think I left him stunned. He wasn't saying or doing anything. I decided this would be a good time to get away, while he was stunned. I got in my car quickly and drove away. I realized what I had just told him, but he was pushing. Dam him it's none of his business. I was in a bad mood by the time I got to Sherburn's.

I found Danelle right away, "Can you go swimming again? I only have a few hours."

"Yeah, let's go."

We relaxed on our tubes and paddled down the shore.

"I don't think I am supposed to go this far out of sight."

"We can go back. I'm not so angry anymore."

"You were really upset when you got here; what happened?"

"Mom and dad have let Jason spend the night the last two nights, and he keeps pushing me for information about James and me. I think that is very private, but I admitted something I didn't want him to know, and it made me angry."

"What was that?"

"Danelle, I really don't want to talk about it."

"He knows you two have done it?"

"We *haven't*. James thinks we should wait till I am 18 years old."

"I thought for sure you had."

"So does everybody else. It helps keep the guys away, so I let them think whatever they want, but mom and dad. I do want my mom and dad to know the truth, but it's really hard to explain that to them."

"Just tell them."

"How would I do that? I want to do it with James, but he keeps pushing me away."

"He pushes you away?"

"Not really. Most of the time he leaves."

"You really haven't done it with him?"

"Almost, but he wouldn't"

"Wow, he's a descent guy." She sounded so surprised.

"You have no idea. I practically begged him. I put him through misery and he still walks away from me."

"I think I like him better now."

"Danelle!" I didn't like that she didn't trust him or like him at all.

"Sarah, you're too young!"

"I know. That's what he says too. When it goes too far he feels so bad."

"Sarah, I can't believe it."

"You are the only person I have talked to about this. So, please don't tell anyone, I mean not one person." I was very firm that I didn't want anyone to get any ideas of us not belonging to each other.

"But if someone asks, Sarah, I should protect your reputation."

"Danelle, it will be him someday. I love him so much."

"So, how far have you gone?"

"We tried."

"What do you mean?"

"We were going to, but it kind of hurt a little and he wouldn't."

"Oh, that's kind of gross."

"You asked." I was embarrassed that I explained this to her, but she was my best friend.

"It hurts?"

"I guess so. He says it's because I'm not ready. He doesn't want to if I'm not ready."

"Well, that's good."

"When we're there, I wanted to so bad. I told him to do it anyway." Here I go being emotional again. The tears were filling my eyes.

"But he didn't?"

"Well, no. He doesn't want to hurt me."

She laughed a little. "Who would have guessed? He's a nice guy."

"Danelle? I want to tell you something *else*, but please, please don't tell anyone."

"I won't"

"Do you promise?" I really needed to share this with someone.

"Yes, I promise."

"He asked me to marry him." I cringed as I said this because I knew she wasn't going to be happy with this.

"What?"

"He gave me a ring and everything."

"You didn't say yes!"

"Yes, I did. It won't happen till I am at least 18 years old. Until then I have to hide the ring. Mom and dad wouldn't understand."

"Sarah, how can you make a decision like that already?"

"I don't know, but I want to be with him forever."

"Okay, let me see the rock." She was trying to be pleasant, but it came out snobbish.

"I tucked it away. I didn't want to lose it. It's kind of big and really noticeable."

"He's okay with you not wearing it?"

"Yeah, I'm too young and people won't understand."

"I don't understand."

"Please, don't tell anyone. I really needed to share this with someone."

"Okay, but you have to tell me before you do anything else. We can talk about it, so you don't make any drastic decisions."

"We have lots of time. It will be 2 years."

"Wow, are you sure?"

"Yes, he is amazing. I don't know how he tolerates me."

"I told you, you are changing and you have so much more confidence. People are noticing."

"I suppose I have to go, but you promised, right?"

"Only, if you promise not to do anything crazy. You need to sort things out before something else happens."

"I will try."

"No, not try. You need to weigh all your options before you do something stupid."

"It's not stupid, it's just different, and not what anyone else is doing. I know I love him, and we will be together forever."

"Sarah, you want me to promise?"

"Yes."

"Then give me this at least."

"Fine, I promise."

She walked with me back to my car. Brian came out."

"I would love to tell him; maybe he would leave you alone."

I smiled, "You said you wouldn't."

"Okay, but he really likes you and it's irritating me that he uses other girls to try and get your attention."

"What? I thought he liked Mykala?"

"Not anymore; he was trying to make you jealous."

"Well, that backfired on him. I showed him how to take things slower, so she would want to kiss him."

She gasped with disbelief, "You didn't?"

"Yes, I did. I will be more careful, maybe make ugly faces, so he'll think I'm weird."

She laughed. "See you, but you need to talk to me before you do anything stupid."

"Yes, I already promised."

"Sarah, do you have a minute?" Brian was trying to get my attention.

I waited for Danelle's approval. She rolled her eyes and nodded. I smiled at her.

"Yeah, what's up?"

Danelle walked away as Brian asked, "Are you going to be back next weekend?"

"I don't know, possibly on Friday."

"Okay, see ya."

"Okay, what's up?"

"Nothing really, I wanted to say thanks."

"That's it?"

"Yeah."

"Well, you're welcome, see ya."

"Wait." He was sounding desperate.

"What?"

"Do you have anything more for me?"

"No, not really."

"We're going to a movie tonight. Can I try to kiss her?"

"Brian you really want to know?" I didn't know if I could believe him.

"Yeah."

"Okay. Hold her hand with your fingers together. It's more than friends."

"Then what?"

"That's it? Well, maybe you could trace her fingers with your other hand."

"What about the kissing?"

"If you do, read the signs. If she is responding then kiss her more, and if she's not, pull away and say thank you."

He smiled, "*That simple?*"

"Yes that simple, but nothing more."

He took my hands in his and kissed me quickly on the cheek and then he let me go to run back in, "Thanks Sarah."

I thought to myself. *That wasn't careful.* Shit. James wouldn't approve of that.

I drove to the trailer thinking *I need to put a stop to Brian.* I didn't want to do anything that would hurt James because he is everything to me. I pulled in to find Jason still at the trailer. I was really getting irritated already with everyone. I put it in park and walked in. Good, they weren't inside. I put my necklace back on, tucked it under my shirt and put the ring in my bra. I got my stuff together and put it in the car. I sat down on the chair and closed my eyes. All of a sudden I was really tried again.

I heard mom, "Sarah are you ready to go?"

I sat up, "Yep, everything is already in the car."

She was concerned again, "You were sleeping?"

"I was swimming for two hours. I'm a little worn out."

"My bags are ready; will you put them in the car?"

I got up and went to get her bags and brought them to the car.

Jason was standing by his truck, "Why did you tell me you already did it?"

I closed my eyes with animosity. *Get it over with, Sarah, he won't stop until he gets it.* I walked over to his truck. I opened the tailgate and sat down on it. He walked over and sat down beside me. I felt so bad that I was going to hurt him, but this had to end.

"Jason, the reason I let you believe that is because you are making it worse for yourself, and I didn't want to see you hurt. Kylie is pretty nasty when she's mad, and I didn't want to see you suffer anymore. If you thought I already did it, maybe you would let go of me and be happy with what you have."

"You did that for me?"

"Jason!" I took a deep breath, "I do care about you, and you made me feel like I was someone and you brought me James. I know you didn't want us together, and when you stopped coming around James was there to pick up the pieces. He didn't hit on me, he was my friend first and it expanded from there."

"Well, it didn't take him long to move in."

"If you haven't noticed, I am kind of a basket case. I cry really easily and when I am really upset I get sick to my stomach. You saw that one for yourself. James took over making me feel liked, then loved. He is so much more than that now. Jason, I am sorry I didn't follow your warning, but now I am with James and *that's* the end of it. I don't have any urge to be with you at all." I slowly peaked at him from the side of my eyes, "I'm sorry, Jason."

"Where is he now? He's not here picking up the pieces now."

"He also didn't leave me wondering where we stood. He is coming back, and he is coming back to me. He's actually very sweet about it. He would have stayed if I asked him to, but he needed to do this so he has a future besides bartending."

"So, why are you spending time with Brian?"

"I am spending time with Danelle, and he happens to be her brother."

"You said you thought you were falling in love with me."

"I did at the time. But things change, besides you left me hanging."

"This could change then!"

"No, this won't change. I think I am way beyond thinking I love him."

"But you two haven't done it."

"Jason, love is way more than doing it."

"What do you mean?"

"That's the whipped cream on top of a Sunday." I laughed remembering where I have heard that one.

"You are so amazingly cute."

"Jason, no! You need to be happy too. If that is with or without Kylie, it's up to you, but it will not be with me."

"I still want to be your first."

"That will not happen, Jason. I love James."

Mom and dad were coming. I stood up and said to Jason, "Thank you for giving him to me."

I watched as mom and dad came closer.

Jason stood up and whispered. "*This* is not over."

I smiled, "Yes it is."

"Not if I can help it."

"But you can't! I have made up my mind already."

"That can change."

I smiled as mom and dad got closer, "I won't let it."

"But I can try."

"I wish you wouldn't."

"Really?"

"Yes."

"You said yes."

"That was only to tell you to stop trying."

Mom and dad were there. Mom noticed that Jason and I were talking, "Nice conversation?"

"Just great." I said with a forced smile.

I gave dad a hug and moved to get in the car, avoiding Jason completely.

"Don't I get one?" Jason was trying to be playful.

I turned to glare at him, "No!"

"Sarah, don't be rude." She liked Jason, maybe because he seemed younger than James.

"I'm not being rude, mom."

Jason walked over to me and put his arms around me.

I pleaded with him, "Jason, please don't."

"I can't help it," as he pulled me close to hug me.

"You can and will, or I will have to tell James."

He turned to whisper in my ear, "You won't, you know he would come home."

I pushed him away and got in my car, "Are you ready, Mom?"

I glared back at Jason. Mom got in and we were on our way. I didn't know how or when I would tell James about this, but I felt like he should know about it.

5. Reading Me

The drive home was peaceful. I was happy to make it through the day not getting sick at all. Mom didn't ask a lot of questions even after we were home.

When I went to bed I remembered the night before and how much better I felt after James came to me in my dream. I wondered if he would do that again. I love his touch. I closed my eyes and drifted away. I tried not to set my mind on anything, other than the soft touch of his hand on my face. I wanted him to come to me again.

As I drifted off, I did feel James. He moved behind me wrapping his arms around me. His head rested on mine with his mouth next to my ear, while his hands moved to my stomach.

"James?"

His whisper came, "Shhhh, my sweet, Sarah. You're safe in my arms."

I opened my eyes, but he wasn't there. I closed them again and he was back. "I love *you* James."

I woke abruptly. I don't remember why, but I couldn't wait for Day 6:

When I see you my heart pounds,
My knees cannot be found.
When I hear you my feelings swell,
This feeling I know well.
My first thought of the day is you,
I wish you knew,
I want to grow old with you,
I hope you feel this too.
With my eternal love,
James

I closed my eyes to try and feel him again, but the feeling was gone. I got up and took a shower. The plan for the day was Urgent Care and work. I closed my eyes and thought 1… 2… 3… breath. I explained everything to the doctor, including the almost with James. I wasn't comfortable, but just in case Sam was wrong. She did a pregnancy test, and of course it came back negative; she did explain that it might be too early to tell. She took blood samples and put me on medicine that helped with upset stomachs. She explained that if it was stress, the acid in my stomach might be over reacting, and this would help with that. She wanted to see me in two weeks to do a follow up. I went to work and the rest of the day went smoothly. When I got home I was really tired, so I relaxed on the couch for a nap and woke to mom coming in. I explained everything to her about my doctor visit except for the pregnancy test. She wasn't happy that she didn't get to go with me, but was proud of me that I was taking care of myself.

I asked if we were going up north next weekend, and she paused for a long moment, "No, if it is stress, why don't we just relax here."

I had to go back out to pick up the prescription and while I was there I picked up a scrapbook for my love notes from James. I made sure it had enough pages, one for each day that he was going to be gone. When I got home I took the six I already had read, some color paper and went to the kitchen. I burned the edges of each of the notes I had already read. I glued them to a color piece of paper and then in the book. I made the cover: My 7 weeks without James. I smiled and brought it to my room with me. I called Tony and explained that I was a little sick last weekend and I wouldn't be there next weekend. I went to bed for the night wanting to feel my James.

No luck on James being there, but I was better now anyway. I'm glad he was saving it for when I really needed him. I went to sleep. I woke to my phone ringing at 2 a.m.

"James?"

"Yeah."

"Thank you for the last two nights, they were wonderful."

"Sarah, did you go to the doctor?"

"Yes, it's just me being stupid and upset; my stomach took it out on me. You sound upset."

"Sarah, if you need me I can come home."

"No, I'm fine. The last two nights helped me so much. I've had two days without getting sick."

"Are you sure?"

"Yes, James."

"Sarah, if you were...I wouldn't be able to forgive myself for not being there with you."

"Two for two on the *'NO's,'* James, and I'm good."

"If you were, Sarah, I would be happy. Something as beautiful as a baby; coming from loving you."

"James, I can tell you right now I am not ready for that."

"I know, I'm not really ready either, but if you are..., don't take care of it without me, please."

"James?"

"Don't destroy *it;* it would be ours."

"James, I'm not. But you are scaring me a little. What are you feeling?"

"I feel like I need to come home."

"I am not going to be the reason you didn't finish this. You are not coming home. If you feel I am, when I go back in two weeks, I will do another test, okay?"

"Okay, two more weeks, but Sarah you have to tell me. I don't know what it feels like either. I'm on the same page as Sam, but it is something."

"You're really scaring me, James."

"I'm sorry, but I just hate being away from you and there *is* something wrong. I feel it."

"Why do you feel that?"

"I held your stomach for hours and I can't tell, but Sarah, make sure you go back in like you're suppose to in two weeks."

"Can we talk about this ring?"

"I see we're changing the subject. Why do you want to talk about the ring?"

"James, it's too big."

"It doesn't even come close to how much I love you."

"Does that mean you love me too much?"

"Maybe." I could tell he was smiling now, "James…"

"Yes, my sweet, Sarah."

"You fill me up."

"What?"

"I love you so much, and you give me what I need when I need it the most."

"How can you say that; when I am so far from you?"

"But you're not. I felt you here last night. How do you do that?"

"I feel that all the time, Sarah. When you dream of me, I feel it like you are here. When you concentrate on needing me, I feel that too. I just shared it with you."

"The other night, wasn't that hard for you?"

"Not as hard as being away from you."

"Only six more weeks, James, we can do this can't we?"

"Do you want me to come to you again? If you close your eyes I could be…?"

"James, it's better when it's real. It's nice, but save your energy for what you need to be doing there. How is it going?"

"Great, but I had a few distractions the last couple of days. I'm not the top guy anymore."

"James, I'm better now. Don't think about it for the next two weeks, and get your spot back. It will help you, us, in the future."

"Yes, but Sarah?"

"No, but Sarah, me. The better you do now the more babies we can have later, a lot later. I am kind of selfish. I want you to myself for awhile."

"How many kids do you want?"

"I never thought about it; all I want is to be with you."

"I see three, but I want five."

"James, you're freaking me out again. We can discuss that after were married."

"That's something we should discuss *before* we're married."

"But we have two years before that. And James, that's *too* much to think about."

"Okay, I just love you so much. I can't wait to spend my life with you."

"You already are."

"I should get some sleep, and my little sickly should too."

"I'm fine, James. I love you so much. Goodnight, James."

"Goodnight my sweet, Sarah."

I hung up the phone and closed my eyes. Again, I felt better than before. James came to me anyway by wrapping his arms around me and kissing my neck and shoulder. I was in for another sleepless night. He hovered, but I told him no, and that he needed to sleep. He lowered himself to me, slightly moving to me to taunt me. I wanted more, but kept in my head a definite no. He needed to sleep. His kisses traced my face, and he moved to hold me tighter. I could feel the want, the urge to push further, but we had to be content with sleeping.

I woke and still felt good, with no illness. I hoped those pills helped me. I pulled out Day 7:

When I think that I love you so much,
You prove me wrong.
My love grows and grows,
And my need for you plays in my head like a song.
With my eternal love,
James

What a way to start the day. I got up and had my normal boring life with no excitement, and no stress. I ended my day the same way: boring, work, sleep, work, and sleep. My life was definitely boring without James. I went to bed wishing I would feel James, but I didn't want him to mess up what he was doing. I tried to push the wanting out of my head as I went to sleep.

I woke another day feeling fine, but my life was a little boring. *Sarah, just get up it will get better with time.* That is what I had to do to tell myself to get going. What was Day 8 going to bring me?

Love is when your love lingers even though you're apart.
True love knows we will be together again.
With my eternal love,
James

It was like James was reading me before he left. He knew just what to put down when I needed it. Okay, I am ready for the day, and off to work I went. It was Wednesday, the hump day. The hump of what; the week? Did everyone feel like they were half way to the weekend or half way through another week? Everyone seems to wait for the weekends. Is everybody's life as boring as mine that we have to wait for the weekends? I made it through the day and went home. Mom was at the second job and wouldn't be home till after 10 p.m. I watched a movie, and I kept thinking about James. I needed to *not* think about him because he was busy. It was okay for us to not be together 24/7, but I loved how much time we had together before he left. There will be a lot more in our future. I waited for mom to get home. I told her I would wait up for her, but I really needed to go to bed.

She was still concerned about me, "How have you been feeling?"

"So far so good. I haven't gotten sick at all."

"Well good."

"Yep, but I still need to sleep a lot, so I am going to bed. Goodnight mom."

"Goodnight."

I fell asleep right away. I wanted to think about James, but it wasn't happening today.

I woke the next morning still feeling good. Wow, I feel really good when I'm not getting sick, or drilled with questions. Life was simpler when I really didn't have that. Let's see what James has for me on Day 9:

When I met you, I was enticed to look at you.
When I looked at you, I was inspired to talk to you.
When I talked to you, I was moved to touch you.
When I touched you, I was motivated to kiss you.
When I kissed you, I was encouraged to hold you.
When I held you, I was convinced to love you.
Now that I love you,
I'm scared I will lose you.
With my eternal love,
James

That was going to make it harder to do without him. I rolled over and thought just for a minute how I would love to touch his chest, his stomach, and his lips. Oh shit, he would feel this when he's really busy. I thought about tracing my fingers along his abs, and how nice it would be to trace them with my lips. *Okay James, hope that wasn't too bad for you.* I got up and went to work. The day went uneventfully. I went home to an empty house again because mom was working. I made dinner and put a plate aside for her. I watched another movie, a love story. I was feeling pretty lonely and needed a love story. It ended and mom wasn't home yet, but I had to go to bed. I was a little sad, and the love story didn't help with that. I went to bed and stared at the ceiling trying to not think about James. I drifted to sleep slowly, but once I did he was there in no time at all, just holding me. He always knew what I needed the most. I slept better this way.

I woke to another day, and it was Friday, the day that everybody waited for, except for me. I had no plans for the weekend. I guess I will have time to lie around and think about James. Was this all I could think about? *Great!* At least I had today to stay busy, because I had to work. Here's my start of Day 10:

You may be out of my reach...
But in my mind we are never apart...
I miss you!!!!
With my eternal love,
James

Oh James, how did you know what I needed before you left? I don't understand how you knew. Can you see how I will feel in advance, too? But then you would have known I was going to get sick, and that Jason was around. James, talk to me, call me, something, anything, please. My phone buzzed with a text.

>"Sarah, I'm busy."

"Sorry."

>"Later."

"K."

I got up and went to work. My mind was going crazy thinking about James. How much does he see and know? Do I have any privacy at all? This was going to drive me crazy. I got home again before mom. She wasn't as late as normal.

We really didn't have much to say, but she was still worried about me. "How are you feeling?"

"Great; I'm still not getting sick. The medicine must be working."

"Good, so what do you have planned for the weekend?"

"Nothing."

"Sarah, it's Friday night, you should go do something."

I was a little disgruntled for not going up north, "Like what?"

"You could hang out with school friends, go to the movies, or something with friends."

"Mom, if you remember that *is* what I did before James, and this is what I do now without him. It's really not that different."

"Yeah, I guess you're right."

The phone rang, so I got up to answer it, "Hello."

"Hey Sarah, how's it going?"

"O-k-a-y, Matt?"

"Yeah, I miss doing homework with you."

"I don't." I laughed a little and then he did too.

"Why didn't you go to Valleyfair? We had an after party that you would have loved."

"Yeah, sorry about that."

"Oh, something you can't talk about?"

"Yeah, not right now." I noticed my mom was listening to me talk to Matt.

"Well, anyway, we're all going to the beach tomorrow, and I wanted to see if you would like to go?"

I was skeptical of him, "You need a ride?"

"Yep, you guessed it."

"Can you behave?"

"Sarah, come on. It's a bunch of people. We're going to play volleyball, cookout, and hang out. Please, say you will take me."

"What time?"

"Pick me up at 10 a.m.?"

"Yes, I will give you a ride. See ya tomorrow."

"Thanks, Sarah, see you tomorrow."

I hung up the phone. I knew this is what she and dad wanted me to do. So, I felt obligated to go and try to have a little fun. To me it was staying busy, so I wouldn't think about James all day.

I had to let mom know, so she would be happy, "I agreed to go to the beach tomorrow with some kids from school. I am supposed to pick Matt up at 10 a.m., and I have no idea how long I will be. I'll have my phone if you need to call me."

"I thought you had a problem with Matt?"

"Yeah, well it's with a bunch of people and he said he would behave."

"That sounds great. You should go and have some fun."

"Yeah, great." I wasn't as excited as she would have liked me to be.

"Mom, I'm going to bed, see ya before you go to work tomorrow."

"Sarah, it's early."

"I know, but I will have a long day tomorrow, and I don't want to get sick again."

"Okay, goodnight, dear."

"Night, mom."

6. Staying Busy

I went to bed and felt really bad about agreeing to go to the beach. I didn't even want to go. I only did it so I wouldn't sit around making James miserable because I would be thinking about him all the time. I tried to fall asleep, but found it troublesome because of what I was going to do tomorrow. I really didn't consider the kids I was going to hang out with friends. The only one I was even close to being friends with was Matt, and he was on friendship probation. I didn't want to lead him on in any way because I love my James. I tossed and turned for hours wondering how I could get out of this. My phone rang at 2 a.m.

"James." I smiled as I answered.

"You're not sleeping?"

"Nope."

"Why not?"

"I think I slept too much this week."

"Sarah, tell me why?"

"How much do you feel?"

"Why?"

"Do I have any privacy at all?"

"Are you worried?"

"No, James, I'm not at all. And I think you would believe me if you feel as much as I think you do."

He chuckled, "Yeah, I know."

"So how much do you know?"

He was being playful, "About what?"

I took a deep breath, "I don't know… everything?"

"First, have you been sick?"

"No. Now my question."

"Sarah, I only feel you, and when your emotions are really strong they are clearer. I can…touch you."

"I knew that much. Do you feel when I get sick?"

"No, maybe. I really feel that you are upset. You call for me."

"I do, but only when I'm stressed out though."

"I know your dad was asking a lot of questions, but was there something else?"

He knows. I know he knows. Is he testing me? "You don't know already?"

"Know what Sarah!?" I could tell he was getting more irritated with me.

"I don't want to tell you."

"Why?"

"You may want to come home and you can't."

"Sarah?" This came out scolding and asking at the same time.

Oh, I didn't want to tell him this, "Jason's been around a lot, and he said I wouldn't tell you because you would come home.

He didn't say a word. I was a little worried now. "James, talk to me?" He still did not respond. "James, you did feel this?" I could hear a bunch of noise in the background. "James, don't even think about it; you can't come home. James, d*am it* James, I tell you everything; talk to me." It got quiet again. He still didn't say anything. I thought about being with him, the way he sees me, and the way I saw him, the way he touched me, the touch of his lips on mine, my body lying next to him, the house, yes, James, the house with the fog swirling, the nightgown I would give myself to him in, and how perfect we fit together.

"Sarah, stop!"

I wanted to make sure he was really distracted from what he was thinking. I thought about the kiss under his chin, the tracing of his mouth on my skin, how badly I wanted to feel him.

"Okay, Sarah, stop please."

I stopped to listen, "James?" I was starting to cry again.

"Oh, don't do that, Sarah, I'm sorry. I have to..."

"James, don't. What kind of future would we have if you don't finish?"

"Oh, Sarah, what am I suppose to do?"

"Finish what you started. I will still be here. You can still feel that, right?" The sick feeling was coming back. "James?" It was silent again. "James, hold on!" I set the phone down and ran to the bathroom. I threw up again. It was stress related. I rinsed my mouth and went back to my room. I picked up the phone and heard a bunch of noise again, "James, are you there?"

"Sarah, I have to come home now. You need me more ways than one."

"Dam it James; I am *not* ruining this for you...for us. James, please don't!"

"Sarah, I need you."

"James, you can have me anytime you want, and you know that. I am here, and I plan to stay. Please, I can handle it. Danelle's happy I spend a lot of time with her now."

He calmed a little when I brought her up, "You do?"

"Yeah, I do."

"But then you're around Brian."

"James, no one can give me what you do, even apart. Please, if I can't handle this you will be the first to know."

"Sarah, you got sick."

"I know, but I am worrying about upsetting you. If you calm down; this will go away."

"Sarah, if I come home it will all go away."

"No, it will get worse, because I will worry about how we are going to get our house we both dream of. The magical place where, where... we're supposed to be together..."

I couldn't finish it. I was done talking him out of coming home. "James, hold on..." I ran to the bathroom again. I got sick again; what could this be if I only get sick when I am upset? I went back to the phone and lay down with it on my ear. "James?"

"Sarah, I *will* do whatever you want me to do, just stop getting sick."

I laughed quietly, "Is this the only way I will get my way?"

He laughed lightly, "Promise me that you won't let anything happen to you. I couldn't live with myself if something happened to you and I wasn't there…"

"Then stop arguing with me."

"Oh, Sarah, this is so hard."

"You promised me two more weeks; you have to stick to that."

"It's not two weeks from now, it's less than that."

"See, you're already closer; just stay till then please."

"I did have a good week."

"See, you have to finish."

"We'll discuss it a week from Monday."

"I will give you that. Besides, I'm not going up north this weekend."

"That helps a little; how about next weekend?"

"Not if I get sick again."

"But you did, so you're not going."

"James, if I tell mom…Well, she already thinks I'm pregnant."

"Shit! Why do you think that?"

"Because I get sick all the time and then I eat like a horse the next day."

"You're eating?"

"James, you know I eat, but after getting sick I am starving the next day."

"No wonder she thinks you are; I kind of do too."

"James we didn't do it. There is no way we could be, and deep in your heart you have got to know that."

"Yes; I don't feel that either, but Sarah…"

"NO buts, James. Don't even think that. You think I'm sick now, can you *imagine* if I was worried about that?"

He laughed with his breath.

"James, can you handle holding me in my dreams?"

"I could hold you for real if I came home."

"I will settle for my dreams, my Cayuse."

"You melt me when you say it that way. Sarah, I have to run five miles in a couple of hours, and this conversation has worn me out. I need to sleep."

"James, its okay if you can't hold me tonight. I can wait for tomorrow. I'm kind of tired too, and my stomach is a little upset. I love you. I will talk to you tomorrow?"

"Yes, Sarah. Goodnight."

I hung up my phone. He didn't know everything or he would have come home. I could keep a few things from him. I did love him so, and I could let him feel that. I dozed off, and he still came to me in my dreams. I was able to face him this time, and I traced my fingers along his face. It was so real, and I could see him there holding me. I knew I was in a dream because he was even more perfect to me. He gazed deep into my eyes.

I woke on Day 11. I didn't like how last night went with James. I couldn't let James know everything. I would have to learn to control my emotions and deal with them on my own. I was ready for my Day 11:

As I close my eyes to touch your skin,
To run my fingers through your hair,
Waking up to see you there.
Is it real or just a dream?
It's one in the same.
I will love you now,
I will love you forever.
I surrender to you,
You are my savior.
With my eternal love,

James

Again, he always knows how to make me feel better. I got up and got ready for the beach.

Mom got up too, "Did you get sick last night?"

"Yeah."

"Where you talking to James?"

"Yeah."

"Maybe you shouldn't have the phone at night?"

"Mom, he's busy and it's the only time I can talk to him, and he keeps it to weekends only."

"But he upset you?"

"I upset myself. He wanted to come home to help take care of me, so I had to push him away so he would stay there and finish."

"*You* pushed him away?"

"Yes I did. It was hard for me and so is talking about it…" I got up and ran to the bathroom for the dreaded throwing up again. It's definitely triggered by my emotions. I walked back out slowly. "I think I should cancel on the beach thing."

"No, you should try to go. It might be good to relax in the sun. Don't try to think about anything."

"Yeah, I guess you're right."

I got my stuff together and went to get Matt.

I got out and opened my trunk. He leaned out the door, "Do you have a bag?"

"Yeah."

"Do you have room in your bag?"

"For what?"

He came out the door with his towel around his neck, no shirt on, a volleyball under his arm, and a Frisbee in the other with a shirt or something. He tossed me the ball. I caught it and dropped it in the trunk.

He asked, "Are you ready?"

"Yep."

"Can I put this in your bag?" He was handing me his shirt and Frisbee.

"Yeah."

Great, he's shirtless and riding with me. Sarah get over it. It's not that big of a deal since we both go in at the same time.

He was trying to make conversation, "So, what have you been doing?"

"I work every day, some days till 4p.m., and other days till 9 p.m."

"You work every day?"

"Monday through Friday. I have to work to pay for my car."

He put his seat back, and put his hands behind his head. "Auh, it's worth it."

"How would you know?"

"Because you get to take me to the beach, and you are the first person I asked.

"Well, thanks." I was sarcastic. "What happened to Alissa?"

"She heard I made a pass at you at the pool party."

"Matt, I didn't tell anyone."

"I know. I think they figured it out when you left."

"Oh, sorry. Matt, you're not going to hit on me today, right? I mean… I just… I had a really bad week, and I want to relax and forget about it."

"Nope. I don't want to be left at the beach without a ride."

"Good." I was happier about going now."

"Why didn't you got to Vallyfair?"

"I was spending the day with a friend, because I'm not really big on rides."

"The *boyfriend*?"

"Yeah." I felt a little guilty now.

"I thought he lived up north?"

I was supposed to be getting James off my mind, "He was down for a day, and I had to take him to the airport." *This is not why I was going to the beach.* Shit here come the tears. I tried to blink to keep them from filling up my eyes, but it was getting harder and harder as Matt was politely asking me questions.

"Where was he going?"

I couldn't talk about it at all, the nausea was coming back. My mouth was watering.

"Sarah, where was he going?"

I was swallowing to hold it in.

He put up his seat, so he could see me better. "I get it, bad week. Sorry Sarah. Would it make you feel better if I told you I was trying to get you to hit on me?"

I smiled, "No!"

"I thought if I didn't have a shirt on, you would be so turned on you would have to like me. I'm so *manly*." He was rubbing his chest and blinking his eyes at me.

I giggled a little. That was very cute of him.

"Are you laughing?"

He was making me feel better. "Yes. Thank you."

We parked and he grabbed my bag for me. We walked over to the rest of the group. I put my mat down and sat on it. I relaxed laying back and closed my eyes. I needed to get rid of the sick feeling. Maybe I can control my throwing up. Relax, take deep breaths, and I could get this to stop.

Matt came and sat next to me, "How are you doing now?"

I opened my eyes, "Better."

"You need to stay busy today! Come play volleyball." He got up and pulled me up. He made sure we were on the same team. We played well together. I played hard, so that way I didn't have time to think about anything. We kept winning and playing new teams. This was great.

"I didn't know you were this good, Sarah. I would have made you play with me a lot more."

After a few hours of playing hard I had to take a break. I told Matt and went back to my mat in the sand. I was tired already and needed to relax.

He only left me alone for a short while, "Sarah, I have an idea."

I didn't open my eyes but I had to smile, "What's that?"

"Well, you're really good and I need a partner, so on the nights you get done working early, can you come play volleyball with me?"

I smiled at him. Boy did that make me feel good. I was actually good at something? "Yes. I would like that." I closed my eyes again.

"Okay, no more rest. I have another idea." He got up and was pulling me up with him.

"No, I need rest, please, more rest." As I dragged my feet he handed me my shorts and tank top. "What are we doing?"

He smiled. "Well, if you're good at volleyball, let's see what else you're good at." He was dragging me to the concession stand. He pulled me past the concessions, down to the dock. He was excited, "Have you ever been canoeing?"

"No, and that is more work; I don't want to work. I want to rest."

"Sarah, you wanted to stay busy, right?"

I rolled my eyes, "Yes."

He rented a canoe for an hour. We went around the whole lake. He was in back and he directed me on where to paddle and how. It was nice and peaceful. We didn't talk about anything else because he didn't want me to get upset. He was telling me what to do most of the time. When we got back everyone was hanging out on the blankets.

Someone asked, "So, where did you two go?"

Matt didn't seem concerned that someone was asking, "Canoeing."

"Yeah, right," was their reply.

I was uncomfortable right away. I was desperate to escape this situation. This wasn't what I needed. I sat down and brought my knees to my chest wrapping my arms around them. He could tell that everything he worked so hard for me to forget came back immediately, and I needed James to hide behind.

Matt smiled at me softly, "Sarah, do you want to go?"

"Yeah, thanks."

He did try to make me feel better as we walked to the car, "You know they don't think you can be friends without liking each other. We can ignore them. It's called stupidity and immaturity."

I smiled, but really didn't have anything to say.

The drive home was kind of quiet. As we pulled up to his house his attention was on me more. I was getting a little uncomfortable again.

"Sarah, you're not changing your mind about playing volleyball with me are you?"

I smiled, "No, I would still like to do that."

"Good."

"Matt?"

He stopped getting out of the car, "Yeah?"

"Thank you for today."

He smiled, "So, we're good?"

"Yes Matt, we're good, and Matt?"

"Yeah."

"Thanks for not asking a lot of questions."

"Can I ask one?"

I smiled mischievously, "You just did."

He showed his disapproval but eased into asking, "Did you two break up?"

"Nope."

"Where did he go?"

"You said one and I really don't want to talk about it." I smiled a fake smile.

"Fine. As long as you will still play volleyball, you don't have to answer my questions."

"Goodbye, Matt."

"I'll call you tomorrow to find out what days you can play on."

"That sounds good."

I went home without feeling sick or sad. I was so tired. I should be able to sleep tonight. Mom was there and she asked how everything went. I told her about my day. I needed a change though, so we planned on frosting my hair on Sunday, something that would make me feel better. I went to bed early. I don't remember much except that I fell asleep right away.

7. Needs

I woke up realizing I slept dreamlessly. I stretched and crawled out of bed. I sat back down to read my Day 12:

True love is what I feel for you,
You are the air that I breathe.
You are the music that I dance to.
Someday you will be mine,
Until the end of time.
With my eternal love,

James

I remember dancing with him at my birthday party and at Tony's. I wanted to stay here in bed all day and think about him. I made myself get up, and mom had the stuff ready to frost my hair. Even if James didn't like it, it would be grown out a little by then. I lounged for a while and then we did the hair. It turned out lighter than I thought. Wow! It's almost really blonde...not too bad. I think I've lost more weight again, but at this point I really wasn't trying to lose any more. Matt called and we set game nights for Tuesday's and Thursday's. I laid around the rest of the day and into the night watching movies and sleeping off and on. I finally went to bed at 10 p.m. I couldn't help myself but think of James as I dosed off.

I woke up realizing today was Day 13, almost 2 weeks since I saw James. No phone call last night; that bums me out a little. I pulled out Day 13: there was only one more in the envelope. What was I going to wake up to after that? I opened it:

I watch the trees to help pass time,
I don't feel the ease,
I want you to see so many things,
For without you I cannot be...
With my eternal love,
James

He felt the same way as I did, but how did he know what I was going to feel like today. I just didn't understand. I went to work as usual and when I got home mom wasn't home yet, but I had another day of not getting sick. So, that was a good thing. I went to bed shortly after she got home. I was down today but not stressed. I went to bed thinking of how much I loved James. My heart was aching for him.

Day 14: The last day in the envelope. Oh how I was going to miss these. I opened it to see what was in store for me.

The emptiness of my heart from missing you,
Does not fill with another,
Because it is you my love
I will love forever
I love you,
James

Oh, James. I feel the same way. I love you more than words can say. I had to push myself to get out of bed. The pain of missing him was worse than ever. I could have stayed in bed all day. Good thing I have my car to help me feel like he was around me, and the thought of having to pay for it kept me motivated. I went to work and had an uneventful day. I got home at 4:30. I sat down on the chair to veg out by myself. I answered the phone and it was Matt.

"Are you on your way to get me, or do you want me to drive? I can barrow my Dad's car if I need to."

"Oh Matt, I forgot. I really need to bail today. I'm not really up to it."

"Sorry, but you can't bail. I have two games set up for us, and I need you."

"Okay, umm. I'll be there in 25 minutes. I just need to get changed, and I will be on my way."

I thought this might help me with the depression. I forced myself to put on a suit and shorts. I left mom a note. I said I would be back shortly after it was dark. I went to pick Matt up. He came running out of the house and jumped in my car.

"Thanks, Sarah, are you ready to work hard?"

"Of course, playing hard will do me good."

He smiled but said, "If you ever need to get whatever it is your upset about off your chest, I can behave myself and listen really well."

"Thanks, but if you want me to be my best, it's not a good idea today."

"Let's play ball."

The night went great. We played doubles and won both games. During the last game it was getting dark, but we fought our way through it. I brought Matt home. He couldn't stop talking about how the game went. I listened to him go on and on about how great we did. I was good at this, and it felt good. I have never felt good at anything here at home before, and it made me happy. I got home and my heart didn't hurt quit as bad. I went in and mom was home.

I knew I made her happy when I walked in smiling. "You seem happy?"

"Yep, we won both games."

"You have a package. It came from Colorado."

I jumped up and grabbed it but sat there holding it. The tears started to fill my eyes.

"Aren't you going to open it?"

"Yes, but in the morning. I feel really good and want to go to bed this way."

She smiled lovingly at me.

I did feel good and wanted to go to bed this way, but I did open the envelope. I just didn't want to open it in front of her. I didn't want her to see how much he fills me up with joy.

There were 14 more notes that had dates on them. I was so happy that I didn't have to go a day without one. There was one without a date so I went ahead and read it.

My sweet Sarah,

Oh how I miss you. My heart is empty and I miss you, your smell, your touch, your taste, your smile, your lips, and oh do I miss your arms. I hope you are living while I am gone. Sometimes that is all we have to keep going. I will come back, into your arms, if you will still have me. I know now how much you fill my days, and I commit myself to filling your days with joy and your nights with pleasure. Please wait for me. I am here in your heart. I love you, Sarah, more than I could ever say.

With all my love,
James

I couldn't stop the tears. I had to wait five more weeks to be with him again. It's only five more weeks. *Okay, I can do this, only five more weeks.* I drifted to sleep with that on my mind.

I felt the trace of his hand down my arm. His breath moved over my face. I woke and turned around; it felt so real. No one was there. Oh James, you have to concentrate on what you are doing, not on me. I will be here when you come home. Please know I will wait for you, and that I would wait a thousand years to be with you again. Even if it was only for a second, I would still wait. I closed my eyes to fall into his arms again. He was there in no time at all, holding me tight to him. He must have felt my depression again.

I woke for Day 15: It was that goofy hump day again. I still don't get what it is about the hump day. Everyone in the world waits for to the weekend. Don't some people work on the weekends? I know quite a few myself, therefore how could this be the middle of the week, or the middle of what. Let's see what James has for me today.

I know were apart,
But space cannot separate our hearts.
With all my love,
James

I went to work feeling depressed again that we were apart, but filled because he loves me. I had a great day knowing how much he loved me. I couldn't stop smiling either. When I got home mom was already there because it was my late day.

She was eager to ask me questions, "So, what was the package you got?"

I thought about James and his notes with a grin on my face. "He has been giving me love notes every day that he is gone. And the envelope that came yesterday has the next two weeks worth."

Mom shook her head in disbelief. I went to bed and fell asleep almost immediately. His arms were there to hold me and protecting me from feeling depressed.

Day 16: I was starting to live for the notes from my Cayuse.

There is nothing that I want more,
Than to be with you.
I miss you!
With all my love,
James

I got up realizing I had forgotten to call Tony to tell him if I was going up there this weekend. I didn't even know yet. I got ready for work and got my stuff for volleyball. I would be ready to play today. I wanted to win more.

I went to the kitchen and had breakfast with mom.

"Are we going to see dad this weekend?"

"How are you feeling?"

"I haven't gotten sick since last Saturday." I was hopeful.

"Do you want to go?"

"Yes and No. It's really hard to be there and not see James, but I like to hang out with Danelle. I'd also like to see Carl."

She shook her head but said, "Then we go."

I headed for work but called Tony from my cell phone. I apologized for not letting him know earlier and I was still up for dancing if it was okay. He agreed it was still a good idea, and we made plans for me to be there at 4 p.m. to get ready. He sounded happy that I was coming. I didn't know how to plan it, but I was going to get to dance my heart out.

When I was done with work I rushed out to stop by home, so I could get dressed there. I called Matt and told him I was on my way.

I arrived at his house and he was waiting outside for me. He was all smiles and couldn't wait to kick some butt.

We had another two great games. I was feeling really good. He went on and on about the games again. "You know, Sarah, we make a great couple."

I wondered if he was getting the wrong idea about this. I was only doing this because it made me feel better about myself.

We pulled up to his house, and he didn't get out. He sat there for a long time before saying anything. "Sarah, we do very well together."

"Yeah, I am having a lot of fun, and we are beating everyone."

He was hesitant, "Are you ready to tell me what's going on?"

"Nope, but thank you, I am having so much fun."

"Okay then. Have a good night."

"Bye."

I went home feeling good. Matt tried to be serious and he didn't push. I was so thankful. I couldn't wait to see Carl.

I got home and found a very cheerful mom. She was happy I was doing okay without James. If she only knew I planned on spending the rest of my life with him, she wouldn't be so pleased.

I went to bed so tired. It was hard working eight hours and then playing volleyball for more than four hours. I closed my eyes awaiting my words in the morning.

I woke to my phone ringing, "James?"

"Say my name again, please?"

"Oh, James, my Cayuse."

"Sarah, I am coming home on Tuesday."

"James, what happened?"

"I love when you say my name."

"I love hearing your voice too. You make a perfect ending to my day, and yet lift me for the next, but James, what happened?"

"Nothing happened Sarah. My heart *aches* for you."

"Oh James, I am empty without you too. But you have to continue. We have our whole lives to be together; this is only temporary. We only have to suffer five more weeks."

"Sarah?"

"Yes, James."

"I'm scared."

"What are you scared of?"

"I can't feel you as much. I don't know how you feel."

"James, you don't get it."

"Get what?"

"When you're not here in my arms, I don't feel anything. My heart is empty."

"So, you're not trying to feel me?"

"It's not that I'm not trying to feel you. I'm just *numb* without you here."

"Sarah, I need to feel you."

I instantly thought about tracing my lips on his. "I could dream about you, us, if you want."

"Did you just think about tracing my lips with yours?"

"You felt that?"

"Oh yes, Sarah, I did. Will you do something else?"

I thought about running my hands over his chest and kissing him.

"Oh Sarah, I need to come home *right now!*"

"You promised you would wait till Tuesday to discuss coming home." I thought about moving my fingertips up and down his back and then wrapping my arms around him."

"I just miss this so much."

"Only five more weeks, James, only five more weeks till we're together."

"That doesn't sound so bad when you say it that way."

"I have to keep telling myself the same thing so I don't go crazy."

"Sarah. I had an idea. We have a break at three weeks and we get a whole day off. I was thinking maybe you could fly out for the day."

I couldn't help but smile, "What?"

"I need to see you, even if it's only for a few hours."

"You want me to come to you?"

"Yes. I need to see you. And you have all that money, you could use some to come and see me."

"I will get on the internet and see what I can find out."

"You think you could do that?"

"To be with you I would do anything. I miss you so much, James. My heart is racing from you asking me."

His joy came through the phone, "You have made me so happy."

My mind was already working on how I was going to make this happen. "I will ask for the day off when I go into work today, and I will try to find a flight."

The relief in his voice was comforting, "Oh my sweet Sarah. I love you so much."

"James, I am so empty without you."

"I don't want to let you go."

"You don't have to. I'm right here, James, and nothing else matters when I have you."

"Are you going up north this weekend?"

"Yes, but my plans are your dad, Danelle, and Tony's."

"Why Tony's? You're not planning on running away again?"

"No, I'm not. He is going to let me play music and dance from 5-8 on Saturday, before people actually get there."

"Don't let anyone get close to you; it drives me crazy." He was being playful now.

"James! You know better than that. You are the only one I want to be with, and you're kind of stuck with me for the rest of your life."

"Good, I want it that way."

"I am so yours, baby, and if you could see the things I want to do to you."

"Okay, Sarah, I still have to sleep."

I thought about kissing his abs.

"Don't do that. It just makes me want to be with you more."

"I will do my best to get there next Wednesday."

"You're really going to try to come see me?"

"You did ask. Did you think I would tell you no?"

"In a way, yes, but I want you to come, so please don't forget to check flights. I need this; I *need* you."

"You already have me, James."

"I am sorry, Sarah, I have to go. I need to sleep a little. We will be running 8 miles in the morning. I will call you tomorrow, and I love you."

"I will be waiting."

"Goodnight my sweet Sarah."

"Goodnight my love.

We hung up but I couldn't sleep. I went out to the computer to see what I could find. My heart was racing still with the thought of seeing him. I found flights to Denver at 8:25 a.m., and back to Minneapolis at 6:00 p.m. It was two hours each way and with time waiting for the flight I would get to see him about 5 to 6 hours. Perfect. I wondered how far the airport was from where he was going to be coming from. That would be something else we would have to consider if we were going to do this. I wrote everything down and put it in my purse. I might actually get to see him. I was completely on a high now. I went back to bed. To my surprise I was able to go to sleep a lot easier, even though my heart was racing. His arms came to comfort and hold me as I slept.

I woke the next morning and I was so happy. Day 17, what did he have in store for me today?

I am waiting for the moment
I can hold and kiss you again.
If all goes well, we shall be together soon.
I miss you, and love you.
With all my love,

James

I couldn't wait to get up today. I got ready for work and was on my way but thought about being up north hanging out with Danelle. She was down to earth, and I promised her I wouldn't do anything crazy till I talked to her, so I would have to tell her about running away for a day to be with him.

Okay, back to work. I smiled to myself, and I guess it showed on the outside too. Everyone at the dealership noticed. More people said hello today and commented on my happiness. I felt guilty for being so happy, but it was spilling out today. I asked for next Wednesday off. With my happiness they couldn't refuse me today.

I went home and packed, remembering my next 2 days of notes from James. I felt really good with no more getting sick. Maybe I was over whatever it was. I put everything in the car and waited a short while for mom to come home.

We were on our way shortly after she got home.

8. Frail

When we got up north, we met dad at Sherburn's. I found Laura at the bar, "Where's Danelle?"

She held out her arms for me, "Come here, Sarah."

I walked behind the bar to her. She took my hands and held me out so she could look at me. "Sarah, you are losing too much weight; I need to feed you."

I was relieved. I thought maybe she was going to scold me for liking James, "I'm fine, Laura. I'm still eating. I have been kind of sick the last few weeks and sometimes things won't stay down."

"Does your mother know?"

"Yes and I have been to the doctor. They gave me some pills to try and help. I haven't gotten sick in almost a week."

She gave me a very serious face, "Well, that's good but I am still going to make you eat."

I sighed, "Where's Danelle."

"In the back; tell her to make you a burger and fries and then you come and eat them in front of me. I want to see you eat."

Great. Someone else thinking I am not eating. I ran to the back and found Brian first.

There was some excitement in his voice, "Sarah, I didn't know you were coming today."

"Where's Danelle?"

"She's taking the trash out."

I tried to walk by him, but he held his arm out to stop me. I turned to him to see what it was that he wanted. "What are you doing?"

"I missed you. Do you want to do something?"

I hesitated on asking, "What do you mean?"

"If I get a hold of someone to come play basketball, will you play?"

That did sound good and I approved, "Yeah. I would like that, but I need to talk to Danelle first."

Danelle was coming in the door as I pushed passed Brian. I rushed to her. "We have to talk."

"It better not be anything crazy."

I raised my eyebrows, "Maybe a little."

She gave me a disapproving look.

"Oh yeah, your mom wants me to eat in front of her, so were suppose to make food and go sit with her while I eat."

"What do you want?"

"How about a Cheeseburger and some fries, but not a whole order of French fries though.

Danelle showed me how to make the stuff. I felt guilty for making her do this for me. We grabbed the food and went to the bar. My mom was laughing because I followed Laura's orders. We sat and I ate very slowly. I didn't know how my stomach was going to take this food.

Laura noticed how slow I was eating, but I think she got the wrong idea because she said, "No wonder you're losing weight; you eat like a snail."

That was correct. I was eating slowly, so it would stay down, but I wasn't done eating. Brian came rushing into the bar. "Danelle, are you up for Basketball? You will be my partner again."

She turned to her mother for approval.

Laura gave her approval with a stipulation. I had to finish eating. Brian sat down next to me and every time Laura went to wait on someone else, he would eat some of my fries. Finally, she stepped away, and he took two huge bites of my cheeseburger. As Laura walked back to us he was trying to chew and swallow as fast as he could. I took the last bite, but there were still fries left.

I leaned to him a little, "Thank you."

He glared at me, "I am not doing this so you don't have to eat. I am trying to hurry you up."

"Good, eat more. I want to go too."

He turned to Danelle, "Pat's on his way down. Go find the basketball; we'll be right there. I am going to try to rush Sarah."

Danelle took off to the house. I sat there and smiled knowing he was going to help me finish eating.

He turned to me as he grabbed more fries, "You are getting too skinny, but you look good." He turned away grinning.

"Brian!"

He sat there smiling, "What?"

I decided he needed to be scolded, "Don't do that. Otherwise I can't be around you."

He turned to me again, "Your restrictions or his?"

I took one last fry, "All mine baby, all mine." I turned to him smiling to see how he took that. I could see the disappointment in his face. Then he squinted his eyes like he was thinking of something to say to me, but it wasn't bad. "Fine, but you said you would play." He turned to his mom holding up the basket. "MOM!"

She nodded for us to be able to go. She wouldn't have let me go if she knew he ate most of the food.

He grabbed my hand and pulled me out of the bar, through the house, and out to where Danelle was already shooting basketballs. I was not happy, "Not fair, you're practicing."

She laughed at me. Pat wasn't there but Tommy was and he was shooting with her. I directed him, "You're my partner, so I hope you're good because I'm not."

He wasn't happy, "Why am I stuck with you?"

I walked up to him and spoke really softly, "Do you want her on the same team as you or would you like to guard her?"

He took a minute to ponder the thought, and when the light bulb went on, he mouthed to me. 'I get it.' He said out loud, "I got the hot shot; I'm good now."

We played, and it was so competitive. I was more willing to fight to win. Since I have been playing volleyball, I found out it was a lot of fun to play hard. It was more hands on and I guarded better than I have ever done before. Brian actually had to work to get past me. He was so close to me our faces were inches apart and nothing. It was so refreshing to play and not be hit on. I noticed his attention went past me, which allowed me to go around him and take a shot.

"You shouldn't lighten up like that. Are you getting tired?"

He wasn't replying to me, so I turned to see what had his attention. I noticed Jason pulled up in his truck and got out.

Danelle was grabbing my arm, "Sarah, do you want to go in? We could play video games."

Brian turned to Danelle. She was pulling me inside. I complained, "You two stop. I am fine."

Brian walked to us and took my other arm and they both escorted me inside.

"Why are you guys doing this?"

Brian spoke to Danelle avoiding answering my questions, "Danelle, open the door." She went in front of me opening the door, so he could drag me into the house.

We got to the kitchen and I stopped, "What is the problem, guys? I am fine and we can still play." I was getting angry, and I wasn't going any further without an explanation.

Brian ignored me and asked Danelle, "Will you please set up the games. I will explain."

Danelle protested, "You *know* we're not supposed to…"

I shifted my attention back and forth between each of them wondering what was going on. "What?"

He still didn't answer my questions, "Danelle, please. I will be careful."

She stormed out of the room, and I was confused about their reactions.

"Sarah, your dad talked to my mom and dad."

"Okay, what are you talking about?"

"We all know."

"Know what?" I wanted to hit someone. This was way over reacting to Jason showing up.

"That when you get upset... well, you've been getting sick."

I was relieved and irritated at the same time. "Brian I am fine. I went to the doctor, and she gave me some pills for my stomach. They are helping, and I haven't gotten sick in a week."

"Really?" He seemed relieved and confused by this.

"Yeah, it's my nerves and my stomach is taking it out on me. Otherwise, I feel perfectly fine."

He moved closer to me with his face down, "Sarah, you're really skinny now. Are you sure you're eating?"

Now I was really mad. "You saw me eat!"

He pleaded, "You didn't even eat half, and I ate most of it."

"Then you shouldn't have hurried me. I would have eaten all of it. I am fine!"

"But your dad asked that we be careful to not upset you or *let* anyone else upset you."

"Well, you're kind of pissing me off now!" I turned to walk away.

He grabbed my arm to stop me. "He's not the only one that cares about you. It's okay to have friends that care too."

"Fine, but I need some alone time with Danelle. We're going to take a walk by the lake. If you want to help, don't let Jason out of the bar."

I walked away and leaned into the living room. "Danelle, can we go for a walk?"

She had no problem with my request, and she jumped up to come with me. We walked slowly down to the dock. "Sarah are you sure you're okay?"

"Yes, I am fine. I haven't gotten sick in a week, but it makes me angry that everyone treats me like I'm going to break.

"It's just that you are so frail. You are too skinny."

"I am fine."

"So, you needed to talk to me about something."

"Well, now I don't want to tell you. You're going to tell me no because it is a little crazy."

"Then don't do it!"

"But I will get to see James."

"You can't wait five weeks?"

"Yes, but if I fly out to Colorado next Wednesday, I could see him for a few hours."

"What do you want to do?!"

"Fly to Colorado in the morning and come back the same afternoon… not even a whole day."

"*That* is crazy. If I were you I wouldn't do it. Wait, time will go by really fast. You're only 16 years old. Will they even let you buy a ticket?"

"I guess I didn't think about that."

"Sarah, think this through. Give me till Sunday and I will give you my answer then."

"That sounds fair."

As we walked back in I had to ask, "What's the big deal with Jason. I told him I didn't like him anymore, and I'm not afraid of him."

"I think Brian was over reacting; you seem so frail."

"I didn't play frail, did I?"

"No, actually you played really good today."

"I have been playing pair volleyball with a guy from school, and we have been winning. I like it a lot."

"So, you hang out with other guys from school?"

"Yeah. I think you are my only girl friend I have. The rest of my friends are guys like your brother."

"But my brother *likes* you."

"No, he doesn't. The only reason he pays attention to me is because I'm not interested in him. If I was, he would run the other way."

"If you think so."

"I know so."

She was curious, "Does James get mad at you?"

"Not mad, maybe a little jealous, but never mad."

"Would you be mad if he hung out with girls as friends?"

"I never thought of it that way. He does like when I hang out with you. No parties, of course."

We both laughed. We moved into the living area with Brian and Tommy and sat down to play video games. We had a bowling tournament in their living room. It was so fun and I didn't get sick, like everybody is freaking out about.

When we were done with that we went out to play pool. I reassured Brian it was okay. Jason wasn't going to stress me out. I was really good now. I've had two weeks to compose myself. We walked out, and Jason sat back in his chair. He was staring the whole time.

Brian came up close to me and I backed away a little leaving a little space between us. He was expressing his disapproval, "I don't like the way he always watches you."

I chuckled, "I didn't notice."

He turned to me, "You didn't?"

I shook my head with disbelief, "Brian he doesn't bother me. He wouldn't bother you either if you ignore him." I winked at Brian, "Maybe he will go away on his own."

"I don't think so."

Our conversation was cut short with the ringing of dad's voice, "Sarah, it's time to go."

I hugged Danelle and said goodbye to Brian and Tommy.

Brian stopped me, "Maybe you should ask if you can stay here tonight."

I was distrustful, "So I can be close to *you*, or to stay away from Jason?"

He glanced over my shoulder, "I'm sure James wouldn't want him to be hanging around like this."

I laughed, "But he would be okay with me staying under the same roof as you?"

"Good point, but I will behave. I promise."

I calmed down and tried to calm him, "If he shows up at the trailer tonight I will ask about tomorrow. Okay?"

He let go in defeat, "Yeah."

I walked over to dad, "I'm ready. Do you want me to wait or should I go?"

"You can go. We will be right behind you."

Danelle and Brian both walked me to my car. Jason did not follow. I was relieved. I got in my car and felt like I was in James's arms immediately. I am going to be okay this weekend. I could feel it.

"Thanks guys, see you tomorrow. I'll try to get dad to let us use the boat for tubing."

Brian was excited again, "We'll pay for the gas."

I was happy too, "Sounds good to me."

I closed my door and drove to the trailer

It was really dark when I got there. Dad didn't leave on any lights. I contemplated if I wanted to go in or wait in my car until they got here. I decided to make a run for it. We didn't even have a yard light, so I was a little nervous. Something about complete darkness was scary to me. I popped the trunk and shut the car off. I got out and hurried to grab moms and my bags running for the safety of the trailer. I flipped on the light as soon as I hit the door. I turned on the outside light so mom and dad could see their way in. I walked back and put mom's bag on her bed. I walked to the front room and put mine in there. I dug out some lounging pants, it was so hot in the trailer I decided on shorts and a tank top. I walked back out and they weren't here yet. Okay, I should have waited for them. They want me to be responsible and then they do stuff like this. I poured myself a glass of water and went to the bathroom to brush my teeth. I heard the truck, and I was relieved that they were here. I heard the door, but they weren't saying anything, so I finished brushing my teeth and walked out to see what they were doing.

To my surprise it wasn't them, "What are *you* doing here?"

Jason didn't give me any expression at all as he replied, "I was going to behave, but your dad and mom wanted some alone time, so they went to neck somewhere. Your dad didn't want you to be up here by yourself."

"Great!" I stood there not knowing what to do with myself. I decided this was awkward, so I moved to the TV and put in a movie and moved to the chair. I didn't pay attention to what he was doing. I was trying to get into the movie, so I wouldn't have to talk to him.

"Sarah, can we do something? The silent treatment is going to bug me."

I wanted to reassure him that I could be left alone, "Jason, I am okay to be here alone. You can go."

He moved to the couch and sat down. He sat with his elbows on his knees. His discomfort was visible in his posture, "I can't leave. Your dad has warned everyone about you getting sick from the stress."

I was irritated again, "Great, so everyone is going to think I'm crazy."

He put his face down and picked at his fingers. "No. A lot of people actually care about you. You are kind of frail."

Now I was angry and I raised my voice, "I have heard that one too many times today. If anyone else treats me like I'm going to break, I am going to get stressed out!"

"You are angry with me because I didn't do anything."

I eased up, "Sorry. I am frustrated because everyone is over reacting to this. I am fine."

My phone rang. I smiled as I answered it, "James!"

"How is it going?"

"Good." I got up and walked outside to talk to James. I gave him a rundown of my day. "I played basketball with Danelle and then we had a bowling tournament with a bunch of people."

I heard Jason come through the first door. I stood up and turned around pointing for him to go back inside. He wasn't going to follow my instructions. He was shaking his head no. I turned away from Jason and continued with my conversation with James.

"Then what did you do?"

"We played pool until it was time to go."

"Was Jason there?"

"Yep, but he didn't try to talk to me, so I am good."

"I hate you being there without me." He sounded bummed out.

"I hate it too." I moved to sit on the steps forgetting Jason was there. "Dad told everyone that I was stressed out. Now *everyone* is acting weird around me."

He sounded relieved that I wanted him here. "I could be home on Tuesday, if you would like."

"James please don't say that. You know I want you to be here, but you are going to finish this."

"Have you been sick at all?"

"Not since last Saturday when I was on the phone with you."

He was really concerned for my well being, "Are you eating?"

"Stop that. You know I eat. And yes, Laura wouldn't let me do anything until I ate."

I could hear the smile on his face, "What did you have?"

"A cheese burger and some French fries."

He knew better. "Who ate most of it for you?"

I was irritated again. "I ate it. Your being as bad as everyone else and you haven't seen me since I lost 20 lbs."

"You what?" He was upset now.

I was careful now. "I lost a little more weight, but James I wasn't trying. I think it happened because of the getting sick."

His voice got deeper, "You have lost enough."

I didn't like how this was going. "I didn't try, James. Can we talk about something else?"

He lightened, "Like what?"

I was winning again. "Maybe about how much I miss…" I thought about kissing his lips.

"Don't do that. I will need to come home then."

I laughed, "I love you so much."

"So, what are you doing now?"

"I'm sitting on the steps talking to you silly."

He was more careful asking, "I know that. Is there anyone there with you?"

"Nope, it's just me."

"Where are your mom and dad?"

"Parking, and they give us a hard time. Hey, do you think they were at Timber Lodge when we brought your mom there? Dad said he saw us there."

He laughed, "I bet they're getting some."

"James, that's *gross*. I don't want to imagine my mom and dad together like that. Yuk."

He was laughing again, "Is it yuk when we're playing?"

"No. I like the playing, but thinking about them…it's gross."

I could hear his laughter. I shook my head in disbelief that he was finding this funny. He finally calmed down, "So, you are by yourself?"

"James you shouldn't worry about me. I only have eyes for you, and I am feeling good. I thought maybe I could use this time to sort things in my head and try to figure out what I want to do..." I tried to say this comically, "...*when* I grow up."

He did chuckle a little but tried to be serious, "Are you listing them out like I told you? Are you listing the pros and cons of each idea?"

"I haven't really started yet. You called me before I could get started. I brushed my teeth and got changed and then you called me."

"So, what are you wearing?" He was being playful again.

"Shorts and a tank top. What are you wearing?" I made the attempt to be playful back.

"Nothing."

"What? Why are you not wearing anything?"

"Everybody is out, and I was thinking about you."

"James, you're torturing yourself again." I felt so bad that he was doing this to himself.

"I'm just kidding. I wanted a reaction."

I laughed and shook my head. "Did you get the reaction you wanted?"

"No, not really."

I laughed a sigh, "I would give you a reaction if you do that with me around."

"Now *that's* what I was wanting."

I started to giggle softly. I totally forgot that Jason was there. James was everything to me, and I loved talking to him.

"Hold on." I held out my phone to take a picture. I looked at it before I was going to send it. I was glad I did because I saw Jason behind me in the picture. I deleted it right away and went back to talking to James. "Sorry."

"What were you doing?"

"I was going to take a picture, but it's too dark."

"Will you send me one tomorrow? Please?"

"I will for sure."

"I want one in a swim suit?"

"James, that's weird."

"No, it's not, plus I miss seeing you that way."

"Okay. Can you send me a picture of you?"

"Sure, but how do you want it?"

"I will take anything."

He laughed and changed the subject, "Did you check on flights?"

"Yep. It would be into Denver at 10:30 a.m. and depart at 6:00 p.m. It would be less than $100 each way."

"That's not bad."

"No. I didn't think that was bad at all. How far are you from Denver?"

"About an hour."

"How would you get there?"

"I'm not sure yet. Did you book the flights?"

"No, two problems; I wanted to make sure everything would work out before I did and, the other thing is I don't know if I can."

"Are you scared to come see me?"

"No, yes, well maybe of the flying."

"Oh, well. That might be a little problem."

"Yes, a little and then booking it; do I have to be 18 years old?"

"I don't know, but you should check."

"I will on Monday, but James? I'm not going to unless you are sure you can get there."

"I'll find out by tomorrow, and I will call you tomorrow night."

"Okay."

"I have to run in the morning. Eight miles is tough."

"Okay. I love you, James."

"Oh, how I love you, my sweet Sarah."

"Bye."

"Bye."

I hung up the phone and sat there for a while. I knew I was in for a lot of questions, but I was cherishing the thought of being with him on Wednesday.

9. Committed

Here came what I was dreading. "So, you really love him?"

I took a deep breath, "Yes. I really do."

He opened the door and held it gesturing for me to come back inside. I got up and walked in. I had to pass him when I was walking in. He leaned closer as I passed him.

"Oh, do I miss you."

I stopped and turned to him, "Please, don't do that."

"He wouldn't have fallen in love with you if it wasn't for me."

"I know that." I was a little angry but tried to recover gracefully, "But that doesn't give you the *right* to do things like that." I walked away to the chair and sat down.

He came over and sat on the floor in front of me. I moved my feet off to the side of the chair. His touching me in any way was not okay with me.

"Are you planning a trip?"

He caught that? "No. I was checking on something for James."

"So, he's coming home?"

"Well, eventually he is."

He was sounding hopeful, "You didn't tell him I was here?"

"Nope."

"I told you. I knew you wouldn't tell him."

"Oh, I told him."

"What did he say?"

"Not a whole lot, but as long as I can handle it he's not going to worry about it."

"That doesn't sound like James. He would have been here already."

"Jason, he knows I love him more than life itself."

"Sarah! I know James. How did you talk him into not coming home?"

I grimaced as I told him, "I got sick and he was willing to do anything to get me to stop."

He chuckled, "He gave into you?"

"Yep."

"I bet he doesn't know you look this sick."

"I don't look sick. I am really thin that is all. And remember I'm frail, so don't upset me!"

He was more concerned, "So, what did the doctor say?"

"If you are asking me if I am pregnant, it was a definite no. She put me on medicine that is supposed to help curb the acids in my stomach. I haven't been sick for a week." I was really proud of this fact.

He was full of sarcasm, "Wow. Amazing. How much have you eaten since then."

Does this ever stop? "Not you too. I really don't want to talk about my eating."

"You're scared to eat, aren't you?"

"No, I eat what I want when I want." I was very direct.

"Okay?"

He scooted down, so he could rest his head on the chair. He turned to me.

If he was going to be here I wanted to get the focus off of me. "Can I ask you a question?"

"Depends."

"Well, maybe a few."

He lightened a little, "What do you want to know?"

"If you and Kylie keep breaking up, why do you *keep* going back to her?"

He sat there quiet and wasn't answering me. Maybe he didn't know how to answer that question, but it worked. He's not talking about me.

"You know, I knew you were going to ask that question someday. I have practiced answering you with many different answers, but I really don't have a good excuse."

"Don't you love her then?"

"You know sometimes she's really fun to be around. She is definitely not bad to look at and other options are obsolete."

I was offended, "What do you *mean* other options?"

"There are not a lot of options for partners up here, and if you have noticed, she is probably the best looking girl around. Of course, nothing compared to you, but you're not from around here."

I was going to let him know I did not approve of his way of thinking, "So, you're telling me you only like her because she looks good and there are no other options."

"No. I not saying that either. We have been together since we were in the 10th grade. That is a lot of years, and we don't know how to be apart. I don't think either one of us is really in love, but we do care about each other. To say we are completely in love with each other, probably not."

"But you still have *sex*?"

"Yeah."

"I don't get that."

"It's better than being alone."

"You really think so? I've seen the way she treats you and it's not right."

"She feels betrayed."

"Yeah, well you shouldn't have done what you did." I was lecturing him a little.

He was defending himself, "We weren't together the whole time I was with you, Sarah." He turned to me and got on his knees. "You were interested in me?"

I felt remorseful, "At one time I was, but Jason…You stopped coming to see me; you left me waiting and wondering. *You* made your choice. I didn't know about Kylie at all, and you just didn't show up anymore without an explanation. How was I supposed to feel? Aren't you with her now?"

He leaned forward and traced his hand across my forehead wiping the hair form my face.

I turned away. "Jason, don't do that. You don't have any right to do that."

"Sarah, I have wanted to have you and be with you, but I thought you needed time to grow up. I see *now* that you can handle this."

"Jason no!"

"Don't you remember how good it felt when we were together?" He wasn't touching me but was too close to me.

"Jason, please stop. I told you this was not going to be. I love James, and you need to stop." I pushed myself off the side of the chair and stood up. "If James is your friend, why would you do this?"

"He stole you from me."

"No, he didn't. You left and I was confused and sad. I didn't understand how you could make me feel that way and then stay away. He was there to be my friend. I think I'm going…"

I pushed him out of the way and ran for the outhouse. Of course, I can never make it. I was throwing up again. *Way too much to handle I guess. I wasn't really getting stressed out though; why am I getting sick.* I think I should stay home until James comes back. I slowly walked back to my car, but the feeling was coming back again. I headed back to the outhouse. I tried to swallow and take deep breaths to calm the feeling but I couldn't stop it. Jason made it to me and pulled back my hair.

"Jason, don't help me!"

He let go. "I'm sorry Sarah, I just thought that…" he trailed off putting his face down. He tried to finish what he wanted to say. "…I thought that if we were alone the feelings would come back."

Now I was angry, because I didn't like getting sick and he was pushing. "I told you, I love James!!! You can't turn it on and off. Why can't you understand that?" I stormed past him walking back to the trailer; he followed me. I walked in and got a glass of water and went to the bathroom to brush my teeth. Jason came and stood in the doorway, but he was beaten down by my scolding. He looked quite pitiful standing there, and I realized I had hurt him again. I didn't want too, but why does he have to keep pushing me?

He finally spoke as I rinsed my mouth and tried to brush my tongue. "I lost my chance with you."

My heart dropped. I didn't want to hurt him anymore. I did think I loved him at one time in my life, but now I love James with all of my heart. It must have shown in my face because he walked away saying, "I am sorry, Sarah."

I let him walk away, so I could have a minute to compose myself and think about how I can make him feel better without giving him the wrong idea. I walked to the living room, and he was sitting on the couch with his head in his hands. My heart hurt because I hurt someone for the first time in my life and I felt awful about it. I sat down on the couch, not too close to him though. "Jason, I am sorry too."

My phone rang. I pulled it out and answered, "James?"

I put my hand on Jason's arm to comfort him while I was talking to my beautiful amazing James.

"What is wrong? You were calling me so strongly, Sarah."

"I'm okay now."

"What happen?"

"Dad and I were fighting, but I'm okay now. I went to bed."

"Are you sure? It felt more like…"

"No James, I'm sure. I love you so much."

"You got sick again, didn't you?"

I sighed, "Yes, I did."

"I think maybe you shouldn't go up there unless I'm home. I don't want you to go through this by yourself."

"James, I will be okay. Remember, I'll send you a picture tomorrow; you will see I am fine."

"Do you need me to stay on the phone with you till you fall asleep?"

He made me feel so good but… "James, remember you are running in the morning. I will let you sleep."

"Sarah, I still feel you."

"I know, James. It will be forever, if you will have me."

"My words escape me for what I want to say to you."

"It's okay James; I woke you. Sleep now and call me tomorrow."

"I love you, my sweet Sarah."

"I love you too, my Cayuse."

I hung up the phone and turned to Jason. "I am sorry for hurting you, Jason, but I do love James and you gave him to me. I can never repay you for that."

"You didn't tell him?"

"You were right; he would come home. I do not want to be the reason he doesn't finish."

"But when he finds out it could hurt him. If he finds out you weren't truthful with him, you could lose him."

"His future is more important than worrying about me. If he finishes and I lose him because I didn't tell him, well, I guess I love him *enough* to let him go."

"Are you sure you haven't done it? Usually you only have that much love for someone if you have been with them."

"Nope, not yet, but Jason, it will be him someday."

"Were you close enough that you may be pregnant?"

"I am not pregnant."

"So, you were that close?"

"Jason we are not going in this direction."

"But Sarah, you have to understand. I still want to be your first. I would make it so special for you."

"Stop right now or I will have to hurt you more. I don't like doing that."

He pushed himself back on the couch more. I moved to the chair. His expression turned to pleading, but I couldn't give in and replied, "This will be easier."

I fell asleep in the chair waiting for mom and dad to show up. Jason stayed on the couch, and that is the last thing I remembered.

I woke to Day 18: I couldn't wait to see what this day would bring me from James. It was still early morning. Jason was sleeping on the couch still. I tried to ease off the chair, but I had a sharp pain in my stomach. I sat back down. I must have thrown up really hard last night. The pain went away when I sat back down. I took a deep breath and tried to get up again. I was a little more careful this time. No sharp pain, but each step I took hurt a little. I still had to get to my daily note. I opened it to read:

When do you know you have found the one?
You may ask this of yourself.
My heart decided for me.
My search was over when I found you.
With all my love,

James

"Hey, are you alright?"

Jason couldn't even give me this time alone? I turned carefully keeping the note tucked behind me. "Yeah, I'm fine."

He walked over and reached behind me to take the note. I couldn't stop him; I was afraid of the pain. I managed to put my hand on his chest to push him back a step.

He was confused, "You're not going to stop me?"

The tears welled up in my eyes, "I don't care if you read it, but please don't wreck it. It's *all* I have while he's gone."

I could see the wonder on his face, "You're not fighting me for it?"

A single tear rolled down my cheek as I pleaded with him to not wreck my note.

"You really do love him?"

I nodded.

He was noticing I wasn't okay, "Are you okay?"

"Yep. Can I have my note back, please?"

He handed it back to me, but I could see the doubt in his face. "You're not okay?"

"Nope. Going to be sick right now and I can't move."

"Why can't you move?"

"Bucket now… please."

I swallowed and tried to hold it back as he ran out of the room. He came back with the dish pan and handed it to me. The feeling was easing a little and I was trying to breathe through my nose to hold it in. I held up the dish pan to ask the question…

"It was all I could find on short notice."

I shook my head disapproving. He stood there looking at me waiting for me to lose it. I closed my eyes and was able to stop it from getting worse.

I finally opened my eyes to see what he was doing. He was still standing there waiting for me to say something.

"Are you okay now?"

I shook my head, "Maybe a little better."

"You're not moving though?"

"Nope, I think I pulled a muscle in my stomach last night. My stomach hurts."

"How bad?"

"Only when I move."

My phone buzzed. I was petrified immediately. James felt this. "Oh shit. That will be James."

"Nobody else calls you?"

"Nope." I pulled my phone out, but it was only a text. I sighed with relief, but opened it to read it.

>"What's wrong?"

I begged Jason, "Shit…, shit…, what should I tell him?"

"Tell him your fine."

I indicated that this would not be believable.

"What?"

"I don't know how to explain this, but he feels everything from me."

"I know he feels things. We have had a lot of fun with it."

"No. When it comes to me, he feels everything. He is stronger than Sam on this one thing. *Me*! He knows everything. If I am upset, sad, happy, anything he feels me. He *knows* something is wrong."

Jason was helping me grasp for something to tell him. "He knows you got sick last night already. Remember, he called you after you got sick."

"Yeah."

"Then tell him you pulled muscles in your stomach when you got sick."

"I'll try."

"I think I pulled muscles in my stomach from getting sick last night, and it kind of hurts."

>*"I'm coming home."*

"No!"

I stared at the phone waiting for his reply. "Shit…Shit, answer me, James. Please?"

Jason moved to read the phone over my shoulder, "What did he say?"

"He's coming home. He has been using everything from me as an excuse to come home. Answer me dam it James, you're not coming home!"

>"Yes I am."

"Can you call me?"

>"No, I leave tonight."

"James, please, NO."

Jason was reading it with me. "Quick Jason give me something that will make him stay."

He didn't understand why I didn't want James to come home. "Why do you want him to stay so bad?"

"It's part of the plan. The part of us is having a future together. If he doesn't finish I'm *afraid* we won't make it."

Jason was a comfort as he said, "Tell him that, Sarah."

"James. It's part of the plan to be together. I'm scared if you don't finish we won't make it forever."

>"Okay. I'll wait only a little while. Go see Sam."

"You want me to see Sam?"

>"Yes Sarah. I need to know if I need to come home now."

I turned to Jason. "Go wake my mom. I need to go see Sam and I don't think I can drive."

"Sarah they didn't come back yet. That is the only reason I am still here."

"Okay. I need to get to my car." I text quickly.

"I am on my way." I was walking to the living room and the pain was a little better.

Jason was walking slowly backwards with his arms up like he was going to catch me or something. I laughed at him, "What are you doing?"

"I am making sure…, I have no idea."

I laughed a little more but held my stomach because laughing did hurt. It wasn't as bad as before. I could walk without pain now. I got to the couch and sat down and got up again. The pain was definitely better. "Jason, I think its better. I need to get some clothes on. Go in my bag and grab me a pair of sweats and a t-shirt please."

I sat back down and text James. "James?"

>"Yeah?"

"I think its better. Do you feel that?"
>"You scared the living crap out of me."
"I'm sorry. I will still see Sam, if you want."
>"Please."
"Call me later?"
>"Yes."
"I love you."
>"You are going to drive me crazy little girl."

I smiled and closed my phone. I noticed Jason was watching me, "Are you two like this *all* the time?"

"Like what?"

"Like you're already married?"

"Mom and dad give me a hard time about it all the time."

"You really do love him."

"I told you that. Where do you think my mom and dad are?"

"Auh, I knew they were getting a room at the Timber Lodge, to be alone."

"I could have stayed at Danelle's if I would have known. What time were they going to be back?"

"They said they would be here by 10 a.m."

"It's only 7:30 a.m. Okay, I need to go see Sam and then maybe Carl."

"What do you want me to do?"

"Jason, I am fine now. I can take myself to see Sam and if I need help getting to Carl, Sam will help me"

I was trying to get dressed as he watched me.

"I don't think you should drive."

"Jason, I don't think it would be good for anyone to see you taking me anywhere. James is too important to me to take that chance. I will tell him everything later."

"Can you leave out the part where I came on to you?"

"Yes, of course. You understand now?"

"Yeah, I don't like it, but I understand."

"So, maybe you could follow me to the Reservation and wait to make sure I leave with Sam."

"I can do that."

I walked out to the car, and I was feeling better.

"Jason, I should leave a note for my mom and dad."

He ran back in the trailer and brought me a piece of paper and pen back out. I wrote that I went to see Carl at the hospital and that I would be back around 11 or 12. He ran it back in.

I yelled from my window. "Thanks, Jason."

He followed me till I got to the Reservation and he pulled over to wait for me to leave again. I went to the house and knocked. Katherine answered the door, and she let me in. Will was sitting on the couch. Katherine went back to the couch to join him.

Will watched me and asked, "What are *you* doing here?"

"James asked me to see Sam. Where is he?"

"He's in James's bedroom."

I headed down the hall, and Will jumped up to follow me, "What is going on, Sarah?"

"It's nothing really."

I knocked on the door, "I'm coming." He opened the door putting on a button up shirt over his muscle shirt. He was so much like my James. I found it hard to look at him.

"We're going to the hospital?"

"If you'll go with me?"

"Of course I will." He followed me to my car and we both got in. He knew already, "You are in pain?"

"Not anymore, but how did you know?"

"It came from James."

I drove down the road a little bit but stopped before Jason could see us.

"Was it that bad?"

I was nodding, "It was a sharp pain, and I couldn't move. It even hurt to walk."

"Okay, let me try."

"What can I do to help?"

He smiled at me. I lifted my shirt a little.

"Oh shit, Sarah."

I turned back to him, "What?"

"You have been getting worse!"

I was feeling bad, "What do you mean?"

He was angry and sad at the same time. Maybe I did look as bad as people were treating me.

"When was the last time James has seen you?"

"Almost three weeks ago."

"How much have you lost since then?"

He was scaring me, "I don't know, maybe 15-20 pounds."

He was shaking his head, "Can you hold food down at all?"

I was a little confused, "Yes I can. I only get sick when I am upset. This was the first time I had sharp pains."

"I am afraid to touch you."

"Sam, please knock it off and try."

I closed my eyes turning to the window. I felt his hand. He pushed my pants down further and then moved up to my abdomen. He took his hand off of me and sat there quietly.

I turned to him for answers. "Do you know anything yet?"

"It's like I told you before. I don't know what it is because I have never felt that before, but I think it's getting worse."

I felt defeated, "Okay, let's go to the hospital.

10. It Will Wait

We drove in silence to the hospital. We both got out and I could feel that it was way better than earlier. I think I did just pull a muscle. It was more like a cramp than anything else. Sam came around the car to walk in with me. He tried to take my hand for moral support or something, but I didn't let him.

"Sam! You can't do that."

"I do care about you. I feel James, and he loves you so much that I feel…I love you too."

"Please don't, Sam. My heart belongs to him and nothing can or will come between us."

"I know that, but I feel like he's telling me to take care of you."

"Not that way Sam and you know it." I was a little angry 'til I saw Clarissa.

She gave me the biggest hug, "How are you my child?"

I smiled at her, but the tears I was holding back were coming so heavily that they started to spill out.

"Actually, I have been a little sick lately, and I have been to the doctor and on Medication for almost three weeks, but nothing is helping."

"It started when James left?"

"No. I got sick the day I brought him to the airport. We had an argument, and I got sick."

She wrapped her arm around me, "Let's go see Carl."

I nodded, "Yes, please."

She led me to his room. As I entered and saw him laying there I felt better. James was so much like his father. I was completely better as I hugged him like the weight of the pain was gone.

He pushed me away, so he could look at me. "Child you are wasting away."

The tears welled up in my eyes again. Did I really look as bad as everyone was telling me? I thought I felt really good. I had more energy, and my clothes fit better. I can play volleyball and be good at it. I am *not* wasting away. If James sees the picture and thinks like everyone else he will come home.

Clarissa explained everything to him as he smiled and watched me. He pulled my hands, so I would be closer to him.

"How are you feeling now?"

"I am doing a lot better. I was upset last night. I have a hard time being up here without…"

He must have seen what I was thinking, which was James holding me. He finished my sentence for me, "My James."

He pulled me back to him, "You love *him* more than you love yourself."

He held me there for a little bit and then pushed me away a little to look at me. He finally said, "Sarah, it's fixable."

I felt relief but confused by this. Clarissa put her arm around my shoulder, "You're going to be fine."

I still didn't get it. I wanted him to tell me more.

"I don't know what it is either, but when James comes home he takes care of you and you will be fine."

"But I don't want him to come home. He has to finish first."

Carl had such a warm smile and he reassured me, "This will wait; he will finish. When he gets home he will take care of you. Don't worry about it anymore."

I was so relieved with this information, but I wanted to know more. "What is it?"

"I don't know, but Sarah you need to not worry."

Well, I definitely felt better. I hugged him tightly. I sat with him for what seemed to be a long time. I realized that I should go. I felt so much better. I couldn't wait to talk to James and tell him what his father said. He doesn't have a choice now; he had to finish.

I went out to the waiting room to find Sam. He was not happy, almost in agony over not being able to tell me what was wrong. I walked up to him grinning.

"What did my dad say?"

I was cheerful, "That I was fine and it's fixable; that my sickness will wait for James to come home and take care of me."

Sam stood up and hugged me so tight. "James has got to quit sending me these feelings. I feel a part of you all the time, and it's driving *me* crazy."

I patted his back, "I will talk to him."

He road with me back to the Reservation. I wanted him to be part of my world too, "Sam, I am going to get my dad's boat, and we're going tubing today. See if you can bring Amelia. If you can, were meeting at Sherburn's at 12:30 p.m."

"I would love that, and I can watch over you."

"Sam, I am going to be okay now that I have talked to your dad. I feel better too."

He got out of the car, "I will try, Sarah."

"Hey, tell her mom and dad there will be a huge group of kids so no alone time. Call me if I need to come get you both."

I drove back to the trailer. Mom and dad were there and, of course, Jason. He was worried. I smiled at him to let him know it went well.

I was ready to move on with my day, "Dad, can we get the boat out and go tubing at Sherburn's today? I kind of promised a lot of kids."

His face grew to a grin, "Sure."

Jason did not approve. I walked by him to go get changed but told him, "Carl said I am fine. James will finish and make it back to take care of me."

He whispered, "You shouldn't push it; you were really bad this morning. *Remember*, I was there."

I kept walking, so I could go get changed. When I walked into the room I sat down to text James. I wanted to let him know I was going to be okay, so he could have a better day not worrying about me.

"James, you don't have to respond until later, but I saw your dad. He says whatever it is; it will wait for you to come home."
>"Oh Sarah, I want to come home now."
"You made me smile James. I love you."
>"My body and soul ache for you."
"It's almost half over, only five more weeks; and maybe Wednesday."
>"I have to go."
"Go and be the best!!!"

I closed my phone and felt more loved. I got changed and went out to start the day right away. This is what I needed, having some fun. Right, that's what everybody waits for, fun for the weekend. I helped with the boat getting everything ready. Jason took it down to the boat launch for me.

"I am meeting you at Sherburn's."

"Jason, I am fine now."

"I will be close if you need something."

"Jason, no, I will be fine until James comes back. His dad said so."

I headed to Sherburn's in the boat. I tied it to the dock and ran up to get Danelle and Brian. I walked in the front. Danelle came out.

I was so excited, "I have the boat. When can you go?"

She laughed, "Come on."

I followed her to the back. As we entered Brian's eyes lit up.

I asked him, "Are you ready? The boat is at the dock."

They both turned to their mother for the answer they both wanted to hear. She couldn't refuse either one, "Fine… go."

We all took off running down to the dock. The lake was smooth as glass.

Brian stopped, "We need more people."

"I invited Sam and his girlfriend. I hope you don't mind."

"Not as long as he brings a girlfriend."

We laughed together. I had to ask, "Who did you invite? Mykala?"

He nodded, "But I don't think she's coming."

"Did you invite anyone else?"

"Just the regulars. Pat never showed up last night, so hopefully he will come. Well, you've got the boat; should we go anyway?"

"Yeah."

"You should go first."

"Okay." I took my shorts off. Danelle was getting things ready in the boat. Brian turned away from me. I took my shirt off.

"Brian, hand me the body suit." He handed it to me without looking at me. I laughed and asked, "What are you doing?"

"Behaving."

I smiled, "Thank you."

Danelle gasped, "Sarah!"

I turned to her to see what shocked her. She was noticing me. I put on the body suit quickly. I knew where she was going with this.

"Sarah, you're *really* thin."

I had it zipped to my belly button before Brian turned around to see what she was talking about. He looked me up and down, and then turned away smiling. It couldn't be that bad. He seemed pleased with what he saw. I couldn't help but grin and I felt better about the way I looked. I handed Danelle my phone, "Take a picture please, for James."

"You are such a cheater."

"Danelle, I haven't been trying to lose weight, but it keeps falling off. Plus, I have been running a lot."

"I'm not saying you look bad, it's just that you are really thin." She leaned into me, "The guys are going to drool."

I laughed a little. "So, I'm not gross looking?"

"No, but you look really grown up, and the blonde, just... wow!"

"Thanks."

She took my picture and I sent it right away. After sending the picture I was trying to zip the suit up, but the zipper wouldn't budge. Danelle tried to help me and couldn't get it either.

Brian jumped out of the boat, "Let me try." He was trying everything but it wasn't budging. He whispered to me, "It's really hard to not kiss you when I'm this close to you, and you're so dam *hot*."

I was trying to not smile and said, "If you can't get it then I will wear a life vest."

"Nope, I'll get it." He was more determined to get the zipper, "Can you take the top part off, so I can flip it over?"

I pulled my arms out and pushed it down so he could flip it over.

"Yep, see, here's the problem." He glanced up at me to show me. "Shit!" He went back to the zipper.

"What?"

"Nothing. I got it. You can put the top back on now."

I pulled it back on.

He zipped it really slowly and when he got to the top his face was really close to mine, "This is going to be harder than I thought."

I pushed him a little, "That is what the body suit is for."

He closed his eyes backing away from me, "You're so…"

"Brian. Knock it off. Remember, water skiing?"

He turned and moved to the boat. I felt way better about how I was looking. My stomach didn't hurt anymore either.

I sat down on the end of the dock and put the ski's on. They were moving away from the dock in the boat to get it set to go. I waved to hit it and we were off. I hadn't done this in a long time, but I waved around to indicate that I wanted to drop a ski. We went all over the place, and I got to go until my legs were so weak I could hardly stay up. I motioned for them to bring me in. When he got me close to the dock I let go. Pat was there and he dove in to come help me with the skies.

I crawled up the ladder after getting to the dock. It was a struggle only because my legs were weak now. I noticed Jason at the top of the shore line shaking his head in disapproval. I waved a small wave to show him I was fine.

Pat came over to me, "He is watching all the time now."

"Pat, its okay, it doesn't bother me anymore. I am fine."

It didn't bother me, but it still bothered Pat and Brian. Brian was now filling Pat in on the Jason situation.

I needed to get their minds off of Jason. He helped me this morning, "Who else is skiing?"

Brian, of course, wanted a turn next. I drove the boat for him. He definitely did more stunts than I could do. When he had his fill we headed in. No one else wanted to water ski, so we put the tube in next. I didn't go at all. I was afraid to lie on my stomach, so I did most of the driving while everyone else took turns going on the inner tube.

When I realized I was supposed to be at Tony's by 4, I headed into the dock. I still had an hour but I wanted some time to get ready for the night.

I pulled up to the dock, "Sorry guys, I have plans at 4. We have to be done for today."

Danelle knew what was up, so she started to help me wrap things up and started putting stuff away. I was trying to hurry and asked Brian, "Can we leave the boat here for the night, so we can do this again tomorrow?"

"Yeah, I will let my dad know."

"Thanks. Danelle, can you go with me?"

"I'm not sure."

Brian wanted in on this. "Where are you going?"

I didn't know if I should tell him or not. But Tony was doing it for the business and Brian could bring his friends. Okay, here it goes.

"I am going dancing at Tony's till 8 p.m. He's opening the doors to the younger crowd, and I am kind of teaching some dance steps."

"You're teaching dance steps?"

I cringed and wanted to get out of there fast, "Yes, I am. I have to go."

"Sarah, you don't have a car."

"Shit, I didn't think about that. I guess I will ask Jason to take me to the trailer."

"What?" Brian grabbed my arm and was storming away from everyone else pulling me with him.

"You're leaving with Jason?"

"Brian, it's not like that. He showed up at the trailer last night, and we had it out. He understands that…I love James. By the end of the argument I hurt him enough that he is not going to…" How do I put this? "Um … not hit on me ever again."

"You're sure about that?"

"I made it pretty clear."

"Well, that's good."

"If you want to come with you can. I'm kind of nervous about it, but he's trying to pick up some business with James not there to be the attraction. If you would like you could bring some of your friends."

"You wouldn't mind?"

"No, but only if you promise not to laugh at me and you help Danelle, so she can go too."

"I will go ask with her."

We were walking back to the dock.

"I suppose I should check to see if Jason is even here."

I got to my stuff on the dock and started to pull the top half of the wet suit down to my waist and put on my tank top, and then I pulled it the rest of the way off. Brian grabbed a towel to shield me. I noticed he was acting funny, "What are you doing?"

"You are going to have to be more careful getting dressed in front of people, and me if you don't want people to hit on you."

I laughed, "Sorry, thank you."

I grabbed my towel and pulled Danelle up to the resort with me. "Brian said he would ask with you. I will be back to see if you can go, but get ready too."

I walked into the bar searching for Jason. I knew he was here because his truck was. I didn't see him anywhere. I searched everywhere and walked back outside. He was standing by his truck. "Did you *need* a ride?" He had a funny smirk on his face like he knew what I needed.

"Do you mind?"

"Nope. Get in."

I hoped I wasn't giving him the wrong idea with asking for his help. I got in and didn't say anything, but I did notice he was smiling smugly. I thought about this. *He was here picking up the pieces James left behind.* I told myself I would not ask for his help anymore after this. We pulled in at the trailer, and I got out right away.

"Sarah, wait."

I turned around but didn't go back to the truck.

"What are you up to?"

"I have to be somewhere at 4 p.m. I will see you later." I ran inside and went to get ready quickly. I tried to pick out something that would make me feel a little older. I put on a tank top that sat short of my jeans. I was hoping this would do the trick.

I took a quick glance in the mirror, and I felt good. Mom and dad weren't here, and I didn't know where they were, but it was my chance to get out of here without explaining anything. I went back out and Jason was still standing there.

"Where are you going?"

"Tony's, but I'm running a little late. I have to go." I didn't wait for any more questions from Jason. I got in my car and headed for Tony's.

I stopped by Sherburn's to see if Danelle could come with me, but she wasn't allowed to. I wanted to scold Brian for not helping her, but she said he went with a bunch of guys somewhere. I left angry, but soon forgot when I got to Tony's.

I walked into the kitchen at Tony's. He smiled as I walked through the door.

"Holy shit girl, James is going to freak."

"Why do you say that?"

"I almost didn't recognize you." He held up my hair, "Blonde, why did you do this?"

"So I would seem older."

"I like the brown better."

"But you have to admit I look older."

"Yeah, but why do you want to look older?"

I was embarrassed now, "If I am going to teach others, like those woman last time...Well, I thought it might go better if I seemed older."

"Okay. You got me there, but James is going to freak when he sees you."

"In a good or bad way?"

He chuckled, "Maybe a little of both."

"Hey Tony, will you take my picture for James?" I was handing him my phone.

He took the picture for me, "Do you want one dancing too?"

"No. This will be good." I sent it right away.

"Are you nervous, Sarah?"

"Yes. I am going to get ready."
"You know where the music is."

I went out and practiced a couple of dances. The two ladies from the last time I was here showed up early and started to go through them with me. Sandy leaned into me, "I thought it might be easier if we started a little early, hope its okay?"

"Yes and thank you. I needed some help today."

A new song came on and I started a new dance. Sandy and her friend, Kate, were on each side of me. It was really fun because it encouraged others to give it a try. It was mostly girls and ladies on the dance floor. I noticed Brian walking in with a bunch of his friends; he noticed me and shook his head. A lot of them joined in the back and tried to follow along. We did the two dances off and on during the night. Sandy and Kate wanted another new one, but I advised them that two was enough. No one else knew the one they already knew.

I saw Jason walk in. He sat down at the bar with Tony. I gave him a slight grin and he shook his head again *not* approving of my activities. I could see Tony scolding him a little. I giggled to myself as I watched. Everyone was ordering food and drinks. I knew this is what Tony wanted, but I felt sorry for him because he was so busy. It couldn't have been that bad because he kept giving me the approval to continue.

At 8 p.m. Tony rang a bell behind the bar. I ran up to the stage and shut the music down. Everyone booed. That made me very happy. They liked this. I announced that our time was up. If you are 21 and older you can stay; everyone else has to leave. I went to the bar. Tony leaned over it and hugged me as I sat down.

"Sarah, your food is almost ready."
"But I didn't order any, Tony."
"James would shoot me if I didn't feed you."

I knew he was right, even though I would not agree with him.

After he brought it out to me he advised me, "You need to hurry. You still have to be out by 8:30 p.m. Jason came and sat by me.

Tony came over quickly, "Jason, I don't want any trouble."

"You're not going to get any from me, right Sarah."

I reassured Tony, "We're okay now." I was directing this more to Jason, "He understands that I love James more than anything, and he will respect James. Right, Jason!"

"Yeah, it's like they are already married anyway."

Tony moved in front of me, "He said you would keep amazing me. By the way, it went really well. Sarah, can you come back next weekend?"

"I'm not sure, I would love to just for this. I had so much fun, but Tony I would like to buy Sandy and Kate dinner, or a drink, or something. They helped me so much."

"It's on me. I'll give them the choice."

"Tony, I can get it."

He gave me a mischievous smile, "Do you know how good this went?"

"Not really."

He laughed, "Very good. I may have to keep you all the time."

I was relieved that he was happy with the results. Tony walked away to wait on another customer. I cut the burger in half and pushed it toward Jason.

"I'm not eating it. *You* have to eat it Sarah."

I knew why he was pushing. James would have too, but I would have won with James. I pulled it back and took a bit from one half. I put ketchup in the basket for the French fries. I ate till 8:30 p.m. Tony noticed I was not finished yet.

"Sarah, you need to eat faster because you have to get out of here."

I picked up the basket and went in the kitchen. I wandered up the stairs to James's room. I sat down on his bed, and the tears started to well in my eyes. No matter how busy I kept myself, I still missed him. I put the basket down on the table next to his bed, grabbed a pillow and curled into a ball. I wasn't there for very long when Tony came to the door.

"Are you okay?"

"Yeah, I just miss him so much."

Tony walked into the room, and nudged me to sit up.

"How did you know I was still here?"

"Jason went to leave and saw your car."

"Oh."

"Before James left and before you two were together…"

I wanted him to give me anything he could about James; I need to feel good.

"Sarah, I can't explain how he felt. He would do this same thing when you weren't here. He was so *in love* with you before you knew. He was so torn on what to do."

I felt the tears streaming down my cheeks. He put his arm around me, "He'll be home in no time, Sarah. I've got to get back down stairs. You can stay as long as you want, but let me know when you're leaving."

He got up and walked to the door. He glanced back at me for a second and walked away. My tears turned into sobbing. I wanted him here to hold me. My heart was aching for him.

After I could contain my tears, I forced myself up and went to the bathroom to get sick again. I rinsed my mouth and walked back in his room to search for a toothbrush. No luck. I went back to the bathroom and rinsed my mouth again, and then I washed my face. I was trying to make it look like I wasn't upset. I walked down the stairs with my food in hand. I couldn't eat anymore even if I wanted too. My stomach wasn't pleased with me because I was so upset. I knew I should try to finish it because Tony went to the trouble to make it for me.

Tony walked into the kitchen and noticed I didn't finish, "You should really try to eat more. James isn't going to be happy with me when he sees you. He's not going to believe me that I tried to feed you."

I took it to the microwave and heated it up.

"Sarah, at least eat the burger."

"I'll try. I am going to take it with me. I am going to go now."

He came and gave me hug again, "He'll be back. I promise you that. He's *not* letting you go."

The microwave beeped and I took out the sandwich wrapping it in a napkin. I walked out knowing I had no intensions of eating it, so I put it in the trash on my way to the car.

I knew I was busted when I hear, "*That's* not eating."

"Jason, I am really not in the mood to do this; I need to go." I went straight to my car and was trying to get in but the tears consumed me.

He came over and opened the door for me not saying a word. I got in and before he closed the door he said, "You might want to get yourself together before you drive."

He closed the door and walked away. I was so relieved.

11. Heart Aches

I walked into Sherburn's hoping no one would notice that I had been upset. I'm surprised James didn't text me or something because he knew when I was feeling this way. He usually does, but maybe he was busy. It was after 9:00 p.m. on Saturday; what could he be doing?'

I walked into the bar and Laura yelled to me, "Danelle's in the back… go ahead. By the way, I heard you did great tonight."

I waved, "Thanks."

I went back letting myself in, and Danelle brightened up.

"We have to do something. I'm kind of bummed out, and I need to get my mind off of him."

Brian walked in with the big group of guys that he showed up with at the dance. Laura was following them in. Brian was going on about how much fun that was and it would have been safe for Danelle. It wasn't like a bar when we were there. She said Danelle could go with me next time. I was happy to hear that; maybe if she was there I wouldn't have time to be depressed. We went out to play pool. Mom and dad showed up around 10:30 p.m., and dad called me over.

"What's up?"

"We haven't seen you much; how was your day?"

"Good, I have been keeping busy."

"I heard about Tony's."

I didn't know what to say. Was I going to be in trouble *again*? "I'm sorry, I would have told you, but I didn't think you would let me."

"No, I probably wouldn't have, but from what Brian said it was a bunch of teenagers and you were having fun."

I was distrusting, "Yeah, it was a lot of fun."

"Then it's okay."

"I left the boat at the dock. Can we go tubing again tomorrow before we put the boat away?"

"If you are having fun, yes."

Jason walked in and sat by my mom and dad. I got up and went to hang with Danelle and all of Brian's friends. I mostly watched, only because I was down. I went to play more music, and as I leaned over the jukebox Brian came over. He leaned on the jukebox but away from me. I saw Jason get up out of the corner of my eye, but he moved to the bar and got another beer and stayed there. I didn't move, but I kept searching for music.

Then I heard Brian, "Do you know what you're wearing *now* is as bad as the bathing suit, for most of us?"

I quit searching for music and turned around. I noticed Danelle was on her way to me, "Do you want to have a pizza?"

I moved to go with her. She sees everything and read what was going on before I knew anything. We were walking to the back and I told her, 'I'm not really hungry. Tony fed me, but I will go with you to make it."

Jason walked by us on his way back to mom and dad, "Sarah, you only had *two* bites of the burger at Tony's, remember?" But he kept walking.

"Thanks a lot, Jason, that helped," I was so irritated now.

Danelle grabbed my hand, "You are eating and that's final."

We went to the back where she put in a pizza, and I stood there feeling really stupid thanks to Jason.

She noticed I wasn't saying anything, "What is up with you? You have been so quiet tonight. You didn't even talk about Tony's and it sounded like you had a lot of fun."

"Being at Tony's was hard for me without James there."

"Do you think it's a good idea to be there then?"

"It helps Tony, so I will do it anyway. Plus, it keeps me busy."

She tried to soothe me, "But Sarah, you still need to eat."

"One favor then."

"What's that?"

"Can we eat with my mom and dad? That way; everyone will see me eat."

She sighed, "Yeah that sounds good. My mom wants to see you eat more."

We waited till the pizza was ready. She handed it to me and grabbed some napkins and we went to sit with my mom and dad. Of course, Jason was still there. He smiled like he was happy he won. I ignored him and sat down. Danelle sat next to me. We ate the pizza. I only had 3 squares and was done. Jason and Danelle were not pleased, but everyone saw me eat. I was worried about how I was going to feel later, but I made a lot of people happy. Danelle and I went back to the pool table area and watched the boys again. Tommy was picking on Danelle again. Brian got a little protective, scolding him as he sat down by me.

He nudged me, "You ate?"

"Yep."

Danelle told on me, "*Only* three pieces, so we need to make her eat more tomorrow."

"Why didn't you make her eat more?"

"How do you make someone eat, Brian, shove it down her throat?"

They were talking about me like I wasn't even there. I felt really stupid. They quit arguing and I said, very quietly, so Brian would be the only one that would hear me, "Sorry, I'll be more careful."

He was confused.

"I'll wear big baggy clothes from now on."

He turned away but spoke, "No. I like what you're wearing. It just looks really good."

I knew I didn't look that bad then. I heard dad yell, "Sarah! It's time to go."

I stood up and spoke to both of them, "Be ready early tomorrow, so we'll have time before I leave."

Danelle walked with me to my mom and dad.

I took on the parenting role, "You two aren't going to disappear again, are you?"

I could see the guilt on their faces.

"Yeah, I am following you two, so you better behave. And next time you want alone time, please let me know and I will stay with Danelle."

Dad smiled, "Like *you're* the responsible one."

Danelle and I walked out. Mom and dad were a little slow again. We shot some hoops while we waited.

Jason came out. He only glanced at me and then went to his truck. He pulled away, but it wasn't for home. I knew he was heading to the trailer. Doesn't he know when to go home? Mom and dad came out, "Okay we're coming."

They got in dad's truck, so I went to my car but yelled back to Danelle, "I'll see you early tomorrow."

"I'll be waiting." She was so sweet. I didn't understand how she could live this way every day.

I followed mom and dad back to the trailer. Jason was waiting by his truck when we pulled in. I moved to go inside right away but told Jason, "You know you really should *go* home; this has to be hard on Kylie."

Dad was laughing. We all went inside, but mom and dad went straight to the back room, and left me to deal with Jason on my own. He was right behind me, and I turned around, "I need to sleep, so I can't keep you company." I continued to walk to the first bedroom. He moved to sit on the couch. I crawled into the squeaky bed not changing clothes at all. I felt so lost without my James, and I wanted to think about my sweet Cayuse. I had a very busy day, so I fell to sleep in no time at all.

My phone ran at 3 a.m. I answered, "Oh, James."

"What? You sound sad."

"I am, but only because you're not here."

"I love you too, Sarah. I felt you earlier, but I couldn't call. What happened?"

I sighed with relief, "I was at Tony's, and I went to your room. The emptiness was over whelming."

"Why are you torturing yourself like that?"

"It's because I miss you."

"What did you do to your hair?" He didn't sound angry.

"I'm sorry. It will grow out if you don't like it."

"Its fine, but you look good no matter what you do. Why did you do it?"

"I needed something, anything that would make me feel better because nothing is working."

"Oh my sweet, adorable, Sarah, I could come home."

"James, don't say that. I told you to finish that first. It's our future together."

"What do you want me to do?"

I sighed again, "Could you talk to me? I need as much as I can. I need your voice, your touch, your smell so bad right now. I can hardly breathe without it."

"Have you been sick today?"

"Once when I was really sad and missing you."

"Sarah, thank you."

"For what?"

He chuckled, "For wearing the wet suit while water skiing."

I took a deep breath. "I remembered no attention for me."

"I will tell you a secret."

"What is that?"

"It made me want to touch you." I felt a trace of his hand on my stomach.

I closed my eyes to enjoy his touch, "Oh, James, I want you here right now."

"I would love to taste your sweet skin." I felt his mouth move from my neck to my ear.

"James, this makes it harder." The feeling him stopped.

"Really?"

"Don't stop... I just need to feel you so bad right now."

I felt his arms wrapping around me. I curled into a ball.

"Sarah, I am coming home."

"No, just help me, talk to me. Tell me a story."

"I can't, Sarah. You know I'm not good on the spot like that."

"I'll take anything, James." The tears welled up in my eyes and trickled down my cheeks.

"You saw my dad today. How was he?"

"He's really well. When he hugs me I feel like it's coming from you. That helps me a little, and yet it makes it hard."

"You went water skiing today?"

"Yeah, and again tomorrow. I am trying to stay busy, so I don't get bummed out without you here."

"Sarah, I love you so much." I felt the trace of his hands down my arms.

"That was nice."

I felt his lips trace mine. I gasped in desperation for him, "James?"

"Sarah this is too hard. I have to take a shower; can I call you back?"

I giggled a little with a breath. "You don't have to do this. I really need to hear your voice."

"Nope, I have to call you back." He was gone in an instant.

I waited for him to call back, but drifted off to a dream. I was at the house. He had his arms around me. His mouth was tracing my arms, my neck, and my lips. I could feel his body next to mine. He pulled me to sit with him as one. It was beautiful and passionate. I gazed deep into his eyes. I wanted to keep him here. I held him tight wanting more of him.

Then the phone rang again, so I answered it. "Hello my Cayuse."

"Sarah?"

"I know; I am sorry. I couldn't help it. I fell asleep."

He breathed a laugh, "I was supposed to be cooling off, not getting hotter."

"I know. I just want to be with you so bad it makes my heart hurt."

I felt his body next to mine, and then he lowered to me. My need was getting filled by feeling him. "How can you do this?"

Replying like it was no big deal, "I'm in the shower."

I felt his lips glide down to my chest.

"Oh, James, this is too hard."

"I love you." He moved against me.

"James, no, you have to stop. The *agony* is making my stomach turn."

"You're going to be sick?"

"No. I just can't do this. It hurts in my heart. I want you to be here so bad. This feels wonderful, but my heart aches more."

I felt his arms move around me to hold me.

"Yes, James. That is what I really need."

"I love you my sweet, Sarah."

"And I love you."

"Ready?"

"For what?"

"1… 2… 3… breathe."

I took a deep breath and laughed a little when I exhaled, "James, we have only 5 more weeks."

"I don't know if I can make it."

"You can and will. I know if you finish we can make it *forever*. I just feel it."

"So, you do get feelings like mine."

"No… not really, but maybe its intuition."

We stayed on the phone not speaking. His arms were around me and his breath at my ear comforted me, so that I could sleep with ease.

I woke to a text, "Goodnight my sweet, Sarah." I rolled over and went back to sleep.

I woke up so hungry this morning. I couldn't wait to go and eat. I could smell the bacon, but first my Day 19: I took a deep breath only to try and contain my crying. I felt weak today.

If I love you too much, if I long for your touch,
You will have to forgive me.
Give me your soul, so this can grow and grow.
The pain when we're apart is not only yours,
For, I love you, and my heart soars.
If you will be mine, it will be till the end of time.
With all my love,

James

Nope, I am okay, and yes, James, I will always be yours.

I went out to the kitchen smiling. I was very hungry, so I went straight to the table to eat. I grabbed two pancakes and bacon. They all were watching me with stunned faces. I just continued to eat not paying attention to their shocked faces.

Dad was cooking, "Do you want an egg?"

"Yes, Please."

"Hash browns?"

"Yep."

"Hungry?"

"I'm starving."

Jason spoke to me, "You're eating?"

"I always eat better in the morning. It gives me energy."

I ate more than the three of them all put together. I got up and poured two glasses of water for brushing my teeth, realizing that I poured one for James. I laughed a little as I walked away with one glass to brush my teeth. I put on a different suit for the day. I wore a skirt to make the change easier and a cover up top for over the suit. I walked out and noticed the three of them talking, but it stopped as I got closer.

I knew they were talking about me, "What?"

Dad was confused, "You are fine?"

"Yeah, why wouldn't I be?"

"Sarah, you were really down last night, and today you're better?"

"I feel better. I think I was tired. If it's alright with you, I am going to go."

Mom was not letting me off that easy, "Sarah, you need to sit down."

I evaluated each of their faces and knew it wasn't going to be good. I didn't want to get sick again, and if I sit down they were going to make me feel bad.

"Um, I don't think so. I don't want to get sick again, and I feel really good right now. If I sit down we are going to discuss something unpleasant, and I really don't want to be in a bad mood or get sick today. So, if you don't mind, I will just go. You can tell me what time to be back to go home. I will be here at that time."

I moved to the fridge and opened it grabbing a bag of carrots and some grapes. I stopped and waited for their reply.

Dad shook his head in disbelief, "Fine go, but be back by 2 p.m., so we can get the boat."

"That sounds good to me."

I hurried out the door. I didn't want them to change their minds, and I knew Jason was trying to change their minds. I heard him ask my dad, "Tucker, you are letting her go, even after…"

I didn't wait to hear what he was going to say. I didn't want to know.

I got to Sherburn's and walked into the store. No one came out. I walked over to the bar, but nobody was there either. I walked behind the counter and knocked on the door going to the back room. No one answered.

I yelled out, "Hey guys. Is there anyone back there?"

The door opened and Brian came out. He pulled me back around the counter toward the front door. Danelle is outside waiting for you down on the dock. My mom is cleaning cabins, and my dad is getting the gas for the boat. I will be down shortly.

I couldn't help but grin. I knew he was with someone in the back room, "Is *Mykala* here with you?"

"No."

"Then who is it?" I was happy for him because he had someone.

"Sarah, it's nobody."

"Brian, I can tell by the way you are acting. You were getting busy with someone."

He closed his eyes in defeat, "Sarah, please."

"Okay, but its okay, Brian. I am happy for you."

He took my hand and started pulling me down into the bar area and next into the cooler, not closing the door. He put me in the corner, but kept his face down.

I tried to make him feel better about it, "Brian, I do want you to be happy. I want you to have someone. Is it Mykala?"

His eyes moved to mine. His thoughts were running across his face. It was like he couldn't tell me, "Sarah, you don't understand. I tried to behave, but sometimes I look at *you* and you're just so… I couldn't help myself; she was willing and I needed to…"

"So, you mean to tell me you did it with whoever is in the other room, and you're here talking to me? Are you crazy? Get back there and make her feel special or you're a *real* jerk."

I pushed him away and walked out. I stormed outside to find Danelle. That was the worst thing I have ever heard. I found Danelle, and she was ready for tubing. Tommy, Pat, and Zach were also there and ready to go.

I didn't say anything but got in the boat, "So, who is first?"

Danelle got in the boat, "I'm spotting first."

I gave her a slight smile.

She didn't smile back, "You're angry?"

"A little, but it's not that big of a deal. I am fine."

She didn't believe me, "Okay, but you're still mad, and I'm not tubing until you aren't mad anymore."

"It might be awhile." I did have an angry tone in my voice.

She was determined, "I'll wait."

Pat went first and then Tommy. The more time that went by the calmer I became. After the third round, Brian and the girl he was with were sitting on the dock when we got back. I couldn't *even* look at him. The anger came back quickly.

I noticed Sam was coming, and he was holding hands with a girl. I quickly got out of the boat and threw the rope to Brian, "Brian, hold the boat."

I ran to Sam, "Hey, you made it, and this is..." I gestured for him to introduce us.

"Sarah, this is my Amelia." He pulled her close and gazed at her as he said this. He stopped a minute as if to cherish her. I could tell she was special to him. Then he came to and introduced me, "Amelia, this is Sarah, James's fiancée."

"Shhh, no one is supposed to know." I smiled at Amelia as I scolded Sam. I put my arm around her but touching his shoulder, "It's so nice to finally meet you. Do you want to water ski or go tubing?"

"I really haven't done either."

"Well, if you want to you can, or you could go swimming."

She put her arm around him to move closer to him. I smiled at Sam over her. He had the most adorable grin on his face, but he asked me, "So, Sarah, how have you been feeling?"

"A lot better today. I invited you yesterday, how did you know to show up today?"

He looked at me like that was a stupid question.

"Oh, I always seem to forget that."

They walked down to the end of the dock with me. I got back in the boat. "Hey, guys, this is Sam and Amelia, and this is Danelle, Tommy, Pat, Zach, Brian, and …" I gestured to Brian so he would introduce the girl he was with.

Brian responded, "This is Liz."

I did look at her and smiled, "Nice to meet you Liz. Okay, who's next?" I turned to Sam wanting him to volunteer.

"Yeah, I would love to go."

"Amelia, you can ride with me. Danelle, are you spotting?"

"Yeah, sure."

I took him for a great ride. Amelia seemed worried. We got back to the dock, and she jumped in to be with Sam. They found a tube and paid a lot of attention to each other. I was happy they got to have time together.

"Who's next?"

Liz spoke up, "I'll go next, if nobody wants to go."

"Great, Danelle, you are still spotting!"

"Okay."

"Nope, I am." And Brian got in the boat.

I glared at him, "You can take her, and I'll wait here."

Liz turned to me, "Um, you look safer; would you mind driving the boat?"

"No, that's fine." I got back in the boat.

Danelle got out, "I'll wait here."

"Danelle, there's not too much weight, so you can stay."

She gestured to Brian, "No, I think I will stay here."

I smirked at her, "Thanks, Danelle."

She smiled evilly.

We were on our way. It was okay because he was sitting in the seat behind me, so he could watch her. That was what he was supposed to do if he was spotting.

I inquired, "Is she doing okay?"

He moved to the seat beside me, but still watched her, "She is fine."

It was silent, but he kept glancing at me out of the corner of his eye. "Sarah?"

"What!!?"

"You're still mad?"

"No." I was sarcastic.

"Can we talk?"

"NOPE!"

"I try not to look, because I know how you feel. I can't help it."

"I *don't* want to hear it."

"Sarah, please?"

"So, Liz... did you make her feel special, or was it just a quickie and it didn't mean anything?"

"I guess you don't want to talk about it." He was ashamed.

"You wanted to talk and I asked a question. Why don't you answer it?"

"It was just... I mean... I wasn't thinking about... she's just..." He quit trying to explain and sat there silently.

I huffed, "That is exactly what I am pissed about. That would have been me if you would have shown me any attention before James, and you wouldn't have given a shit about *me* or how I would have *felt*. You are an asshole."

He sat there for the longest time not saying a word. When we got back to the dock Brian got out of the boat and jumped in to help Liz.

Danelle got back in the boat, "Are you still mad?"

"Yep. What time is it? I have to be back by 2 p.m., so we can load up the boat and I have to go home."

"Its 1 p.m."

"Does anyone else want a turn?"

Nobody answered, "Well, if everyone is tired out I'll go."

"I'll go next."

I glared at Brian but spoke to Danelle, "Danelle, you are spotting."

"Nope, not for him." She leaned to me, "I might *let* you hurt him."

I laughed, "Liz do you want to go with me? You just have to watch to make sure I don't dump or hurt him."

She said, "Sure," as she was getting in.

I took him on the ride of his life. He couldn't do many tricks this time, but I couldn't dump him like I wanted to. At least I got to try.

Liz was uncomfortable with how rough I was being, "Should you be so hard on him?"

"Yes. He was a jerk."

"To you?"

Why was she asking me that? "No!"

"To who?" She really didn't know.

I couldn't say anything.

"Was that you at the door earlier?"

"Yep."

"He likes you?"

"No, he doesn't! He was being stupid and you deserve better."

"I was using him too."

Now I was really confused. "What? How can you do something like *that* if you don't love the person?"

"Do *you* like Brian?"

"No. I just think that the guy is suppose to feel you are special, not a piece of meat. My James…" I couldn't talk about it anymore.

"I'm sorry. I thought he was being a jerk to you."

I eased up on Brian and brought him in. I docked the boat and looked around at everyone. I was surrounded by people, and I still thought of how happy I was to have my James. He loved me so much that he didn't want to hurt me. He would wait. How can people take that so lightly?

"Hey, Sam, I have to go. Do you two need a ride?"

"No, I have James's car."

"Sam, you're not supposed to…"

"We'll be good."

I gave him an approving look, "Patience Sam, you have a long wait."

"Danelle, see you in a week or two."

"Hey, Brian, I'm sorry."

12. So In Love

I walked up to my car to leave. I was so confused now. It was such a big deal for me to be with James. He had been with so many women. *Why was he so respectful of me? Was he just that smooth that he made me want to be with him or did he really love me?* I was pretty sure he loves me, or why would he try to make me feel so happy.

I shook it off and drove back to the trailer. I walked in, "I am ready to get the boat. Who is helping me?"

Jason was there with mom and dad. I noticed he turned to my dad waiting for an answer.

I was getting impatient, "Okay people. I am on time and we need to get the boat loaded up."

Dad finally spoke, "Jason, would you mind?"

"Yes, no problem." He was to his feet immediately.

I walked back out. I was a little angry that I was finding this all out. *What world was I living in?* I didn't know or care about this less than a year ago. I always thought you fall in love with someone; you get married, had kids, and lived happily ever after. I got in his truck, but my mind was going a million miles an hour.

"Hey, are you okay?" Jason was driving me to Sherburn's.

"Yeah, just a little confused about some things. I need time to work them out in my head, not text book things."

"Like what?" Was he trying to *pick up the pieces* while James was away?

"Have you been with anyone besides Kylie?"

"What? Why would you ask such a question? What are you thinking about?"

"I was just wondering. Can you answer me honestly?"

"Yeah."

"Yeah you can answer me honestly, or yeah you have?"

"Sarah, what happened today?"

"Nothing. Just answer the question."

"Yeah, I have."

"What happened?"

"What are you asking?"

"Why aren't you with her, or them?"

"You really want to know?"

"Yes."

"The first time we were too young, and it wasn't right."

"How many?"

"James has been…"

I interrupted him, "I know it's a lot. He already told me about it and them; I need to understand something. Can you just tell me?"

"A few." He looked up at me from the tops of his eyes.

"Before Kylie, or when you were with her, or while you were apart?"

"Sarah, why do you want to know this?"

"It's just something I need to sort out, and it's good to hear different situations."

"The first was before Kylie, the rest while we were broken up."

"Were you looking for something, someone better?"

"I don't know; I never thought about it."

We pulled into Sherburn's and I got out, "Meet you at the launch."

"Sarah, you're not going to explain?"

"There is nothing to explain. I need to figure something out."

I walked down to the boat. I really wanted to hurry up and leave before anyone saw me. I untied the boat and got in, almost stepping on Brian.

"What are you doing lying in the boat?"

"I am waiting for you. *We* need to talk."

I sat down on one of the seats. We really didn't need to talk, but maybe I can get more answers.

"You said you were sorry, why?"

"When Liz road with me, she knew you were using her and she was using you too. Did you know *that*?"

"Yeah, I did. Does that mean you're not mad at me anymore?"

"No, I'm not mad, but I didn't understand. I guess I still don't. How can you be with someone you are not in love with?"

"For guys, it's easy. But you said something that I need to talk to you about."

"What's that?"

"You said if I would have shown you attention before James, we would have done that?"

"I had a crush on you, but you didn't even take a second look at me till I was with James. So, explain how can you be with someone you don't love?"

"It's easy. That feeling is so good, that it really doesn't matter. If someone came on to you and was willing to do it, would you stop?"

"Yes, I would stop. It wouldn't mean anything and that's suppose to be something special between two people. It's letting them into your soul."

"Is that what you think?"

I was embarrassed. Was I that naïve?

"Brian how many girls have you been with?"

"A few; why?"

"Is that three or more than three?"

"Why are you asking me these questions?"

"Curiosity."

"Quite a few more than three, but it's not my fault though."

"What?"

"Girls, they come up here, and they are escaping from reality. They can let themselves do whatever they want, but it doesn't go home with them. They come on to me, and I give them what they want."

"What about you're first? Did you love her? Was it special?"

"No and no. My first was with a girl that was two years older than me and she showed me how. She thought I was cute."

I frowned, so how can *this* be taken so lightly? This was supposed to be something two people that love each other share.

"Brian, I have to go. They are waiting at the launch for me."

"Sarah, what is with all the questions? I wanted to talk about…"

I stopped him from talking by putting my hand over his mouth. "Don't try to tell me; my heart belongs to James and I have to go."

He moved really close to me. "Can I just try one thing?" I put up my hand to hold him at a distance, "No, you need to get out. I need to go."

He climbed out of the boat watching me, "Sarah, I still need to talk to you."

"Later." I drove off in the boat. Jason already had the trailer in the water for loading the boat. I steered it into the trailer and cut the engine. I threw Jason the rope and jumped out to help guide it in. I got in the truck after getting the boat secured, but my mind was somewhere else."

"Sarah, what are you up to?"

I didn't know what to say. I was still working things out in my head. "What?"

"What are you thinking about?"

I gave him a half hearty smile, "It's nothing really." Then I went back to looking out the window.

We got back to the trailer; I helped put the boat away and started walking to the trailer dazed, because it was too much to understand.

"Sarah?"

I turned around to see what Jason wanted.

"Are you okay?"

I was kind of numb in a way, "Yep, just fine."

I turned away to walk inside. I went straight to the room and got dressed in regular clothes. I put the necklace back on and tucked it away in my shirt. I packed my bag and put it in the car, then went to sit on the couch to wait for going home. I wasn't paying attention to anything going on around me. I was thinking about all the info I had gotten today. Maybe I need to get some girls opinions on things. I was going to work on that next, but first I would have to make friends with girls.

"Sarah?" Mom's voice rang out. I came to noticing that the three of them were looking at me again.

"Are you ready to go?" My mom asked.

"Yep, any time. My stuff is in the car; do you want me to get your bags?"

"No. I can get it."

I shrugged my shoulders, and my mind was wandering off again. I really needed to get home to my boring life. It was much simpler. How can anybody look forward to the weekends? I needed my weeks to overcome my weekends. I got up and walked out. I sat on the steps. I was getting irritated with them staring at me. Jason came out and stepped around me so he could face me. *What now?*

I looked up at him, "What?"

"Your mom and dad are a little worried about you."

I shook my head. "Really, Jason, I am fine. I don't think I will be sick anymore. I think I understand things better."

"Really?"

"Yeah, I really only got sick when I couldn't handle things. I think I can handle things better. I feel less confused."

He reached down to my neck and pulled on the necklace, "Did James give you this?" as he pulled a little more the ring fell out. I took the ring in my hand and tucked it back in my shirt. I didn't say anything, and he sat down on the stairs in front of me, but not facing me.

"Is *that* what I think it is?"

"Yep."

"You're not wearing it where it should be?"

"Nope, I'm too young for this."

"Then why do you have it?"

"I think he was afraid?"

"Of what?"

"That I would think he wasn't coming back. When he gets back I will give it back to him, so he can hold onto it for a couple of years."

"So, you're going to tell him no?"

"Jason, I already said yes."

"Then why will you give it back?"

"People won't understand, maybe in another year or two."

"So, you do want to marry him?"
"Yes, with all my heart."
"What was with all the questions?"
"I just don't understand how he can feel this way about me?"
"I do."
"Please don't start. It doesn't make sense. I already have too much to think about?"
"If you love James that much then you don't have to think about it."
We sat there after that not saying anything. Mom came out, "Are you ready to go?"
"Yep, whenever you are."

She put her stuff in the car. I gave dad a hug and kiss. "Dad, I am fine now. Quit telling people I am having a nervous breakdown. That made everything worse." I did give him a reassuring smile and then headed to the car.

Jason came up and put his arm around my shoulders like a big brother would do. "Sarah, you're just different, that's what makes you special. Don't think about it too hard."

I gave him a side hug, "Thank you."

I got in the car, and then mom got in. We didn't say a whole lot.

When we got home I threw in a movie and waited for the night to come. I still didn't know if James could work it out to get to Denver on Wednesday. If he can, I think I have to go. It would help me so much just to see him. I went to bed early; I did have to work in the morning. Matt called at 10 p.m. making sure we were still good for Tuesday and Thursday. He wanted to know about next Saturday and Sunday for a tournament. I would have to get back to him on this. I wanted to talk to mom first. When we hung up the phone, I closed my eyes. I needed to sleep. I really did feel so much better. I was happy to love James.

I woke to my phone about 2 a.m. "James."
"You sound happy?"
"I am. You make me happy."
"You were so miserable that I wanted to come home."

"I told you, you could help me by talking to me. I think I am done being sick too."

"What do you mean?"

"I understand things a little better now. I did some sorting and I feel better."

"So, what did you sort out?"

"That I was lucky to have you, and your love."

"You had doubts?"

"No, not doubts. I didn't understand how you could be so sure about loving me, but Jason told me I didn't have to understand it. If I love you as much as I do, then it doesn't matter. And James, I love you more than life itself."

"Sarah, I told you. I love you more than I can ever show you. You saw Jason this weekend?"

"Yep, I let him explain. And James, it helped me see more clearly that you are the only person I need and want in my life."

"Did he do what I think he did?"

"What's that?"

"Did he try to touch you, kiss you?"

"No actually he didn't. More like a lot of talking."

"Sarah, I think it's time I just come home. This really isn't that important. I can go to school; this was just a specialty that might help in the end, but it really isn't going to help right away."

"James just finish. I will be waiting, forever if I have to. I love you!"

"So, you will come here to Denver, to be with me for a day?"

"I would follow you anywhere. Did you find a ride to the airport?"

"No, not yet, but I will keep trying. So, what else did you do?"

"Not much. Sam and Amelia showed up today to go tubing with us, but they spent most of their time hiding in the water." I laughed a little.

"You're not supposed to be helping him to get some."

"James, they really do love each other. Why would I stand in the way of love?"

"You are so adorable."

"Yeah, that's what you think."

"Yes I do."

"So, what have you been doing?"

"I've been running, running, and more running, studying some wind charts, learning how to plan fighting fires, and researching the preservation of the land. A lot of stuff. I should be able to cut out three classes in college with this certificate. When you were at Tony's, you looked a little thin."

"I know. I think it was from getting sick all the time, but I don't think that will happen anymore. I am so clear on a lot of things now. Hey, you didn't send me a picture."

"Oh, hold on. There."

"That's not right. What was that?"

"Guess."

"Send me one, please?"

"Wait, okay there."

"Abs; nice. Now send me a real picture."

"That is real. Didn't you notice something?"

"What that they're more cut and your thinner?"

I could hear his satisfaction that I did notice, "You did notice."

"Of course I noticed. What do you do… workout non stop there?"

"Yeah, I have to keep up with you."

"Whatever, I'm nowhere near that. Now I'm going to have to work harder. Thanks. The Volleyball is helping, though."

"You're playing volleyball?"

"Yep, every Tuesday and Thursday. Can you please send me a whole picture, not just part of one?"

"Okay, hold on. There you go."

"There you are. Oh… my… god!"

"What?"

"You look so good to me."

"You are terrible."

"Yep, hold on. There look at that."

"What is that?"

"My puny abs."

"What abs?"

"That's what I mean; there are none."

"It looks yummy to me."

I laughed, "Yeah, it would."

"You are totally back to yourself."

"When wasn't I myself?"

"You have been so depressed lately; it's been driving me crazy."

"That's what you do for me."

"I make you depressed?"

"No, you drive me crazy."

"How do I drive you crazy?"

"James, there are things I want to do to you and then I remember that I shouldn't have those feelings."

"Why shouldn't you? Maybe you should tell me."

"I am only sixteen and I want to…"

"What?" He was anxious.

"I'll show you later."

"You are going to make me wait five weeks to find out?"

"Maybe only three days."

"I have to go!"

"Why?" I didn't want this to be over yet.

"Because… I really have to find a ride to the airport."

"You're not getting rid of me for that."

"Hey, you haven't put all the money away yet, have you?"

"No. Why?"

"We may need a place to be alone. I may need to kiss you so passionately that I would get arrested for indecent exposure."

"Okay! Um, how am I going to get it to you?"

"Just deposit it in my account."

"How much?"

"Like $400."

"That's a lot."

"We may need a suite."

He gave me the name of the bank and his account number.

"No problem, I will get it in there tomorrow. Is there anything else I can do for you?"

"You can do a lot for me."

"Like what?"

"Take a picture of your eyes."

"Hold on…there." I sent the picture.

"You are smiling."

"How can you tell?"

"I see it in those beautiful green eyes."

"They are not green, maybe hazel, but not green."

"Hold on… there. Look for yourself."

"They are green, but that is usually only when I am really mischievous."

"So, what are you up too?"

"Running away to see you."

"Don't say it like that. I don't like to hear you running away, in any way."

"I am not running away; I just want to see you."

"You know if you ever need to get away, I left you a key."

"What? Where?"

"I had Wilson put it in a box right by the bike. You won't miss it."

"It wouldn't be the same without you there."

"I know, but if you need it. One promise though?"

"What is that?"

"No running away."

"Even if it is to you?"

"Well, that might be okay. That reminds me, you are going back to the doctor, right?"

"James, I feel so much better. Do I have too?"

"Yes. Just to be safe. Plus, if you are carrying my baby, I want you to be well taken care of."

"James, I better not be. I really couldn't handle that."

"We could be together sooner."

"But I would have to share you and I really want you to myself for awhile. Plus, we didn't even do it yet. If you're saying it's not going to happen until I am eighteen, then I just don't see it."

"Do you really pay attention to how you feel?"

"Yeah, my body screams at me and makes me sick when I am upset, remember?"

"Do you think you are?"

"No!"

"Then it's got to be something else. If you were, I think you would feel it."

"I'm not the one that feels things."
"Oh yeah, feel this." I felt his mouth tracing my face.
"James, don't distract me like that. We're talking."
"We could be…" I felt like he was breathing in my ear.
"James, you'll bum me out."
"Okay, okay. I'll behave 'til Wednesday."
"Maybe on Wednesday."
"It's going to have to be. I need a little of you."
"What little, a hand or finger?"
"No, more like a mouth and body."
"James, do you have to run in the morning?"
"Yeah, why?"
"We have been on the phone for more than two hours."
"Shit! Really?"
"Yeah, I should let you go."
"Sarah…"
"What?"
"I love talking to you. I miss you."
"I miss you too. How am I going to know if I should book the tickets?"
"Um, I will try to text you. Once tomorrow comes, I will be busy 'til Wednesday morning."
"So, I won't hear from you, except for a text?"
"Yes. I am sorry about that, but plan on seeing me one way or another on Wednesday. Don't make plans for anything else. Please."
"I'm all yours."
"Sarah, I love you so much."
"And I you, my Cayuse."
"Goodnight Sarah."
"Bye."

I hung up the phone. I was *so* in love with him.

13. Broken Plan

I woke with a smile on my face. I was going to be okay from now on, and it was time for Day 20:

After I see you in my dreams
I can't breathe thou it seems,
I reach for your touch
I know it's not much.
It will be awhile so don't hold your breath
Just know without you I feel death.
So I ask myself if this is a dream or is it true
Am I lucky enough to spend my life with you?
With all my love,

James

I swear he knew what was going to happen before it did. His notes were so good about being on the subjects we talked about. Like he could read my mood, but before I was feeling it.

I looked at my phone just in case he found a ride this morning, but nothing. I got ready for work. Today was my late work day.

Mom had breakfast with me. She seemed pleased this morning. "You seem better, lighter."

"I feel better. I think I was really depressed when James left, but it's going okay. The key is staying busy, and talking to him a little."

"I heard you talking to him for a long while last night."

"I do miss him and he keeps it to the weekends. I won't hear from him 'til next Saturday morning."

"You look better, that is all I was saying."

"Thanks mom. I do feel better."

"You talked to Jason a lot this weekend?"

"Yes, I did."

"Are you two friends again?"

"Yes, as long as he behaves."

"Behaves?"

"It's nothing. I have to go to work. Love you mom."

I got up and grabbed my stuff then headed out the door for work.

I had the best day at work. Everybody was so nice there. Allen, my boss, even called me into his office to make sure everything was still good with my car. He walked out with me to show me how to check my oil and windshield wash. Then he checked the miles. He advised me I needed the oil changed. The car would last longer if I took good care of it. He took care of it with the mechanics. It would only cost me $23.00 for the filters and oil. He made sure they put a card in my car, so I could keep track of it myself. "Now Sarah, make sure you get the oil changed every 3000 miles or at least every six months. You have a specialty car. Make sure you take care of it."

He made me feel special because I had a unique car. I was so happy someone else cared enough to make sure I was okay. People are naturally good hearted. The day was long and they were killers for me. I got home late and mom was already home. We both went to bed shortly after I got home. I didn't get a text from James, but I still went to bed happy. Tomorrow would have to be the deciding day. Otherwise, it was going to be the full five more weeks before I saw him. I closed my eyes. I needed to sleep, so I would be full strength for volleyball tomorrow.

I woke to Day 21: Now it was a full three weeks that he has been gone and my heart is still beating, and I still loved my James. I smiled and got ready for my love note of the day.

> *What happened to yesterday?*
> *Will today be the day?*
> *Where will you be tomorrow?*
> *I will not fear*
> *For you will be near.*
> *With my all my love,*
>
> *James*

I knew it. I knew it. He knew what we would talk about, or how I would feel when he wrote these. They fit perfectly to what is going on so much. I should just book the flight and plan on going. We could figure out the rest after I got there. Nope, I didn't want to get stuck at the airport without seeing him. That might make me more depressed. I am going on with my day like normal, and I am not going to worry about it.

I have a busy day today starting with going to the doctors' for a follow up. I rushed to get ready and told mom I was leaving early, so I could go get the check up before going to work.

I went to urgent care and saw the same doctor, thank goodness. I always hate going to the clinics where you see a different doctor every time you go. I didn't want to have to explain everything again. I did advise her that I was still getting sick, but I did feel better for the most part. She took another pregnancy test at my request. I needed the reassurance of it not being that. She advised me that my white blood count was up from the last blood work she did. She explained that this meant that my body was trying to fight something off. She wanted to do some more tests. The pregnancy test came back while they were doing all the other tests, and of course it was a '*no.*' I had to give another urine sample, and they took five more vials of blood. I felt drained and light headed. She also didn't like that I actually lost 23 pounds in the last two weeks. I was at less than 10% body fat now. She encouraged me to eat stuff that had natural fats: yogurt, sour cream, and butter on everything. And encouraged a candy bar midday, to try to get the weight to stop falling off. She wanted me to come back in a week. I agreed, but what was so *urgent* that I had to come back in a week?

I went to work with mixed feelings. I knew it was something, but James would be home to take care of me, so it wasn't going to be too bad. It would wait.

I kept checking my phone to see if James had text me. No text from him. This was not going to help my mood, which was going downward again.

Work went okay considering my mood. Everyone was asking me what I was going to do on my day off. I didn't know how to answer them anymore. Maybe I would go to the beach for the day if I wasn't going to see him. I would give him until bedtime before I gave up on seeing him tomorrow. Finally my work day was over.

I rushed home and got ready for volleyball and called Matt to see if he was ready. I laughed when he replied, "Yes, will you hurry up. I need to warm up. I didn't play this weekend. Did you ask your mom about next weekend?"

"No, but I will tonight when I get home. I'm on my way."

"I will be waiting out front. Just hurry up."

"I'm already driving. Calm down. I feel good and I will carry us if you're not good enough."

"You'll carry me? Ha. Will you get here already?"

"I'm less than a mile away."

I hung up the phone and checked my phone to see if James had text me yet. There was nothing. I pulled up to Matt's house. He was outside and ran to the car getting in right away.

We were on our way and he smiled over at me, "You seem better?"

"Yep, I feel really good today."

"Good. Are you ready to talk?"

"Nope." I smiled like I had a secret. He was suspicious of me. I laughed with playfulness. He shook his head.

We had the best two games ever. They were complete blow outs with us winning both. We worked so well together. It was like we could read each other's minds when it came to setting and blocking. I felt so good when I played. After the second game he hugged me. You are getting better! Then he ran and gave high fives to a bunch of people. I was a little nervous with the hug, but realized he was just excited and relieved that we got the first game over with.

When we were in the car on the way home he went on and on about how good we were together. He finally broke down and came down on me heavy. "Sarah, we are good enough to play in that tournament this weekend and we can enter for free. They want us to play. They keep calling and asking me."

"Matt, tell them we'll play. I will tell mom I am not going even if she does."

"What, you would do that for me?"

"No. It's for me. I feel really good when I play."

He laughed, "That's fine. I will take you any way I can get you."

"Matt!"

He frowned at me, "I didn't mean it that way. We're winning that's all."

I giggled because he was looking pitiful. "Okay, Matt."

He got out of my car as soon as we were at his house. He didn't even try to get me to talk about James. Keeping him distracted with volleyball was working. I was in heaven until I headed toward home. I checked my phone and there was nothing from James. I knew I would not see him tomorrow.

When I got home mom was there. She was eager to hear about my day, "So, how did it go?"

I plopped down in the chair, "We won both games again, and Matt signed us up for a tournament this weekend, so if you don't mind I am staying home this weekend."

"I wasn't planning on going up north this weekend anyway. I need to work."

"Good, than I am not ruining your plans."

"Nope. How did the doctors go today?"

"They are doing more blood work. She said my white blood count was up. She said there was an infection somewhere, so they are testing for everything. I do feel better, so whatever it is, it can't be that bad."

I could tell this did not make her happy, but almost sad. If she thought this was bad, I didn't want to know about it. I got up to head for my room, "Sorry mom, I am tired and I need to get some sleep. Tomorrow is my long day." I didn't want to give her the opportunity to elaborate on what she was thinking. I went to bed looking at my phone. I knew I wasn't going to see my James tomorrow and I was going to sleep sad again.

My phone rang at 3 a.m.

I answered sadly, "James?"

"Of course, who else calls you at 3 a.m.?"

"I love you. I'm not going to get to see you?"

"Nope, I couldn't get it worked out for tomorrow; I am really sorry."

"James, it's okay. I'm fine; it's just hard to get my hopes up and then be let down."

"I love you. How did it go at the doctors today?"

"Third time's a charm; I got another no."

"OH!"

"James, you weren't hoping I was, were you?"

"In a way I was. We could be together forever sooner."

"James, you know I couldn't handle that."

"I know, but I want you to be all mine all of the time. I don't like letting you go."

I laughed a little. I liked that he loved me that much.

"So, what else then?"

"What do you mean? What else?" I really couldn't hide things well with James.

"Did they find out what's wrong?"

"There is nothing wrong with me."

"Sarah, there is something. I *felt* it."

"Fine, my white blood count is up, so there is an infection somewhere that my body is trying to fight off, but they did a whole bunch of other tests, and that's all I know."

"Sarah."

"James, please don't say what you're thinking. I don't want to know. I don't want to be upset."

"Okay, now did you make plans for tomorrow?"

"No. I was still hoping to see you."

"Well, I can't help you there, but I do have a surprise for you."

"What? You don't have to get me anything. You have already given me too much."

"It's really not like that, but here is the plan. You need to go to my mom's. Wilson will be there around 10:30 or 11:00 a.m."

"I don't want to go *there* without you. The memory will be too hard."

"Do you trust me?"

"Of course I do. James, the last three weeks have been so hard for me."

"Sarah, you have to do this. I can't explain how important this is for me."

"Fine, explain it again."

"Simple. Go to my mom's house. Be there before 10:30 am. Wilson will be there between 10:30 and 11:00 a.m. Wait by the pool. He will tell you what to do next."

"Is this like a treasure hunt or something?"

"That is it exactly. It will take you all day, so don't make plans."

"All day?"

"Sarah, you took the day off and it's your late work day. So, I did plan it to last all day."

"I wish you were going to be with me for this. Is it going to depress me?"

"I promise it will be like I am with you all day."

I laughed with a sigh, "Okay, because I don't want to be depressed again. I feel so much better."

"You will like it. It will definitely be fun."

"It's not going to be that fun if I am alone."

"You won't feel alone, please tell me you *will* do this."

"I will, but if it makes me sad you may have to come home. I don't think I can handle getting sick anymore."

"Did they say how much you lost?"

"Yeah, but I am not telling you."

"Sarah…"

"You will think I'm not eating, but James I am. I eat good food more, but because I won't eat a burger, or pizza everyone thinks I'm not eating. You saw me eat, so don't believe them."

"Sarah, how much?"

"I'm not telling you."

"Yes, you are!"

"Make me."

"Sarah, please don't make me worry. Just tell me."

"You'll worry more if I tell you. So no, I'm not saying."

"You'll make me angry if you don't tell me."

"Fine… 10 pounds."

"You are so lying."

"I am not!" I tried to sound offended.

"You are too. How much and this time tell me the truth."

"James, trust me on this one. I look good and you will like it."

"That doesn't matter if your body gets weak. Your body won't be able to fight off whatever it is that's making you sick."

"I feel really good though. I have more energy now and we won two more games last night. I am also getting to play in a tournament this weekend. They asked us to play because we are beating everyone we play."

"Who exactly are you playing with?"

"Kids from school."

"You don't want to tell me that either?"

"James, what are you doing tomorrow?"

"I will be talking to you a lot."

"On the phone?"

"Yes, and you're avoiding my questions."

"Yes, and you're not helping me."

"Helping what?"

"Letting me not answer your questions."

"You will answer my questions, but I will let you off the hook tonight. You have a big day tomorrow, and I want you well rested for it, but you will answer my questions!"

"We'll see." I giggled a little.

"I'm *done* playing this game with you."

"Are you getting mad? I don't think I have ever really seen you mad."

"Yes I am because you are avoiding my questions; you think it's funny, and I can't feel the answers."

"You can't?" I was trying to be playful. "So, when you're mad the feelings go away?"

"No. I feel you and you are avoiding my questions."

"I love you."

"I will let it go for now; you go to sleep."

"I won't be able to because I will miss your voice."

His voice softened, "Sleep, my sweet Sarah; you have a long day tomorrow."

"Fine, I will try to sleep."

"Goodnight, my sweet Sarah."

"Goodnight, James."

I hung up my phone and grinned. I won the argument, and I was not going to tell him how much I lost. I would, hopefully, gain it back before I saw him again. I had four weeks to work on it. I closed my eyes waiting for my tomorrow. I did drift off with a smile on my face.

I woke to Day 22: What did he have in store for me. I got my daily note out.

When we're together my heart thumps, and pumps; taking my breath away.
The energy that flows
Makes me glow
I want you to be mine all of the time; to have you next to me.
My body yearns for you, my heart aches for you.
I pray to be by your side
And that I will survive.
With all my love,
James

Again, he amazes me. I got up and got ready for my day. I left like I was going to work, so I was way early for what James had planned, but I would go and wait.

14. Surprise

As I drove to James mom's house, I felt weird. I was going to be there alone or at least 'til Wilson got there. I pulled into the driveway, and the nausea came over me. I kept swallowing, telling myself *I could do this. Why was I getting upset now? This is going to be a good day.* Nope, I was going to be sick. I went straight to where James told me the key would be. I opened the box. The key was there on a key chain that read, 'Sarah". After getting the door open I ran to the bathroom to get sick. Great, I wasn't going to do this anymore. I went to the sink to rinse my mouth noticing a basket with all my essentials, from personal hygiene to make up, everything I use. Did he read my mind or snoop? I didn't understand how he knew this stuff about me. I pulled a toothbrush from it and brushed my teeth. I turned to walk out and noticed a scale. I shook my head. He was not going to find that out, not if I can help it. I went back out and sat down in a lawn chair by the pool I closed my eyes to wait. It was still early. I must have been dreaming because I could almost smell him, his presence. I smiled taking a deep inhale to enjoy him.

"Sarah?"

I opened my eyes to see Wilson had arrived. He smiled at me and handed me a box and walked away. I traced my hands over it. I sat up and opened it. There was a note in the box.

I read:

You need to smile first. Now, Wilson will give you something, bring it with you and go to the dock. Finish it then you will get the next box. By the way, you have to finish it before you get the next box!!

I laughed and looked up. Wilson was handing me a small container. I smiled shaking my head, "Is this the salad you made the last time I was here?"

"Yes, it is."

"I love this salad."

"That is what James said."

I got up and walked down to the dock and sat on the chair that was put there for me, at least that is what I am assuming. I was in jeans and a dress tank top, for work of course, so this was a little warm. I ate very slowly, enjoying every morsel. It wasn't too little or too much; it was *just right*. I felt like I was in a fairy tale. I finished it and set the bowl down and took a deep breath.

"Are you ready for the next one?"

I looked up at Wilson. He was kind of sneaky. I was starting to feel sad without James, "Yes."

He handed me the next box. I traced over it with my hands again. I could feel him, like he put the box together himself, but I knew it was Wilson. I opened it. Wilson walked away taking the bowl with him. It was another note:

You can go back to the house. There is a basket of your stuff on the counter in the bathroom. You can brush your teeth; I know how you are about brushing. The next box will be in there.

I walked back to the house and into his apartment. I already used it, but I went in and brushed my teeth tracing my hand over the next box. It wasn't there before when I brushed my teeth. I opened it while I was brushing. The front of the note said,

No! Finish first.

I chuckled. I knew he could feel what was going to happen before I did it. I finished and opened the note:

Next, you need to put the ring where it belongs, I'll wait...

I laughed to myself taking the necklace off and took the ring from it and placed it on my finger. I admired it on my hand that was shaking now. I shook my head and went back to reading the note,

Next, you will go to the lounge couch where there is a tray of fruit for you to nibble on. Your next box is waiting there for you.

I walked to the lounge, and I picked up the huge tray and moved it to the end table, so I could sit down and put my feet up. I traced my hand where James would be if he were here. The box was a little smaller. I took a deep breath as I opened it. There was a note and a book underneath it. I pulled out the book and sat it on my lap. I opened the note,

How are you doing? I hope still okay. Open the book to page 45. Read it and close your eyes. Remember 1-, 2-, 3-, breathe.

I took a deep breath and opened the book to page 45.

My love is so deep so strong
My heart is so weak and alone
I have waited for so long,
To be with you from now until the end of time.

I smiled and traced my hand over it. I scooted all the way back and leaned against the back of the lounge and closed my eyes. I took another deep breath, and then I felt his breath trace my face.

"James, not like *this*. It won't be the same."

"How do you know?"

I slowly opened my eyes, and I could see him. Was this real? I touched his face slowly tracing his cheeks with my finger tip as I looked deep in his eyes. They were sweet, loving, and full of desire. I heaved a breath, "Are you really…?"

A smiled grew on his face as he slowly leaned to me to kiss me so softly. The tears moved quickly to my eyes and a few were leaking out.

"You're not supposed to cry."

I wrapped my arms around his neck and started to kiss him deeply. I continued to touch him, but moved my hand to his back, his arms, and his chest. I was making sure he was really here. He took my hands to stop them from touching him everywhere. I was breathing so hard from the confusion and excitement. I wanted to kiss him more, but his smile comforted me. He pulled my hands to his mouth and kissed my finger tips individually. I moved to replace my finger tips with my mouth. I kept my eyes open to make sure he wouldn't disappear from me. I moved to my knees putting both hands on his face to cup it and hold it, so I could keep kissing him. He wrapped his arms around me pulling me closer. "Oh shit, girl."

I kissed him so deep. He was trying to talk during the kiss, "Girl…"

I bit his bottom lip to lure him in. I loved to kiss him and be kissed by him.

"You…"

I moved to wrap my lips around his top lip in a kiss.

"There's..."

I kissed him deeply holding his mouth to mine. I used my tongue to play with his. He could hardly breathe either. I felt like my heart was going to burst.

I gasped for air and he was able to get out, "Nothing…" His hands traced under my shirt to pull it up. He got to my ribs and his hands stopped moving as he traced his thumbs over my ribs. I could see the sadness coming to his eyes. I closed my eyes to not see the hurt that was filling him. I tried to kiss him more to distract him from what he was touching. I wanted to bring him back to the heat of the moment. I moved to his lap and pulled his shirt up. He had to let go of me so he could raise his hands to allow me to remove his shirt. The kiss only broke for a second to get his shirt over his head. I got the shirt to his wrists, and I tangled the shirt around them. I pushed him back to lie down, and his hands struggled to freedom coming back to my waist. I felt him move against me. I knew he had already forgotten about my weight loss.

"Oh Sarah, you have to stop."

I moved against him. I needed for him to stay focused. I leaned down and glided my lips across his chest. I wanted to touch every part of him. I was having a hard time believing he was here with me. I moved back to his mouth and moved my lips with his and we breathed heavily as our lips touched and moved together to complement each other. I felt him pull my hips to him, so we could feel each other. I bit my bottom lip because I was filled with mixed emotions. I moved to him wrapping my arms around him and rested my head on his chest. I didn't want him to see the tears running down my face, "James?"

He pulled my face, cupping it in his hands, to look at him.

I had to make sure this was real, "You are real?" I couldn't stop it now. I was crying.

"Sarah, what's wrong?"

I was trembling with excitement for him, but I had to confess how I was feeling. "I was missing you so bad it hurts, James. My heart felt like it was going to stop because I didn't have you. I tried to block it out, to stay numb, but it was killing me inside. I just can't believe you are here." I put my head back down to his chest. This was too much; I needed to catch my breath and slow my heart.

"Ahu Sarah? We have a problem here."

I looked at him a little worried. He was unbuttoning his pants and then mine; his breathing was still increasing. I kissed his lips carefully.

"Sarah, you have me so horny; you either have to help me or I need a shower... *now*!"

He was so intense and was pulling my shirt off. He unsnapped my bra and pulled it off with my shirt. He rolled me off him so he was hovering, but only to pull off my pants. He stood up and pulled them the rest of the way off. He looked at me to see if it was okay. I could hardly breathe as I looked at him wanting him to come back to me. He pulled me up to be next to him. He lifted one of my legs to his waist as we moved to the bed. I wrapped the other one around him too. He sat me down and I could feel the confusion of wanting and not wanting at the same time. I stared into his eyes. I wanted to help him, but I couldn't say a word. He pushed his pants off not taking his eyes off of mine. He was crawling over me stopping at my stomach kissing and sucking it. I felt my body move to the pleasure of his kiss. He moved up to my breasts looking at me again, "Are you okay?" I nodded to let him know I liked the way I was feeling. He licked and sucked on one breast as I held his head to me. He moved to the other one as I watched his mouth moved around my breast. His mouth moved up sucking my neck and then searching for my mouth as his body grazed mine. He whispered to my lips, "If I try I will tear you apart; we have to settle." He lowered to me, so I could feel him against me. He moved in ways that would give me pleasure. It wasn't hard, but it was taunting and sexy. It was moist and I wanted to feel him badly. He moved to me and moaned quietly, but his body tensed and I heard him again, "Oh Sarah." He did it again and moaned more. I could feel the pleasure coming slowly, especially when he would be closest to me. He moaned again and again. His movements were so fast and I couldn't keep up with him. I felt his rush as he pushed to me harder, "Oh shit, Sarah." He continued to move to me at a much slower pace rubbing against me. He was touching the spot that drove me crazy for him. I could feel the tingling in my toes and it started to rise. "James, I feel it. You should try now."

His fingers traced my cheek as he watched my face, "Do you want a baby?"

I shook my head but the extreme feeling was coming. "I want you now." I moved my hands down to help him find me. I wanted him to try.

He pulled away and moved to create the most pleasure for me, "You have to settle for this." His movements were amazing and I was gasping from the pleasure I was feeling, "Oh James…" As I breathed out so did a moan of pleasure, and it was increasing. I couldn't stop it and it was coming, "James?" He smiled sweetly as I felt the rush. His mouth came to mine so quickly to kiss me over and over so softly. My body was trembling as he held me there and kissed me. He was pleased that he could do this for me. He watched my face carefully as he kissed me, to see when I would calm. He traced my lips with his fingers and looked into my eyes, "What you do to me little girl."

When there was some control in my desire for him, he rolled off of me to his back trying to catch his breath. I rolled to my side curling up to him resting my lips on his shoulder looking at him. I needed more attention, so I traced my fingers over his chest. Then his arm that was still under me wrapped around my waist and pulled me closer to him. His eyes were closed, but he spoke to me, "Sarah, what is your body fat, less than 10%?"

It made me sad, that after that he wants to talk about my weight. He rolled to face me and entangled his legs in mine. This was better than discussing my weight.

He held me so tight and was very serious, "If you want me to try, you are going to have to let me be in control."

I was confused.

His face grew to a grin, "When you come on to me aggressive like that, I *get so turned on*. You take me past the point of being in control right away."

I was searching his face, "*When?*"

He laughed with a sigh, "As soon as you kissed me aggressively."

I still didn't understand, "But that was the first kiss."

He chuckled, "I know, after that I couldn't stop it."

I wanted to be with him, "Can we try again?"

He shook his head no, "*This* wasn't part of the plan."

"It wasn't?"

That playful grin came to his face, "No, you were in for a whole day of eating, board games, a movie, and maybe cards."

"You're kidding?"

"How about a shower to wash all this off, we don't want to chance any of it getting in." He smiled sweetly at me, "Then Sarah, we can…we can *try*."

I was happy about this.

"We also need to eat. We will need more energy."

I glared at him.

"Okay, fine. I need more energy." He kissed me seductively and mouthed to me, "Why do you want this so bad? Wasn't what we shared enough for you?"

I swallowed and took a deep breath. "You have needs…"

He tried to stop me with a kiss.

I pushed him away, "I want to be the *one* that satisfies those needs."

He moved his hands to cup my face, "I have many needs Sarah, and you fill them all." He kissed me deeply and I was getting lost in him again, but he whispered to my lips, "Shower and food, or we're not trying anything."

He wrapped the sheet around me and picked me up throwing me over his shoulder.

"Ahu, James, you might want to put me down."

"You're lighter than anything I have been doing."

"No! James, put me down now."

He set me down, and I ran for the bathroom. I was throwing up again.

He was right there holding me up, "I am so sorry, Sarah, what can I do?"

"Nothing, I'm fine. You might want to wait in the other room."

"I am not leaving you to deal with this on your own."

I moved to the sink and rinsed my mouth out, and then I brushed my teeth. He was holding me around my mid section, but he was very careful to not hold tight. I didn't want to see his face, but the mirror made it impossible. He felt so bad that the tears were actually welling up in his eyes. I put my free hand on his arm that was around me, "James, I'm fine. Nothing hurts. It just kind of comes on."

He couldn't look at me. I turned around and wrapped my arms around him with the sheet covering him. I put my cheek to his chest, "Please, don't be upset with me. I can't stop it sometimes." I was searching his face for what he was thinking. I tried to reassure him again. "I ate a while ago, so I must have gotten a little food processed."

He was angry, "*Me*, be upset with *you*?"

"Aren't you?"

"*No*, I'm the one that is making you sick!"

"Stop that right now. You are not making me sick. I can't even believe you said that." I was feeling it coming on again. Maybe too many emotions were causing this. Okay, I can stop this, just concentrate. I swallowed and pushed him away just a little.

"What?"

I swallowed again and tried to breathe through my nose. Nope, it wasn't working. I turned to move away from him back to the toilet, throwing up again. In-between the heaves I got out, "Dam it."

He was holding me again.

"This sucks."

He laughed a little.

I almost wanted to laugh with him, but I knew it would hurt. "James, don't make me laugh; it will hurt. Do you have a better description for it?"

"No, but you're cute when irritated."

"James, this is not cute. Sink, please."

He helped me to the sink, so I could brush my teeth again. I put my hands on the counter and leaned over it. I looked up in the mirror to find his face full of worry. I wanted to ease this, "Shower?"

His eyes came slowly up to meet mine, "Are you better?"

"As far as I can tell I am."

He walked us over to the shower, holding me so carefully and tenderly. I rested my body against his as he held me. He slowly removed the sheet from us and walked into the shower.

It was too hot and I felt light headed, "James, cooler."

He turned down the hot so it was warm, "Better?"

I leaned my head back to his chest as he helped me wash up, "Can you sit for a couple of minutes?"

"Yeah, I am okay now."

He helped me to the seat in the shower. I put my head in my hands leaning forward.

"Sarah, you don't seem good."

"I'm just weak from getting sick."

"A couple more seconds."

"James, I'm fine."

The water shut off and he was toweling off. He had a towel around his waist and one wrapped around me. We walked out to the room. I was getting colder by the minute, and I was starting to shiver. He rubbed my arms with his hands, moving us to the dresser, and he opened a drawer that was full of lingerie.

I had to give him a hard time, "Cross dresser?"

"I don't think any of this would fit me." He pulled out silky girl shorts and helped me step into them. He pulled out a very plain camisole and slid it over my head.

"So, why do you have a drawer of this?"

The most playful and mischievous grin came to his face, "I was fantasizing."

"I hope it's all with me." I was serious but he just laughed.

He moved closer to me and traced his hand down the front of me, stopping at my stomach, "Do you feel any better?"

I entangled my fingers with his and stepped closer, "James, I really don't feel sick or bad at all, except when I actually throw up." I grimaced when I said this, but I tried to get off the subject, "How long do I get to keep you?"

"What time are you supposed to work 'til?"

"It's my late night, so it would be 9:00 p.m."

"Then we have until 9:00 p.m."

"When is your flight?"

"Later." He was avoiding answering me.

"How much later?"

He just looked at me so seriously, "We have until 9 o'clock."

"James, you *are* going back?"

"Can you eat?" He was putting boxers on avoiding my glare.

"I can try, James."

He moved to me bending a little moving up to my ear like he was taking in my scent and whispering, "What do you want to eat?"

He took my breath away. I turned my face to him and breathed in his ear and nudged it with my nose. He didn't move and his eyes closed in enjoyment. He liked it. I used my tongue to lift his ear lobe to my teeth and gently pulled away. He must have really liked it because his hands moved around me to trace my back carefully, "Food, Sarah."

"Yes." I breathed in his ear.

I closed my lips around his lobe sucking on it and then I opened my mouth to breath. His hands traced down to my butt as he pulled me to him. I felt him and gasped a little in his ear. He lifted me and carried me to the bed, "I can't believe you want this from me; you just got sick."

I nuzzled into this neck and touched his face. I still couldn't believe he was here with me. He sat me down and picked up his phone, "Hello Wilson…"

"Remember what we talked about?"

"If you could have that ready in an hour, we'll be up."

His desire was back, "We have 45 minutes; if I can't please you by then, you'll have to trade me in."

He moved to me slowly and glided the camisole off me and traced his hands down the side of me. "Scoot up to the pillows."

As I did this he moved with me. I rolled to my side, so I could feel him.

"No not yet. Lay back and close your eyes."

"Why?"

"Do you trust me?"

I was nervous again and I tried to smile, but felt the twitch in my lips so I said softly, "Yes."

He pulled out the feather and smiled at me. I knew this meant we would try. I eased back and closed my eyes. He leaned over me to trace his lips against mine. The kiss was so sweet and luring, "Are you sure you really want to do this? Sarah, you're still not ready; I feel it."

I opened my eyes to show him I was ready, "To be with you, *yes*."

I closed my eyes and waited for him. I felt the feather over my face, and felt his body move closer to mine. He browsed my body with the feather moving down my front, then up again, and down each arm and then back up. It tickled slightly as he moved down my middle again. He stopped to play with it on my stomach. I felt the warmth of my heart rising in my body. I stretched a little and he laughed a little. He moved… I didn't open my eyes, but I felt the feather along my legs. I brought my legs up, so I had them bent. "Sarah," he pushed them down, "You have to be completely relaxed."

He went back to tracing my stomach with the feather, then back up all the way to my face, around my neck, my collarbone and back down. I was falling into enjoying this so much. I felt like I was drifting into a dream, almost like a trance of some sort. He stopped for a second. When he resumed I felt his fingers behind the feather as he traced everything again. He moved more slowly tracing over my body and went even slower over the parts of my body he wanted to touch longer. When he was back to my face he started the tracing all over again, but this time he followed with his lips… over my face, my lips, my jaw line, and down my neck to my heaving chest, down each arm and back up. He took the hand that was closest to him and sucked on each finger. When he let go I moved both my arms up to the pillow; I was in heaven. He moved over my stomach quickly to my legs. He was still tracing each one with the feather and his mouth. I felt ready with yearning and wanting him. I spread my legs to show him I was ready, but he pushed them together and moved upward tracing his face to run between them. I was starting to tremble. He moved to my stomach and then back up to my breasts. He nibbled and sucked on each one. I wanted to feel his body next to mine. I moved my hands to run my fingers through his hair. He took my hands and moved them to my sides, so I grabbed the sheets on my sides. He moved to my stomach, at first lightly, but the taunting slowly became more intense. I couldn't stand it, and I wanted him to try now. The tingling was in my toes and was rising. He pushed the shorts down as far as he could without leaving me indecent. The licking, kissing, and sucking made the rush come. I moaned and he continued. Every breath I made was a moan. I was in complete pleasure. I rolled to my side; I had to stop. He pulled my shorts off and came to lie next to me. I felt him pull my leg up and around him. He put himself next to me, so he could be in me. The trance was distracting and taking over. I moved closer to him because I wanted what was coming next. The trembling was over coming me, and I nuzzled into him as I felt his desire push hard against me. I knew this was what I was waiting for, and then there was nothing.

15. How Close

"Sarah?" I opened my eyes slowly to look at the most beautiful face in the world. I was wrapped in blankets and the camisole was back on me. I gazed at James and was afraid to ask. If we did and I didn't remember, would he feel bad?

His face went down but he smiled, "We didn't, you fell asleep."

I felt bad, "You shouldn't have let me sleep, James; we only have a little time."

"Sarah, you got sick. I couldn't wake you. You needed rest."

"I felt you; I was ready. We could have been together."

He shook his head no. "You aren't ready. You need to quit trying so hard." He was avoiding my eyes. What was he thinking?

"I'm not thinking anything, Sarah. Okay, maybe that you need to eat for energy." He was pulling a tray over to me, and I pushed to sit up.

"It's time to eat, and I know you eat better when you wake up." He was right; I was starving.

The plate had a huge porterhouse on it with mushrooms all over it and a side plate of hash browns. He was cutting the meat up into tiny pieces. "Do you like mushrooms?"

"Yes."

He took one piece of meat and a mushroom and held it up for me to take a bite. I took the bite and looked at him, "Aren't you eating?"

"I ate while you were sleeping." He traced his fingers along my forehead.

"Are you going to feed me this whole thing?"

His caring eyes scanned my face as he was getting some hash browns next. I was thankful it was a small forkful. As he brought it up to me he said, "Only as much as you want."

I took the bite and tried to talk at the same time, "What time is it?"

He was getting another bite ready for me, "It's 5 p.m."

I was excited, "So, we still have time?"

He shook his head bringing the fork to my mouth for another bite, "No way, girl. You have worn me out."

I glared, "Liar."

He prepared another forkful for me. I wanted to protest to not eat if he wasn't going to give into me. He held it up and waved it a little in front of me. I took the bite but I wasn't happy.

"You are leaving again, right?"

He grinned and got another forkful for me. He held it up for me, "Quit asking so many quest and eat."

I took the bite and replied, "James, you know I eat! It's the throwing up I can't control."

I could see the sadness coming over his face even though he wouldn't look at me. He was getting a forkful of hash browns ready for me.

"James, why won't you answer me about going back?"

"It doesn't matter, and I am not going to argue with you because you are not going to get sick on my time…not anymore."

He held up the fork for me and I took the bite.

I tried to talk again with my mouth full, "Do you remember what I told you what your dad said to me?"

"Sarah!" He was trying to sound happy. "It doesn't matter." His smile wasn't real; it was forced.

"James, I can't eat anymore."

"You had six bites."

I closed my eyes, leaned back into the pillows, and took a deep breath.

"What? What's wrong Sarah?"

"I was just thinking."

"Nope, no thinking." He moved the tray to the floor and moved to me kissing me so softly. I was getting lost in it.

"So, you have enough energy to try again?"

"No, Sarah. Stop please."

"Then you are going to go back?"

"You are infuriating."

"No, you're just avoiding what I want."

He pulled me down and started to unbutton his pants, "Fine, if this is what will get you to stop asking questions."

I got up and walked away from him. Surprisingly I did not feel sick. I walked to the lounge couch and sat down and put my feet up. He didn't follow, so he must be really mad or something. I scooted down and peaked around the side. He wasn't even looking this way. He slowly turned his head to face me looking right into my eyes, "Remember Sarah, I feel you."

I turned around and thought. *If you feel me, why didn't you follow me?*

I heard him reply, "Because I am not going to argue with you."

I tried again. *But I love you and I want to be with you. I want to spend the rest of our lives together.* I turned to peak around the side again. He wasn't there anymore and I huffed.

I felt him take my hand in his. He was sitting next to me on the other side. I leaned into his shoulder. "So, what did you have planned for the day, now that we have deviated from it?"

He had a guilty smile, "Just to make you so happy that you wouldn't want anyone else."

I kissed his shoulder, "I don't want anyone else already. That's part of the reason why I feel you need to go back. You are the one that believes in plans, and I need you to finish this."

"Sarah, you're sick. I could feel it when I touched you."

"What?"

"Here," he laid me down and pulled up the camisole.

He used his mouth, "The worst part is right here. He put his mouth on my stomach off to the side a little and then started to trace it across my stomach, "But it spreads across here, like this."

"So, you can actually feel it?"

"Yeah, but I don't know what it is. I would have had to have felt it before and have someone actually tell me what it was.

"So, let's think about this. What is there?"

"I don't want to leave until I know it's gone, and you are getting better. I just love you so much and I can't lose you."

We sat quietly for a while until he couldn't take it anymore, "If I say I will go back, will you eat a little more?"

"Can I feed myself?"

"But then you win twice."

"James, you like when I win. That's why you let me."

He got up shaking his head in disbelief, but brought the tray of food to me, and sat down facing me.

"James, are you going to watch me eat? It's not like I can feed it to someone else."

"No, but I like to look at you. Plus, I have a surprise for you, so don't get too full either."

I took a bite and he kissed my cheek.

"Do I get that with every bite?"

"Maybe more, it depends."

"On what?"

"How much energy you will have." He looked down in defeat.

I placed my hand on his face to pull him back to looking at me, "What?"

"You were so relaxed and …" He leaned to me and kissed me.

"What is it, James?"

His eyes were so sad, maybe ashamed, "Nothing, I just don't want you to hurt in anyway."

I didn't understand where this was coming from. Maybe it was too much to help me with getting sick. "James, you're not telling me something?"

He tried to put on a happy face, "You can have as many kisses as you want. No more arguing though. I just want to be with you."

I took a huge bite to make him happy, "James, eating is *not* the problem; it's the keeping it down that is hard."

He was miserable again. Talking about it wasn't helping.

I tried again, "It's usually bad food that makes it worse, so I avoid it. James you always feed me good food."

I was making it worse as I tried to explain. I was afraid I would make him want to stay more, "James, let's not think or talk about it. I feel fine. I play volleyball, water ski, and a whole bunch of things. I am fine."

His sadness was spreading to me and my heart, "I want to stay here with you."

I put down the tray and moved to kneel in front of him, "You can't watch over me 24/7."

"No, but I want you to come here and live with me."

I threw my arms around his neck and kissed him so hard. *He really does love me.*

"Yes, I do."

I hated when he felt my feelings and answered them without me saying a word, "You have to stop doing that."

He grinned.

"Then, you also know I can't do that yet. It wouldn't be fair to my mom with leaving her there alone. I am also only 16 years old."

"Okay, your surprise!" He was pulling me up. He grabbed the tray to bring it to the kitchen with us. He pushed me to the counter right next to him. "Close your eyes."

I disapproved.

"Sarah, please. You will like this."

I closed my eyes.

"Now, open your mouth."

I stood there with my mouth open. He placed a fork in my mouth. I took the bite and smiled with pleasure and opened my eyes. "My favorite; cheesecake. It's almost as good as…" I leaned to kiss his lips. He wrapped his arms around me and kissed me so deep. Our lips moved together, complimenting each other as we moved them. He was taking my breath away.

"I could…" his kiss was deeper; "live with…" my heart was pounding harder, "you. While…" he pulled me closer, "I go to school." He was so distracting.

"I would love that." The thought of sleeping in his arms everyday was so comforting to me. I would be able to kiss him all the time. He reached for another forkful of cheesecake and fed it to me. He came in for a deep kiss sharing it with me.

"Oh, this is so good."

He did it again, but this was so good with flavor, the moving our lips together was luring. It was so hot. He took another forkful and put it to my mouth. I tried to take a huge bite but got it all over my lips. He put down the fork to cup my face with his hands and came in for the best kiss ever. I was turning to jelly in his arms and my knees were getting weak. I could feel my heart pounding. I loved when he kissed me like this. I could do this forever. He moved closer and he pushed to me. I grabbed his face to look him in the eyes, "James, yes."

He picked me up and sat me on the counter. His body was so tense and he lifted the camisole up enough so he could play with my breasts. He licked, nibbled, and sucked them. His body was trembling a little. He lifted me down and turned me away from him. One arm wrapped around me up to my chest while he was kissing my neck and ear. His other hand moved down under the shorts and he traced his hand over me. He touched me in a spot that made the tingling start immediately. I was so scared because he never touched me this way and he was trembling so badly. I moaned because he was making the rush come already, "Oh, James."

He turned me to face him; he took himself in his hand and put it down my shorts. I could hardly breathe. He was tracing it against me; he was very hard and ready. I wanted him to push to me. He stopped and pulled away from me, "Wait here, I'll be right back."

"What? James, don't leave me." I was so hot and wanted him so bad. I didn't realize I was trembling too. I heard the shower. No, I didn't want him to stop. I went to the door and it was locked. "James?"

"Sarah, I would have hurt you."

"No, you wouldn't have. Open the door, and I can help you."

"No, Sarah. Not this time."

I leaned my head to the door. I was in agony from wanting him so bad. My heart hurt for him.

"Sarah, I will be right there. I will help you, just give me a second."

I was trembling and I felt wet down there. I went to use Will's bathroom. It was a good thing I did, it was my period. *Great timing.* I looked in the vanity and then in the medicine cabinet. I didn't have anything with me. I found a box of feminine products. Clarissa was so great, she thought of everything. I put in a tampon; it was really uncomfortable. I washed out the shorts and wrapped a towel around my waist. This was going to be embarrassing. I walked out; I could still hear the shower. I hurried to the room and put on my underwear and jeans. He came out of the bathroom with a towel on. He took one look at me and came to me getting on his knees kissing my stomach, "Sarah, I am so sorry. Please forgive me. I couldn't stop."

"James, its okay and I got my period. It would have been really gross."

He looked up at me, but tears were running down his face. I wrapped my hands around his head, "James, its okay."

He put his head to my stomach and held me there. "So, you are not hurting there?"

"No James. I'm okay." *We didn't do anything, so why was he asking if I was hurting.*

"I shouldn't have Sarah. I am so sorry; what can I do to make it up to you?"

I was completely confused with his reaction. "James, what are you talking about?"

"I was out of control." He was so miserable.

"James, you stopped when it was too intense." I didn't know if I was asking him or telling him. He was way over reacting for walking away from me.

He glanced up at me, "I never want to hurt you; I wouldn't forgive myself."

I touched his face lovingly, "If you want to make me feel good you could hold me."

He moved up to pull me to a hug and held me tight as he twirled me around like that was the perfect thing to say.

We walked out to the living room, but I stopped him. "I am starving now."

He smiled, but still walked me to the couch and sat me down, "It's safer to have you here."

He turned on the TV and handed me the remote, "Look for a movie."

I started to flip through the channels. He went to the kitchen and warmed up the steak and hash browns. He brought them to me on a tray. He stepped on the couch to squeeze in to sit behind me. I ate and he traced his hands over my back and messaged it. He would kiss my shoulder and back once in awhile. I finished the whole thing and scooted back into him, snuggling into him.

"You really feel okay? You're not in any pain?"

"NO! Why do you keep asking me?"

"I did things that weren't right Sarah, things I promised myself that I wouldn't do, because it may hurt you."

"James, you have only given me pleasure today." I leaned into him more.

He kissed my cheek.

"I have to go to the bathroom."

"You're not going to get sick are you?"

"Nope, it's the girly thing."

He was getting up with me.

I pushed him to stop him, "I can do this myself."

He smiled at me and took my hand in his, "I'll wait for you by the door."

He walked with me to the bathroom, and I stopped to look at him. This was kind of weird.

I slowly closed the door noticing he was miserable again. The tampon was hurting me so I went to find more supplies. Of course I found them in the same place. I tried another tampon but it still hurt. I decided on a pad. I realized my day with James was almost over. I wanted to hurry to get back to him. I hurried and opened the door, and he was waiting for me. He looked so upset. He moved to hold my hand immediately and was being really clingy. I like when he did this, but it was a little different. We walked to the living room holding hands. He laid down patting the couch where he wanted me. I curled up to him. He took my hand and kissed it, then my shoulder and my neck.

I turned to him. "Why were you so upset before?"

"I love you so much sometimes." He closed his eyes and put his face next to mine to take in my scent. "The self control is getting harder." He shuttered a little.

"Will you tell me when your flight is?"

"Sarah, I don't want to think about being away from you."

"So, tell me and get it over with and we don't have to think about it again."

"Why do you want to know so badly?"

"I could call mom and tell her I am going to get ice cream or something with the volleyball kids, so I could buy more time with you."

His smile was enlightening. "I like the way you think; 12:20 a.m."

"So, you have to be there by 10:20 p.m. That would work out great. I will call her and tell her I am meeting them at DQ, and I'll be home around 10 p.m. That's plenty of time for you to get there." I smiled at him, "See was that so hard?"

He moved to kiss me again. "How come you love me?"

I was lost in his kiss but mouthed to him. "You make me feel special. You make me so happy. I can't explain it."

"Oh, you are special, Sarah."

He moved to lay more on me putting his hands on each side of my face looking at me in the eyes. "Sarah, I..." he swallowed, "Before, we..." He closed his eyes and pushed to me. He was taking my breath away again.

"James, I wanted to and you tried. It's okay. We have a lifetime to be together; it's just too gross now."

He moved to the side a little, "That's not what I am trying to say, Sarah."

He put his head next to mine. He put his hand on my stomach and rested it there. "Are you sure you are not hurting, not hurting at all?"

I turned searching for his lips as I found them, "I feel wonderful and with no pain."

I kissed him lightly which turned into full kissing and then making out for hours. He traced my face and kept touching my stomach. I didn't know if he was really turned on or if he kept checking to feel if I was going to be sick. He was so sweet and adoring. *I would have attacked him if I wasn't gross right now.* He smiled like he heard me. I knew he was reading my mind. We continued to kiss. The news came on and we both looked at the TV. The tears welled up in my eyes.

"Oh Sarah, don't do that. I won't be able to leave. You are the one making me go." His kiss came deeper and more desperate. "If you don't want me to go, just tell me. I will stay. I will find another way."

"I'm okay. I'm just scared."

"Of what?"

"The emptiness." The tears spilled over and ran down my cheeks.

"I can't leave."

"No, James, I can't be the reason you didn't finish. You will regret, and regress against me. You have to go back. It's the plan."

"But I will be hurting you." He traced his fingers to wipe my tears from my face.

"James, remember I am very emotional, but I will be fine. And when you come back I will make sure I don't fall asleep."

He turned away from me, "It really wasn't sleeping; you were more in a trance."

"What?"

"I love you more than you know, Sarah."

I was confused again. *What was he saying?* He kissed me to distract me, but oh was this good.

I stopped kissing him, "I have to call my mom."

I got up and got my phone and sat back down beside him. I had eight phone calls. I listened to the messages. Oh, shit, Matt called about Volleyball.

I called mom, "Hi mom."

"Hello, what's up?"

"I'm going to meet some of the kids from volleyball at DQ. I will be a little late."

"You're going to have fun?"

"Yes."

"See you later than. Don't be too late."

"I won't. I love you mom."

"Love you too, bye."

I smiled and hung up. I have to call one more person. He smiled at me.

I called Matt, "Hey what's up?"

"I have been trying to call you all day."

"I have been working." I looked at James. He got up and went to his room.

"You have not been working. I called there."

"I've been busy."

"You are with the boyfriend again?"

I smiled, "Um, yah I am with James." My grin got even bigger.

"We're still on this weekend, right?"

"Yeah, I told you that already."

"I had to fork out some doe; Paul couldn't swing it for free."

"So, you need me to pitch in?"

"No. I just wanted to make sure you were still in."

"Yep."

"So, what are you two doing?"

"None of your business."

"Is he back for good?"

"Not yet, but soon."

"Are you going to be depressed again?"

"Maybe." The tears started again, "Matt I need a favor."

"What?"

"Just don't call my house; Mom thinks I am with you guys. The people we play volleyball with."

"He doesn't know you play with me?"

"Thanks, I'll see you tomorrow."

"You are so going to owe me."

"I can't talk to you now; my time is limited with my James. I'll talk to you tomorrow."

"Fine, but you owe me big."

"Bye."

I hung up the phone and got up to find James. He was getting his stuff ready when I walked in and put my arms around his waist and kissed his back.

"You are playing with Matt?"

"Yep, he promised to not make passes. He knows I love you with all my heart."

"I don't like you spending time with him."

"James, I promised I would play this weekend, after that I will stop if that is what you want. I would do anything you want me to."

He turned around and kissed me so deep, "I won't ask you to do that." He kissed me more but said to my lips, "I am being stupid and jealous."

"It's not stupid because its how you feel. I will stop if it hurts you."

He lifted me into another great kiss. He made my knees so week. "You like playing?"

"Not if it hurts you."

His kissing was so wonderful; I would give up living if it meant I would be with him forever.

"You will play if it makes you feel good."

I jumped into his arms and attacked him with the deepest kiss, if we didn't have to go I would have been asking him to take me right now… mess or no mess.

It was already 9:20 p.m. We had to head that way. He looked at me. "Can I drive you home?"

"How will you get to the airport? Do I need to drop you off?"

"No. Wilson is going to follow me so I can stop a couple blocks from your house. He will take me."

"I want to stay with you until you leave."

"It will be too hard for me to leave if you are standing there." His eyes moved down to avoid my look.

"James, it's just four more weeks. Then we have to plan, to work out things to be together all the time."

"Anything you want, Sarah, I am at your command."

"I am not commanding anything, we're partners. We can do anything together."

"All I know is; I want to be with you for the rest of my life. I will do anything, and give you anything you want, if you ask me."

"James, I only want your love."

He traced his hands over my face. He was so serious and stared into my eyes, but I could see the hurt in them. "You have my love, more than you know."

I always felt like he wasn't telling me something when he said that. He grabbed a small bag and led me out of the room, through the living room, and out the door. He locked it and turned to guide me out the gate, but my heart was breaking all over again. *Was this going to devastate me? Was I going to have a nervous breakdown without him here?*

"You will be fine, but if you don't want me to go I will stay."

I put my head on his chest; I couldn't reply. I wanted to ask him to stay but I couldn't. He deserved so much better. *Oh James, I wish you would stay here with me forever.*

"Okay."

"No James, I didn't mean to ask you to stay, you have to go. I am so sorry." I was walking backwards to the car looking at him, pleading with him. He needed to not change his mind.

"I will be here forever, but just a little ways away from you temporarily."

I was relieved, "I love you."

He opened my door for me to get in. He got on his phone as he walked around the car to get in. He hung up before he got in. He held out his hand for me to take. As I place my hand in his he brought it to his mouth and kissed it. He drove much more comfortably than I did. I watched him the whole drive. *I was so amazed that he loved me. I was so average and he was so amazing.* He smiled, "I can feel what you are thinking again. Sarah, it's so strong again. I feel like I can do this again." He look down the road like he was glaring at the road and I felt a sensation of him touching me.

"James, don't do that. I will attack you while you're driving."

"That's what you do to me all the time when you think about me."

"Oh shit. How do you handle that?"

"Most of the time cold showers, except now that you let me…"

"Let you, what?"

He peaked out the corner of his eye at me. "Sarah you kind of let me… um, we sort of…" then he looked at me.

"James what are you trying to say to me?"

Disappointment came to his face, "You let me play and be satisfied."

"James?"

"I just love you so much Sarah, that's all."

I felt that feeling again.

"James, please don't do that. It's making me really hot for you."

He chuckled, "Good! I want you to want me as much as I want to be with you all of the time."

I was taken with him; he was so amazing to look at. I wasn't paying much attention to where we were because I couldn't take my eyes off of him. He pulled down a block that was one over from my house and he stopped. Wilson pulled up behind us.

He grabbed my arm. "Wait." He got out and came to open my door for me taking my hand in his. He hit the door shut with his hip and he walked backwards 'til we got to the driver's side.

He was pulling me closer to him, "Are you sure you're not in any pain?" He placed his hand on my stomach. "You really feel fine?"

I took his hand and brought it up to my heart and gazed deeply into his beautiful deep brown eyes.

"Oh, Sarah, don't do that; I won't be able to leave."

We stood there mesmerized with each other, not knowing how to say good-bye. He entangled our fingers to hold me tight. I couldn't deal with this and I broke down. "Okay, James, please don't go. I can't handle being away from you anymore. I want to spend every minute of every hour with you, for the rest of my life."

16. Last Attempt

He lifted me up and brought me slowly down to him to the most magnificent kiss. He broke that kiss but rested his forehead on mine. "Oh my god, Sarah, I needed you to say that so bad." He slowly pulled the necklace over my head. He took my hand, lifting it to his face. He put my ring finger all the way in his mouth. I cupped his face with my free hand to watch him. He sucked off the ring and took it with his hand to place it on the necklace again. He put it back over my head. He slid the ring down my shirt and placed his hand where it rested. "It's forever my sweet, Sarah."

"James, we should get going. You will be late." Wilson was there to get James to the airport.

I could see the regret on his face, "Sarah?"

"I know you're still going." My heart was breaking.

"Four more weeks my sweet little girl. Four more weeks and I will give you everything you want."

I begged him with my eyes and said, "You?"

He leaned into kiss my cheek and whispered, "You were ready."

He turned me to kiss him deeply. He let go hurrying to the truck Wilson was in. I couldn't move. *What did he mean I was ready? Was I ready for* him? Did that mean we could have if I didn't fall asleep? Were we that close and I ruined it? Was he miserable? Would we try to be together as soon as he got home?

I could not move an inch; he had taken my breath away. My phone buzzed, I fumbled around trying to take it out. I opened it to find a message from James:

>"Sarah, first 1- 2- 3- breath. Then go home. I love you more than you know."

I looked at the time on my phone, only 10:05 p.m. I could still make it. I got in my car and drove. The only true friend I had was Matt, so I called him as I drove to his house, "Sarah, what are you doing calling me?"

"I need your help. Can you come with me right now?"

"Auh, yeah I guess."

"Meet me out front of your house; I will be there in 3 minutes."

I hung up the phone. I pulled up to his house. I saw him come out, and I got out from the driver's seat to move to the passenger side of the car. He walked up to me and I held out the keys. He didn't take the keys; he looked at me, "Are you okay?"

I jingled them in front of his face, "Nope."

He took the keys. I got in and then he got in but didn't start it. I could tell he was looking at me.

"Where too?"

"The airport."

"I am not helping you run away!"

I turned to him and tried to smile the best I could holding back my tears, "I'm not going anywhere, Matt! Please!"

He started the car and took off.

"Matt, one more thing, just play along with what I am going to say."

"What are you talking about?"

I took out my phone and dialed home putting it on speaker phone.

"Sarah?"

"Yeah, mom, Matt and I found a court with lights. We're going to practice a few things and then I'll be home."

"Sarah, it's after 10 p.m. and you have to work in the morning."

I waved for Matt to say something.

"Hey Mrs. Sullivan, we'll just be…" He looked at me… I held up my thumb and pointer, oh so much… to show him a little. "…a little bit."

"Okay, but not too late, Sarah."

"Love you mom." I hung up the phone.

Matt was shaking his head, "You so *owe* me, big."

"You have my permission to go as fast as you want because we have to hurry." I looked at him as the tears flowed down my cheeks.

"Sarah, did he break up with you?"

I turned to look out the window, "Nope."

"But he's leaving?"

"Yep, hurry, please, Matt." I looked up to see the planes flying over us as I prayed I would get to see him one more time before he has to leave.

Matt pulled in and parked. He was getting out with me. I was running in, and he was right behind me. "Sarah, what are we looking for?"

"I'm not sure about the airline, but Denver 12:20 a.m. departure."

"Sarah!"

I turned because he was stopped and looking at the flights. There it is, Sarah, this way." He grabbed my hand and pulled me in the right direction. I felt like we were running forever. Matt stopped and pulled me to a stop. He looked over, my eyes followed where he was looking. Wilson was sitting next to my James. He had his hand on James's back, but my James was leaning forward with his head in his hands.

"James!" I yelled. He stood up. I let go of Matt's hand and ran to my Cayuse throwing myself into his arms.

"Oh, Sarah, you are so asking for trouble. What are you doing here?"

I hugged him tighter and kissed his neck, "I don't want to let you go."

He moved his hands to cup my face and pulled it to gaze into my eyes; when I saw his face he looked as miserable as I felt. He kissed me and held me there. We only broke so we could breath. His attention went over me and he released me so that I was standing. He held me close as we moved to Matt. He put out his hand to shake Matt's hand, but only taking his eyes off me long enough to shake Matt's hand. "You must be Matt, Thanks for entertaining my…", and that is when his stare came back to me, "…Sarah. And if you could, please don't hit on her again. I get a little jealous." He continued to smile at me; he held me tight and traced one hand down my face.

I had to scold him, "James, if it wasn't for Matt, I wouldn't be here. You should be thankful."

"Sorry, Matt, thank you." He started to move us toward a corner to have a little more privacy, but he spoke to Wilson. "Wilson, could you please get him anything he wants; this may take awhile." He was grinning at me mischievously.

"Yes, James, but you don't have awhile; make it quick."

He took my hands and kissed them as he led me away. I couldn't take my eyes off of his. He was hurting as bad as I was. The emptiness was showing through.

"You are crazy little girl."

"I am only crazy about you. I don't want to let you go."

"I love you too, Sarah, but this is harder for me…"

He leaned his forehead to mine, cupping my face with his hands.

I nudged his chin, "I do have one question for you, and it wouldn't wait."

"What is that?"

"What did you mean I was ready?"

He closed his eyes, "Sarah we can't, and I can't talk about that here, not now." He kissed me so softly parting my lips with his."

"Excuse me, James, but the flight is boarding. James, you made me promise, you have to go son." Wilson took his arm and started to walk him to where they were boarding. I moved with him holding his hands. Wilson was pleading with me, "Sarah, you have to let him go now."

I couldn't let go and I heard Wilson again, "Matt, could you help me by holding her back."

I kept holding James hand's because he wasn't letting go either. Matt moved in front of me and James had to let go.

In my last desperate chance at him staying I yelled for him, "James?"

He broke away from Wilson and came back to me and kissed me so passionately, "I love you more than you know. I will be back; be patient, Sarah. I am not going anywhere in here." He was patting his heart. He turned and walked down the boarding ramp and turned once to look at me. My heart was breaking and the tears streamed down my face.

Wilson walked back over to me, "I'm sorry, Sarah, you know he needs to finish."

I started to sob, "I know. I want him too, but I miss him so much when he is gone."

Wilson put his arm around me, so I could bury my face in his chest as we walked back out of the airport. He walked us all the way to my car opening the door for me. "Sarah, you are part of James's family. If you need anything, anything at all my Clarissa has instructed me to help you." He held my hand, but there was a piece of paper in it.

"You call or stop by. It's as much yours as it is his." He smiled and kissed my hand like a gentleman would do. He looked at Matt, "You must be a very good friend. You can get her home?"

He nodded. We both got in the car for the ride home. I didn't want to talk at all, so I looked out the window. I was trembling and couldn't keep my hands from shaking. I tried to hold them together, but that didn't work. I shook them and then sat on them.

"Um, Sarah?"

Oh shit, what did he want now? Can't he see I'm having a nervous breakdown here? I tried to calm myself, "Yeah?"

"You don't owe me anything."

"What?"

"I didn't realize."

"Matt, you need to pull over now; I'm going to be sick."

"Where?"

"Anywhere, soon please."

He took the next off ramp and pulled over. I had the door open before he stopped. I felt like throwing up but it wasn't as bad as before. I paced. The cool night air helped. I shook my hands thinking this would help with the trembling.

He got out, but watched from a distance, "Are you okay?"

I laughed to myself as I thought: The difference between a boy and a man. Or maybe it was because the two that have helped me actually care about me.

"Yeah, it's getting better." I paced a few more times. I sat down in the grass and laid back.

"Sarah, I thought you were feeling better?"

"Yeah, I am. It's just too much sometimes. This stupid thing I have."

'What do you have?"

"I don't know what it is yet. The doctor keeps doing different tests, but they don't know what it is. But to make it simpler to understand, if I get upset, I get sick."

"Is that why you keep getting skinnier?"

"Yeah, I go back in on Monday."

"Is that why he had a hard time leaving?"

"I think that's part of it."

"And the other?"

"I think he really loves me."

"That's kind of obvious."

He came and sat by me, "Do you think you can play tomorrow? I would understand if you can't."

"I will be fine tomorrow, and I will do great. I promise."

"But if you're sick?"

"Its only when I get upset."

I sat up and felt a little better. I can't believe I made it through that without getting sick.

"Sarah, it's getting late. Do you think we should go?"

"Yeah."

He got up and put his hand out to help pull me up. I stood up but my head was still dizzy. I stumbled, and he caught me. His face was so near to mine as he held me there for more than I was comfortable with.

"Are you okay?"

"Yep, I am just getting my legs back. I'm fine."

He stood me up and followed me back to the car with his arms extended out, in case I lost my balance again. "Matt, I'm okay now."

"If I let you get hurt, I think your James would kill me."

"Really, he doesn't do stuff like that. He mostly scolds me for doing things I shouldn't be doing, like chasing him to the airport."

"He scolded you?"

"Only a little."

"I have never seen anything like that."

I took a deep breath, "Like what?"

"Two people so torn about being apart, and the desire for each other."

I looked at him and the tears where welling up again, "Matt, you need to distract me. Don't talk about it."

He started talking about volleyball and strategies for tomorrow and this weekend. I didn't hear a word he said, but I nodded, said okay, yeah, and hummed and hawed. I was only hoping I was doing it at the right time. We pulled up to his house, so I took a deep breath and got out. He did the same, meeting me in front of the car. He handed me my keys. He looked at me funny.

"What?"

"Why did you tell him I hit on you?"

"I had too. He already knew."

"Yeah right."

"Matt you wouldn't understand, but there is a connection that I can't explain. He feels my feelings and that's all I can say."

"'So, he feels you?"

"Yes. Good and bad."

He was trying to figure it out in his head, so he was distant. I hugged him so tight, "Thank you! I owe you big."

He didn't hug me back. I let him go to see what the problem was, "He didn't look at you the way he looked at me."

I laughed a sigh, "He's okay with us being friends, playing volleyball.

"So, we're good for tomorrow?"

"Yep."

"Do I get to drive again?"

I disapproved but then grinned, "I owe you."

He smiled and almost hugged me but then moved away and took my hand to shake it.

"It's a deal."

He walked to his house and I drove home.

Mom was sleeping when I got home so I didn't have to explain anything.

I woke in a rush, not realizing what time it was. I was panicking because I had fallen asleep so fast and I didn't have time to get everything ready for the day.

I still had to read my note for the day. Day 23:

When I look into your eyes
They make me melt
I can't believe the way that felt.
When I touch your soft skin
It makes me want to grin
As if it was a sin.
When I kiss your lips
I cannot breath
You knock me to my knees.
I love you more than you know,
I love you more than I can show,
But I will love you so."
With all my love,
James

I had this note before yesterday. That is so amazing. He knew how to fit these notes perfectly. I had to get going if I was going to be on time. I noticed my period was already over, not even a full day. Maybe it had something to do with what's wrong with me. I would bring it up on Monday to the doctor.

I went to work, but I also brought my volleyball stuff with me. I did so good not thinking about James at work. The phone kept me busy. I called Matt as soon as I left work. He came out ready, but looked at me funny.

"You're not bailing on me, right?"

I was still in my work clothes, "Can I get dressed here?"

"Yeah." He walked me up to his room taking my bag from me and set it in the bathroom on the floor. He moved out of my way carefully and went to leave. He stopped at the door not turning around, "Why didn't you get dressed at home?"

"I didn't stop there. I didn't want to be alone. I might have bailed."

"Are you okay?"

"Yes, but not if you keep asking me questions… door please."

He moved to close the door and paused like he was going to say something, but then closed the door. I got dressed quickly and came out.

"Ready?"

"Yep."

We were a little early, but he had me warm up. I am sure he wanted to make sure I could handle playing, "I think you're ready."

I knew I was ready. I was so ready to work out my frustrations on the ball. I worked really hard and it showed in the game. We kicked butt winning both games. I was in such a great mood that I dangled my car keys in front of him.

"You're going to let me drive?"

"I owe you!" I was grinning.

"We win and I get to drive your car. You have made my night."

He talked the whole time he drove. He went the longest way he could possibly go. I was laughing to myself. I didn't even mind dropping him off because he didn't ask any questions or bring up James at all.

When I got home mom was waiting for me, but she just asked how everything went. She seemed happy that I was having fun playing volleyball with Matt. I went to bed hoping to fall asleep quickly. It couldn't come fast enough today.

I laid down holding my pillow, and it didn't come fast enough. The tears were streaming down my face. I didn't want to do this anymore. Why was I torturing myself and probably him for not being apart for a single day? I cried myself to sleep.

17. A Good Day

When I woke it was Day 24, and I felt a little better. I made it a whole day without getting sick. There was a message for me. I opened my phone.
>"1-, 2-, 3-, breath. One thing I know is I love you."

The world stops when I am with you
Nothing else matters but to touch your soul,
It's my goal
The smile on your face, the bite of your bottom lip
It makes me feel good when you're happy
It makes me sappy.
You amaze me in every way,
How can you love me?
I know it's meant to be.
With all my love,

James

I had more time this morning. I put the notes in my book with the other notes from James. My day was boring and uneventful, except for the thought of James. He was right, this was how I was going to get through each day.

I started a new day with Day 25: I had the note in my hand before I even opened my eyes.

I hate having one day without you
I hate having on minute without you
It is the thought of you that gets me through.
I love you more than you know,
James

I got a bag ready for Saturday. I packed a lot of snacks, because I was feeling like eating again. I was starving this morning and ate two bowls of cereal. I was still hungry, but I didn't know if I was going to pay for it later. I went to work happy. I counted days… he was actually going to be gone 47 days if he was flying in on that Sunday. We could work out plans later. I made my way to work. I had a great day; my boss even called me in to talk more about my car and how special it was and how to take care of it. I tried to listen, but my mind drifted elsewhere.

"Sarah, do you have a boyfriend?" When I heard that I looked at him, what an inappropriate question.

"Yes, I do?" I was confused.

"Sometimes you are so happy and other times you seem distant, almost sad."

"I will try to be better about that."

"I'm not talking about your performance; you do just fine. We just worry about you, and you are a very pretty girl. We all want you to be happy all the time."

I was getting a little creeped out, "Well if that's all, I'll go back to work."

"Some of us are going out to eat after work; you could come with us."

"I have a volleyball tournament tomorrow; I need to get some sleep so I have energy, but thank you."

I walked out. I took a deep breath. That was really creepy. I didn't know how to feel other than that.

At the end of my day, I punched the clock and went to get in my car, but my boss, Mr. Allen Kretton, was at my car door. I rolled down my window, "Did I forget something?"

"No. I just wanted to offer again. I can pay for you if you will come?"

Okay, *now*, I am really freaked out, "Nope, I'm sure. Thanks though."

He bent down to lean on my window, and I leaned away from it. Was he making a pass at me? He's like old; he has to be at least 30 years old.

"Promise me next time you will come with us?"

I just wanted him away from my window, "Yeah, of course, next time."

He stood up pleased with himself, "I'll plan on next Friday, then."

"Yeah, okay." I was leaving town next Friday, so I knew I could get out of going. I'll tell him that my mom wasn't giving me a choice or something. I rolled up my window and drove away.

I started to feel like I needed to throw up again. I didn't' want too; I was trying everything to keep from getting sick while I was driving home. I pulled in and took a deep breath and was able to stop it. I only have to fall asleep, and I would have made it two days. Now I had to deal with mom. Hopefully, she wouldn't bug me into this feeling again by asking too many questions.

I walked in and mom was sitting in her chair. I went in and hugged her, and then went to the kitchen to eat something. Instead of getting sick; all I could think about was eating. I took some left over's out and threw them in the microwave.

"You're eating?"

"Yeah, I am so...hungry. I haven't eaten this much in a long time. It's like I can't get enough."

"So, you have been so busy lately I haven't had much time to see you."

I looked at her feeling bad that I was leaving her home alone. "I'm sorry."

"Oh, don't be. I am happy you are keeping busy. So, Matt and you... are spending a lot of time together?"

"Mom, were just friends. That's it."

"Okay, have you talked to James lately?"

"Last weekend. I told you he keeps it to the weekends. Oh, it's Friday, maybe tonight?"

"Sarah, you do know it's okay to explore other options."

"Mom, I am going to marry him someday." I was getting angry.

"Sarah, I am just saying things change. How do you know he's not exploring other options?"

I smiled, knowing that he loved me. I thought of how miserable he was when he left; that's what told me 'it's only me,' "I trust him, and you shouldn't do that."

"Do what?"

"Try to make me doubt him. He is very good to me, and you have to realize I love him and he is mine. That is it."

"You are too young to make that decision."

"Fine, I won't right now. I will in a couple years, but it will be him."

I finished eating and didn't feel sick, even after arguing with my mother. I think I am actually getting better, finally. I got up to go to bed. "Good night mom. Sorry for arguing."

I walked to my room. I really needed James to call me, just to prove her wrong, that he might be interested in someone else. Even though I knew deep in my heart he loved me. I crawled in bed with my phone, putting my lips on my phone and fell asleep. My phone rang at 2 a.m.

"James?"

"Who else would call you at 2 a.m.?"

"Well I don't know." I was being playful.

"You shouldn't tease me like that."

"I'm sorry. Are you okay, James?"

"Why are you asking me?"

"I know you didn't get much sleep the other day with flying and then the drive."

"You were worried about me weren't you?"

"Yes, I am. If you feel what I feel, it hurts all the time."

"Sarah, what happened today, when you were upset?"

"James, why do you do that?"

"Sarah, I don't try. I can feel everything more than I have ever. It's so clear I can almost see your face when it happens, so don't try to change the subject. What happened?"

"Don't get mad."

"Sarah!"

"I was just very uncomfortable."

"With what?"

"Okay. I think my boss came on to me, but I'm not sure. He just gave me the creeps."

"Quit. There is enough money in that account that you could have three months to find another job. It's your money too."

"James, I can't do that."

"If you are mine, then everything I have is yours. Just quit."

"If you don't mind I will stay a little longer, but if he is creeps me out again…"

"You will quit."

"Only if I have to, James."

"Do you realize that tomorrow is our hump day?"

"What?"

"Were halfway through this, and then I can come home to you. We'll have to figure a way to convince your mom on letting me live with you. I can't be away from you ever again."

"James, that might be harder than you think."

"I can be very persuasive when I want to be."

"Really, how's that?"

"I have you."

"But, I liked you before you showed me any affection."

"You were feeling me call to you. You are my soul mate. Otherwise, you couldn't feel me like this."

I felt his touch on my face.

"James, I'm okay right now, and if you do that the hurting and the desire will overwhelm me and I will be miserable."

I felt his finger tips glide along my jaw line and then over my lips.

"Yep, the pain of you not being here is coming back."

"Sarah, close your eyes. I need to do something."

"James, it's going to hurt." But I closed my eyes anyway.

He laughed, "You closed your eyes?"
"Yes."
"I wasn't asking; I feel you that much."
I felt his kiss so soft on my lips, his hand moving slowly down to my neck just to feel the shape of it.
"You are lying on your side, but you are hugging a pillow where your head is laying."
"Oh, James, how are you going to concentrate if you feel me all the time?"
"I am actually stronger, and I can stop it, or block some of it."
The kissing resumed. It felt like he was there in front of me, but his focus stayed on my face and my neck.
"James, I'm going to fall asleep like this."
"Go ahead; I want to stay here for awhile, if it's okay with you."
"Yes, please."
His touch was relaxing and soothing. I fell asleep with no pain in my heart.

My alarm was buzzing, and I woke to a fuzzy day. I was ready but I had to move. My rest was amazing. I haven't slept this good in a long time. I took a deep breath and pulled out my Day 26: As I opened it I realized he wasn't right. We were over half way there. Our hump day would have been yesterday, half way through the day. I couldn't wait to tell him he was wrong.

I would travel through wind and fire
Just to feel your desire
Through the ocean and over the sand
Just to feel grand.
Remember I am far, but near,
So don't fret because I am right here.
I love you more than you know,
James

He touched my heart in such a special way. But I had a big day ahead of me. I got dressed quickly putting on sun block so I wouldn't get burnt.

I grabbed my bag and I needed to eat because I was starving again. I fried three eggs and had some toast with them. I grabbed my water jug knowing it was going to get hot, and I ran out the door.

Matt was waiting outside for me. He didn't say much of anything; his mind was on today.

"Are you feeling good?"

I was feeling really good and rested, "Better than you look."

"What do you mean?"

I chuckled, "You look nervous."

"I am a little."

"Remember, this is supposed to be fun. Keep your focus on that."

"You sound like a mom."

"Thanks." I was sarcastic.

The morning went good, and we won both games, and now we had a break 'til 11 a.m. I was starving again. I made Matt sit with me to eat some of the snacks I brought. We had veggies and an energy bar. He lay down on the mat in front of me. I fed him veggies, trying to get him motivated for the next game. He propped himself up on his side, resting on his elbow, but looked at me.

"Do you want to know something?"

"What?"

"You are the real thing, not a phony."

My eyes widened. Where was this going? What was he thinking? I replied, "Okay?"

"No, I mean when I made a pass at you, it was because you are hot. But that was it. I really didn't know you."

"What are you trying to say, Matt?"

"That, I am sorry." He looked at me to see how I was taking that. He must have felt safe to elaborate because he continued, "And now, now that I have spent so much time with you and after seeing you with James... I guess I see why he looks at you that way."

I was embarrassed, "What way?"

He lay back down, "He sees past the surface, that's all."

"So, are you saying there is more to me than a great body?" I was being playful. He was being too serious, and I had to lighten the mood. Have fun, win games.

A mischievous smile came to his face, "Yes, there is more to you than a great body, but I am shallow and I get girls with my sexy body." He traced his hand down his chest.

That was better, lighter. I giggled as I watched him worship his own body.

We started warming up for the next game. We had three in a row this time. The first game we did good, and the second we struggled. It was neck and neck to the end. The third was a blow out. Matt was on a high. A bunch of people showed up from school to watch. After these games he went to hang with them. They were congratulating him and cheering for him. I was getting too hot and we still had games. We had a two hour break, so I grabbed my towel and walked to the lake. I needed to cool down, and after that I could eat some more. I took my hair out of my pony and went under water to get completely cooled off. I did it again because if felt refreshing. When I came up Matt was moving in front of me tracing my mid section, more to let me know he was there than anything else.

"Why didn't you tell me you were going swimming? I would have come with you. I needed to cool off too."

I didn't want to interrupt his fun. "You were hanging with a bunch of kids from school. I am okay to be alone once in a while."

"But we're partners, and I would rather be here with you. You're mine today. They can worship my body some other day."

He made me laugh again. "Thanks, but you're kind of their ring leader. You have to live up to their needs too, the god that you are."

"You're teasing me?""

"I'm sorry, but the girls over there have been drooling all day."

"Really, where?"

"See, you're still a dog."

He looked ashamed, but then he glanced up at me through his eyelashes, "I don't want to be. I wish I could find someone real, someone like you, Sarah."

"I can help you with that."

"Okay." He was so eager to learn.

"Pretend they all have boyfriends that would kill you if you hit on them and just be their friends. You will be most desirable this way."

"Ha, you are funny."

"No, you are very cute when you're not being a jerk."

"So, you think I am desirable?"

"If I didn't have my James; yes, very much so."

"So, you are turned on by my body?"

"No, I am saying you are very sweet when you aren't trying to get someone turned on with your body."

"So, you're not turned on by my body?"

"Matt, you are my best friend next to James, so don't be a jerk. We have games to play."

He pushed me under the water saying, "You need to cool off."

We went back to our spots by the courts, and I pulled out more food.

"You're eating again?"

"Yes, we need to keep our energy up."

I pulled out a tuna salad and some fruit.

"You came prepared?"

"Yeah, I want to win the trophy."

"I can't wait to have it on my shelf."

"I have never had one."

"You are kidding?"

"No, I have never done anything that was competitive."

"Well, we're going to get it for you."

I started to eat my tuna salad and watched Matt. He lay back down in front of me. I fed him a forkful. He closed his eyes and ate it without saying anything. He moved his head closer to me. If I was watching us, it would have looked like we were a couple. I was hoping that he would stop that. Girls' might be turned off by this. He opened his mouth waiting for more. I gave him another forkful and giggled.

"What's so funny?"

"You look like a baby bird looking for food."

"Good thing you brought food. I would have been starving by now."

I pulled out the grapes and was feeding the both of us. When they were gone we started warming up again. I ate a protein bar because I needed more energy. It was almost time for our next game. We were getting to the finals, so our games would go every other hour now.

Thank goodness we had a blow out and then break time again. We sat and watched the next game. We might have to play against this team.

"No food this time?"

"No, did you need some? I have more."

He smiled and shook his head no.

We were up shortly, so we started to get ready.

We won the 5 p.m. game and the next one would be at 7 p.m. We had an hour. I pulled out what I had left for food; we were getting down to the last of it. He laid down propping himself to look at me.

"Do you treat James this good?"

I was happy, "He treats me this good."

"The other day, when you both were so torn to be apart, my heart actually hurt for you." He paused to think about something and then he asked, "He is a lot older than us?"

"I told you before he is 19 years old."

"But you guys don't have sex?"

I couldn't answer him and I watched the other team playing. "Matt, I really don't want to talk about James. It's hard for me to be away from him."

He sat up and moved closer, "I'm sorry; not a good time either. Are you still okay?"

"Yep." I had to take a deep breath and swallow a couple of times, but I was going to be okay.

"I'm so sorry. I just want someone to feel that way about me."

"You will someday, but like I said you have to spend time with them before it even gets that way."

"How long?"

"Until you know."

"Know what?"

I smiled thinking of my James, "We actually fought a lot when I first met him. He was kind of a jerk."

"What changed your mind?"

"The time he spent with me was comforting. He was always there and he was my friend first."

A grin grew on his face as he looked at me. I was getting it, which is where we were now. I put that thought out of my mind. I loved my James, more than I could ever explain.

We went out for the 7 p.m. game. I was getting nervous, and he could tell. "Sarah, remember have some fun out there."

I grimaced at him. I didn't want to lose this one for him. It was a challenge; we were struggling, but it wasn't me this time. I had to get him back in the game. I called a time out. We walked to the side and I took a drink of water.

"So, are you okay?"

"Yeah, I'm fine." He was short with me.

"Do you need to throw up? It works for me."

He laughed. "No."

"Do you need to cry and have a nervous breakdown? I could show you how."

"What are you saying?"

"The girls need something to drool over; flex the muscles and show them what you can do."

"I'm good now."

"Yes, you are."

We went back out, and he was more relaxed. He started to get better, then better, and then great. We ended up winning the game. We were in for the championship at 9 p.m. He walked up to me and hugged me, but almost holding me like James would, gentle and tender. His mouth came to my ear, "Thank you."

I was happy too, but this was not comfortable for me. I turned him so he would be facing the group of girls, "Matt, you need to get your rewards from them."

He moved away from me and looked back at me, "I get it. Sorry."

He went to the group of girls who congratulated him the way he deserved. I was happy for him. I decided to walk to the concessions because I needed more food. I can't believe that I was eating this way. I was feeling better. I got a hot dog and some chips; oh I added another hot dog in case Matt needed food. I walked back to the court slowly. He saw me and came running to me.

"Why do you keep running off on me?"

"I was getting food." I handed him a hot dog.

"You're eating again?"

"Yeah, it's weird. I haven't eaten this much in one day in …" I thought about it and it started the day he left. "…Three weeks?"

"Sarah, what's wrong?"

I shook my head, "I just realized something, but I don't know what to make of it."

"What's that?"

"I started getting sick when he left."

"He's making you sick?"

"No, but maybe the being apart makes it worse."

"Oh."

We went back and got ready for the last game. We were working hard but the team we were playing against had been together for three years. They were in their early twenties, so we didn't have a chance to win. We lost by 2. Not bad, but I felt bad for Matt, after working hard all day.

We walked to the car and I dangled the keys in front of his face.

"Not in the mood. Sorry."

I drove him home. He got out without saying too much. "Sarah? I…, I just…, I'll call you."

He walked away depressed, and I felt bad. I went home and to bed feeling sad.

18. Sharing Souls

I woke to my phone ringing, "James!"
"My sweet, Sarah."
"I have missed you so much today."
"Good, you were with Matt today?"
"Yeah, but I only thought of you, and how much I love and miss you."
"Tell me what you miss?"
"I miss your soft touch on the indentation of my back when you're leading me. The tracing of your hand down my back to show me I'm special to you. The soft kiss of your lips on my hand and then turning it over to kiss my palm to show me you adore me. The way you move to me and talk in my ear making my heart race. And the..."
He interrupted me, "Wait!"
"What, James?"
"I want you here next to me, so I can share this with you."
"Share what with me?"
I felt this amazing rush through my whole body, as if he moved into my body and then out.
"Oh, James, what was that?"

"I wanted to touch you with my soul. What does it feel like for you?"

"It's like I can feel every part of you move through me."

He laughed, "It's a little erotic, so I am by the shower."

"How are you doing?"

"If I do it…"

"Oh, shit, James."

"Yep, I have to call you back."

He was gone. I closed my phone and curled up in my bed to enjoy what he just shared with me. I was dozing again when my phone rang again, "Oh, James."

"So, how did today go?"

"We won all day, except for the last game. We only took second."

"I'm sorry."

"I love you."

"Did he behave?"

"You know that answer to that James, especially if you feel me stronger than ever."

His laughter was so quiet, but he knew I got it now.

"You must feel something else too."

"What's that my love?"

"I haven't gotten sick for a total of three days."

"I didn't feel that. So, you feel better?"

"I still get the nausea feeling, but I have been able to hold it in, and I am eating like a pig."

"What?"

"I ate all day. I even had a hot dog. You really didn't feel that?"

"No, but you may feel this."

I felt the movement through me again. "Oh, James, you have to stop doing that. I am getting so…my heart will hurt."

"I'm sorry; I just want you to feel the joy and pleasure you gave me."

"James, I still feel bad about falling asleep, don't say I gave you pleasure."

"Sarah, you did give me pleasure. I really need to confess something."

"Will it make me mad, sad, or happy?"

"I'm not sure."

"Do you love me? You're not breaking my heart are you?"

"No. Of course not."

"Okay, I am ready then."

"Sarah I..., we.... Dam it! I just can't explain how I feel about you no matter how much I try. The desire is worse than ever. If I spend one more minute without you I am going to explode."

"Okay."

"Okay what?"

"You can do whatever you need to; I am here for you."

"You are giving me permission to come to you?"

"Yes. The pain will go away eventually."

I felt his touch on my neck and the trace of his lips on mine. I felt his hands gliding over my body and a push to me.

"Oh, James, how real is this?"

"Do you feel me?"

"Yes, James. That's why I am asking; how real is this?"

I felt wonderful; his touch was making it hard for me to breath. I grabbed the sheet because the desire was increasing. I could feel his movement, and the tingling started.

"How does this feel to you?"

"Like...Oh, my god, James!" I rolled to my side but I felt him push me back and the feeling came stronger.

"Sarah, I am going to... Tell me what it feels like?"

I could feel myself tightening.

"Sarah! What did you just do? That felt amazing."

I squeezed more. It did feel good. "Oh, Sarah, am I hurting you? I am going to."

I felt the rush, but it was in me, and my body liked it so much. I felt a rush, but it seemed more like an explosion, "James, if this is real, I want to be with you right now... I felt it. There was..."

He finished my sentence, "An *explosion*, you felt that?"

"Yes."

"Shit, Sarah. Think about it. If you really felt it, then I really came inside you. There is a possibility that you could..."

"Shut up, James, it's already done if that could happen. James?"

"Yes?"

"I need more. Can you do that again please?"

The pleasure was way better than I could explain. I wanted to keep feeling this. *Is this what it felt like for real? I wasn't going to let him walk away again.* He chuckled, "Sarah, I know what you're thinking."

"Oh, James, why wouldn't you do this to me for real?"

"Sarah." He was breathing as hard as I was. The noises we were sharing were such a turn on. I loved what he was doing, and I wanted it to never end.

"You said I was ready; how could you stop?"

"Sarah, you have no idea."

"James!" It was so extreme. I put the pillow over my mouth. I wanted to scream to him to hurry and make it come now. I was having a hard time holding in the noises.

"Sarah. Are you in pain?"

"No." I could hardly get it out. I was afraid I would be so loud that my mom would hear me.

"Are you okay?"

"Need more James. Hurry it's almost…"

I felt it move deeper, harder. If I wasn't ready before I am surely ready now. I squeezed as hard as I could and the rush from him came again, which triggered the rush for me. He moved very slowly after that.

"James?" I could hear him; he was in pleasure too. I felt his hands cupping my face, the tracing with his lips over my face.

"Sarah, I shouldn't have done that."

"Oh, yes, you should have. I will not be able to keep my hands off of you."

"That's why I shouldn't have. We should not be doing this. Honestly Sarah, I could go to jail for being with you."

"But, we haven't."

"Sarah, how are you? Does it hurt you at all?"

"No, it felt…" I thought about the explosion and how it was for me. I could feel the smile in his reply, "It feels that good for you too?"

"Oh, yes, James. I will not let you stop the next time I see you."

"Can I stay here till you sleep?"

"You still feel like…?"

"Oh, Sarah, I am and I don't want to let this feeling go. I feel so good when I feel the heat of you. And I can't help but…"

He started to move again. I didn't think I could handle this again. My body took over and moved to him complimenting his movements to me.

"Sarah? What are you doing?"

"It's not me. My body is doing it."

He slowed to a softer rhythm, so the pleasure was different. I wanted him faster; the feeling wanted to come.

"James more, harder."

"Oh, Sarah, you will feel so much better this way... like this."

I had to put the pillow over my mouth right away. It was like a constant pleasure with each movement. It was so slow, but I felt the wanting with each movement. I had to keep my mouth open to breathe, maybe more like gasping. As the pleasure came it was a complete release into him, and I started to cry.

"Sarah?"

"Yes." I was shuttering with the crying.

"Are you crying?"

"I can't help it. I have never felt this way."

"Oh, Sarah, I shouldn't have. We should be together, so I can hold you. I am so sorry, Sarah. I was in agony without you and I was being selfish."

I turned to my side. I couldn't handle this anymore. It had to stop. I felt him move around me, holding me. I felt him whispering in my ear, "Sarah, I love you so much, I shouldn't have done that."

"James, shhhh."

"You are sad?"

"No, extremely happy. I am feeling really good right now and just need to enjoy this."

"So, you're not mad at me for...?"

"James, you will pay for this when I see you!"

"Oh, Sarah, I am so sorry."

"James, what I mean is you better plan on a place that we can be alone for awhile, because you will not take a shower, not if I can feel like this."

"I have to admit something, Sarah."

"Okay, I really wasn't paying attention, and I could hardly open my eyes.

"Sarah, baby, I was jealous of Matt today."

"I'm sorry."

"That's why I had to come to you tonight. I wanted you to want to be with me more than him."

"James, you didn't have to do that for me to want to be with you."

"I was desperate for you to want to be with me. I needed to feel your desire."

"I am glad you did this. I have never felt so good in my life, but I would have rather you be here for it."

"I wish I could show and tell you how much you mean to me." I felt him tracing his hand on my face and my neck. I was falling asleep.

"James, I could fall asleep. This has made me so tired."

"Sarah, don't go to sleep, I still need to tell you something."

"What's that?"

"Sarah, we..., I..."

"James?"

"When I moved through you; I was giving you *my soul*."

"What do you mean?"

"We are now as one. This is *marriage in the heritage world*, and I couldn't wait for you to be ready; I hope you don't mind."

"So, how do I have a part in this? How do I marry you?"

"What?"

"You gave me your soul. Now what do I give you?"

"You already did it."

"What did I do?"

"You let me *use the feather* with you."

I yawned. I was falling asleep. It was so comforting to talk to him. "But I fell asleep."

"Sarah, it was more like a trance, that's all. The use of the feather allows me to come to you."

I didn't hear anything after that because I was asleep. I still felt him there which made me sleep deeply.

19. Cancer

Day 27: I was in no hurry to get out of bed. I was still dreamy from the night with my Cayuse. I remembered the feelings that overcame me and shivered. I made myself stop thinking about it, because he would feel my thoughts. I rolled over to hug my pillow. I was so relaxed and satisfied and I closed my eyes stretching my arms out. I grabbed my note for the day.

I was empty
You brought me fullness.
I was searching
You brought me discovery.
I was lost
You brought me home.
I gave you my soul
You gave me you.
I love you more than you know,

James

I wish I could feel him now. I needed to trace my hands over his face to read how deep his love is. I know he loves me, but the look in his eyes would tell me how much. They were a warm brown that looked lighter when his look softened with tenderness for me. I closed my eyes to see his. Okay, the heart was hurting a little. I have to make myself get up now, or I would succumb to it. I was still not in any hurry. I only had to do my laundry today to get ready for the week. Mom was working until 7 p.m., so I had the day to myself, not exactly a good thing.

I was hungry again and still felt really well. I decided to make myself an egg and cheese sandwich. Protein gave me more energy, so it was good for me to have. I started working on my laundry. I hadn't done it in awhile. I was glad to not work today. I needed to catch up on my daily tasks, and I could care less to spend any time with my boss, now that I was uncomfortable around him.

I put in a movie to wait for the next load to be ready to fold and curled up in the chair. I watched half the movie and then paused it to go start another load. I went right back to the movie and watched the rest of it. I really didn't feel like another movie. I went down and put in another load and when I came back up I decided to check on my fall classes. I was only in school for two hours a day and then college for whatever classes I was going to take. I was going to do my PSEO at Normandale Community College. I was going to get my generals done before I was done with High School. I was glad to be away from the endless hallways of desolation because I really didn't enjoy the High School life. My entrance exam was good, and I was ready to go. I was searching for an English class and a Math class. I was going to go to High School my first two hours of the day. The English classes were available Monday, Wednesday, and Friday's at 11 a.m. for almost two hours each. That would work. I could be done by 12:45 pm., which sounds good to me. I locked in the class. So, that was one down, now on to the second. These didn't seem too pleasing to me, but I had to go with Monday, Tuesday, and Thursday at 1 p.m. I would be done on these days by 2:45 p.m. So Monday's would be my worst day for school, but I could handle that. I locked in this class and I printed my schedules. I then went in to see what books I would need. I could get them free, but I would have to turn in the books at the end of the classes. I thought that would be okay. James would be impressed with me planning things out. I smiled to myself and couldn't wait to talk to him. I was still curious where he was going to school. I went to search some different programs for what he was looking for: Forestry, Game Warden, or maybe a Sheriff, something on those lines. I didn't know if he had anything lined up.

University of Minnesota offers a Natural resource program. He could go into any of them, but they have the field station in Cloquet, MN. That would be close to his home so he could see his family. That might be perfect for him. I printed out the information sheet for him and book marked the page on the computer, so he could look again. I couldn't wait to talk to him again, but it was Sunday, I didn't know if he would call me tonight. He had to work so hard, so he needs to rest. He needed to be strong. He had to focus on me less and himself more.

The doorbell rang. I closed the pages I was looking at and moved to the door. I opened it and there was a beautiful boy, Matt, standing there. I hugged him and pulled him inside.

"What are you doing here?"

"I wanted to apologize for last night. We had a great day and I was pretty crabby last night when you dropped me off. We did really well and I brought you food to thank you."

I pulled him to the kitchen, "So, what did you bring?"

He put the bag on the table and grinned, "Well, after yesterday, I figured you try to eat healthy, so…Do you like Caesar Salad?"

"I think so."

"How about Chicken and Wild Rice soup?"

"Maybe."

"And, of course, a tray of fruit."

I chuckled with the biggest smile on my face. He continued to pull stuff out of the bag and I got two plates, two bowls, and some tooth picks. Then he held up a movie. "Can we watch this while we eat?"

"What is it?"

"A really old movie about Volleyball; 'Sideout'."

"Sure."

He started putting salad on the plates, and pouring soup into the bowls. I went to set up TV trays for us. I put one in front of the couch and the other in front of the chair. I didn't want to give him any false hope. He walked out with the plates putting one on the tray by the couch and then the other, but picking up the tray and moved it to the front of the couch, so we would have to sit together.

"Sarah, after yesterday you don't trust me?"

I gave him my guilty look, "Matt, it's not that I don't trust you. I just don't want you to get the wrong impression. We're just friends and I don't want to hurt your feelings. I know it's hard to understand, but I do care about you and your friendship."

He pulled me to sit down, "I saw the desperate attempt to be together, and I understand that you are in love with…him. We're just friends."

We started to eat as the movie played. He was commenting on the movie, to parts he wanted me to watch, mostly the playing volleyball parts. He pointed out how we were better because we did this or that. He was quite funny to watch, especially the excitement over the game. After we were done eating the soup and salad he paused the movie. He got up, "Fruit now?"

I got up and grabbed the plates and bowls and brought them to the kitchen and he followed to grab the tray of fruit. I put one TV tray away and he put the plate of fruit on the other and moved it to be in-between us. He sat back down and started the movie again. I think I watched his excitement more than the movie. As it ended, he looked at me, "Did you get your schedule for school yet?"

"Nope, but I am doing PSEO this year, and I just signed up for those classes. I will only be at school for the first two classes each day." He didn't seem too happy, but I had to do what was best for James and our future. He let the subject end but asked about the 4th of July.

"Do you have plans for the 4th?"

"I know we were going up north next weekend, but I haven't talked to my mom about what day we were going up."

"If you don't have plans, will you come to the carnival and fireworks with me?"

He could see the hesitation in my look.

"It would be with a group of people; so far there are eight of us going together and you should come hang with us."

"When mom gets home, I will ask what her plans are."

He settled for this answer. He stood up and got the movie out and put it away. He glanced up at me, "Well, I better go." He was walking to the door. I got up to let him out. He stopped at the door and turned to look at me. I was nervous because I didn't want him to come on to me at all. He didn't do anything but reminded me, "Call me and let me know either way, please."

I reassured him, "I will." He leaned into me to give me a hug, but it was short and sweet, more like a friend would do. That made me very happy and relieved. I closed the door and felt better about the friendship with Matt. I went back to finishing my laundry.

Mom got home at 7:30 pm. I fed her the left over's from Matt and me, and she seemed happy that he stopped by today. I was going in for the kill about next weekend."

"Mom, we are going up north next weekend, right?"

"Yeah, that could be the plan."

"Well the 4th is Wednesday; when were you thinking of going up north?"

"I was hoping we could leave early Wednesday."

"Okay!"

"Why, did you take the time off from work?"

"I think they weren't going to need me those three days, but I will check."

I didn't want to stay just because she would be happy. I was spending time with someone other than James. I was getting tired of them pushing me away from him. He was my forever.

"Do you have another Doctors appointment tomorrow?"

"Yep. I suppose more testing and find out what happened with the last tests."

"Okay, would you like me to go with you?"

"No, I'll be fine."

"Will you at least call me and let me know?"

"Of course, mom."

I went to bed early; I was happy for the day and fell asleep right away.

Day 28: I had to stay on track today. I had to get back to the doctors this morning. I took out my note for a fresh start to my day.

You wrinkle your nose
When I pull you close,
Your eyes glimmer
As I pause to linger.
I shiver at your touch
I love you so much,
I love you more than you know,

James

I smiled but didn't linger. I had breakfast and got ready to go.

When the doctor came in she didn't seem too pleased, and she was very careful how she spoke to me, "Well, we didn't find anything that would tell us what is causing you to get sick."

"I haven't gotten sick for four days, and I am eating a lot now."

"That is very good, but your white blood count was very high last week and you have lost another 7 pounds, so I think we need to do some more in-depth tests."

"Like what?"

"Well, I don't want to alarm you, but I think we need to do a scan. It will maybe show something we are missing."

"I was thinking I should have birth control too."

"I will give you the prescription, but with what's going on you should really think things through before you do anything like that."

"I am just being safe."

"Okay."

The tears started to well up in my eyes. She tried to reassure me. "I really don't think it is *cancer*, but we're just making sure."

"I was instantly fearful. She didn't say that word before. Now I was really scared and the stream from my eyes was heavier. I wondered *how someone my age can have cancer.*

She had someone come in and gave me a radiation pill. I was kind of freaked out. The tech had on a radiation suit and I was going to put this into my body. I was here alone and very scared. I took the pill and they scheduled the scan for the next morning. The doctor gave me a note for work, so they wouldn't question me on trying to get time off in the morning. When I left the office I was a mess. I didn't know what to do or where to go. I really didn't want to be alone. I knew I had to go to work, so I just took a lot of deep breaths.

When I got to work, I got started right away. I needed to not think about this. I did fairly well on trying to not think about it, but at the end of the day I had to talk to my creepy boss. I walked in, "Um, Mr. Kretton. I have a doctor's note for tomorrow. I have to have some test done in the morning."

"You have been sick?"

"Yeah, and they can't find out what is wrong with me. So I am having a scan tomorrow." I took a deep breath as he read the note.

His look was horrifying, "A PET scan, isn't that for…Cancer?"

My heart dropped, hearing it from someone else's lips made it worse. The tears were welling up in my eyes and I could hardly breathe. He nodded, "Of course, whatever you need."

I didn't want to push my luck, but I wanted to take advantage of the situation. "Um, my mom wants to take me out of town on Wednesday. Is it possible to have Wednesday through Friday off too?"

"After this, you may want a few days, of course."

He was writing something down and stood up walking over to me handing me a piece of paper. "This is my cell phone number. You can call me anytime, if you need to talk or something."

I took it from him and excused myself. I hurried to my car. This was just so overwhelming. I was having a hard time dealing with it and the way he looked at me made it worse. Now I really wished I did have James here. I needed him so bad right now. I went home. It was already late. I didn't want to worry my mom, so I stopped at a gas station and used their bathroom. I washed my face and reapplied makeup, so she wouldn't notice. I got home and mom was ready for bed.

"So, how did it go today?"

"Just more tests, and I have to go back tomorrow. They still haven't found anything. Oh, I have off Wednesday through Friday, so we can go up early."

"Okay, what time would you like to go?"

"Like around noon or something like that, whatever time. I really don't care. I'm just tired. I had a long day, so I am going to bed."

"Are you sure you are okay?"

"Yep. I haven't got sick in five days and counting." I couldn't worry her; she was working so hard lately, and she didn't need to worry about this too.

I went to bed holding my phone and curling up with a pillow. The tears streamed down my face, but I held back the sobbing. I woke to my phone ringing. I wanted to talk to him as bad as I didn't. My pillow was soaked. I answered, "James." I tried to say it with a smile.

"You have been upset all day. What is going on?"

"I'm just over reacting; you know my insecurities."

"Sarah!"

"James, tell me a story. Make me laugh."

"On the spot again; you know I am not good at this."

"Please, James."

He told me about a course that was very challenging and that everyone was wiping out on. It would have been funnier if I wasn't so upset. He was silent, so I didn't know if he was done.

"Sarah?"

"Yep."

"You need to tell me what happened today."

I couldn't talk because if I did, I would sob.

"I'll ask you questions and you can say yes or no, okay?"

"Yes."

"Was it your boss?"

"No."

"Your mom?"

"No."

I could hear the hesitation, "The doctors?"

"Yes."

I could hear him moving and doing something. He wasn't saying anything. Finally he blurted out, "I'm on my way."

I started to cry immediately.

"James, I'm just over reacting. As bad as I want you here, you can't."

"Sarah, please tell me?"

"I signed up for classes today. I will only have to be at school 'til 2:45 p.m. on Mondays, Tuesdays, and Thursdays. Wednesdays and Fridays I will be done at 1 p.m."

"That's good, Sarah. Making plans for the next step, but what are you upset about?"

"I looked for stuff for you too."

He eased, "You need to not talk about it?"

"Yep."

"Okay, but I still need to know."

"Yep."

"Please, just tell me. I can feel you and my heart is breaking."

"Dr. Jenson said she didn't think it was, but we are doing a scan tomorrow for …" I couldn't even say the word, let alone think it. James said he couldn't live without me. He is going to be so sad.

"Sarah, your thoughts are driving me crazy and I can't live without you. What are you talking about?"

"…for cancer."

"But, that's *not* it!"

"What?"

"Sarah, I have felt cancer before. It's not that."

I gasped with relieve. I could not believe he was so confident on this. "So, I am over reacting?"

"Oh, my sweet Sarah. I should have told you that. I would have reacted the same way, but no, baby, it's not cancer."

"But I took a radiation pill."

"You did what? I don't like that."

"Well neither do I and it was scary. They had on a radiation suit to give me the pill and now it's in me."

"Oh, Sarah, I really need to come home."

"Well, now that I know it's not cancer. I am fine. I haven't gotten sick in 5 days and counting, James."

"I think I will come home anyway. I just need to be around you."

"I need that too, but I am not going to be the reason you quit. So, suck it up and finish."

"You're tough."

"No, I'm not, but I want to be with you forever, and if you do something for me that you will regret latter you will be mad at me and it will fester in you. I will not let you be mad at me. I want you to be obsessed with me for the rest of your life. So, maybe I can win some arguments."

He laughed with this. "I love you more than you know, my sweet Sarah. So, what did you search for me?"

"The University of Minnesota has a Natural Resource program that you may want to look into. There are lots of options and the field work is done in Cloquet, which isn't too far from your dads place."

"You looked that up for me?"

"Yes. That's what you said you were interested in, and I wanted to make sure you knew what the next step of your plan would be."

"Sarah, I love you."

"Well, if it's not Cancer, you're stuck with me for a while."

He laughed quietly. "Good, I like that idea. So, are you better now?"

"Yes."

"I hate to say this, but I have to go. I have a big day tomorrow."

"I love you, James."

"Is your mom going with you tomorrow?"

"NO! I didn't want her to worry."

"So, you have been dealing with all this by yourself?"

"No, I have you."

"But I'm not there. Is there someone that can go with you?"

"No."

"Sarah?"

"NO James! Now that you told me it's not cancer I will be fine."

"You could ask…" He didn't want to say what he was thinking. "…Matt?"

"Nope, only you."

"Then I guess I have to come home."

"You're not funny."

"Sarah, it's okay. You need someone to lean on and I will have to deal with my jealousy a different way."

"No, James, if not you than nobody."

"I don't like that you are doing this alone."

"I'm not. I feel you all the time now. I will be fine."

"Just in case you change your mind, I will be okay with it."

"No, you won't, you're just putting me first before your feelings. I appreciate it, but James, that would hurt you and I don't want to hurt you ever. I will be fine."

I felt him touch my face. I closed my eyes to enjoy this. Then he traced his lips against mine, "James, you have a big day tomorrow."

"Yep." I felt his hands glide down my neck with his mouth following.

"James, you have to go."

"Yep." I could feel his breath tracing my jaw line.

"James…I will want more."

A whisper came to my ear, "I know."

My heart was racing and I could hardly breathe. He knew how to touch me to make all the sadness fade away. I cuddled into my pillow. I loved the way he turned my world upside down. I went into a beautiful dream of lying in his bed and him looking at me and touching my face, not eagerly, but caring, comforting, but his eyes were *sad*.

20. Girl Talk

Day 29: Today was my scan. I felt a lot better about it after talking to James. I pulled my daily note out. I only had 3 left. Maybe a package would come for me today. I hoped so, or I was going to miss a few days being up north.

I will spend my life with you
For you are the one.
You make me smile, cry, and fly.
I will fill your needs;
I will fill your desires.
Spend your life with me.
Say it is so, for I will take care of you.
I love you more than you know,

James

I smiled and got up to start my day. I headed to the hospital for my scan. Matt called me as I was driving there.

"Are we still on for today?"

"Oh yeah, I forgot. Yeah, I'll be there after work."
"Are you on your way to work now?"
"No."
"Where are you off too?"
"The hospital."
"For what?"
"I am having a scan done this morning."
"Is your mom with you?"
"Nope, I am okay though."
"Sarah, you shouldn't be doing this alone."
"Remember how I told you that James feels things?"
"Sarah?"
"The scan is for cancer, but James knows it's not that, so I am really fine."
"What hospital are you going to?"
"United Hospital in St. Paul. That is where they do the scans, but Matt, I am fine. I will pick you up at 5 p.m. if that is okay. I have to stop home to get changed."
"Yeah. Call me when you're done though. Promise me."
"Okay, bye."

I went in and waited a short while, almost a half hour past my appointment time. Even though I knew it wasn't cancer, I was getting impatient. I finally got called into the back where I changed and then had to lay on a moveable bed. I was getting frustrated waiting to find out nothing. They weren't going to find anything. I should really walk out. This wasn't going to do any good.

The nurse walked up to me, "It's just going to be a little longer, but someone is here to entertain you while you wait."

"James?"

Matt came around the corner looking at me.

I sighed with relief, "Matt, I told you I am fine."

"I know but…if he can't be here, and you said I was your best friend next to him, I felt it was my duty."

I started to tear up. I couldn't believe he was here. I couldn't help myself and I stared at him. He pulled up a chair and handed me a couple magazines. I laughed a little.

"See, you do feel better."

I was embarrassed, "Yeah."

"May I?" as he reached for my hand. I took a hold of his and tightened my grip. We started to look at a magazine together. I disapproved of his selection, "Sports Illustrated, Swim Suit edition?"

"Well, you may want to see what would look good on you."

"None of them, I don't have boobs like that."

He laughed. He kept me entertained pretty good, not thinking about how long this was taking. They finally took me back. He walked with me as far as they let him. The tech did a series of scans. When we were done, she pulled me aside to have me get changed. She could see the anxiety in my face. "If it helps, I'm not supposed to say anything, but I saw no cancer cells anywhere. The doctor will have to look at it, so you can't hold me to that."

I smiled at her, but I already knew that. I went in and got changed. I came out and Matt was waiting for me.

"Are you ready to go?"

"Yep."

We started to walk out and he took my hand. It made me feel better.

"So, what did they say?"

"She's not authorized to say, but she said she didn't see any cancer cells."

He moved to put his arm around me, "That's good then, right?"

I took his arm from around me and put his hand back in mine. "Yeah, I guess."

"You're supposed to be happy about this."

"I told you, James knew it wasn't cancer."

"Okay, but if he feels things... why can't he tell you what it is?"

"He has never felt what this is before. See, he has to have felt it before, then someone would have had to tell him what it was, and then he could tell me what it is."

"You lost me."

"Like cancer, he felt what cancer feels like in someone else, so he knew what that felt like. He has never felt whatever it is in me to be able to tell me what is wrong with me."

"This is just too farfetched for me. It's mind boggling."

"You're telling me."

"Where did you park?"

"In the green lot. Where are you?"

"I got dropped off, so I'm driving you home."

"I have to go to work."

"You can take the day off, Sarah."

"No, I have a car to pay for, and I have Wednesday through Friday off. I am going up north."

"So, you can't come with me for the 4th and you're not playing volleyball on Thursday with me?"

"Oh, Matt, I am sorry. I forgot about Thursday, but I really need to get away and not think about all this crappie stuff."

"James, isn't up there?"

"No, but I go see his Dad. I actually have a dance class that I put on at one of the bars and, oh shit."

"What?"

"I forgot to call Tony. Do you mind?" I held up my phone gesturing a phone call.

"Nope."

I called Tony and it was great to hear his voice. "Sarah, I am so glad to hear from you. How have you been?"

"Okay, but Tony I am coming up on Wednesday. Could we set up the class for both Friday and Saturday? I need to dance."

"Anything you want, Sarah. Have you talked to James?"

"Yeah, he came home to see me last Wednesday. He's working hard."

"Did you two behave?"

"Tony, I can't tell you that."

"Sarah, he made me promise to not let him take advantage of you. He loves you."

"He didn't take advantage of me."

I could see Matt look at me out of the corner of his eyes, smiling. He knew what I was talking about.

"So, you are good for Friday and Saturday?"

"Well, not actually, but I will do my homework before I come up. I will try to have 5 dances to teach. I will be ready."

"Okay, I'll see you about 4 p.m. on Friday."

"Yes, thanks Tony."

"Bye Sarah. And if you talk to James, tell him I said good boy."

I rolled my eyes, "Bye Tony.

I hung up the phone, and was content. I looked at Matt, and he was smiling bigger than ever.

I was irritated, "What?"

"You two still *haven't done it.*"

"Matt, that's none of your business."

"But, I thought for sure with how you both acted at the airport that you had."

"There is more to a relationship than just doing it."

"So, you are having sex, you just haven't done it yet?"

"You're over stepping the friendship boundaries."

"If I was a girlfriend, you would talk to me about this, right?"

"I don't know. I've never had a friend that close to talk to about that kind of stuff."

"We'll, that's what friends do. They help each other evaluate the situation and make decisions."

"I don't think it's something I am comfortable talking about it, with anyone."

"Okay, we'll start simple. Are you on birth control?"

I looked at him funny, "No, but I am starting after my next period."

"So you want to be with him?"

I couldn't answer him; it was too weird

"Sarah, obviously you love him. It's okay to want to be with him. Look at the girls I hang out with. Some of them I don't even like, but I still want to do it with them.

"Have you done it?"

He was uncomfortable. He didn't want to answer me.

"See it's not easy talking about it with me either. The last thing I remembered was you haven't yet."

"Fine, no."

"I'm sure you could have a few times, why haven't you?"

"I just haven't found anyone that would be worth sharing that with. But I do have sex, some are very eager to pleasure me."

"That's gross."

"It's the truth. Oral sex is really good for the male." He stopped and questioned me with his eyes like he was asking me if I did that with James.

"Sorry, not for me. I get grossed out."

"Oh, so, what do you two do?"

"Okay, we're getting close to your house, and I am really not going to talk about it anymore."

"Later than."

He pulled up to his house, "Are you okay to get yourself to work?"

"Yep, I'll be fine."

Work went uneventful and I headed home to change. I called Matt when I was on my way. We went to the park and played our two games without any questions. I was relieved he didn't bring up the subject again. We were walking to the car and I dangled my keys in front of his face. He tried to grab them, and I pulled them away, "You have to promise me no more questions."

He put down his hand, "The thrill is wearing away. That's okay you can drive."

Shit, that *wasn't* the reaction I was looking for.

We got in the car, but I wasn't looking forward to the drive. He did pretty well until we got close to his house.

"Sarah, if I'm your best friend next to James, why won't you let me help you."

"Help me do what?"

"Make decisions."

"About what?"

"If you are going to do it with him."

"But I am. It's just a matter of timing."

"So, you want to be with him that way?"

"Yes I do."

"Why?"

"Because he is good to me."

"How is he good to you?"

"Matt here's the truth. The only reason he wouldn't do it with me is because he is afraid he will hurt me. So, if it gets too hot or too close, he takes a shower. He is miserable over it, but he puts me first every time. He watches movies, plays card games, and just spends time with me because he says it's a privilege to be with me. I don't want him to be miserable anymore, and I love him more than life itself. There you have it all."

"Wow, he walks away from you?"

"Most of the time."

"But not every time?"

"We were very close a couple of times, but he could see I was scared and once it was close enough to hurt."

"So, he leaves?"

"That time we waited too long, and it was kind of messy. How close have you been?"

"Not that close, I get messy way before I get that far. Maybe it's the age thing?"

"Or the experience thing." *Oops that slipped out.*

"Experience?"

Great, now I would have to explain, "James has been with a few women before we were together."

"And you're okay with that?"

"If you knew the whole story you would understand, but I think the more you do it the more you can control it."

"So, there is hope for me yet?"

I chuckled with his comment, but I was still uncomfortable talking about this with Matt. I was glad I was with my James, because he had more control. It would be worse to be with someone who hadn't done it. I bet there would be no control.

We pulled up to his house, and he had a funny grin on his face, "Did you know that the more a guy does it the bigger he will get?"

"Okay, that's more information than I wanted to know."

"I'm just saying that it might be easier to be with someone that hasn't done it yet."

"But that's not the goal, Matt. I want to be with James, because I love him. I plan on marring him."

"You *can't* be serious?"

I grabbed my bag and pulled out my necklace. He grabbed it from me, "This is huge."

I laughed, "I know it's too big, but I already said yes. I will be with him forever."

"After seeing you two at the airport, I kind of believe that."

"Good."

He took my hand, "I am glad you let me be there for you today. If you ever need someone to go with you, please, please call me. We can be '*just friends*'."

"Thank you, Matt."

"Call me Sunday when you get back? So we can have more girl talk."

I giggled, "You got it."

Mom was waiting up for me. I walked in and she handed me a large envelope. I grabbed it and brought it to my chest. I knew what it was.

"What does he keep sending you?"

"Love notes, kind of like poems."

"Oh, well that's sweet."

"Yep, that's my James, sweet."

I got on the internet and was looking for more dance steps. I picked out 5 songs and practiced a few things in my room before lying down for the night. I knew my James would call tonight, just to make sure everything was okay. I stayed awake 'til he called. I had a lot of work to do before Friday. But if I knew the rest of the dances I could work on them for the next two days. When he called I was out of breath.

"James!"

"You are out of breath?"

"Yeah, I have been working on a few dances for Tony's on Friday."

"What are you talking about?"

"Oh, I have agreed to put on a dance class on the Saturdays that I am up north, at Tony's from 5-8 p.m. for the younger crowd. He makes a lot of money when everyone shows up, and I get to dance my heart out. There are two ladies that love what I do, so they show up and learn the dances early. Then they help me. It's really fun."

"So, you are dancing without me?"

"James, it makes me feel better about myself. Can't I please keep doing it?"

"Sarah, why are you asking me? You know you can do whatever you want. I just hate that I am not there to protect you from all the guys that show up to watch you."

"James, I don't even notice them. I only see you with my whole heart."

"How did today go?"

"You were right, but I was irritated about the wait."

"Matt was there with you?"

"How did you know that?"

"You were at ease, I could tell the difference. I wish it was me."

"I didn't ask him to come with me."

"I know. Sarah you are so irresistible that people are drawn to you naturally; you don't have to try. If my feelings are right, you pushed him away?"

"James, you are right. He's not you."

"Was he trying something?"

"No, it was more like a half hug, but you are the only one I want that close to me. I feel really yucky when anyone is that close to me and it's not you."

"So, other guys make you sick?"

"Yes, you could put it that way."

"Oh, I do love you my little girl."

"You know, you are going to have to quit calling me your little girl."

"Why would I do that? You're a girl, you're mine, and you're little."

"I thought you were referencing my age."

"Nope, you're my little girl. My sweet, Sarah, with skin so soft. I want to kiss every part of you. I would give up tomorrow just to take in your scent, to taste your lips. I can't wait to have you in my bed every night, just to hear you breath, to watch your chest as your heart beats."

"James."

"I need to feel your touch, so tender, so soft. To kiss your fingers tip by tip, for it is what you touch me with. To run my fingers through your hair, so I can feel the silk of it falling through my fingers."

"James. What is up with you?"

"I don't want to lose you, not to another guy, but to something I have no control over. You don't like to hear why I desire you?"

"I love hearing you talk about me that way, but why do you think you are going to lose me; you know how I feel about you. I also make sure everyone knows how I feel about you."

"I know, but can I come home now? I really need to be in your presence. You make me feel so good all the time. It's not about the sex. It's about you being you."

"James, we are at four weeks, it's just a little over two more weeks. You can make it, and the reunion will be so sweet; I promise you that, better than any movie could be."

I thought of us being together, and the pleasure that filled my head was so sweet to remember.

"Oh Sarah, it's so much more than that. I feel that when I get to put my arm around you. Please, don't make it about the sex. I love you so much more than that. It's more like this."

I felt him move through me; like he did the other night when he shared his soul with me.

"Oh, James."

"Yes, Sarah, that is what it is like for me to be around you all the time."

"I am sorry, James."

"For what?"

"If that is how you feel when you are around me, I just don't understand how you can even walk. My knees are jelly."

He laughed quietly, "So, now you know how I feel; how do you feel?"

"I am great now."

"How did the scan go?"

"You, of course, were right."

"No cancer, I told you."

"Yeah, that word scared me."

"I know my sweet, Sarah. We will find out what it is when I come home. I promise. I will search every hospital 'til I find something that feels like that."

"Okay, that will be faster than going to the doctors every week."

"If you can wait until I get home?"

"James, I haven't been sick for six whole days."

"And you're still eating?"

"Yes, since I saw you I feel wonderful all the time."

"Sarah, I..., we..., I can't wait to see you."

"James, you are not telling me something and I am not like you. I can't read your feelings. You have to talk to me."

"I need to be with you to share this with you. It's something you want, so I don't think you will be unhappy, but I need to see you face to face. Okay?"

"Okay, I love you."

"Sarah, you need to sleep, I will stay 'til you do."

"No, James, you keep me from sleep, because I don't want to let you go."

"Okay, we will say goodnight then."

"Not yet, James. I mean... okay. I love you so much, James."

"Sarah, I am so in love with you. I will come home if you will let me. Don't think I could ever regret not finishing. You are more important than anything. I can figure it out a different way."

"No, I love you James. Goodnight."

"Okay baby, Goodnight."

21. The Guard Dog

Day 30: Only 19 days 'til he was home full time. Depending on where he was staying would make the decision of how much time I would get to see him. I got up and went for my daily note. I was in a great mood.

From the deepest ocean
Which is my heart,
To the endless sky
Which is my soul,
My love for you will never die.
You touch every part of me and I will survive.
I love you more than you know,

James

I worked on the dances all morning 'til mom was ready to go. My bag was larger than normal because it would be four nights and five days to dress for. I was ready whenever mom was. By noon we had everything in the car.

Our drive was nice. I talked about volleyball and our wins. I talked about getting school set up. I avoided telling her about doing research for James. I knew how she felt, and 16 years old is too young to make any decisions for lifelong partners. Deep down I knew I loved my James, and I knew I *was going to marry him some day.*

We got up there by 2:30 p.m. We went straight to the trailer, and dad was there. We unpacked and I realized I was very nervous about Friday and Saturday.

"So, what's the plan you two? Do I need to get lost for awhile?" I understood their need to be alone more than ever.

They both glared at me with funny faces and dad replied, "Where do you want to go?"

"Tony's, I have two dance sessions this weekend, and I want to practice there if I can."

"Well, let's see, how long do you think?"

"I will take any time you will give me. I will meet you at Sherburn's when you tell me. I want to see Danelle anyway."

"Meet us up there by 7 p.m. and we'll have dinner."

"Is four hours going to be enough time for the two of you?"

"Sarah!"

"Well, last time you abandoned me and left Jason to watch over me, which I wasn't too happy about."

"Go! Get out of here before we change our minds."

I smiled and put on something a little more grown up, just in case Tony had customers. I had bought a couple special tops for Friday and Saturday, but today I was just going to wear a cute short tank top. I ran out the door before they could say anything about what I was wearing, and I hopped in my car. As I drove past Sherburn's, Brian was outside and he saw me, so I had to stop. I rolled down my window because I didn't want to get out.

"Where are you going?"

"Tony's, I need to practice. I will be there both Friday and Saturday this week, so I need to be ready."

"Do you want me to come with you?"

"Nope, I really don't want an audience."

"When will you be back?"

"At 7 p.m., so get your tennis shoes on because I am going to whip you this time."

"We've got a volleyball net. I heard you have been playing."

"I can whip you in that too."

"Hurry back, you are in for it."

"Good, tell Danelle for me."

"Yep."

I pulled into the back of Tony's and walked into the kitchen. There was somebody in the fridge.

"Tony?"

"Um, you're not supposed to be in here; customers use the other door."

The fridge closed, and there was a gorgeous man, or boy turning to face me. I wondered to myself, how old is this guy? I couldn't tell, but he was standing there looking at me.

"I'm not a customer, where is Tony?"

"Well, if you used the right door you would have found him."

I started walking to the bar, but he moved in front of me, "You will have to go around; you can't walk in here like that."

"Just go get Tony, and he will tell you." I was disgusted with his actions. No one up here has ever been so rude to me. Tony walked into the kitchen, but didn't notice I was there.

I needed to get his attention, "Tony?"

He set everything down, "Oh, sweet little Sarah." He moved to me to give me a great big hug, lifting me off the ground and turned me around in a circle. As he did this I glared at this perfectly rude guy.

I complained to Tony, "I almost got ran off by your guard dog."

"Sarah! Be nice. He protects my assets and he is helping me while James is gone. I will also have Jason this Friday and Saturday."

"How many people are we talking about? You're making me nervous."

"I don't know, but I have been advertising since Monday."

"Tony, now I am scared."

I heard the voice from behind me, "The famous Sarah is scared?"

I looked up at Tony, "He knows who I am, and he tried to keep me out?"

"Only 'cuz I hugged you like my own."

"I brought the music for a couple new dances; can I practice for awhile? It's still really early."

"You know how to work the equipment. Oh, by the way this is Jake. Formally, Jake, this is James's Sarah."

I gave him a mocking smile, "Nice to meet you." I turned back to Tony, "Can I use James room for a minute?"

"Um, it's not James's room anymore, but I am working on making a small apartment over the kitchen here. Do you want to see it? It will give you… I mean James, more privacy."

I smiled but looked at Jake, now grinning smugly, "Yes please."

We walked up the stairs on the outside of the building. He opened the door for me. Tony was explaining as I walked in, "Clarissa insisted that if you were going to be spending time here with him it had to be nice. She has been helping me." It was like a one room studio apartment or maybe like a hotel room. It was very small, but I did notice the bed was very close to the bathroom. I turned to look at Tony. He was embarrassed, "You know that's how he controls himself."

I shook my head in disbelief and I noticed a small kitchenette with a fridge, microwave, and a very small oven. It also had a tiny little table for two with a single candle on it. I grinned; that had Clarissa's influence all over it. The bed was, of course, very large and was filled with tons of pillows.

I turned to Tony, "That doesn't look like he will have much control in that."

He chuckled as he said, "That was all Clarissa." He was handing me a key, "Here… any time you need to get away, Sarah. You know what is his, is also yours."

"Not yet."

"Yeah, I think we both know better than that."

"I have to practice, but what's with the *guard dog* down stairs?"

We were heading back down the stairs. "Sarah, I had to have a good looking kid working here to keep up the business. James will always have a home here, but I had to keep my business going. He protects my business and the ladies like to look at him."

"His personality needs work. He needs to lighten up and flirt with the girls, or he's not going to make much money."

"Not that he needs the money, but you should tell him that. Maybe you can rub off on him too."

"I just might tell him to not be rude."

We were walking into the kitchen and we finally got to it. Tony had to bring it up. "Sarah, how are you feeling?"

I noticed that Jake guy standing there and I really didn't want anyone else feeling sorry for me. "Tony, I am not really sure."

"You look good."

"Not really, but I have made it 7 days without being sick."

"So, I can feed you? You know James would be angry with me if I didn't at least try."

"Of course you can."

I noticed that Jake guy was paying attention to me and Tony.

"Tony, I am going to go practice, okay?"

"Anything you want." He waved me out.

I had five songs ready for the weekend: two country songs, two hip hop songs, and one easy listening song.

I started the CD and went through the dances one by one. Then I started them over.

I heard Tony yell from the bar, "Are you sure people are going to like this type of music?"

"Tony, do you trust me?"

"Yeah, but you're scaring me."

"I wanted a variety. So, we would get a large group, but I think you took care of that for me."

"Yes, I did."

I could see Tony and Jake talking but I was wondering what about. I hated having an audience. I continued to work through the five songs, five times each.

"Sarah, food is ready."

I shut the music off and walked to the bar. I sat at the end. Tony handed me the ketchup.

I heard Jake, "You really shouldn't give her free food."

"Jake, she will make me more money than you can imagine... settle down."

I didn't say anything, but I took a bite of my burger as I laughed to myself. Tony put us in the right order and I liked it. He came to sit with me while I ate, and he asked about James. How he was doing and what the plan was when he came back. I wasn't able to fill him in because we hadn't figured anything out yet. The only thing we knew fore sure was that we didn't want to be apart ever again.

Tony moved to the kitchen to take care of some things, and Jake was on a mission to irritate me. I tried to ignore him, but it wasn't going to work.

"Well, Sarah the great, what wise wisdom do you have for me?"

"What?"

"I swear everyone up here knows who you are and how great you can be. So, do something great."

"I don't know what you are talking about, and I am not great. In fact I am very average, so nothing great from me."

I resumed eating, avoiding his look, but it persisted, and he was making me really uncomfortable, "What is your problem with me? Did I do something that has pissed you off? You don't even know me."

"I know your type. The girls think you're great, honest, and not up here to steal their guys away. The guys all want a piece of you, and the adults think you are just the sweetest thing on this earth. So, my idea is you are hiding something."

"Nope. I am an open book, and I am not as great as everyone says I am, so you can get over this crap of being nasty to me."

"I just don't trust you."

"You don't have to, but you can quit staring at me because it makes me nervous."

"The great Sarah is nervous?"

Tony walked back out. I was in panic mode turning to him. My stomach was beginning to turn. He put both hands on my arms looking into my eyes, "Sarah, honey no. No, you don't, do not do that. James will get mad at me."

I took a deep breath trying to keep it down. He questioned Jake, "What happen? What changed?"

He looked at us puzzled as I shook my head, "Tony, I am so sorry, but I can't eat anymore. I have to go. Can I practice tomorrow after I see Carl?"

"Anytime and you have a key now. Are you sure you're okay, Sarah?"

I nodded and got up hugging him so tight. Anyone or anything that had to do with James was comforting to me.

"You know, if you need to run away, you have a key now."

I smiled softly, but I was kind of feeling a little weak. I started to walk out but remembered Jake, "Oh, I guess it was nice to meet you."

When I left I really didn't feel like it was nice to meet him, and I don't know why I even said it. I felt like I was in high school, and I wasn't fitting in. I had come such a long way, and in one meeting he took it away for me. Yuk.

I went to Sherburn's early. Brian and Danelle were waiting. Tommy was there too, "Are you guys ready to play ball?"

Danelle ran up to me and gave me the biggest hug, "Have you lost any more weight."

"Nope, haven't been sick in almost 7 days. I just have to get through the night."

"That is so good, Sarah. What did you do?"

"Nothing."

She grabbed my hand dragging me out the door. She yelled back at Brian, "Stay here, we need to talk first."

I gave him that blank expression as she led me out. I followed her all the way to the dock before she turned to me, "Did you run to Denver to see him?"

'Nope, didn't have to."

"So, why are you better?"

"I don't know why I'm better, but he came to see me. He planned the whole day to be with me."

"Did you do it?"

"Nope, but it was very hot."

"How hot?"

"Hot enough to be an almost, but the shower came into play again."

"Why does he do that?"

"To get cooled off. Now that you know I didn't do anything stupid, can we play ball?"

"Did you go to the doctors?"

"Yep and they still don't know what it is, but I definitely do not have cancer."

"Well, that's good. I didn't realize they thought it was that."

"It was just a make sure test. Can we play now?"

"For now, yes."

We had a long night ahead of us, so I hoped they were ready. I had more energy than I ever did before.

Tommy and I were partners again, and Brian seemed to be pouting. As we played Brian would make comments to me, "We didn't finish our talk." I ignored him, but he was distracted, so I got past him easily. Danelle was getting frustrated. "So, when can we talk?" I was still avoiding him. I wasn't in the mood for any serious talks, especially since they involved me, "You will talk to me this weekend." I went past him again.

Danelle yelled at him, "Brian, get your head out of your pants."

I turned to her, "That's disgusting, Danelle."

She complained, "But he is letting you get by."

Tommy had the ball and I moved around Brian for the pass, "You can't keep avoiding me." I grabbed the ball and went for the shot. He grabbed me around the waist and stopped me completely. "Brian, that's a foul, you can't do that."

I was trying to breathe because he knocked the wind out of me.

"Shit, Sarah, I am sorry. Just say you will talk to me this weekend, and I will drop the subject for now."

"Fine, but you better get your game on 'cuz you are in trouble now."

If he wanted to play dirty, I was going to make sure to do it good. Every time he had the ball I grabbed his arms, so he couldn't make the shot. He got it now, and he was being more competitive. Danelle and Brian won. I was worn out and had to sit down, "That was better."

"Yeah, you like to play rough."

"No, you started it."

Tommy and Danelle walked away down toward the dock. I watched as they walked away.

"So, you feel better?"

"Yeah, a lot better. I haven't gotten sick in almost 7 days, so it would be really good if you didn't upset me, okay?"

"But we need to talk about this."

"Brian, I didn't lose any more weight in the last week, and I would like to keep it that way."

"Fine. Does that mean we can't talk about what you said the last time you were up here?"

"Yeah, I think I am. So, when did that happen?" I gestured to Danelle and Tommy.

"He doesn't touch her; I warned him."

"But it's cute."

"No, it's not. She is only 15 and he is 17 and he is having urges."

"Yuk, Brian!"

"Are you saying you don't have urges?"

I thought about that and boy did I, but it was with my James. I acted innocent, "I am too young for that."

"Yeah right, do you really think he will wait for you to be ready?"

"Yep, I know he will and we're getting to the dangerous line of me getting upset, Brian."

"But you said we would have done it if I showed you attention before you found James."

I was going to really give it to him now. "You didn't even notice me. You can be a jerk and if you knew I would have been an easy target you would have without having any feelings for me. Then you would have dogged me. There, are you happy we talked about it? Can we play volleyball now?"

"Yeah, I guess so." He looked like someone kicked him in the chest.

He was following me down to the beach. I called for Danelle to see if they wanted to play. They both got up and walked back to us. They didn't seem happy about my wanting to stay busy. We didn't play very well. We mostly tried to keep it going over the net. I helped Danelle, by showing her how to set. When everyone else got tired of playing, I headed up to meet mom and dad for dinner. I walked into the bar looking for them, but they weren't there yet. Laura gestured for me to come to her, "You look better."

I hugged her, "I haven't lost any weight in the last week. I do feel better."

She was pleased with this, "That is good Sarah. Are you eating?"

"Yeah, mom and dad were supposed to meet me here for dinner. Have you seen them yet?"

"Nope, not yet. What do you want to eat?"

"I don't know. I had half a burger about three hours ago, so I'm not terribly hungry."

"How about chicken drummies and some potato wedges; we got them in new and they are great."

"That sounds good to me."

"Where are Brian and Danelle?"

"I think they are still on the beach; I wore them out."

"You do look better."

I sat down at the bar to wait. Jason came and sat down by me, "What are you doing here?"

Like he doesn't know the answer to that one, "Where else would I be?"

He let that go, "Where are your mom and dad? I was supposed to have dinner with them."

"So was I, but I just ordered with Laura."

"Can I eat with you?"

"Yeah, then I would have some company."

"What did you order?"

"Chicken drummies and potato wedges."

Laura walked out and Jason asked if he could have the same order. She wasn't please but went to put the food on.

He glanced at me quickly, "So, you look better?"

"I feel better." I truly did feel tons better.

"Does James have anything to do with that?"

"Yeah, but that's none of your business and I am not talking about it." I gave him a warning smile.

"So, I will be working at Tony's Friday and Saturday when you're there."

"Yep. So, what is up with the new guy?"

"Sarah, you weren't attracted to him?"

"No, he's a total jerk."

"Why do you say that?"

"He was really mean to me, and how many people up here are mean to me? He doesn't even know me."

"Sarah, we all warned him that he will fall in love with you and you belong to James, so he was probably on the defense to not like you."

"Well, that's okay then."

"You don't want him to like you?"

"No. I don't want anyone to like me. I was happy in my very educated boring life, but then you had to look at me all sweet and nice. You had to bring me out of my shell, and now look at me; I'm hopelessly in love."

"With James, I know."

"It's your fault, really."

"I know, but I am not happy about it."

"You didn't talk about me to Jake the way you talked about me to James, did you?"

The guilty look on his face told me the answer I didn't want.

"Kind of."

"Did you like making more competition? Isn't James enough?"

"I do miss you."

"Jason, you really don't know me. It was just the attraction of someone looking at you, that's all. I wasn't even good looking. I am a dork."

"Um, that's not true. You are totally gorgeous and get better looking every day, even though you're a little thin."

"I didn't lose any weight last week. Please, don't say I'm too skinny. It's not my fault."

"No, Sarah, you look hot."

"I didn't want to hear that either."

"I just cannot please you today."

"Not when we have to talk about me. So, how is it going with Kylie?"

"Right now, she's after Jake."

"Oh, but isn't he a lot younger than her?"

He looked at me unjustly. "In her words, 'If I can do it, so can she.'"

"I am so sorry."

"You could get him to forget about her, just flirt with him a little."

"Sorry Jason, I can't do that."

"Can you just charm him a little?"

"Are you telling me you still love Kylie?"

"I have told you before, we don't know how to be apart; it has been too long."

I grinned, "I will not flirt with him, but I will try to help if I can, without doing that."

Laura brought out our food, and mom and dad walked in. I grabbed my food and nudged Jason with my elbow to move to the table to sit with them. He grabbed his food too.

I sat down looking at the two of them, "I told you that wasn't enough time for you two."

They both were guilty. I wanted to tease them more. "They are setting an example for me, so I will behave when James comes home." I gave him a grin

"Sarah, you are only 16 years old."

I gave them an innocent look but Jason laughed.

"We didn't wait, but I want to get back outside to see if anyone will play volleyball with me again."

Mom scolded me, "Haven't you had enough volleyball?"

"Nope."

"Did Sarah tell you, that she and her partner, Matt, took second in a beach volleyball tournament last Saturday?"

"No, she didn't. With Matt, I see."

I looked at him evidently, "James already knows, so get that out of your head. He is okay with us being friends." I leaned into him, "I will tell you the rest of that later."

He chuckled, "I knew there was more to it than that."

22. So Tired

I went in the back to find Danelle, Brian, and Tommy. They were all vegetating on the couch. I think Brian would have come to find me, but he didn't want to leave them alone.

"So, what are we doing now? I ate and I have energy again."

Brian looked at me but was sad. I didn't understand his sadness. He finally replied, "I have fireworks, so we could go down to the dock and light them off once it gets dark."

"That shouldn't be too long of a wait." I squeezed in between Brian and Tommy.

Brian turned to whisper in my ear, "You shouldn't sit so close to me, and I am really turned on by you."

I got up instantly and moved to the bed which was behind the couch, "What about you two? Will you go down for fireworks?"

Danelle turned to me and nodded her head, "Yeah, we'll go with." I grinned even more. I fell back on the bed with satisfaction that I was going to stay busy, but I was already getting tired. I closed my eyes, but it was suppose to be for just a second.

"Sarah? Are you coming?"

I opened my eyes, "Yeah, I guess I am a little tired."

Brian put his hand out to help me up, but pretended like I pulled him. He fell down next to me.

"Brian I can't do this." I sat up and moved away from him. "Where are Danelle and Tommy?"

"They are waiting for us on the dock."

"You're letting them sit there by themselves?"

"You were sleeping. I said I would wake you. Sarah, why do you have to be in love with him?"

"I just am." I stood up and lost my balance a little.

He caught me, "You're actually doing better?"

"Yeah, I thought so." I sat back down and shook my head, "I guess I was really tired. I might have to go to the trailer after the fireworks."

"Here, lay back down."

I wasn't in the trusting mood anymore.

"I won't try anything, Sarah."

He got up and left the room as I lay back down and closed my eyes. I didn't feel sick. Maybe I just got up too quickly. I felt a cold rag on my forehead, and Brian was sitting down next to me.

"Do you think you're trying too hard to be normal?"

"Maybe. I do have good news though."

"What's that?"

"I don't have cancer. I had the test on Tuesday."

He was patting my head with the rag and leaning over me more. I still had my eyes closed, but I put up my hand to hold him at a distance.

He took my hand lowering it, "Sarah, it's okay."

He turned the rag over and patted more.

"I think I am okay now." I grabbed his hand to move it from my forehead as I tried to sit up. I didn't get very far because he was in my way. I opened my eyes and we were face to face, "Brian, you can let me up now."

He moved to trace his lips on mine. I couldn't do this. I loved my James. My heart was racing for fear that this would hurt him.

"Brian, stop!"

"This doesn't feel good, Sarah?"

"It feels nice, but I love James and this is not going to happen." I tried to push him away.

He wrapped his arms around me pulling my head closer to his, "Just one, Sarah, please."

He kissed me so deep, but I couldn't respond. I didn't want this. I was still pushing him.

He released me, "You feel *nothing*?"

"Brian, if I didn't love James so much, that would have been amazing, but I do love James."

He moved away from me and stood there. He took my hand in his and kissed the back of it, but looked defeated, "I will behave. You will not have to deal with that again. I am sorry."

I lifted his chin, so I could see his eyes. "That was perfect, but not for me. I am sorry, Brian. Can we go light some fireworks now?"

He took my hand and led me out and to the dock. I noticed Tommy looking at Brian, but he shook his head. Tommy felt sorry for Brian. I was beginning to feel really bad, but he shouldn't have done that anyway. He knows I love James. I felt the anger growing as I justified why he did this to himself. He shouldn't have kissed me. This was going to be a very long weekend. I sat down on the beach while Tommy and Brian got ready to do the fireworks. I smiled at Danelle. She looked at me with guilty eyes.

I had a feeling, "You knew?"

"Yeah, but it was the only way Tommy and I could be together, alone."

"That was wrong. Did you at least kiss him?"

"No. We just hold hands and talk. But when Brian is around Tommy has a hard time with that, and Brian is around a lot. Did Brian try to kiss you?"

"Yes, but I couldn't respond. You know how I feel about James. I couldn't no matter how nice it was."

"So, you liked it?"

"He would be a good kisser if I wanted him to kiss me, but, no, I didn't like it."

She was sorry. I put my arm around her shoulder. "I really understand wanting to spend time with him. I feel that way all the time about my James."

We watched as they lit the fireworks until they were all gone. I got up, "I think I have to go back to the trailer. I really need some sleep."

Brian came running over, "I said I would behave."

"Brian, it's not that. I just feel really tired, especially since I fell asleep in the bed. I just don't feel right."

"We should drive you?"

"No, I will be fine. Be ready for skiing tomorrow, and I'll get the boat again."

He walked me to my car. Danelle and Tommy were being allowed to be alone again.

"Sarah, are you sure you're okay?"

"Yep, I just need some rest."

"Is this part of the sickness, or are you upset with me?"

"I am not upset with you; just don't do *that* again. As far as the sickness, I have no idea, but I need to go."

I got in and he closed my door. I didn't feel sick at all, but I could hardly keep my eyes open on my way to the trailer. I pulled in and it was completely dark. I took a deep breath and got out of my car, almost falling back into it. I pushed myself up and walked to the trailer, but I had to rest on the steps. Okay, maybe somebody should have helped me get to the trailer. I sat there taking deep breaths. I still didn't feel sick, just really weak. Jason's truck pulled in. I didn't want him to help me, or even see me this week. I tried to stand up, but it didn't work. He was out of his truck slamming it into park before he stopped. He came running, "Sarah, I think I should take you to the hospital."

"What? I'm fine. I am just a little tired."

"You can't even get up."

"Yeah, I can. I just don't want to."

"Why are you being stubborn?"

"How did you know to come here?"

"Brian came in and pulled me out to my truck. He said there was something wrong with you."

"Oh, I am really tired, maybe a little weak." I extended my hand for him to pull me up. He took me by the elbow and pulled me up.

"See, I can stand. I am fine. I just need to lay down for a little bit."

"Has this happen before?"

"Nope, it's a new symptom."

"Does your doctor know?"

"Not this one. Haven't felt like this before."

"Give me your phone."

"Why?"

"I am calling James. Maybe he can talk some sense into you."

"I'm not giving you my phone to call him."

He walked me in and helped me to the couch. I lay down and closed my eyes. I needed to sleep now.

I was almost asleep when I heard Jason talking to someone. Maybe mom and dad were back.

"I don't know because I wasn't with her."

"I tried, but she won't go."

"Brian and Danelle were with her. He said they played basketball, and she got really tired after that."

"I don't know that either."

"He said they went to play volleyball after that."

"Yeah, that's when I saw her."

"Yes, she ate. We all watched her."

"No, she didn't."

"She went in the back and Brian said she almost passed out."

"He gave her a cold rag for her head and it helped, but then she went down to watch fireworks."

"He said she decided she had to leave, and she wouldn't take anyone's help."

"No, he came and got me."

"James, I'm calling you. What do you want me to do?"

"You have to talk to her then, because she doesn't listen to anyone except you."

"Sarah, you have to wake up." I opened my eyes and looked at him, "Jason, leave me alone. I need to sleep."

"No, Sarah, you have to wake up. Someone wants to talk to you."

"Jason, go home. I am fine and I need to sleep now." I rolled over. I knew it was my James, and he was going to scold me.

"James, I am going to put the phone by her ear since she won't get up."

"Sarah, honey, I need to talk to you."

"Oh, my sweet, James. I need to sleep. Call me tomorrow."

"Sarah!"

"What, James?"

"I need you to sit up, or I am coming home now."

"Okay, okay, I am up."

"No, you're not, get up now. If you sit up I will take that."

"Okay, I am."

"NO YOU ARE NOT, SARAH!" He was sounding so upset.

I pushed myself up. "James, what is wrong?"

"You!"

I glared at Jason, but he only shrugged his shoulders.

"James, I'm tired. That's it. I think I did too much today."

"Sarah, you are still sick even though they said you don't have cancer."

"I know, but I have felt so good since I saw you."

Jason's expression became inquiring. I knew I was going to have to answer questions now. I held up my hand to keep him from doing it now.

"But, Sarah, you're pushing yourself too hard."

"I have made it seven days without getting sick, James, and I am still eating like a pig. I even ate at Tony's."

"You went to Tony's?"

"Yes, I had to practice for Friday and Saturday."

"How much did you do?"

"I tried to get through each dance a few times. I think maybe five times each."

"And how many dances, Sarah?"

"Five, I have to be ready."

"Sarah! You played basketball, volleyball, and then you practiced that much?"

"James, I really need to sleep now. I can't keep my eyes open."

"You must be tired. You're at the trailer and it's before 11 p.m., but I am so worried about you. If Jason called me others are worried too."

"James, I didn't pass out. You know that because you feel me. Channel it and you will see I am not in any pain. I don't feel sick, and that I am just tired. Please, can I lay down now?"

"Yes, my sweet, Sarah, you sleep, but do me a favor and take it easy tomorrow."

"Yes, James, I promise. Will you call me tomorrow?"

"I'll try. Let me talk to Jason."

I handed Jason my phone and rolled over on the couch to sleep. I could still hear Jason's side of the conversation even though I didn't want to. I only wanted to sleep.

"I told you, she will only listen to you."

"Yeah, I will stay."

"Somebody did what?"

"Did she kiss him back?"

Oh shit, James knows already. I should have told him, but I am so tired. I can't explain it to him. He will come home for sure. *I am so sorry my sweet Cayuse, but I can't deal with this today. Let me explain it tomorrow.*

"Then you have nothing to worry about."

"You know that's hard for me."

"I will try, but she really loves you. I see it in her eyes."

"James, honestly she doesn't even like it when people help her. Like tonight when I had to help her inside. I had to lift her by her arm and if she could have flatly refused she would have."

"No way, he wouldn't be that stupid, would he?"

I rolled back over and held my hand out for the phone. I was trying to sit up.

"Um, I think she wants to talk to you."

"Yeah, she's awake and she is looking at me."

I stood up and walked towards him with my hand out.

"Yep."

I took the phone out of his hand and walked out the door. "James."

"Sarah, you are supposed to be sleeping."

"Well, obviously I need to talk more, and you are more important than how I feel."

"Sarah, don't do this. It's okay and I know you are really tired."

"No, it's not. So, here it goes… so listen up because I am not going to make it very long." I took a deep breath and started to walk down the road. I didn't want Jason to listen to me talk with my James.

"Yes, Brian kissed me. No, I didn't want him too. Yes, I did try to stop him. Yes, it was when I almost passed out. No, I didn't pass out. Yes, I am really weak. Yes, I am really tired. No, I'm not playing games with you. I do love you with my heart, my soul, and everything. If you still want to come home, great, I would love that. Then we can figure out how we can be together every day because I was trying not to be selfish, but my heart gets more and more hurt every day that you are gone."

"Sarah?"

"There is more, so just listen. I am so tired of being strong and taking care of myself. I am only trying to keep myself busy, so I don't have a nervous breakdown without you here. I like when you're here to take care of me."

"Sarah."

"James, the only lips I ever want to feel ever again is yours. So if you want to argue anymore it will have to wait until tomorrow because I am so tired and I need to lie down right now."

I found a large rock and sat down on it. I wasn't going to make it much longer. I needed to go back in, but how far did I walk? *Shit, where am I?*

"You are absolutely adorable."

I was scared and so tired I didn't know what to do, "James…?"

"Sarah, what's wrong?"

"I was walking while I was talking to you, and now I am so tired."

"Where are you?"

"Don't know, I don't think I can walk back. James, I am so tired."

"Sarah, you are kidding me?"

"James, I need to lay down now. " I moved to sit on the ground and rested my head on the rock. I need to close my eyes for 10 minutes. Can you stay on the phone with me 'til I fall asleep???"

"Sarah, get up. Get up now!"

"Just a couple of minutes, I can't go anymore."

I closed my eyes. I could hardly hold the phone.

"Sarah, don't you dare do this to me. Get up now, Sarah. I need you to stay awake a little longer, baby. I know you can do this. I won't be mad… about the kiss if you get up right now."

I could hear him, but I was so tired. I tried to get up, but I only made it up enough to sit on the rock.

Sarah, you can't do this when I'm not there to help you. Please, get up now."

"James, I am so tired."

"I know but you have to keep moving. Start walking, don't sit down."

"Too late, I can't stand up yet. I just need to close my eyes."

"Sarah, I gave you my soul. If something happens to you, it will happen to me too."

"What do you mean?"

"If you die… so will I."

"I'm not dying, I just need to sleep."

"You're outside on the side of the road, something could happen to you. Please, get up and start walking."

"Okay, James." I leaned my head against a tree and closed my eyes."

"Sarah?"

"Sarah."

"Sarah! You are killing me here."

"Sorry, I only need a couple of minutes."

"Not yet, get up and start walking."

I couldn't move, but I could see headlights. They were pulling over. James was still on the phone with me, so I would be safe. I closed my eyes, "James, what did you ask Jason to do?"

"I didn't want to, but I asked him to watch over you. I don't want anyone else to kiss those soft lips. Sarah, please get up, I need you to keep going."

I looked up and saw Jason. I was relieved and closed my eyes. I was done. He took the phone from me and I heard him talk to James. "James, I am here with her. Hold on because I need to get her to the truck."

I felt him lift me. I was glad that I didn't have to try and walk. He sat me in the truck and I fell to the seat. He got in and lifted my head to his leg. I heard him tell James I was safe now. I was happy he let him know I was okay now, "Tell him I love him."

I heard Jason tell James what I had said. I don't know if they kept talking because I was happy to be able to sleep now.

I woke up suddenly. I was on the bed in the 1st bedroom of the trailer. I didn't remember how I got here, but I knew being here I didn't have to be up at any special time. I could hear talking from the other room, but I didn't want to face the world without James yet. I rolled over and closed my eyes. I heard a truck start and pull away. I went back to sleep.

23. Staying Busy

I woke again feeling so much better, but I was also starving. I got dressed for going swimming but put shorts and a tank top over it. I got out my Day 31:

This is not a poem, this is my love so deep so divine.
You mean everything to me and I need you to survive.
My heart hurts with the pain of loss
Though, I still have you here in my mind.
I can only dream of the time we have to bind,
Sarah, I love you, more than you know.

James

He knew what I needed to hear yet again. How does he know these things? I wanted to go see Carl today. I felt so much better when I could see him, and I wanted to thank Clarissa for all the nice things she has done for me. I went out to eat breakfast. Jason was on the chair with his eyes closed. I was searching for mom and dad. The truck was gone when I opened the window, so I went to the kitchen to eat breakfast. I poured a bowl and opened the fridge to find the milk. When I closed it Jason was standing there.

He startled me, "Shit Jason, you scared me."

"Um, you scared me last night. How are you feeling?"

"Great. I told you I just needed to sleep." I moved to the table to pour the milk. I tried to not look at him, but I had an eerie feeling he was staring.

"You're eating?"

"Yeah, I am starving." I turned the box, so I would have something to read while I was eating. It also gave me something to do while avoiding Jason's stare.

"Do you have any idea of what time it is?"

"No. Why? What time is it?"

"It's 2 p.m."

I was shocked, "I wanted to see Carl today. I promised to go water skiing, and I still have to practice." I was trying to eat as fast as I could and tried to plan it all out in my head. I would still practice, but maybe only a couple of times each, and then I could get the boat down to Sherburn's. That way it would at least be there for the rest of the weekend. Then I will go see Carl for a couple hours, and I could still be back to meet mom and dad at Sherburn's at a decent time.

"Sarah, what are you thinking?"

"I need to hurry. I have a lot of stuff to do today."

"Ah, no you don't. I promised that I would keep an eye on you."

"You didn't tell my mom and dad, did you?"

"No, but I did promised James."

The tears started to well up in my eyes. I was avoiding his look and tried to hurry to get done eating. The swallowing became difficult.

"Sarah? You said you would take it easy today. Do you remember last night at all?"

As I raised my face to him the tears were already running down my checks. I had to work really hard to get out, "I have to stay busy, so it doesn't hurt so badly."

He pulled out the chair and sat down not saying a word. I continued to try to swallow my food, but the lump in my throat was not helping me at all. I knew I couldn't eat anymore and I covered my face with my hands.

I knew I had to get busy right now or the nervous breakdown would take over. I finally pushed the bowl away and stood up to get some water. I proceed to the bathroom to brush my teeth. Jason came to the door to watch me for some reason. I remembered brushing my teeth with James and how playful he was when we did this. Shit the tears were coming again. I leaned with one hand on the counter and avoided looking in the mirror.

"You have memories in here too?"

I raised my eyes till they reflected his face.

"You must have spent more time with him than I know."

Oops the tears were leaking out now. I rinsed and wiped my mouth and face. I walked back out and into the first bedroom to grab my bag. Next, I went to the living room, but I just wandered around since I didn't know what I was looking for.

"Sarah?"

I turned to Jason.

"What are you doing?"

"I have to go to Tony's to practice."

"But you said you would take it easy."

"I will only run through them a couple of times. Where are my mom and dad?"

"They went to town to get food and then the flea market. I said I would keep an eye on you today, so you're stuck with me."

"Are you ready? I need to go."

"Yep. Should we *take your* car or my truck?"

"I guess the truck, in case I need a nap."

"Sarah, if you're tired just stay here and go back to sleep."

"Nope, my mind will take over, and I can't stop to think; let's go."

I went to the truck and threw my stuff in the back. He looked at me as he started the truck.

"Do you want to go to Tony's first?"

"Yes."

I tried to not think about James, but today was not going to be easy for that. I felt so bad about the kiss from Brian. I wouldn't let anyone get that close again. It would have to be two feet or more. No more chances.

I loved him so much. I wish he would come back right now. *James I am sorry, stay and finish. I will be here when you come home.*

I gazed out the window as Jason was driving. His slowness was going to drive me crazy. I blurted out, "We'll have to take my car next time."

"Why is that?"

"You drive too slowly."

He shook his head. When we finally got to Tony's I was jumping out before he could stop, "Sarah!"

I walked in trying to go through the kitchen, but that stupid Jake guy was there to be in my way.

"You are supposed to use the other door."

"I thought we finished this yesterday. Tony treats me like family. Put a muzzle on the bite and let me go practice."

Jason came through the door and looked at Jake. "I'm with her today."

"I thought she was with James?"

I turned to glare at them both. I gave up on trying to yell at either of them, and I walked out to the bar where Tony was. He gave me a huge hug, "How are you today?"

I couldn't say anything, and the tears welled up in my eyes again.

"Oh Sarah, it's a hard one today. Go dance away the sadness. Take as long as you want."

I swallowed and took a deep breath and went to start the music. I listened through them once to get in the mood to dance. I started to feel better and ignored what everyone else was doing. I had to try to get rid of this mood today, or I wasn't going to get everything done. I stayed on the stage behind the equipment going through the routines. I really wasn't ready for an audience, and I was trying to push the sadness out and I couldn't shake it.

I started it again and I heard Jason yell, "You said a couple of times, Sarah. James is going to shoot me."

I leaned forward, so he could see me, "Have I even been out there on the dance floor doing any of them?"

"Sarah, I don't want to have to call him again today."

"Jason, don't threaten me or you can take me home and I will go on my own today."

I didn't hear a reply, so I guess he decided to drop the subject. I closed my eyes and imagined the dance floor, and then I worked through the routines in my head as I did a very small amount of foot work. I did what James always does with me. *1..., 2..., 3..., breath.* I took a deep breath.

I heard a deep voice, but it was a voice I really didn't want to hear.

"Why don't you come out here and go through them; it might help."

I opened my eyes, but I was guarded and it was that crabby Jake guy.

"Come on, I will go through them with you."

I really didn't know what to make of this, maybe a breakthrough that he wasn't quite the jerk I thought he was.

"Come on; I won't bite."

I started the music over and went out. He started to do my moves. I couldn't believe he knew them. My surprise must have shown on my face because he commented, "Yesterday, I paid attention."

I shook my head and ran back to the stage to start it over again. He went through all the dances with me. We both goofed up a couple of times, but he was helping me through my sadness. I started it over again and everything went smoother this time.

In my relief from the sadness I said, "You're not so bad when you're not barking."

I knew he was easing because he only laughed with my comment. I went up and started them again. I was actually laughing, giggling, and having a good time.

We made it through three songs when Tony and Jason walked back in. I heard Tony yell from the bar, "Jake, you're working."

He took off back to the bar but gave me a quick grin and said, "You will do fine tomorrow."

I wanted to hug him and say thank you, but that would violate my rules for today, so I didn't say anything. I went up and turned off the music and walked to the bar. Jason and Tony had moved to the kitchen again so Jake was the only one there. I still felt like I should say something. He really helped me to stop feeling like I was losing it. I decided that maybe I should just go, so I moved to the kitchen door but looked back at him.

He chuckled, "Fine, go through the kitchen."

I giggled a little, but I heard Jason talking to Tony.
"She wasn't in good shape. I had to call James."
"What happened? What do you mean?"
"She was so tired that she couldn't even hold herself up."

I was starting to feel sad again, and I looked back at Jake. He must have seen something in my face because he lowered his eyebrows with a question in them. I put my finger to my lips to make sure he was quiet, and I went back to listening as he shook his head in disbelief that I was eaves dropping.

"Why did you hire him anyway?"
"He's nice to look at for the girls and I needed him for the business. I have been busy since he started here."
"You know he is going to fall in love with her like the rest of us."
"No, he is irritated that everyone loves her. He is determined not to. He knows she belongs with James and doesn't want to even be friends with her."

I looked back at Jake. I realized that I must be a really terrible person if someone has to make up their mind to not like me. He started to move closer to me and smiled. Shit, was I doing it again? I listened again.

"I just don't want anything to happen to her and I don't want her to get upset. James would kill me if anything happened to her."

I quickly peeked back at Jake with an apologetic look, "Thank you for your help today." I pushed through the door to the kitchen.

They both stopped talking as soon as I entered. I walked over to Tony and gave him a great big hug. "Thank you. I needed that."

I turned to Jason, "Carl is next on my list. Skiing will have to wait."

Jason shook Tony's hand, "I guess we're leaving?"

I was headed out the door but Tony had to let me know things were okay now, "Sarah you can come here anytime. You have a key now, but I do have one rule."

I stopped and turned to look at him.

"You have to let me know you are here."

I smiled at him, "I promise to let you know if I am here."

We headed out to the truck. Once we were both in, Jason turned to me, "How are you doing?"

I grinned, "Better now."

"So, Carl is next?"

"Yep, I think he is still at the hospital."

"To the hospital it is."

We drove in silence, so I gazed out the window. I was noticing the trees and how green they were, and the sky and how blue it was. The clouds were white and fluffy. How everything was so beautiful, even when I didn't have my James. If he was here, I would be noticing him: The contour of his face, his brown skin, his soft brown eyes, and the strength of his body. I was on my way to being miserable again.

24. No More Goofing Around

The smile on Carl's face as I entered the room was amazing. He had the same mouth as my James but aged with weather. Clarissa gracefully swept to me to give me a hug. Jason followed me into the room.

When Clarissa released me I held her face to mine, "Clarissa, you have helped us so much. I cannot thank you enough and Mr. Wilson was so nice to us. I love his cooking."

She smiled and kissed my cheek, "My James loves you, so you matter to us."

I hugged her again so tight and then she spoke again, "Carl wants to look at you." She slowly let me go, so I could turn to him.

He spoke but it wasn't to me, "Well, son, we haven't seen you for awhile. You are here with Sarah?"

"James asked me to keep an eye on her. How are you doing sir?"

Carl got this funny grin on his face, "Much better now. It's good to see you, but if he asked you to keep an eye on…" he looked at me, "You are getting worse?"

I tried to be happy and put on a fake smile but he knew.

"Come here child?"

I walked over to him, and he was pushing himself to sit up more. I grabbed pillows to help him and so did Clarissa. I sat down on the side of the bed next to him, and he opened his arms to pull my face to his chest. I felt at home here.

"Okay, everybody out. Sorry, my sweet Clarissa, I need to talk to my daughter in law." He pulled my face up to look at him. "Tell me what is going on."

I took a deep breath and started to ramble. "I haven't been sick at all since James came home last week, so it's been a whole week. I can eat all the time now and I am hungry. I had a scan for cancer but it wasn't that, and now I get tired. Last night it was so bad that I couldn't keep my eyes open. I had no strength at all."

"May I feel?"

I grimaced because this always made me feel weird. I stood up and he placed his hand on my stomach, "You and James have been together?"

Why was he asking that? I just told him James came home last week.

His smile was confusing to me, "Maybe close?"

I still didn't get what he was talking about.

His face lightened as he pulled me back to him, "My mistake. It is still there, but your body is fighting it better. That is where the resting comes into it. If you rest more, your body will continue to fight better."

"Well, I guess I will rest more."

He pulled me to lay down with him like a small child would do when her daddy would tell her a story. He told me about Clarissa and his story. It was quite beautiful. The love they shared in the little time that they have together. He was reassuring me that he was okay with James and me being together, but they didn't feel they had a choice at the time. He went to explain about the feather. I was trying to listen so carefully. He was explaining how precious this gift was because it was very powerful and after it's used the connection between the two would be stronger. That made sense. James said feeling me was so much stronger after he left again. Carl also explained that sometimes the power is too much, so it was to be used carefully and we needed to learn how to use it properly. All I could think was, *all it did for me was put me to sleep.*

He continued with story after story. I lost track and was almost falling asleep.

Before I knew it, Clarissa was helping me out of the bed, "Sarah, sweetheart. Carl needs to rest."

I rolled out into her arms, tipped a little to the side, off balance.

"You are not okay?"

"No. I am okay…just fallen asleep. I need to get my feet back."

Jason came over to help hold me up. She wasn't pleased as she looked up at him. "Have you seen her like this before?"

"Last night."

She pushed me into a chair and squatted in front of me. "They haven't found anything yet?"

I shrugged, and gave her a quaint smile, "They know it's not cancer."

"But you have gotten so thin."

"Only 30 pounds now and last week I hadn't lost anything."

I could see her concern and the pain in her eyes as they filled with tears, "Does James know?"

"Yes, he knows most of it anyway, but maybe not exactly how much I've lost."

Jason took a step back and fell into a chair. He distracted me from Clarissa for a brief moment but long enough that I could see the horror on his face. "You need to keep your mouth shut. He doesn't need to worry."

Clarissa pulled my attention back to her.

I pleaded with her, "Please don't tell him that. It would make him upset."

She was not happy, "Did you tell Carl?"

I looked at him resting, "I couldn't, not about the weight."

She got up and grabbed her purse. "No more goofing around Sarah, I am coming home and we will go see a specialist until we find out what it is. Start here on Monday." She gave me a phone number with a Doctor's name on it. She continued, "He will know where to start. I will try to be home by Tuesday. It's no wonder why you don't have any energy."

I felt relief as I hugged her again. I stood up more slowly and I wasn't weak anymore. "I will call him on Monday, I promise."

She glanced over to Jason, "I think it is time for James to come home."

I pulled her back to me, "NO! He has to finish."

"Sarah, if he knew how bad it is he would be here."

I was pleading with her in the way I looked at her. *No one would understand this, but he needed to finish for us to be together forever. I know I am being silly, and I don't know why, but if he didn't finish this, we wouldn't make it.* So I begged, "Clarissa, Carl told me last time that this would wait. James would finish and he would be here in time to take care of me. That's what has to happen. I will keep fighting until then. I will be more careful, please let him stay. I will see every specialist you want me to 'til then. Please…?"

She kissed my forehead, "Fine, but I am stepping in; I get to take you to the doctors."

I agreed, but they would all have to keep the secret form my Cayuse. I knew he would be home to take care of me and to love me forever.

On our drive back Jason didn't say a word. He didn't even look at me. I was confused and relieved at the same time. I put my feet on the dashboard and leaned back as far as I could and closed my eyes.

He finally spoke, "Are you okay?"

"Yep, I am just resting."

"So, James, doesn't know you lost 30 pounds?"

"We'll actually he doesn't know the number, but he came home and spent the day with me last Wednesday. So, he did see me this way. If I remember correctly he spent the whole day trying to feed me." I laughed to myself. The thought of how angry he was at me when I peaked around the couch at him after refusing to eat anymore.

"Where to next?"

"What time is it?"

"It's…almost 7 p.m."

"Well, I haven't done everything I wanted to do today."

"You have all weekend; what is the rush?"

"I need to stay busy, Jason, that is all."

"So where to?"

"The trailer; I need to change. No water skiing today."

He was grinning and it was irritating me, "James and you are not winning, I just ran out of time. Why did you let me sleep so long?"

"I couldn't wake you."

"Yes, you could have. I would have woken up."

"No, I am saying I couldn't be in the bed room with you to wake you."

Shit, this was hard for him. "I guess, I should say thank you then. The drama wears me out."

He laughed, "That's not the only thing that wears you out."

I let that go. I didn't want to know what he was talking about. I took a couple of deep breaths to relax more, "I think I need food?"

"What do you want?"

"Protein, maybe a steak."

"Do you want to stop somewhere?"

"No, I'll see what they've got when we get to the trailer."

Dad smiled as we pulled in. I didn't want them to see my weakness. "Jason, if you don't keep your mouth shut, I will make sure I will never ever see you again."

"Sarah, they need to know how sick you are."

"Jason, they have enough problems. Mom is already working three jobs, and dad is almost starving up here, so not a word."

I jumped out of his truck as happy as could be, "So, what have you two been up to all day?"

Dad shook his head, "I think we're supposed to be asking you that question."

"I went to see Carl and Clarissa. Oh yeah, I went to Tony's to practice again for tomorrow. I wanted to go water skiing, but that didn't pan out.

"We're making steaks; are you hungry?"

"I think you read my mind dad. Where is mom?"

"She's inside making potatoes. I think hash browns."

I ran inside to see if she needed help. I got the table ready and went to check on dad. Steaks were ready. I hopped happily inside and sat at the table. Jason sat down across from me. I think he was waiting for me to pass out. I felt so much better than yesterday. I grabbed a steak right away and it seemed like they all stopped doing what they were doing.

I tried to not pay attention, but felt I needed to say something. "I am not going to break. All of you should not freak out every time I eat. I feel better and I have been eating a lot for more than a week now."

Mom and dad eased and smiled. Jason did not. He was more like glaring at me. Mom offered me some potatoes, but I was hungry for just meat. I tried to explain that I needed protein, and I would get more if I didn't eat anything else. I ate a whole steak by myself and could have eaten more, but I didn't know how it would sit later.

I wanted to know what I was being allowed to do, "What are the plans for tonight? Sherburn's?"

"Of course, you will want to see Danelle?"

"Yes, and play basketball or volleyball."

"Hum hum." Jason was trying to remind me I was supposed to be taking it easy.

"Or maybe just pool and video games." I was grimacing at him. Now I needed my space, so I could stay busy again.

"So…if we're meeting there. Can I go now?"

It was cute the way they looked at each other not knowing what to say. Dad finally grinned, "Fine go."

Jason stood up to go with me. I was trying to get some free time, "I can take myself; you're not done eating."

I went to the room to change quickly and ran for the door not giving them a chance to change their minds.

When I got to Sherburn's, I walked into the bar. I saw Laura, so I went to the bar. "Where is Danelle?"

"In the back, but are you alright?"

"Yeah, I just needed to sleep, about fifteen hours of sleep."

She shook her head and pointed for me to go to the back.

As I entered the kitchen Brian was there and was looking miserable. When he saw me he walked up to me and wrapped his arms around me in the biggest hug. "I am so sorry, Sarah. I thought you would never come back."

"Um, Brian." I tried to be careful, "I like to spend time here, but this is not going to be. You have to not hug me like this, and no more kissing. James already knows."

"You told him?"

"Nope, but he knew."

"Jason! I bet he is spying on you."

"Whatever the reason, you need to keep a distance, and then I can still come here."

He let go but continued to try to keep my attention, "What happened to you today?"

"I over slept by a lot of hours. I slept fifteen hours."

"Wow, you were tired."

"I told you, but I am ready to take you on."

"I thought you said no kissing or hugging."

"Brian, stop that! Who is the girl this week?"

"Only the one I can't have."

"Brian, please. You have to stop, or I won't want to come here, and I will spend all my time at Tony's."

"Did you meet the bartender?"

"Yeah," I laughed and said, "The guard dog."

He started to laugh too but asked, "He didn't turn your head?"

"Really, Brian. You know my heart belongs to one man."

"Okay. It's getting too deep. What will it be, Basketball or Volleyball?"

"I like both, so why don't you choose."

I hurried to the living room. Danelle was sitting next to Tommy. Her legs were lying over his lap and they were holding hands watching TV. I sat next to her cuddling into her but wrapped my arms around her reaching to hug Tommy.

"Sarah, stop that."

I laughed, "How is my partner today. Are you ready to win?"

"Do we have to play? We're watching a movie."

I hugged them tighter, "Nope. I can stay right here and cuddle with the two of you." I snuggled into her shoulder and hugged him tighter.

"If we play will you please let go of us?"

"Yes."

"Fine, we will play with you."

I jumped up and grabbed the basketball, "Well, come on."

Brian pulled me out the door. "You do know they haven't even kissed yet."

"Good, she is only 15 years old. She is too young."

"You are only 16 years old, and what have you done?"

"Shut up."

They came out embarrassed, so I knew they kissed while Brian was with me. I went up to her pulling her aside, "How was it?"

"What?"

"The kiss?"

"How did you know?"

"Mine wasn't that long ago and I can tell because your face is all red."

"Will you shut up? Brian will hit him."

I smiled, "Fine, but you will tell me later."

"We're not supposed to talk about it."

"I know how that is. Can you go with me tomorrow to Tony's?"

"I will ask."

"Do you want to go? I will ask with you."

"Yes, I do."

"Is Tommy going?"

"He said he would go with Brian. Brian asked a bunch of girls, but they all think he's a jerk now."

"Why? What did he do now?"

"He's not dating anyone. He kind of likes…" She looked up at me. This was making me feel bad, but I loved James.

"Danelle, that isn't going to happen, and he knows that."

"Good… because that would be weird."

We played a hard game. I felt really good and made it challenging for Brian with no dirty play today. I saw mom and dad pull in, but Jason wasn't following in his truck. I glanced down the road and there were no lights. If he was so worried and James asked him to keep an eye on me why wouldn't he show up? He got out of the truck with my mom and dad. He didn't drive himself. I grinned as I realized he was planning on hitching a ride with me later if I was too weak to get myself home. I really didn't want him looking out for me. I could handle myself better today, and I knew this was hard for him.

We continued to play and Tommy and I won today. I sat down and Brian came over watching me.

I noticed what he was doing and tried to relieve his worry, "Don't worry. It's only a breather."

"What happened last night?"

"I'm glad you got Jason; I couldn't even make it in the trailer. I got so tired that I couldn't stand up on my own. Jason called James and told on me. He told him I passed out, so now I have 24 hours supervision while I am up here."

"I'm sorry. I shouldn't have gotten him. I should have insisted on driving you."

"It's okay, but James asked him to watch over me, so now I can't go anywhere without Jason there. I would be fine on my own."

"Last night you had me really worried."

"But as you can see I am fine now."

"Yes, you are. Shit. Sarah?"

"Yeah." He had me worried that he was going to try something.

"I screwed up last night."

"Just don't let it happen again."

"No, I mean I am sorry. You looked so soft and sweet and my hormones got in the way of our friendship."

"You won't kiss me again, right?"

"Not unless you ask me too."

"Okay. So, what is next?"

I searched for Danelle and Tommy because I had been distracted by Brian. They were wrapped in each other's arms standing, talking, and waiting for us. It seemed simple. The cuddling and how sweet it was. It seemed so long ago when I was there, and I didn't stay there for long.

"Do you want to play video games?"

"Sure."

We headed in, but I looked back at those two, "Danelle, you can do that in here too."

They followed arm in arm. Now she would understand why I wanted to spend every minute with James that I could. It was so sweet and innocent.

We played video games till my finger hurt. I wasn't exhausted like I was the night before. Sleep agreed with me. I wandered to the bar to find mom, dad, and Jason. Jason moved to me quickly and spoke very quietly, "Is he behaving himself?"

I looked at him and our faces were less than two inches apart. I swallowed, "Yes, and he even apologized for doing that."

He turned away from me. I took a step back to stay within my new two foot rule.

"Are you ready to go then?"

I was irritated, "No. I'd like to play pool next."

"You should get some rest. Carl said that you would heal better if you rest."

"Jason, I feel fine."

"How am I going to tell James that you wouldn't behave?"

I was mocking him, "James, she won't listen to me. And then I will deal with him. I like the making up. It's so good."

"I don't want to hear about that."

"Sorry. I will behave. How about midnight?"

He looked at the clock on the wall and then back at me, "Fine, but I'm not going to look for you. Be ready to go, and I'll meet you at the car."

"Fine."

"Fine."

Oh I was finding him infuriating. I went back to play pool with Brian, Tommy, and Danelle. We played until 10 minutes before I was supposed to meet Jason.

Brian was trying to get me to stay longer and wasn't happy that Jason had a say in what time I had to leave by. "He's putting time frames on you?"

"No, actually it is helping me. I want to go water skiing tomorrow, and then I have the dance at 5 pm., and I need to rest so I can do it all tomorrow."

"Sarah, are you really that weak?"

"I guess so. Yesterday was the first time I was that tired, but today I have gotten tired a couple of times and I don't want to push it."

"So, you will be here early?"

"I will try, but we will go water skiing."

He walked me out to the car but saw Jason standing there.

"I would hug you goodbye, but Jason would probably tell, so I guess I shouldn't do that."

I turned and gave him a quick side hug, "Hope this will be enough for the friendship."

He was smiling as I let go and walked away to Jason.

"You're early?"

"I need my rest."

"You hugged him?"

"Kind of. It was a friendship hug, and you get those too, even when I didn't want to give you one, so you shouldn't talk."

He rolled his eyes, "Keys please?"

I was hesitant, "Can you handle my car?"

"Sarah, I am not playing games. Get in and give me the keys."

"Fine." I tossed him my keys.

"Fine." He got in and we headed for the trailer.

I was able to get myself in this time. I went to the bedroom and got ready for bed putting on a t-shirt and shorts. I crawled into the bottom bunk to sleep. I couldn't believe I was tired after sleeping fifteen hours today.

"Are you decent?" Jason was outside of the room.

"Yeah, but I am lying down already."

He turned so he was in the doorway looking down at me through the bars that were holding the top bunk up, "You know this is hard for me?"

"Jason, don't do it then. I am fine now. I release you from your duty of the Sarah watch program. I will tell James I flatly refused."

"You know I love you too?"

"Jason, no. I am doing better, so please don't do this. I can't handle anymore drama, so please let me be with James. That is where my heart belongs."

"There is nothing more that I want than to feel your lips again, but I know I would not get the response I want. I am sorry for that, but just know that I love you." He walked away. I was sad and thankful that he knew to walk away. I closed my eyes to yet another day of not being sick. I was up to eight days in a row of not throwing up.

25. A Day In The Sun

I fell to sleep quickly only to be awakened by a phone call. I picked up my phone happily, "James!"

"Sarah, I have been miserable all day. How are you my love?"

"I am so much better. I slept for fifteen hours yesterday. I was really tired." I got up as I was talking to James and looked at the back room. Mom and dad were back and sleeping. I turned to check the living room. Jason was sleeping on the couch. I closed the door as quietly as I could and crawled back into bed.

"Oh Sarah, you had me so worried."

"I am fine now. I saw your mom and dad today."

"How is my dad?"

"He looks amazing. He told me stories, but one has me concerned. I will ask you about that when I see you."

"No tell me. I have nothing to hide from you."

"Okay, but you won't answer me."

"Yes I will. Quit playing with me."

"It was about the feather."

"You're right. It will wait till I get home."

"James, did we over use it?"

"Maybe, but please let us discuss it when we are together again."

"See! I told you and one other thing…"

"What is that?"

"You have to let Jason off the hook on looking after me."

"Why? I am worried about you."

I thought about touching his lips with my fingertips. I closed my eyes to enjoy the thought.

"Sarah! You're trying to distract me. Why? He hasn't tried anything has he?"

"You know the answer to that. Can I have a taste?"

"Well, then, what are you telling me?"

"James, your dad said you did something to me that was helping my body to fight. Could it be from you sharing your soul with me, because if that is it, I could really use a dose of feeling better."

I heard him whisper, "Sarah…are your eyes closed?"

My distraction was working, "Yes."

"Then you need to sleep."

"James, don't tease me. Please, just once. I will sleep better."

"You know you don't like it when it's not real."

"But you thought maybe it was?"

"Sarah."

"I will just have to be okay with it. Please?"

I felt the rush through my whole body, "Oh James, I needed that."

I felt his lips on mine. His mouth moved to mine as I parted to let our lips move together. His tongue brought my mouth to his more. Oh my heart was beginning to hurt. "Okay James, that's enough. I can't handle any more."

The feeling eased and lessened, "We have only 17 more days left."

"I know. Can you talk me to sleep?"

He kept me comfortable in his arms and whispered sweet nothings in my ear till I fell asleep. I don't think it was very long.

Day 32: It was only 16 more days till he would be home. I can do this. I was feeling so good today already. I was ready for water skiing. I think I am anyway. I pulled out my note from my bag and sat back down.

The stars from heaven
The sand from the Sea
It will always be me
In love with you.
I love you more than you know,
James

I was in heaven. I had love notes from my James that would last me a life time. I still didn't understand how he did it. I got up and realized I had my period. I had it a week ago, so why was I getting it again. Maybe because it only lasted a day last time I was going to pay for it now. I could start the pills on Sunday. I knew that this would make it so our time to be together would seem closer. I realized that this was probably why I was so tired and weak. I would have to take it easy. I wanted to have a really good night dancing.

I went to the kitchen and it smelt great. Mom and dad were making steak and eggs. They did pay attention and they were trying to help by giving me as much protein as they could.

I sat down at the table and started to fill my plate, "Can I use the boat today?"

The weirdest thing happened. They both looked at Jason for the answer. Now I was going in for the kill, "So that would be a yes and Jason will you please help her to the launch."

Dad was irritated, "Wait a minute. That is not what we're saying at all."

I took a deep breath getting ready for the negotiations realizing Jason probably said something about me sleeping fifteen hours yesterday.

"Okay, I won't water ski or go tubing. I will just drive the boat, and I will have someone who can drive with me at all times."

I could see they were thinking about it. They were torn over worrying about me being sick, and me being happy doing stuff without James.

Jason was going to ruin it, because he couldn't keep his mouth shut. "I suppose Brian will be the driver with you?"

I knew this was actually going to help them say yes. They wanted me to keep my options open.

"Probably, unless we train Danelle on how to drive it. I think I could do that. Thank you Jason that is a really good idea. Unless... Do you want to go?"

"Nope, I only go on the lake to fish."

I was waiting for mom and dad to decide, "So, what is the verdict?"

"You're not skiing or tubing?" Mom asked.

"I'll even leave the wet suit here if you want."

Dad laughed quietly, "Fine... go."

I was excited, "Who is bringing the boat to the launch for me?"

They both turned to Jason. He wasn't happy, "Fine, but I wouldn't let her go if I were you guys."

My mom was concerned now. I don't think she wanted to let me go either, "Is there a specific reason why she shouldn't go?"

He didn't say anything and walked out of the trailer. He was mad. We were kind of using him a lot lately and it was bothering me. I walked out and up to the boat to help get it ready. He came up with his truck and backed into the trailer for hooking it up. I took the wet suit out and threw it in the back of his truck to make him feel better. He still gave me a nasty look. I got in the truck but didn't say anything until we were pulling out.

"Wait, I have to ask mom or dad to bring down my car by 3:30 p.m. so I can get to Tony's early."

"Let me use your car and I will pick you up."

"Jason, you don't have to take care of me today. I am fine."

He grimaced at me.

"You will be there at 3:30 p.m.?"

"Yeah." He was sarcastic.

"I hate asking you to do any more favors; you have already done so much for me."

His face showed disappointment in what I had said, so I handed him my keys hoping to rectify it.

"Please be there at 3:30 p.m."

"I can't stay and watch over you. I can't watch your attempt to kill yourself."

"Okay, but please, please..." I was giving him my biggest pouty look I could muster, "Please don't be late."

"I am going to Tony's to help set up."

"You can do whatever you want, but please don't be late."

"I will be there at 3:30 p.m. on the nose."

We were at the boat launch and I got in to head to Sherburn's. I glanced at him one last time worried he would try to control me by not showing up. I had to trust him. I didn't have much of a choice.

Brian was on the dock when I got there. He was grabbing the rope form me pulling it to tie it to the dock.

"It's just you and me today."

"Where's Danelle?"

"She has to watch the store."

"Don't you have to watch the store too?"

"Nope, it's her turn."

"Is Tommy here?"

"Yep."

"And you're going to leave them alone?"

"Yep. My mom is there."

"Then why does Danelle have to watch the store?"

"My mom doesn't feel good 'til she gets at least 8 hours of sleep."

"We can't go without a spotter."

"Nope."

"Can you invite anyone else?"

"Yeah, but they are all girls."

"Brian that's fine. I don't mind at all."

I sat down on the bench with him. "I had to agree to not water ski or go tubing myself to get the boat today."

"Really? Why did you get the boat then?"

"Because I told you I would."

We sat there for the longest time not saying anything. I didn't like the silence, "So, what should we do?"

I could see this funny grin on his face.

I nudged him with my shoulder, "Stop that thought right now. I already had an argument with James and I don't want to do that again."

"So, what do you want to do?"

"All I know is that I don't want to do anything that will make me tired."

"Should we lay in the sun and take it easy than?"

"Getting some color might help me to not look so sick."

"Really?" He was surprised that I agreed so easily.

"I get the tubing tube, it's bigger." I got up and grabbed it out of the boat and put it in the water.

He was smiling from ear to ear, "I have to go get one."

"Okay?"

"I'll be right back." He was acting kind of bummed out and I felt bad. I took off my shorts, my tank top, and got on the tube before he got back.

As he returned, walking down the dock he said out loud, "Danelle and Tommy are coming down in an hour or so."

"Did you call anybody else?"

"Yep."

"Good."

He put the tube behind him and fell into the water splashing me. I sat back up. "Okay, wasn't ready for that." I laid back down and closed my eyes.

"Did you know you are so skinny that your hip bones stick out at least an inch farther than your stomach?"

"I really didn't want to talk about my body, "Nope, I try to not pay attention to it, and you shouldn't either. Why are you looking anyway? You're making it harder on yourself."

"I can't help it. You don't really sit in a bathing suit every day."

"Close your eyes and don't think about it."

"That's easy for you to say."

I was quiet again, but Brian couldn't help himself, "Does James have a hard time keeping his hands off of you?"

"Brian, we are going to have to do something else if you can't behave."

"I'm not touching!"

"Change the subject please."

"To what?"

"Who did you call?"

"Mykala, Tammy, Katie, and Pam."
"Are they coming?"
"Maybe."
"I only have 'til 3:30 p.m."
"Why?"
"I have to get ready for tonight. I like to look good because it makes me feel better."
"What time do you have to be there?"
"Not until 5 p.m., but I want to run through the songs once before people show up."

It was peaceful after that. He didn't say much. I must have dozed off as we drifted. Brian was at my side holding my tube.

"Sarah? Danelle and Tommy are on their way down."
I sat up to see Danelle, "Did you guys want to go tubing?"
"No. We're going to swim if that's alright?"
I laid back down, "That's great for me."

Brian pulled my tube to get my attention again. "Sarah, you're getting very pink. You might want to roll over."

I didn't know if there was an ulterior motive, but I did it anyway. He moved back to holding the tube more. I went back to sleep as soon as I turned over.

"Hey, Sarah?"
I tried to open my eyes and propped myself up on my elbows to see what he wanted. He was in front of me, "You were sleeping."
"Yeah, relaxing."
"No, you have been sleeping for almost an hour and a half. You are pretty fried."
"Great."
"Some girls showed up. Can I take them tubing?"
"Yep." I started to push myself up.
"Sarah, shit."
"What?" I was in panic mode now.
He was looking down the front of me, "You are such a turn on for me."

"Brian, swim out as far as you can and go under deep."

"Why?" He was crawling on the tube towards me.

"The cold water will help."

"I can think of something else that would help me."

"Don't even think about it." I pushed him back and under the water. I slipped off the other side of the tube, so I could put as much room between us as possible. I swam to the dock. I was going up the stairs and greeted the girls as I came up. Mykala was one of them and she introduced me to the other girls that were with her. I shook each of their hands as Mykala said their names. When she was done she moved closer to me and whispered, "You and Brian?"

I smiled shaking my head, "Nope."

She gave me a questioning look and raised her eyebrows, "The one from your party?"

As I thought about him I couldn't help but smile, "Yeah. His name is James."

"I know who he is and he is hot."

I didn't know if I liked her noticing, but he was mine and I grinned even more. "I know."

"I would let him do me any day."

No, I didn't like that at all. She needs to stay away from my James. "Mykala!"

"Sarah, you do know Brian likes you?"

"No, actually, he invited you even with me here. He still likes you."

"You really think so?"

"Yep. You know if you give him a chance you will notice the improvements. He's been working really hard to be a gentleman."

"I just might. He is gorgeous."

I shook my head and turned to grin at Brian. He noticed and gave me that innocent questioning look.

"Mykala, there is one rule for tubing. Someone has to be in the boat at all times watching the person on the tube. Brian, please be careful."

Mykala grabbed my arm, "You not staying?"

"No. I need to get ready for Tony's. Are you coming?"

"I wouldn't miss it. What time are you going to be there?"

"I will be there at 4:30 pm, but it doesn't actually start until 5 pm."

"We'll see you then."

It was only 2:30 pm, but I had my fill of the sun. I went to see if Jason was early. He wasn't, so I started to walk to the trailer. If it took me a half hour, by the time Jason got there I could be ready. I really wanted to be ready for tonight. It didn't take me long to walk. I was able to wash my hair and blow dry it. I wore a tank top, but I also had on one of James's white button up dress shirts. I put it over and left it open down to my waist and tied a knot in front. I wrapped my arms around to give myself a hug and imagined it to be James. I smiled and opened my eyes and noticed I looked really good. My hair turned out gorgeous, but I pulled it up and pulled strands down to dangle. Why couldn't I look this good when my James was here? Oh, I would rather spend time with him than fixing myself. All the jeans I owned were too big for me now, so I had to wear a belt. I turned and looked and it didn't look too bad because they were baggy in the right places. I put on a little makeup but lightly. I liked the down to earth soft look. I put some lip gloss on to shine those lips. I looked at myself again. I didn't look sick at all and I was happy.

26. New Young Hottie

"Sarah...Sarah! Are you here?" I heard Jason storming in the trailer.

"Yeah, I am getting ready."

He was frantic as he was coming down the hall, "Why didn't you wait for me?"

"I had too much sun, and some girls showed up to play with Brian. I didn't want to cramp his style."

I heard Jason almost to the bathroom door, "Are you decent?"

I leaned out the door to answer him, "Yeah, I just have to brush my teeth." I went back to putting toothpaste on my brush.

"Sarah?"

"What?" I started to brush my teeth.

"Is that really you?"

"What?" I now had a mouthful of toothpaste and foam. I looked out the door again, and he had stopped before getting to the bathroom.

"Oh, shit, Sarah. You shouldn't look that good. It's going to be torture for everyone."

I chuckled, "Shut up. I feel good."

He moved to lean against the wall across from the bathroom, but looked like a large cat getting ready to pounce. Once I noticed him I turned away quickly. *Shit that is not good,* I thought to myself.

"Um, Jason, I can drive myself if you want to go. It's only until 8 pm, and I think I can get myself home if it's that early."

"Nope. I promised James." He moved to brace himself on the doorframe to stop him self from coming in.

I turned to him with a firm look, "Let's go then." I gestured for him to start walking, but he only dropped one hand to let me through. I knew he was to that point of not being able to trust himself. I took a breath and tried to ease the moment, "I think I should drive myself. This is not easy for you."

"Nope, but let's go."

I walked by him carefully to keep as much distance as I could, but I felt his hand almost touch my waist. I was firm with him, "Jason, NO!" I tried to walk a little faster down the hall to put distance between us. He grabbed my hand to stop me and turned me so my back was against the wall. He moved closer and gazed into my eyes deeply.

I was pleading with him as I reminded him, "James feels everything. You don't want to do that."

His desire didn't seem to ease, and I was really scared, "Jason, no!"

He finally closed his eyes and let his arm drop down, so I could walk away from him, and that is exactly what I did. I walked away quickly and kept going out of the trailer and to my car. I got in and realized I didn't have my keys, "Shit!"

If I go back in there, will I be asking for trouble? But I can't leave 'til I have keys. Do I dare call James? He will be furious and will want to come home. I couldn't jeopardize what he has gotten done in the last four weeks. I can handle this. I feel really good and strong right now. I will just go in and ask for my keys. I took a deep breath and clinched my fists. I opened my car door and left it open in case I had to hurry. I walked up to the trailer slowly opening the door. I didn't see him. I looked in the kitchen and then at the chair in the living room. I took a step further and looked on the couch. Shit what was he doing? "Jason, I need my keys."

"Yeah, I know." I turned and he was sitting on the counter in the kitchen behind the fridge. He must have been watching out the window.

"Can I have them please?"

"Not until you go put some more clothes on."

"What?"

"Sarah, if I can't control myself how is anyone else? I have more control than James; you know that."

"Jason, give me the keys now!"

He held them out for me to take, dangling them from his hand, "See you are afraid of me."

"No, I just don't want to make this worse. Toss them to me."

"Um, no. You need to change, or put more clothes on."

"I am not going to the bedroom for clothes or anything else. Give me the keys, and I will walk out the door and this never happen. Please, Jason?"

He closed his eyes. He was showing weakness, so I took a step towards him, "Jason, I am so happy you have been here to help me, but if you don't stop this right now, I won't be able to be around you at all. Please, please… give me the keys."

As his look came back to my face, I could see his eyes were soft and sad, "Go put more clothes on. I will wait in the car."

"I think I need to drive myself. You need space from me. You can go… take your truck. I will be behind you shortly."

He set the keys on the table and walked out. I didn't move until I heard his truck leave. I walked over to the couch and collapsed with relief. I was going to have to avoid any alone time with Jason. When I finally was able to calm my heart and I was able to swallow again, I got up and went to grab a sweatshirt. Then I was off to Tony's.

I stopped to see if Danelle was going with me. She was going, but she had to ride with Brian, so I was off and on my own again. I pulled into Tony's, but I noticed Jason's truck wasn't here. I hope I didn't upset him too badly, but he shouldn't let himself feel like that.

I went in through the kitchen, and Jake was there.

He glanced at me, "Ma'am, you have to use the other door."

"Jake, haven't we discussed this already?"

He turned to me and his jaw dropped, "Sarah?"

"What?"

He turned away from me, "Tony's in the bar."

I proceeded out to the bar, and I saw Tony.

"Oh my, Sarah. You don't look sick at all." He hugged me, "Are you ready?"

"Not really." I was trembling in my skin. "I will try to do my best though."

"Color looks good on you."

"Thanks."

"Where's, Jason?"

"I don't know. We had an argument about what I am wearing, and he left pretty mad."

"So, we might be on our own?"

"I don't think he will abandon you. I think he will be here. He needed time to calm down."

"You know where the stage is."

"Yes, I do."

I hurried to the stand and started the music. I was shaking a little. I didn't know if it was from Jason, or if it was because there were going to be a lot of people here watching me. I closed my eyes trying to calm my nerves.

"Are you nervous?"

I chuckled and opened my eyes to look at Jake, "Yes."

"You need to relax. You are a very good dancer."

I gave him a smirk, "I don't feel so good."

"Tony said you are sick. Are you going to throw up?"

"No, it's not that kind of not feeling good. It's just nerves."

"Go ahead and start the music again and come here. I will go through them with you again."

I was relieved, "Really?"

"I said I would. Come on."

I started the music and ran down to the dance floor, "Is Tony going to get mad at you?"

"No. We are totally ready. Actually, we're more than what I think is necessary."

"You will be surprised." I shook my hands to loosen up a little. We went through all the songs.

He asked politely, "Are you using all of them today?"

"No. I think just a couple. I was going to start with the ones from the last time I did this, because everyone knows those and then I'll add a couple more."

"I like the reggae one. Can we do that one tonight?"

"Sure." I was feeling better and more relaxed.

Sandy and Kate walked in and moved to the dance floor right away. We started with the new ones, so they would know how to do them. I made sure to use the one that Jake liked. He helped me, so I wanted to make him happy. I noticed that Jake had moved back to the bar when I started working with the woman. He was really nice when he wasn't trying to be nasty to me. We made it through the songs twice before people started showing up. I ran up to change the music to one of the old dances while they were arriving. I wanted to keep the new ones for later in the night. People started dancing right away as they arrived. When the dance floor was full I put in the other country song I had picked out, and we went through the dance. We were having so much fun. When the song was over I put some other music on, and let everyone dance freely and then I went to the bar to sit for a moment.

Tony came over to me right away, "Are you okay?"

"Yeah, but can I get a drink?"

"Sarah, no alcohol." He was trying to be playful. That was the first thing he had ever said to me, so I chuckled a little.

"Okay, I will get you a soda."

He brought me one, and I took a large drink and looked at Tony, "Did Jason show up?"

"Yeah. He is taking care of the kitchen. He can't watch you, not today, anyway."

I was relieved, "I am okay with that, Tony."

"What happened?"

"Nothing really... It was just my attire; we didn't agree on what I should wear."

"But you look so much older and so good, Sarah."

I lifted my eyebrows, "I think that is what the problem is."

"Oh, yeah I didn't think about it that way."

"Neither did I, Tony."

Jake walked over, "I think you look amazing." He walked away, but he never looked up or at me as he made his comment.

I ignored it, but secretly it made me feel good, "Tony, do you think I should bring out the next song?"

"No, not yet, because I need orders to keep Jason busy."

"I will break the music for 15 minutes. Are you ready now?"

"Yeah, good idea."

I went up to the stage and after the song was over I interrupted, "Hey, we're going to take a 15 minute break. Get your drinks and food orders while you can."

"I went to the kitchen to help Jason. I started a bag of fries and said softly to Jason, "I am sorry."

"What are you doing?" He was still angry with me.

"I was apologizing to you and helping you."

"I see you don't listen."

"I have to have some faults."

The heat was getting to me and the arguing wasn't helping. I stopped and grabbed the counter.

Jason's tone changed instantly, "Sarah?"

I was still angry, "Jason, don't! I am fine. It's just too hot in here for me."

"Get out then. I can do this."

I grabbed a tray of glasses to bring out to the bar. I heard him scold me, "Don't do that, Sarah."

"Jason, I am fine."

I walked out to the bar to stack the glasses. Jake came over and grabbed the tray, "What do you think you're doing?"

I looked at him sternly, "I am helping." Then I weakened, "Let me do this."

He took his hands off the tray, but I had to sit it down. I was getting weaker.

Tony noticed and walked up to me, "Sarah, you're not okay?"

I didn't want to feel this way. I didn't want to be weak, "Tony, I am fine. Let me do this. Let me finish tonight before you start to worry about me. I am having fun."

He didn't know what to do, so he agreed, "Okay, but James will be angry with me."

"I will deal with my James and his fury."

I walked back out to the stage. Brian came up to me, "What did you say to Mykala?"

"Nothing, why?"

"She can't keep her hands off of me." I had to chuckle but he scolded, "You did say something?"

I had to correct him, "Actually, she thinks you are gorgeous, and I just suggested that she give it another try. Was that okay?"

"Well, if I can't have you, I guess she will be okay for now."

"Brian, remember to treat her like she has a boyfriend; it's more seductive that way."

"You find me seductive?"

"Sometimes, but don't get any ideas. I love James."

He smiled, "Thanks."

"Where is Danelle?"

"He looked to a corner where she and Tommy were sitting and talking to each other. I felt warmth with her happiness, "Tell her I want to see her before she leaves."

"You got it."

I started to flick the lights, "Is everybody ready for more?"

The cheering was loud. I started the music. I needed to breathe before I started the next training. I walked back to the bar, "Tony?"

"What sweetheart?"

"When it slows down, can I borrow Jake for the next training?"

"Are you okay?"

"Um, just getting tired. I could use a little help."

"All you have to do is say so."

I gave him a grin to let him know I was thankful, "Did you get a lot of orders?'

He grabbed my cheeks, "You are amazing, Sarah, and I love you myself." He kissed my cheek, and then he went to get more orders from the kitchen.

Jason walked out and came to me right away, "Tony said you were...?"

"Jason, I am fine. I just need to sit for a couple of minutes."

I realized the music was almost done, so I ran up to the stage and set it up to run through a couple more songs. I sat down behind the equipment to try and catch my breath. It was getting harder. When those songs were coming to an end, I put in another track of three songs.

Kate and Sandy came up, "Are you ready for the next one? I think the people want more."

I smiled, but I didn't know if I could do it, "Okay."

As the song ended I started announcing, "Okay ladies, we have a guest to dance with us, so if we can get the New Young Hottie, Jake, on the dance floor."

He was so cute when he was happy. He jumped over the bar in one leap, but stopped to see if Tony approved. Tony waved him to go. Jason emerged from the kitchen to watch.

"Watch out ladies, because he is hot."

I started the song and he came to the stage putting out his hand for mine. I shook my head, "You need to get all the ladies to dance, not me."

"I will start here."

I gave him my hand, and he led me to the dance floor. We started to dance the routine, but he did something different. He was facing me as he did them, "Are you okay?"

I shook my head no, "Go get more girls to dance."

"Are you sure?"

"Yes."

He moved to all the girls that were sitting and pulled them to the dance floor giving each on a private lesson on the routine. I went back to the stage and watched him work the crowd. This was a really good song, and the girls were going crazy over him. I even replayed the song, so they would have more time with him. He was enjoying himself. When it finally came to an end the second time, I set up for it to play regular music for a while. I took a deep breath and sat back down. I looked at the clock, and we only had a half hour left. I was going to make it. I searched for Tony who was behind the bar dancing away. Jake had made it back to the bar and was helping with orders. It was amazing how many girls were ordering things from him now. I glanced back at Tony, and I swear, his smile was a mile long. This was going good, and I only had to make it one more day and then I could rest.

When Tony rang the bell, I let the last song play out. I announced that we were doing this again tomorrow, but only if we hurried to get out. I also reminded people to bring more friends. I liked that I was helping Tony. I shut down everything and walked to the bar.

Tony came to me again kissing my cheeks once on each side, "I love you, Sarah. Do you know how much business you bring me? It was a good idea to have Jake help. Over half the orders were after he went out and danced. I think they all wanted a closer look."

I was pleased with his happiness.

"What can I get you to eat?"

I didn't want them to worry, but I was done, "No food Tony. I need to go up stairs and rest."

The worry came over his face as it turned pale white, "What? Are you okay? Sarah, you shouldn't have."

I tried to ease his worry, "I am going to be okay, but I need to lay down for a little bit."

I headed to the kitchen and passed through not even looking at Jason. I was avoiding him in fact. I had one goal in mind and that was up the stairs to the bed. I made it to the forth step and had to sit down. I put my head in my hands. Shit, I hated this. *What is wrong with me?*

I heard someone coming and I was afraid it was Jason. I forced myself up as he came around the corner. I was relieved it was Jake. I turned to walk up the stairs, and he put a bag of garbage in the dumpster. I made it one more step and then another. I didn't want any help. I grabbed the railing to help pull myself up another one.

He must have noticed because he asked, "Hey, are you alright?"

I didn't want to answer, "Why did Tony make this for James way up there?"

"Do you want help?"

"Nope. I am getting there."

"Um, you're not even halfway. Are you sure you don't need help?"

I didn't want to feel this way anymore. The tears were welling up in my eyes. I was determined to not cry, "Can you keep your mouth shut?"

"Yeah."

I looked back carefully, "Then yeah, I could use your help."

He came up the steps to me quickly, "What are you trying to do?"

"Go up stairs and lay down for awhile."

He didn't try to help me at all. He picked me up and carried me up the stairs and into the apartment. He laid me down on the bed. I rolled away from him and curled up with a pillow.

"Are you sure I shouldn't tell someone?"

"Please don't. Everyone tends to over react. I just need a little nap. I will be fine. Can you do me one more favor though?"

"What's that?"

"Wake me up by 10 pm, or else I won't be able to come back tomorrow."

"Yes, I can do that."

"Thanks."

27. Easing The Pain

I started to move slowly. I didn't remember where I was. This was so comfortable. I reached out, "James?" I felt around but he wasn't there. I opened my eyes and realized I was somewhere I wasn't used to. I sat up looking around.

"You're awake?"

I turned to where the voice came from. It was Jake.

"What time is it?"

"Almost 11 pm."

I was panicking trying to get up and hurry to go, "Shit. I told you I had to be up at 10 pm." I moved off the bed and lost my balance. He didn't move closer to me, but instead he sat there and watched me.

"Your mom called, and I had to tell Tony. He talked to her and you are fine. He sent me up here to check on you."

"How long have you been here?"

"About five minutes. I think I woke you a little when I walked in."

I lay back down to compose myself. I needed to get up more slowly. Jake was distant and cold, "So, what is wrong with you?"

"I don't know."

"Do you pass out all the time?"

"I didn't pass out. I just get really tired. Wednesday it started."

"From what Jason said, you have lost 30 pounds in the last month."

"I knew he wouldn't keep his mouth shut."

"He was talking to Tony. I pay attention."

"Hey, thanks for helping me earlier." I curled up on the bed looking at him.

"So, you are not this great, strong, opinionated girl that everyone talks about."

"I told you that the other day."

"So, can you come tomorrow? Will you feel up to it?"

"I already promised Tony. He seems to do good when we put these on."

"He must have. I made almost $300. in those three hours."

"That's good."

"How much does Tony pay you?"

"I get a meal, and he lets me dance here."

"He doesn't pay you?"

"No, it's more like I do a favor for him, and he feeds me and lets me dance. Almost… anytime I want.

His look became distrustful, almost a glare, "So, are you running a fever?"

I didn't know what to think of this, "A little now and then, maybe a couple of degrees."

"All the time?"

Why was he asking me these questions? "Well, if you are asking if I run a temperature when I was throwing up? No, I didn't feel sick at all."

"You were throwing up?"

"Yeah, but only when I got upset."

"Okay, there was more with the fever?"

"Yeah, if you are asking about the fever when I am really tired; I have no idea. I just get tired and I don't seem to have any strength."

This was weird, but I felt like I could tell him anything. He wasn't like after me or trying to flirt with me at all. I felt very safe.

"So, there is an infection somewhere. What tests have they run?"

"I really don't know. They take a lot of blood samples and I guess my white blood cell count was up really high a week or so ago. Why are you asking all these questions?"

"Trying to understand what is wrong with you."

"It's not cancer. I had a scan done last Tuesday. Hey, is Jason still here?"

"Yeah, do you want me to go get him?"

"Nope, I was hoping to get out of here without him knowing."

"I don't think he will notice. When was the last time you got sick?"

I was really proud of myself, "Nine days ago. Why won't he notice?"

"How do you feel when you eat?" His eyes moved to me, "His old girlfriend showed up."

I was grinning from ear to ear, "Really, were they together? Was she nice to him?"

I could tell he was confused by the look on his face, "I personally don't like her at all. I wouldn't give her the time of day, so she turned her attention back to him. She was all over him and it was sickening. I asked how you feel when you eat."

"I feel fine as long as it is good food. I think I threw up more when I had junk food. Lately I have been hungry for red meat. She hit on you in front of him?"

"Do you still have feelings for him or something?"

"No. I only want him to be happy. She is a little abusive and I don't like that, but if he is happy with her than it's none of my business. How did you know I once had feelings for him?"

"A little birdie told me."

I was sitting up now testing the waters of the weak knee thing. I moved a little and wasn't dizzy at all. I had a little more strength.

"Shouldn't you be helping Tony? I am okay now."

"No. It got really slow before he sent me up here."

I stood up and moved around. I was feeling better, but he was watching me walk back and forth.

"Do you have a problem with walking, too?"

"No, just when I am weak I get a little light headed. How did you get stuck checking on me?"

He laughed, "Tony said I was the safest choice."

I shook my head knowing Tony was right. "I think I am ready to go."

I fixed the bed up and smiled as I looked at it. I turned and he was watching me but got up to go to the door. I walked over to leave.

"I will walk down in front of you just in case." He went out the door and down a couple of steps to wait for me.

As I locked the door he looked back up at me, "One more question. Do you have your period?"

"Don't you think that is kind of personal?"

"Well, if they have been taking a lot of blood and your craving red meet which means protein…If you had your period and your iron levels could be way down which would explain the feeling of weakness, the hunger for protein, and the sleepiness."

I was feeling better already. "Well, yeah. How do you know this stuff?"

"School and I pay attention. You should eat a steak tonight while you're feeling better."

He started to go down the stairs and I followed.

I looked out over the parking lot and I saw Jason and Kylie. It was very hot and aggressive. I grinned and thought about how much I missed James. Then Jason looked right at me and his eyes were sad. I don't think he liked me seeing him with her, but I was happy for him and I mouthed, "It's okay."

Kylie looked to see what he was looking at. She saw me and I stopped in my tracks. He was with her and he was looking at me which was not a good thing. She smiled and was even more aggressive to get his attention back, which was not that hard for her to do. She would have done it right there in front of me, just to show me she could. He crawled into the truck with her. Jake turned around to see why I had stopped. I was smiling again because she didn't come after me; that was a very good thing.

He questioned me, "You just spent two days with him and you're not upset by this?"

"No! My heart belongs to James. I am happy for them. Jason should spend as much time with her as he does with me. His relationship would go a lot better."

We continued down the stairs and into the kitchen. I got to the door to the bar and I stopped. He was holding the door open, so I could walk through.

"I can't go in there. It's after 8:30 pm. I am not allowed."

He laughed, "So, you do follow the rules?"

I had the most serious face as I looked at him, "Only when I have to."

Tony came in giving me a huge hug, "Are you okay for tomorrow?"

"I will be great tomorrow."

He leaned really close to me, "Your spell is already working."

I was confused.

"Jake, he's already walking around here smiling, and the girls are going nuts."

"But Tony, I don't want him to…"

"He knows you love James. He's just not as serious as he was a couple of days ago."

"Where did he come from?"

"He moved here to work at the hospital. He took this job to meet people."

"Tony, I better go or I won't be able to come back."

He kissed my forehead. "You are sure you are okay?"

I reassured him, "Yes, I just needed to rest."

I hugged him and headed to my car. I was all alone again. I got in my car and noticed Jake taking out the garbage as I started my car. He put up his hand to stop me and came over quickly. I rolled down my window.

"Can I do that again tomorrow? I had a lot of fun."

"Yeah, as long as Tony doesn't mind."

"See you tomorrow."

"Yeah, see yah."

He walked away like it was nothing. It was so refreshing to not get hit on. James would like that too.

I went to Sherburn's and found Danelle and Tommy playing pool after checking in with mom and dad. They were just finishing up with their game. "So, what are we doing tonight?"

Danelle looked at me with puppy dog eyes. "We were going for a walk."

"Okay, where is Brian?"

"You should come with us for a walk."

"You two don't want a third wheel."

"You don't want to hang with Brian. Mykala is here."

I smiled. What else could I do? "That's good." I was trying to be happy for both of them.

"Where is Jason?" Danelle asked.

"Where he should be, with Kylie."

"Well, we could play another game of pool."

"No, that's okay. I'll go back and talk to mom and dad for awhile."

"Sarah, really, it's okay. We don't mind."

"No, I will be fine."

I went to go sit with mom and dad. Mom asked me, "So, you took a nap?"

"Yeah I did. Sorry."

"What are you up to now?"

"Nothing, everybody is busy."

"Where is Jason?"

"With Kylie."

"And Danelle?"

"With Tommy on a walk."

"What is Brian up too?"

"Mykala is over."

"So, what else could you do?"

"I could go to the trailer and sleep some more."

"Sarah, didn't you just take a nap?"

"Yeah, but I don't have anything else to do."

"Well, I am sure you can think of something to do."

"I could go back to Tony's and do the dishes."

"I don't think so."

"James isn't there, so what's the big deal?"

"It's not that we don't want you with James. He is good to you, but you are very young and as far as Tony's you will have to find something else to do."

"Okay, I'll just go back to the trailer then."

Jason and Kylie walked in holding hands and were walking to our table. I got up, "I'm going to go."

As they got to the table Jason asked, "Can we join you?"

Dad of course encouraged them, "Yes, we can pull up another chair."

"I am leaving. You can take mine."

Jason spoke up, "Where are you going?"

I was irritated that everyone had someone except for me even though I wanted it that way. "I am going to call James and go to bed." I tried to smile politely, but it may have come across as snotty.

Kylie grabbed my arm to stop me, "You don't have to go."

I smiled at her, "Thanks, but I need more sleep and tomorrow is going to be a long day."

She did scare me only because I had seen her mad before. I walked out but I didn't want to be alone. I was afraid the sadness would consume me. I decided to go back to Tony's. At least I could stay busy and I could still be home before mom and dad, so they wouldn't know the difference.

I pulled into the back and walked into the kitchen. I noticed the dishes weren't even started. I hung James's dress shirt on the back of a chair by the desk and went to work."

"And what do you think you are doing little girl?"

I gasped, oh shit, "James?" as I turned to see him the tears were already welling up in my eyes.

"No. Sorry. I didn't mean to startle you."

It was Jake but he called me what James called me. He was confused by my despair. "Are you alright?"

"Yep." I turned back around and tried to keep washing the dishes. I was holding the tears back, but they were dripping into the water. I could hardly see. I just kept washing the same thing until I could see again. I heard the door flap and I knew he had left the room. I put one hand on the side of the sink to hold myself up and the other I tried to wipe the tears away as quickly as I could.

I felt a hand touch my shoulder and I lost it. I couldn't hole the tears back anymore. "Sarah, what are you doing?"

I knew the voice but I couldn't look at Tony. "If it's okay, I need to stay busy for awhile. I will stay out of the way."

"Sarah, are you okay?"

"Yep, just didn't want to be alone right now."

"Wash away. Do you want me to make you something?"

"Nope, I can't eat right now."

"Maybe, later than?"

"Yeah, that's fine."

I knew he walked back out because I heard the door flap again. I needed to get rid of the sadness. I knew I would be all right tomorrow if I could keep myself busy. I started with the dishes and then the pans. When they were all done I moved to the counter tops as I danced from one to the next. I was feeling a little better. It was like James was there, only busy working in the other room.

Tony walked in, "More dishes, sweetheart…Shit!"

I stopped and looked at him. What did I do wrong? "What?"

"My kitchen is beautiful again. I swear if James doesn't marry you…I will. In ten years of course."

I giggled and took the dishes from him. I washed them up and took a tray of glasses out to the bar. I knelt down to stack them. Jake walked over by me.

"Are you better now?"

"Yep." I looked up and grinned evilly. "See those girls down at the end?"

"Yes."

"They are loaded. Pay them some attention and you will get a huge tip."

He dropped his face to me, "Are you telling me to flirt with girls?"

"Yes. I am. Trust me. You may even get a phone number."

He was disgusted, "I don't want that. They are slutty."

I hit his leg, "You don't have to use the number, but the tip is great." I got up and stopped and raised my eyebrows at him then turned to go back to the kitchen. Next I was cleaning the shelves.

Tony walked in, "Sarah, get up now. You are doing too much. Let me make you something to eat."

"No, I'm staying busy."

Jake walked in. "Tony she needs protein, make her a steak."

"What?"

"Trust me. If you want her to come back tomorrow full of energy, make her a steak."

"You got it, Doc."

The look on Jake's face was disapproving but Tony started to make me a steak. Jake went back out to the bar.

I moved closer to Tony and talked quietly, "What did you mean 'Doc'?"

"Oh, that is someone else doctoring you and looking out for you so you feel better. That's all."

Tony was trying too hard to make it light, "What does he do at the hospital?"

"I don't know. You are going to eat this if I make it for you?"

"Of course, but I am a little hungry now."

The steak was ready but Tony was walking away from me to the bar. It smelt so good I was already drooling. Why was he walking away with it?

"Well, come on. You don't have to eat alone."

"Really?"

He was nodding, "It's not busy at all."

I stopped to grab a fork and knife and then followed out to the bar. I was salting it.

Tony scolded, "You might want to taste that before you put too much on it."

Jake moved down to this end of the bar, "Craving salt?"

I was confused about their reactions. I looked up at Jake to question what he said, "What do you mean?"

"I told you. You need iron and craving salt is a symptom."

I shook my head not believing his knowledge and took a huge bite. Ahu, this was so good. I took another bite and closed my eyes to enjoy it. I had never had a steak this good before. I took another bite because it was going down so easily.

Jake moved to Tony, "I told you. I wouldn't feed her burgers anymore."

I took another bite. I enjoyed this so much as each piece was melting in my mouth. It was medium rare, so it was very tender. I took another bite before I noticed they were watching me. I was embarrassed and cringed a little.

Tony was excited, "I did good?"

I was trying to finish the bite in my mouth to answer. Tony was a little worried when I was trying to swallow, but I got it down and let him know, "It is perfect."

I wasn't expecting Tony's reaction of clapping his hands and cheering, "Yeah."

I took another bite as I laughed at his happiness.

"You never finish anything I make, Sarah, and you have almost eaten all of it. Can I make you another one?"

"No! This is good." I took another bite. I was enjoying watching him over react.

"That is it. You are getting steak from now on."

I tried to talk with my mouth full, "Tony, no. They are too expensive. I like your burgers."

"No arguments from you. I can't wait to tell James you let me feed you."

I felt a jab to my heart immediately. James; how I miss my James. I felt the hurt coming back into my heart, and I was finding it hard to swallow again.

"Sarah, don't you dare stop eating. I'm sorry; I was so excited I didn't think when I said… Come on Sarah, you can do this. There are only three bites left."

I swallowed and slowly forced down the last three pieces but the hole in my heart was making it hard for me to breathe again. I could tell Jake was watching me with curiosity now.

"You're not going to get sick now?"

"No. It was great, Tony. I'll go finish the dishes and then I should go."

"Whatever you want, Sarah. I am sorry." I could see how concerned he was.

I wanted to let him know it wasn't his fault, so I smiled as much as I could, "I am fine."

He knew I wasn't, but I got up and went to the kitchen anyway. I could hear him and he was angry with himself for bringing up James and upsetting me. I tried to not get upset, but sometimes it was so hard.

I finished the dishes as I listened and danced to the music. I was working on blocking the sadness. I heard the door flap, "I'm almost done. I'm just rinsing the sink now. Then I am going to go."

"You don't have to explain to me."

Jake knew how to make me laugh without trying. It was like he was the only one that wasn't fussing over me. I turned to look at him. "I thought you were Tony."

"Nope. You did the entire cleanup?"

"Yeah. I needed to stay busy."

"I get why he treats you special, Sarah."

I swallowed. I did not want him to tell me he liked me. Please not that.

He was very frank, "Well, let's list them."

No, please no. I am not special at all. I am average and I love James.

"You put on a show for free. You drive his business up. You don't ask him for anything. You come here and clean up our mess, and you save him time that it would take him to do the work."

I was relieved. I chuckled to myself as I closed my eyes to enjoy this none hitting on compliment. I had to take advantage of the situation. "So, you won't tell me to use the other door anymore?"

He started to laugh, "No, you can use the back door."

I gave him a stern face, "Thanks. I'm glad you approve."

He shook his head. "Do you want to practice the other three dances? I don't have to clean the kitchen anymore, and Tony said it would be okay."

"Really?" He was making me so happy the tears were filling my eyes again.

He was a little put off, "Yeah, but none of that. It makes me nervous."

I grabbed a paper towel and wiped them away the best I could.

He walked away from me giving me the time to compose myself but said, "Come on then."

I followed him out of the kitchen and he was already on the stage. I looked at Tony to make sure he was okay with this. Tony gave me a nod, so I knew it was okay and I hurried to the dance floor.

"Sarah, I can't find the music. What did you do with it?"

I ran up to the stage and reached in front of him, "I put it right here."

I flipped it and looked at him. He was less than two feet and nothing. No feeling of it being weird or wrong. I smiled and took a step back.

He got up and moved to the dance floor. He had no ulterior motive. I chuckled and followed to the dance floor and we went through the dances. I couldn't believe he remembered them almost better than me. He did some other moves to jazz it up a little. I was hoping I could remember them tomorrow. We went through them a few times and by the third time I was feeling no pain. I knew it would be best if I left feeling good.

"I better go. I should try to be home before the parents get there."

"Yeah, I should get to bed too."

I was heading to say good bye to Tony, but I stopped and turned on Jake, "A few of us are going water skiing tomorrow around 11 am. Do you want to come?"

"Nope. I am working 'til 4 pm."

"Oh, okay then."

"I'll be here before people show up."

I shrugged and headed to Tony. I gave him the biggest hug and whispered in his ear. "I am okay, Tony."

He released the hug but held me out to look at me, "It will be steak tomorrow."

"You do know you don't have to do that."

"Yes, I know, Sarah, but you ate my food and you made me happy." He kissed my forehead and made sure I got to my car okay.

I was driving to the trailer and the heaviness was coming back. The hole was getting bigger and started to ache. I grabbed my chest wondering *'Can a sixteen year old girl have a heart attack?'* or *'Can a heart actually break in two?'*

28. Over Reacting

When I pulled in mom and dad's truck was already there, and so was Jason. Great, they were going to interrogate me on where I have been. There were a lot of cars here. I hope they weren't all out looking for me. *Shit*, it wasn't even 2 am yet. What are they all doing here?

When I got out of my car I noticed there was a bonfire in the back, so this wasn't about me. Thank goodness. I walked into the trailer. Of course mom, dad, and Jason all had to be inside waiting for me to show up. I cannot win today. I knew they were discussing me because they quit talking when I walked in.

My mom was furious with me, "Where did you go?"

"I went to Tony's and washed dishes. If you were worried why didn't you call me?"

"We did."

I lost my breath as I pulled out my phone and opened it to check. It was dead. "Shit."

"What is the excuse this time?"

I held it up and the tears were coming. Not because they were mad at me, but because if it was dead James couldn't call me either. I only let them look long enough to see I didn't have a screen at all. I walked away to the front bedroom and searched for my power cord. I plugged it in and tried to turn it on. It must be really dead because it still didn't come on even after plugging it in. I stood there holding it willing it to turn on.

Mom walked in, "I thought we told you no!"

I could hardly look at her. The tears were running down my face, "What is the big deal? James isn't here. I don't want to be with anyone else, so there is no reason to not trust me. I can't be bad if he isn't here."

"That is it. *You are not seeing him anymore!*"

"Oh, yes, I am! I don't care what anyone says. I will leave again if you forbid me to see him."

I heard the door to the trailer, "She's back?" I knew that was Kylie. Great, more people to be in my business.

"Sarah, how can you treat us this way?"

"What way? I love you, but please don't tell me I can't see him anymore. I will do whatever you want, but do not take him away from me. That is one thing I cannot take."

I heard Jason address Kylie in the front room, "Kylie, just go back outside. I will be there in a minute."

"Don't put her before me, Jason!" I could hear him pleading with her. "I'm not, it's just James asked me too, and you know I love you." I was surprised to hear him say that. He does love her, but I heard the door open and slam shut. Then the door opened again and I heard Jason, "Sorry, I have to go after her."

Mom was still yelling at me, "Why did you go back to Tony's after we said no?"

"I didn't want to be alone and I needed to stay busy. I miss James and sometimes my heart hurts so bad that I can't breathe. Tony lets me be busy and doesn't ask me a lot of questions. If I stay busy it's not so bad."

"Sarah, I think you are going too fast with James. You have your whole life ahead of you. I thought you were having fun going out with a bunch of guys. What about Matt, Brian, and Jason?"

I pointed outside like Jason was even a choice.

"But Sarah, you have so many choices, why are you making decisions now?"

"I am not making a decision now. We're not going to get married for two years."

"That is kind of making a decision."

"I really don't want to talk about this anymore. Can you call Tony and verify or something. I wasn't doing anything wrong."

"It was wrong because we already told you no!" She stormed out of the room and I fell to the floor grabbing a pillow to bury my face into. I held my phone hoping it would come on. I needed to talk to him so badly. He would have to give into me now. I would go live with him. I couldn't deal with life without him anymore. I knew I couldn't leave, it would ruin tomorrow and I had plans. I had to behave, but I wasn't happy here.

I heard the door again, "Hello, I am Clarissa, James's mother. Is Sarah okay?"

My dad wasn't happy and I could hear it in his voice, "Yes. She is just over reacting and trying to get her way."

"May I see her? James is worried. He hasn't been able to get through for the last couple of hours."

My heart leapt. I hurried to my feet and went around the corner of the door pleading as I looked at her. The tears were streaming down my face. I almost ran to her. She held me in her arms as she traced my face with her hand.

"Is it alright if we take a drive? She will have a better outlook on things when we get back. I promise you that."

"James is too old for her. We think maybe they need time apart."

Clarissa stayed calm and collected. She stated, "Well, obviously that is not working, because they are apart now. She will be better after I talk to her. Please allow her to come with me. It will not be long."

Dad was so angry and I knew I was hurting my mother by hugging and clinging to Clarissa, but she understood so much better than them, "Fine, but we better see improvements."

She guided me out the door and to her truck. I got in and she didn't say a word. She drove a short distance and picked up her phone. She pulled over to the side and stopped. She handed me the phone, so I got out of the truck, "James, I am so sorry. I didn't know my phone was dead."

"Oh, my sweet, Sarah, you had me so worried. You are hurting so bad right now. What is going on?"

"They told me I couldn't see you."

"Why?"

"Because I didn't listen to them and went back to Tony's. James, I couldn't be alone and Tony lets me do the dishes. He fed me a steak."

"How do you rank?"

"James, don't make me laugh. I just want you to be here. I try to stay busy, so I don't miss you as much. I have been pushing so hard that I can't even keep my eyes open at the end of the day, so it doesn't hurt so much."

"Slow down and tell me what happened?"

"After the dance was over, I was so tired I laid down in your room and took a nap."

"You were that tired you couldn't leave?"

"James, we're not discussing how I am doing. Anyway, I woke up late… it was almost 11 pm, but Tony talked to my mom and everything was okay. I went to Sherburn's and Danelle has a boyfriend now and they wanted to spend time together alone. Brian had a girl over, so I couldn't bug him either."

"Where was Jason?"

"Where he should be, James, with Kylie. It wasn't good for him to be around me all the time. I had to push him away, James."

"Okay, but I felt all this. The feeling I am getting is a lot worse."

"I went back to Tony's and did dishes. I didn't want to be alone."

"Sarah, that isn't why they said I couldn't see you any more."

"No, I screwed up. I told them that you weren't here, so there was no reason to not trust me, and that I only wanted to be with you."

"Sarah, you just admitted that you wanted to be with me. You know what they are thinking."

"James, I kind of threatened to run away too. I am so sorry, James. They were pushing and forbidding me to see you. I am not going to allow it. They don't have that right. I love you."

"Okay, its okay, Sarah. We will just have to take things slower. Let them see us together being good. No more hot nights for a while. We do have the rest of our lives. Don't get so upset. I am not going anywhere; I promise. How are you doing otherwise?"

"I still haven't gotten sick, but the getting tired real easily happened again."

"Okay. I know this is going to be hard, but you need to go back and agree with them on everything."

"*Except you, James.* I will not agree to not see you. I can't live without you. If you haven't noticed I have been deteriorating since you left."

"Do you really believe that?"

"Let's just say you can't plan any trips for longer than three weeks. I was pretty weak by then."

"I am making you sick?"

"No. I am making myself sick because I can't live without you."

"Sixteen more days, baby, sixteen more days, and I will kiss you till you are better, but in the mean time you need to follow the rules. Please, Sarah, bite your lip and do what you are told."

"Yes James, everything except for not seeing you."

Clarissa came around the truck, "James, call me later."

"I will, but what are you doing?"

I handed Clarissa the phone and ran to the back of her truck. It was the first time I threw up in 10 full days. I could hear her talking to James.

"Yes."

"I do believe she is getting worse."

"You know how she feels, you need to finish."

"Did you check out what I told you?"

"Then do it."

"I called my friend who is a Doctor and he will see her."

"Yes, but you need to hurry. I don't know if she can wait the two weeks."

I walked around the truck to face her, "I am better now, but I need to sleep." I crawled into her truck and curled up on the seat.

She got in, "Sarah, we need to discuss something."

I opened my eyes to pay attention to what she wanted to say.

"If you want them to respect you and your opinions you have to use more self control. Agree with them and use what they say as an excuse to why you are doing what you're doing. Don't disrespect them. They do love you and want to protect you as much as James does."

"Okay."

"When we get back you will need to be on your best behavior. Can you promise me that?"

"Yes." I closed my eyes.

Someone was picking me up from the truck, "James?" I nuzzled into his neck.

"NO, Sarah, it's Jason."

I stopped nuzzling and I heard Clarissa trying to get my attention as I was being carried in, "Sarah, Sarah!"

I opened my eyes to look at her, but could hardly keep them open. She was trying again, "Sarah, I need you to promise me something."

I opened my eyes again looking at her as she cupped my face with her hands, "James loves you and wants you to wait until you are 18. Carl waited three years for me. James loves you and wants you to wait too. So, promise me you will try to do that?"

"I will." I closed my eyes again.

I heard her but she wasn't talking to me anymore, "Jason, have Kylie help you with her to the room." I heard her address my mom and dad again, "James does want her to follow your rules. He knows you love her and want to protect her. She is still young and over reacts to things."

I could hear the anger in my dad's voice, "I love your Son, like he was my own, but when it comes to Sarah, she makes bad choices because of him."

"Did you call Tony and check her story out?"

"It doesn't matter. She did not listen to us."

"Call Tony. You will see she wasn't doing anything bad. With her being so sick you might want to pick your battles."

"So sick?"

"She hasn't told you all of it? I think maybe you should sit down. She has been handling everything on her own because she knows you work so hard and she didn't want to worry you."

I was drifting back out as Jason lowered me to the bed. Kylie sat down next to me on the bed. I reached over her lap for my phone, "James." She grabbed the phone for me and put it in my hand. I hugged her waist, "You two look good together when you're not mad." I rolled over and put the phone to my lips. I heard them a little.

"She really loves James?"

"I told you. That is the only reason he asked and you know I owed him that. Remember?"

"So, what is wrong with her?"

"They don't know. Come on, let's let her sleep."

I worked up enough energy to say, "Close the door; James may call." I was holding up my phone.

I closed my eyes waiting for his call, but I drifted to sleep.

It must have been awhile because I felt a little rested when he finally called.

"James."

"Your phone is working?"

"It's plugged in. I am so sorry I worried you."

"For what, my sweet?"

"Everything, I make you miserable."

"You give me life."

"I think your mom told them everything about how sick I have been. James, I have been so good 'til tonight."

"Sarah, don't think about it. It will be fine." I felt his face next to mine, "I am here. You can sleep now."

"But you just called. I want to hear your voice."

"I know, Sarah, but your body heals better while you sleep. I need you to make it 'til I can get there."

"James, please."

"I will stay until you are sleeping."

"I love you."

"And I love you more than you know.

I could feel his hand trace over my face, and his warm sweet breath was at my ear. It was easier to fall asleep with him holding me.

29. Restrictions Not Restricting

Today was glorious because it was day 33: Just over two weeks and my sweet James will be home. I put my phone down and got my note.

I will find you when you are lost,
I will cheer you when you are sad,
I will warm you when you are chilled,
I will marry you when you are ready,
I love you more than you know,

James

I smelled the note to see if his scent lingered, but there was nothing there. I didn't want to face the wrath from last night, but I had to go to the bathroom. I opened the door quietly and looked to the back room. They were sleeping. I tiptoed out to the living room. Jason and Kylie were on the couch together. I tried to pass them as quietly as possible.

Kylie grabbed my hand, "Where are you going?"

"I have to go to the bathroom."

"Do you want me to go with you?"

I reassured her it was okay, "No, I slept so I feel better. Stay with Jason because he seems happy." I noticed he had a smile on his face.

I went to the bathroom in the outhouse. I hated going out here, because of the bug thing. I came out stretching.

"Clarissa told them everything, Sarah."

I rolled my eyes, "There really isn't that much to tell them. Mom knew I was getting sick and I hadn't in ten days. She knew I was sleeping a lot. She knew I was going to the Doctors. The only thing she didn't know about was the cancer test and that was negative. I only told them portions so they wouldn't worry so much."

"Are you hungry?"

"Yes, I'm starving. I did get sick when I was with Clarissa last night, so my stomach is empty."

"You got sick last night?"

"I didn't hide it. Clarissa knows. She had to talk to James when it happened."

"So, James knows too?"

"Yes."

"What do you want to eat?"

"Someone told me that with them taking so much blood that my iron levels could be down and that is what was making me weak. So, steak and eggs would probably be good."

"Okay, right on that one."

"You asked." We were walking back to the trailer and he put his arm around my shoulder. I shrugged him off.

"Thanks for dealing with Kylie last night."

"As long as she doesn't want to kill me; I am okay with her."

He laughed, "And I'm sorry that you had to see that yesterday."

"Jason, does she make you happy? I mean I saw the smile on your face this morning."

He was embarrassed and tried to tease me a little, "Well, I was kind of hot from...you know."

I couldn't believe he said that, so I hit him in the arm, "Stop that!"

He laughed and rubbed his arm at the same time. We walked in and I sat by Kylie on the couch and leaned into her, "You shouldn't have woken him."

"I was told to not leave you alone."

"But I didn't want his help. He is yours!"

She coddled me a little, "You're not so bad when I don't have to fight you for him."

"I wouldn't have fought you. I knew I would lose that one. Plus, I didn't know about you when I went fishing with him that day."

"I know that now. I was really jealous."

"I would have been too, if it would have been James doing that."

She turned to look at Jason in the kitchen. I saw that look in her eye. "Do you love him?"

She turned back to me, "I always have, but we do stupid stuff that…" Her face had a smirk, "Are you okay to help with breakfast?"

She didn't answer my question, "Um, if you don't mind, I think I will sit here awhile."

She touched my hand, "We'll get you when it's ready."

"Hey Kylie, how angry are my mom and dad at me?"

"I think they are more worried than anything. Clarissa didn't sugar coat anything."

"Great! Now, I won't get to do anything."

She was enjoying my misery, I think. She went to the kitchen to help Jason and they were very playful. I was happy for both of them. I slowly lay down and closed my eyes. I must have been still worn out because I fell back to sleep.

"Sarah, food is ready." I sat up and still felt okay. I stumbled to the table. Mom and dad were already sitting at the table, but I moved around it to squeeze into the corner. I was trying to stay calm, and I took a deep breath and swallowed a couple of times. I avoided everyone's looks by eating. I knew they weren't going to be pleasant.

Okay, here it goes, "So, am I going to be allowed to do anything?"

"Don't start, Sarah." I guess I found out Dad was still angry with me.

I ate a little more and decided to try again, "Did you call Tony to check on me last night?"

Dad looked at me, and I could feel the anger. My eyes were wide open looking back at him waiting for his reply, "You don't stop do you?"

Mom tried to ease the situation, "Yes, we did. But Sarah, first of all we told you *no* and you didn't listen to us. Second of all, you need to let someone know where you are at *all* times. Especially now, since we don't know what is wrong with you."

I was trying to hold back my grin. I knew this was going better than I had planned. "Okay. I know I screwed up, but my phone is completely charged now. I can call you every minute and give you updates."

"What are you thinking?" Dad was easing up. Oh, yeah, this is going good.

I took a deep breath. I was getting up the nerve to ask, "Well, I know that the last place you want me to go is Tony's, but that helps his business and he spent money on advertising. It's for him more than me."

"You can stop right there!" Great, that wasn't what I was expecting. I thought for sure he was going to flatly refuse. "Jason is working and Kylie said she would go too. So, we already decided you can do that, but you will come back as soon as it's over."

I pleaded, "But Tony usually feeds me. Can't I stay and eat with him?"

Dad turned to Jason, "What time will you be done?"

"I don't think I have to help clean up, so about 10 pm."

Jason was smiling as he took his next bite. I knew he was helping me buy a little time. I went back to eating myself to not give anything away.

"If you leave when Jason is done you will be back here by 10:30!"

"Okay."

I wasn't going to push anymore. I got what I wanted out of the deal. I finished eating and got up putting my plate in the sink. I poured a glass of water to brush my teeth with and went to the bathroom. After brushing I walked back out and put the rest of my stuff away walking to the first bedroom.

Dad was on his toes, "Where do you think you're going?"

"Back to bed, I really didn't want anything else."

"You're not going to push for anything else?"

"Nope, that was the only thing that was important to me."

"What about waterskiing or tubing?"

"Brian can take the boat without me, and I am just happy to go to Tony's tonight." I continued to walk away.

Dad stopped me, "How are you feeling today?"

He actually sounded worried, so I turned to him, "All better. I slept."

"Do you need more sleep?"

"No, not really, I just didn't want to push my luck."

He eased and caved, "You can go down to Sherburn's if you would like, but don't get so crazy."

"Really?"

"Yes…go."

I ran to him and hugged him tight, "Thank you." Then I ran to the bedroom to get changed. I put on my suit with only a cover up over the top. I couldn't believe I had restrictions that weren't restricting at all. I wouldn't go for very long. I didn't want to be weak tonight. It was still early enough that I could take a nap before going to Tony's. I walked out with my bag and grabbed carrots and grapes and turned to look at them all watching me. "Thanks. You do know I am not going to break? I am okay most of the time."

Dad stood up and hugged me like I was leaving forever.

"Dad, I feel good. Tony fed me steak last night, big on the protein thing."

"Sarah, you have to tell someone where you are all the time, *please*."

"I will. My phone is charged today."

I hurried to my car. I didn't want them to change their minds. I was out free, clear, and on my way to Sherburn's.

It was still pretty quiet at Sherburn's, but I found Laura in the bar cleaning and stocking things.

"Where's Danelle?"

"Hey, how are you doing today?"

"Great. It's amazing what sleep does."

She breathed a laugh, "She's still sleeping."

"Can she go swimming and tubing with me if I can get her up?"

"Yes."

I was on a roll, so I thought I would ask, "Can she go to Tony's with me tonight?"

The way she looked at me, I knew she was thinking about it, "What time will you be back?"

"I have to be back here by 10:30 pm."

"If she goes she will have to ride with Brian. He will be back by 8:30 pm."

"That's good enough for me." I was giddy, "Can I go wake her?"

"Good luck with that. She was up late."

I sprinted into the back. Today was starting way better than I was hoping for. I looked for her in the house where there was a living room and a bedroom, but no one was there. I went back through the kitchen and up the stairs. Danelle was sleeping on the couch and Brian was sleeping on a mattress. They shared this room? Reminder for myself; no sleep over's with Danelle at her house. I woke Danelle, "It's time to get up and go swimming with me."

"Sarah, it is too early."

"I only have 'til 1 pm, then I have to take a nap, so I have energy for tonight."

"Fine, I will get up." She slowly got up and grabbed some stuff and headed down to the bathroom.

I looked at Brian. How was I going to get him up with as much distance as I could? I went to the foot of the mattress and started jumping on it a little, "Brian, time to get up and play."

He didn't move. I jumped a little closer to him. There wasn't much give in the mattress. He still didn't move. I nudged him with my foot, "Brian, let's go water skiing. Get up."

It came so swiftly, he knocked me off my feet and pulled me into him. I was almost underneath him.

"Brian!" I was trying to push myself free. "Brian, get off me. Let me up."

He pulled me closer and nuzzled into my neck and started kissing me there.

"Brian, I'm Sarah. You need to stop now."

He opened his eyes and pushed me away covering himself with the sheet. He was…shit…nude.

"Sarah, shit, I'm sorry. I mean…"

I got up and avoided his eyes, "I think I will wait outside."

I walked down the stairs. I was a little freaked out. That was bad.

Another reminder to myself, don't wake Brian again. I went out to the dock to wait for them. I took off my cover up and dove into the water. It was refreshing. They were taking a long time, so I got out and moved to the bench. I was enjoying the peacefulness of the lake and leaned back closing my eyes.

"Sarah?"

I sat up and knew it was Brian.

"Where is Danelle?"

"I asked her to wait a little bit. I have to…" he was hesitant as he moved to sit down next to me.

I knew he was worried that I was upset with him again, so I was going to try and ease the tension, "You know it was my fault. I should have left you sleep."

He didn't say anything for a while and then he finally turned to me, "What are you thinking?"

"Honestly?"

He nodded.

"Why were you sleeping in the nude? Danelle was in the same room?"

"I heard you stopped by last night."

"Are you avoiding my question?"

He shook his head, "No, actually, I'm trying to explain."

"O-k-a-y?"

"You stopped last night and Mykala was here…"

I was confused at his leading into explaining, but when he raised his eyebrows I got it. Shit, they did it already. I turned away and huffed looking at the lake. I wondered, *am I a freak or what?*

He was pleading with me, "I pushed her away, Sarah. The harder I pushed the more aggressive she got and…"

I got up not paying attention to what he was saying, "Let's go water skiing or tubing. Is there anyone else coming?" I glanced back at him and he was miserable, "It's none of my business, Brian. You don't have to tell me anything."

He reached for my hand, "Sarah, you were the voice in my head. It kept telling me no, and I tried to push her away. Frankly, Sarah, I don't know how you do it. She was attacking me and did things I couldn't turn down. I was weak and I..."

"Brian, don't. I just can't believe you would do that with her in the room."

"What?"

"Danelle, she sleeps in the same room as you. That's not right."

"Mykala was gone and I was sleeping before she even came up, Sarah."

"But you were sleeping in the nude. She is your sister and you share the room. She shouldn't see you like that."

"So, you're more upset about that than about Mykala?"

"Brian that is what you wanted, right? To be with her and if that is what you wanted then why would I be mad? You really like her, right? Like maybe even love her?"

"I don't know if I would say that."

"I think I should get Danelle and you should get Mykala and her friends to come tubing."

"Sarah, you were in my head the whole time."

"If you don't want to be a jerk you should spend time with her, especially after that. I know that is what I would want." I glared at him, "I would want to know that it meant something to you."

I was thinking of how wonderful and attentive James was after we would try, or get too hot. Why was my James so patient with me? I sat back down. I didn't realize that thinking about him was causing the heaviness to come back and it was getting harder to breath.

"Sarah, are you okay?"

"Yeah, I'm just thinking about something. It's really hard for me to think or talk about all this, so can we get some more people. I really need to stay busy."

"One more question?"

I was pleading for him to not talk about what I was avoiding to think about.

"Sarah, you love, James. You tell me all the time your heart belongs to him."

"Yes, but Brian I can't talk about this." The tears were welling up in my eyes. I could hardly swallow and I was almost gasping for air.

"Honestly, have you made love to him?"

"Yes, but no if you mean did we *do it*." I took my towel and wiped my face. I held it there to not reveal my face again.

"Sarah, that doesn't make since."

I tried to speak, but of course it came out muffled, "He won't do it. He is afraid he will hurt me, so we settle for something less. But I want to be with him that way, so we have been working up to it. He is afraid I will hate him if he hurts me."

"There is that possibility. I think I have lost at least four girls I was completely whipped over for doing it too soon."

I lowered the towel to see his face. I loved James and I never wanted it to end.

"Sarah, it does sound like he loves you, if it makes you feel any better, but don't tempt him if you're not ready. It is very hard to turn it down even if you love the person. Look at me, I can't walk away from it or stop. I just hope it wasn't too early for Mykala. I guess we'll find out today."

I slowly lowered the towel from my face, "She is coming?"

"I hope so."

I was excited for him, "Be very attentive. I know I love that." My mind wandered off to my James. "I like when he kisses my hands, and holds me close to him. Then he kisses my cheek so soft and traces my face with his fingers." I closed my eyes to enjoy the thought.

"We can stop talking about it, or I will get really hot right now."

"*Brian*! That is so wrong."

"I am a guy and you're saying things that…"

I could hear footsteps coming down the dock, so I turned to see who it was.

Danelle was on her way to us, "Is it a good time yet? I took a couple of phone calls and people are on their way."

"Yep, you have perfect timing." I was glad our conversation was over for now.

Brian got up and went into the boat to get everything ready. I got in the boat too. We got in each other's way and avoided touching in anyway.

Danelle noticed, "Are you *two* okay?"

We both stopped and turned to each other and busted out laughing, "Yeah, we're fine. Was *Mykala* one of those phone calls?"

"Yeah."

I reminded Brian in a scolding way, "Be *very* attentive."

"I will. Stop telling me what to do."

"Well, it works. Remember the *voice* in your head?"

He shook his head in disbelief that I would bring that up again.

Tommy came first and got in the boat with me. He came and sat down next to me, so I couldn't help myself, "Are you behaving with Danelle? Or do I need to put my partner down?"

He was embarrassed by my comment. He glanced at Danelle, "I like that she wants to spend time with me."

He was being sweet, but I needed to know how advanced this guy was. "Are you a virgin, cuz I am?" I was hoping with my confession he would open up to me.

He was aghast, "You are so blunt sometimes, Sarah. Why would you ask me that?"

"Because if you are then I know you will take things slow. She is only 15 years old."

The color in his face changed twice, to two different shades of red. I was happy with that as my answer. "I hope that means you are."

He nodded.

"That's good enough for me." I didn't want to embarrass him anymore than I had already, so I didn't bug him about it.

Mykala and a few other girls showed up next. I ran through their names, so I could remember them. Tammy, Pam, and …shit I couldn't remember the other one's name.

I wanted to get things rolling, "Who's first?"

Of course, Brian had to be. I pulled Mykala in to spot for him. She wasn't watching as carefully as I wanted her to. We circled once and he dropped a ski. She was biting her nails. I was getting disgusted about her non interest in the matter at hand, "Hey, you need to watch him carefully because we're coming to a jump."

She watched him for a brief moment and then went back to not watching. I was expecting more than this. I pulled out so he wouldn't get another jump right away. I noticed she was really looking nervous, "Hey, are you okay?"

She raised her face to me but was giving me a funny look. Shit I wasn't expecting this reaction. I turned into another jump and looked at her, "Do me a favor and watch him carefully this time; there is another jump coming up."

She watched only long enough for him to get through the jump. I need to get him in this boat fast for her. She was having doubts. I took him jump over jump and he was not dumping at all. I finally gave up trying to dump him and fake that something was wrong with the boat. I slowed it down and as Brian went down I yelled to him, "Something is wrong. You need to come here. I don't know what it is."

He started to pull himself to the boat with the rope. I knew I only had a couple of seconds and went back to Mykala, "He is going to get in here any second. What is wrong?"

She looked up to me with the saddest puppy eyes, "We did it last night. I don't know if it was right."

"I talked to him this morning and he does really care about you, if that makes you feel any better."

I could see the fear in her face. I went back to help pull him in. He handed me the ski, and I leaned over the boat trying to talk to him quietly, "She needs attention."

He was confused, "What?"

"She is feeling insecure. You need to make her feel good about last night."

He handed me the rope, and I put it in a safe place at the back of the boat. I leaned back over to grab his hand to pull him in.

"What did she say?"

I glared at him, "Nothing, I can see it. Treat her special, sweet, charm her. She needs it right now." I pulled him in the boat.

He went back to the motor and fiddled around a little, "The oil just got disconnected. It's okay."

He came up to where she was sitting. He grabbed her hands and looked into her eyes but spoke to me, "Sarah, can you take us for a little ride on the way in?"

"Yep."

I turned to face the front and started the boat. I went really slowly around the shore line. I tried to peak over my shoulder but Brian scolded, "Sarah, face forward, please."

I giggled and continued to go slow. We were getting closer, so I felt I needed to warn them, "Guys, we're getting close to the dock." I took a quick glance and he was being attentive. At least he listens well. As we approached the dock I noticed Pat standing there. I hadn't seen or heard from him in awhile. I tossed him the rope and he helped pull us in and tied it to the dock. I got out and gave him a huge hug. "How are you? Where have you been? What have you been up too? You haven't called forever!"

He stood there in awe until he could get out, "Family problems."

I was so happy to see him, "Better now?"

"Not really, but I get a break today. You look thin. What's happened to you? There is nothing left!"

"I have been a little sick myself."

"Are you better?"

I grinned, "Not yet, but I will be in two weeks."

He was confused, but he didn't know about my James being gone.

I smiled, "Who's next?"

Two of the girls wanted to tube together. I looked around to see who could spot for us. Brian and Mykala were cozy in the water. Danelle and Tommy were floating around on tubes. I finally got back to Pat and one of the girls, "You two have to spot for me."

They both got in. I took them for the safest fast ride I could give them and they were screaming. "Pat this is..." I looked at her for her name.

"Patty."

"Patty this is Pat." We all started laughing hysterically. We finally got back to the dock and I saw Jason and Kylie coming down the dock.

I pulled up to it, "Did you guys want to go?"

Jason looked at Kylie smiling and then back at me, "We are checking on you."

I got out of the boat, "I am fine. What time is it?"

Jason shook his head, "You were supposed to go rest a half hour ago."

I rushed back to the boat and grabbed my bag and my phone, "Hey Brian, I have to go. If they want to go you will have to drive them."

He yelled out, "Where are you going?"

I was heading down the dock, "I have to rest before tonight."

Pat tried to stop me, "You are really sick?"

"Kind of." I gave him the 'sorry I have to go' look and took off to walk in front of Jason and Kylie.

Jason noticed what was going on at the lake, "You have gotten to be a little match maker."

I turned around, "You two are happy, right?"

He pulled Kylie closer to him.

"Thanks for coming and getting me." I hurried to my car.

"Sarah, we'll see you there."

"Okay."

I hurried into the trailer. When I got there mom and dad were stressed with worry. I wanted to ease the tension.

"Thanks for sending Jason and Kylie. I lost track of time and I need a nap before tonight."

"What time did you want to get up?"

"By 2:30 pm. I want to get cleaned up before tonight."

"We were going into town. Can you get yourself up?"

"Yeah, no problem."

I went into the bedroom and then I heard them leave. I started packing my stuff for tonight. I had an idea. I was going to take a nap in James's bed at Tony's. I was out the door quickly.

I pulled into Tony's and of course I checked in with him. "Tony, can you make sure I am up by 3:30 pm so I can get ready?"

"Do your mom and dad know where you are?"

"Not really, but they went into town and they knew I wanted to be her by 3:30 pm."

"I am not covering for you."

"Okay, you won't have to."

I went up stairs and set the alarm for 3:30 pm and closed my eyes curling up with the pillows around me. I was going to get real rest in this bed.

30. A Little Temperature

I woke to knocking on the door, but I was so tired I couldn't get up. The door was opening, but I couldn't open my eyes.

"Sarah?"

The door opened more.

"Are you decent?"

I made no attempt to get up or open my eyes, "Yeah, my alarm hasn't gone off yet. Let me sleep till then."

I heard footsteps coming towards me, "Sarah, you have it set for am, not pm."

"Oh shit." I sat up really fast. The dizziness took over and I thought I was going to be sick. I lay back down immediately, but realized it was Jake. He wasn't supposed to be here 'till 5 o'clock. Was it 5 pm now? Shit, I can't go down like this.

He walked over to the bed, "It's only 3:40 pm, but we didn't hear the alarm or you walking around, so Tony sent me up here. You're not doing well?"

"I'll be fine. I just need to get up slower."

He walked over to me and sat on the bed grabbing my wrist. He put two fingers on it and looked at his watch.

"What are you doing?"

"I'm checking your pulse. Quiet please."

I laid there and closed my eyes. I felt him touch my forehead. I opened my eyes, "What are you doing now?"

He gave me a disapproving look, "You have a temperature."

"Yeah, I have been warm a lot lately."

"No. I mean its pretty high." He walked over and grabbed something from the cupboard bringing it back to me. It was a thermometer to take my temp, and I was refusing.

"Open up or I'm telling Tony."

I opened my mouth, so he could take my temperature. I moved to sit up.

"No. Not yet. Wait until I find out how high it is."

I lay back down but tried to talk, "What do you do at the hospital?"

"Take temperatures and pulses." He smiled at me with a disapproving look.

"Like a nurse or something? Aren't you kind of young for that?"

"Yes, something like that. Now, shhhh, or I will make you do it again.

I laid there impatient because I needed to get ready. The dizziness was gone, or at least I thought it would be. I couldn't handle it anymore, "You weren't supposed to be here until 5 pm."

"I got done early... shhh."

I was tapping my feet and rapping my fingers on the bed.

"That is not going to help."

I stopped, but I had to get moving. It beeped three times, so I took it out of my mouth and sat up looking at it, "See, only 100." I stood up and I was okay now. I felt well rested.

He took it from me to evaluate it, "They really can't figure out what it is; with all the testing they have done?"

"Nope, and if you wouldn't mind I need to get ready."

"Can I try one thing?"

I didn't even know him, and I didn't need any more drama, "What?"

"It's just a hunch. Lay back down, it will only take a second and then I will leave."

"You will leave me alone to get ready?"

He was a little put off, "Yes."

I lay back down, but was leery of what he was going to do.

"Does your stomach hurt at all?"

"Only when I get sick."

He took both his hands and placed them on my stomach, pushing and moving them around. He wasn't even looking at me, so I didn't feel threatened by this. You could tell he was thinking as he felt around for something.

"Does it hurt if I push right…"

I felt it, maybe discomfort, but not painful.

"Not really." He was pushing the spot that James said it was, "Why, what is there?"

"Nothing, I was just curious." He put out his hand to help me sit up, "You may want to take a cool shower. It will help with the fever."

He started walking to the door, and I couldn't help myself, "What were you looking for?"

"Nothing, I thought maybe it was something, but it wasn't that."

He was really confusing. As he walked out the door he looked back at me, "You're going to get ready? Can you make it down by yourself, or do I need to come back?"

"Nope, I feel fine. I will make it on my own."

I took his suggestion because he was already right about the protein thing. I got ready in one of my new shirts that was loose but flattering, and then I put on a pair of jeans. If I had to be carried in a skirt it wouldn't be good. I stopped to see myself in the mirror. Well, definitely not as good as yesterday, but it would do. It was only 4:30 pm, so I knew Sandy and Kate would be there. I took a deep breath and went down and walked through the kitchen.

"Hey, you're supposed to use the other door,"

I turned to Jake. He had a funny grin on his face.

"You are trying to be funny?"

"How are you now that you've showered?"

"Great."

I went straight to the stage and started to play music. Sandy and Kate were there, so we started with the songs from Friday. They helped make me feel so comfortable to do this. I played it again as people were arriving. Brian was there with Mykala, but I didn't see Danelle. I searched everywhere and finally found her in the back with Tommy. He was trying to get her to dance, but she didn't like dancing much. That was probably the biggest difference between Danelle and me. I went and set up the music, so it would play three songs in a row. I went back out to dance with Kate and Sandy. I was having so much fun. When it was close to one hour, I announced a ten minute break for refreshments. I added this because it helped a lot with people buying stuff. Tony gave me thumbs up. I noticed Jake was holding up a glass for me, so I nodded, but he got really busy after I called a break. He shrugged his shoulders, so I would see he wasn't going to bring it to me. My plan for the next training was to have Jake out, so I had to do it right before the next break. We did the first training right when we started up and it went well. I continued to play music. Everyone was having fun including me. I really didn't feel tired at all, and I was having a blast. Brian even came and danced with me.

He was so close I whispered in his ear, "You did really well."

"I swear I hear you in my head all the time now."

"She is very happy."

"Because of you."

"I only told you what I would have wanted. You did the work."

He pulled me close to hug me, "Thank you. If you ever decide that…"

"Brian, I won't."

He let go of me and worked his way back to Mykala. I tried to find Jason and Kylie. They were supposed to be here. I laughed with a sigh realizing they must be preoccupied. She was a lot nicer when she wasn't going to kill me. It was almost time for the next training. I was trying to get Tony's and Jake's attention. Tony nodded, so I knew it would be a good time for Jake to come out. I got on stage and announced the next training.

"Okay ladies, who wants more of what we got a sweet taste of last night?"

The roar of the crowd was amazing.

"Who wants our hot new bartender to come out here?"

The cheering got louder. I was laughing as I saw Jake shaking his head, but he had a great big grin on his face.

"I think if you ladies cheer louder he will come over the bar for you."

They were all screaming. I gestured for him to come up, "Are you going to give them what they want, Jake?"

He came over the bar in one leap. He moved to the middle of the dance floor, and I started the music, "Come on ladies, he doesn't want to dance by himself."

That worked. They all wanted to be close to him. He put his finger up curling it for me to come out there. I shook my head and announced, "They want you."

He did it again and I went out to the dance floor. He had already started the moves, so I stayed behind him doing them too. He grabbed me and pushed me in front of him. I shook my head no, but he didn't give me a choice. We were dancing, laughing, and having so much fun. The song was coming to an end, so I ran back to the stage.

"Ladies, how about one more time before we take a break?"

The cheering was unreal. I replayed the song and went back out and stayed further back from Jake. I wanted him to enjoy himself. That was what this was all about, people having fun, and I was enjoying myself watching him. The girls were all over him, but he kept his distance. He did look like he was having fun. The song was almost over again, so I ran up to the stage.

"Okay, okay. Sorry, ladies, he has to go back to work."

The girls were all booing. I was finding this very funny. He waved at everyone on the dance floor and went back to the bar as I said, "If you want to see him more, you can get your orders from him. We're taking another ten minute break.

I was happy and still felt great. Maybe yesterday I did too much. I walked up to the bar as Tony made his way to me, "I like it, I like it, I like it. Sarah, you are so special."

I smiled at him.

"Did you want something to drink?"

I gave him a playful smile, "I thought you said no drinking?"

He laughed, "You are better today!"

"Yep."

He went to get me a soda and set it in front of me. I took a couple of sips and went back to the stage and set it to play a few songs in a row again. I went out to dance and felt so good to not think about being sick or weak.

When there was only a half hour left, I asked everyone, "Do you guys want one more new dance?"

The cheering was loud again. I put in the last one and went out between Kate and Sandy. They did the whole dance with me. They were so great. I loved that I had people that wanted me there. After going through it, I put on other music. Kate and Sandy continued with the last dance over and over again. Pretty soon almost everybody was on the dance floor doing this one. Even Danelle and Tommy were trying it. I went out to the back letting the system play three songs in a row again. I heard Tony ring the bell. I made my way to the stage as the last song played out.

I didn't want it to end either, but it was over, "Okay guys, that's it for today, but check to see if we will be here next week. Will everyone be here?"

The cheering was almost as loud as it was for Jake. I was smiling from ear to ear.

"If you want me back next weekend, we have fifteen minutes to clear out. So, help me out and vacate as soon as possible."

I turned up the lights and shut everything down. I walked to the bar and sat down.

Jake came over right away, "Are you still doing okay?"

I gave him a great big smile, "Great."

Tony came out from the kitchen, "Your steak will be ready in a couple."

"Hey, Tony, can I buy Sandy and Kate something? They have helped me so much."

"It's on me."

"No, Tony, please I can pay you for it."

"Not on my shift. Jake, will you see what they want?"

He walked down to them, and they both looked at me and said a voiceless 'thank you'. I could read their lips fairly easily. I smiled back and mouthed, "No, thank you." They really did make it easier for me. Tony came out with my steak, and Jake came to tell him what the ladies would like. It wasn't much, so I felt better about that. I started to eat my steak and it was so good. The adrenaline was wearing off and I was getting tired. I propped myself up on the bar with one hand leaning into it, while I was trying to eat my steak with my other hand.

Tony put his arm around me, "Dishes tonight?"

"I can't. I have to leave by 10 pm. Did Jason show up?"

"He's in the back, and Kylie is with him."

"Good."

"You're not going to run are you?"

"Nope, we have an understanding now." I felt myself nod off a little, and the sleepiness was overwhelming.

"Sarah, honey, are you okay?"

"Yep, I'm getting tired. Can I lay down upstairs for awhile? Will you wake me so I can leave by 10 pm?" I felt myself almost fall off my hand that was propping me.

"Sarah?"

I opened my eyes and blinked a few times trying to brush it off. I heard Tony say, 'Jake' with fear in his voice.

"Tony, I'm fine. I just need to rest."

I felt Jake pick me up and was walking me out of the bar. We were in the kitchen when I heard him yell at Jason, "If you were supposed to be watching her, you should have been doing a better job."

I was struggling, "Jake, he is with Kylie, so be nice."

"Shhh… Sarah sleep. I will bring you upstairs."

I couldn't stay awake anymore.

31. A Little Magic

Jake:

I was totally pissed off. I thought all these people cared about her, but they are letting her get sicker by the day. They are all standing by letting her get worse. Jason was behind me following me up the stairs. I didn't even want him to follow. She was light as a feather. I tried to open the door; shit, she must have locked it. I had to ask for his help.

I turned, "She locked the door. Check her pockets."

"I can't"

"Jason, I can't do it, or I will drop her. You have to get the keys."

Jason's girlfriend came from behind him, "I will."

I tried to stretch Sarah out so she could get in her pocket easier, but she was holding tighter to me. She was so pale, so fragile, and her skin was shallow. Kylie found the keys and opened the door for me. I laid her on the bed.

"Sarah, let me check your pulse."

She gave me her arm. She didn't pass out, she is just that tired. Her pulse was slightly elevated.

"Jason, Kylie, get some towels and wet them down with cold water. We need to get her temperature down."

I was going through this in my mind. I really needed to take her to the hospital. I was torn on what to do. I wasn't any better than them if I just let her deteriorate like this. I was here to help her. I touched her forehead and it was burning up. I wiped the hair from her face. She needed more than a couple of cool towels on her arms and forehead.

"Guys, we need to get more clothes off of her. We need to get her temperature down right now."

I looked at them and they both looked at me like I was crazy.

"What does James have for clothes here?"

They both still didn't move. I was getting frustrated with them so I got up and started going through his drawers. I found some boxers that might work, and a large T-shirt. I grabbed them and put them on the bed.

"I am going to take her pants off and you guys put the boxers on. We can put cold towels on her legs."

I noticed the fear on Jason's face, "I have to leave." He turned and walked out. Kylie was going to follow him.

"Kylie, please, I need help. Can you please stay and help me?"

She stayed.

"You need to unbutton and unzip her jeans and then I will pull them from the bottom. You need to help her put the boxers on her, okay?"

She looked at me not trusting me.

"It wouldn't be right if I did it."

She nodded and undid them. I pulled from the bottom and turned away. I left the room to grab more towels and wet them while Kylie took care of her.

"Kylie, do you have them on?"

"Almost, um...Yeah."

I walked out with the towels and laid them on her legs. I looked at Kylie, "Okay, are you ready for the next one."

I think she was in shock because she just stared at me.

"I am going to hold her up, and you need to change her shirt."

I sat down on the bed and lifted her, so she was facing away from me. I could hold her up in front of me with my hands on her shoulders under her shirt so Kylie could take it off. I kept my eyes on Kylie. She pulled the one off and put on the t-shirt. I laid her back down and went in the bathroom for more towels. I placed one on her stomach, her neck, arms, and one on her head.

"Sarah, can you hear me?"

"I need to sleep, James."

I looked at Kylie and smiled because she was responding, "Thank you. I will get Jason now. I need to make a phone call."

I walked out and Jason was standing on the landing. I was disgusted with him, "Can you go in and keep the cold rags going and help Kylie? I need to make a phone call."

He was full of remorse and walked by me inside.

I called Clarissa.

"Jake, what is it?"

"Sarah! She is doing okay right now, but she wore herself out and almost fell asleep at the bar tonight. I had to carry her to James's room. We had to undress her to get her cooled down. Her temperature was very high. What do you want me to do?"

"I am on my way."

I hung up the phone and walked back in and looked at Jason and Kylie. They were both sitting there looking at her.

"You two can leave now. I will take care of her."

Jason got defensive with me, "James wouldn't approve. He might even kill me for leaving her. No way we're staying."

He looked at Kylie, who was now sitting the closest to Sarah. She nodded. I couldn't handle this. I didn't want anyone here. I was here to help her. I stepped away leaning against the counter. I can't just let them let her do this to herself. Why were they letting her do stuff if she was this sick? I was getting more and more angry. If James loved her as much as everyone seemed to act, why wasn't he here? When I glanced back at her, I noticed the compassion was rising with emotions. I had to keep my distance. I was only here to look after her, and not to have feelings toward her. Clarissa would be very angry with me if I…I can't even think that way… stop it.

It didn't take long before there was knocking on the door. I went to open it and Clarissa came in and went to the bed right away, "Did she pass out? Should we take her to the hospital?"

"She didn't pass out; she just went into a deep sleep."

I walked over to the other side of the bed and sat down. I looked at Clarissa, "Watch...Sarah, I need to take your pulse again."

She didn't move this time. That was strange because she had just responded to me. I moved closer and looked at her, "Sarah! I need to take your pulse, or we are calling James."

She moved her arm out for me to check. I took it and felt for the pulse watching my watch timing it.

I looked at Clarissa, "See, she responds and her pulse is strong and not racing at all. It's like she is completely exhausted and needs to sleep."

I grabbed the thermometer, "Sarah, we have to take your temperature. Open your mouth."

No response once again.

"Do you want me to call your mom and dad?"

There was still no movement from her, "I will call James."

She opened her mouth. The James threat worked every time... how strange. I put the thermometer under her tongue. She rolled to me and put her hand on my leg. I wanted to hold her so bad and to make her feel better. I looked at Clarissa and very carefully moved her hand back to rest on the bed. It beeped; it was ready. I took it out and looked at it. It was down to 99. I handed it to Clarissa, "I think she needs to rest, but she really needs to find out what is wrong.

"I am going to the cities on Tuesday and I am taking her myself. We should get her home."

"I really don't think we should move her."

I knew I shouldn't keep her here, but...

"Her parents are on their way, but you don't think we should move her?"

"No. She should sleep here. I'm sure if I ask Jason and Kylie they would agree to stay, so we can take turns watching her."

I looked at both of them to see if they would agree. Kylie nodded right away.

Jason looked at Sarah for a long moment, "If Kylie will stay then I will."

Kylie smiled at him. He was still in love with Sarah, but wanted to love Kylie like he does her. I understand now why he left.

"Fine, but we'll have to see what her parents want to do. I am going down to calm Tony. He is worried sick. I will wait for her parents there."

I got up to walk her out. I carefully closed the door, so we could talk privately.

She turned on me, "What happened? You were supposed to watch her."

"Honestly, I don't know. She was fine with no sign of weakness at all. When she sat down she was almost sleeping in less than six minutes. I was watching, and I was watching carefully. I have never seen anything like this."

I waited for her reply because I knew she wasn't pleased. I didn't know what she was thinking. I was holding my breath waiting to hear what she wanted me to do. I wanted to make Sarah better, so I could spend more time with her. She just had such a good heart and she was selfless. I didn't know that many people that wanted the best for someone else like she does. I have only known her for a few days and I wanted to be around her all the time. No, that is not why I am here. Just tell me to take her to the hospital. We could get her fixed up and I could go home. Why didn't I stay distant from her? I know she loves this James guy, so I had to keep a cold heart and not let her in. Clarissa was reading my face. I was trying to be cold, think cold. I don't care.

Clarissa's look softened, "Your heart is opening to her, isn't it?"

"No, I am here for one reason. I owe you everything."

"You don't owe me anything. You have worked for everything you have done, but please don't fall for her. You will get hurt, because she loves James. They are meant to be together."

"I know that. I am not. I am here to find out what is wrong, that is all."

She smiled at me as my guilt was driving me crazy, "Are you sure?"

"Yes. What do you want me to do?"

"If you are sure you will stay, if you are not…"

She was waiting for me to change my plea, but I held strong, so she finished her sentence, "If not, than she will go home with her parents, no matter what happens."

"I can handle it." What was I saying? I don't know if I can handle this. I have to; that is what I am here for.

"Then I will advise them to let her sleep here, and you will stay."

"How about Jason and Kylie?"

"I think they should stay too, if they will."

"You know Jason is in love with her?" I was trying to get the attention off of me.

"Yes, I know. So, does James, but she does not love him and she has made her point clear. James had to trust someone and Jason was one of his best friends."

She turned to walk down the stairs. I watched 'till she was gone. I walked back in. Jason and Kylie were sitting at the table talking. I looked at them angry again. I walked over to Sarah, and she was shivering. I felt her forehead and she was cold. I got the thermometer, "Sarah, we need to take your temperature, now."

She wasn't responding, "Sarah, do I have to call James?"

She rolled toward my voice opening her mouth. I put it under her tongue.

"Jason, do you know if she had been like this before?"

"Yeah, Thursday night." He looked at Kylie, "That is why James asked me to stay. I called him because she wouldn't respond to me. Once I got him on the phone she got up, she was walking and talking to him."

"I need her to tell me how she is feeling, like pain or anything. Can we call him?"

"We can try. I know he calls her in the middle of the night. I have heard her talking to him."

"So, he keeps her up at night, and she runs all day?"

"Pretty much, she thinks she will miss him less if she stays busy."

The thermometer beeped. I looked at it, and it was 96.8, now too low. I started pulling the towels off of her. "She's on the cold side, and it worked." She was really starting to shiver.

Kylie came over and started grabbing them off with me, "She looks really cold."

"Really, she's not, but let's get her covered up. Her parents might feel better if they didn't know we undressed her."

She smiled at me and took the towels to the bathroom. I covered her up with blankets. Jason wasn't much help. I didn't know if it was because it was too much for him or if he didn't' want Kylie to see how much he really cared about her.

The knock on the door came a little too soon for me. I got up to answer. Clarissa came in followed by, whom I am assuming were, Sarah's parents. Her mom walked over to her and placed her hand on her head. I stepped back. I knew it would be better coming from Clarissa.

"What happened?" Her mom was asking as she looked around the room at all of us.

Clarissa stepped up to explain, "She was eating with Tony after the dance and she got sleepy. We had her checked out, and she is just sleeping. She is responding to us, but it seems that this is making her very tired, and she loses strength easily. Jake, will you show them?"

I noticed her dad walked back out; I don't think he could handle seeing her like this. I walked to the opposite side of the bed from where her mom was. I sat down trying to get a little closer. I did not want to use the James threat, from what Clarissa said they already did not approve of him being with her. I didn't want to do anything that would upset Clarissa.

"Sarah." I was repeating in my mind, *please answer me, please move a little*. "Sarah, I need to take your pulse again."

"Just let me sleep. I am so tired."

I gasped with relief, "Sarah, we need to do this now."

"I said no! I am tired… need sleep."

I was so relieved she was responding. I looked up and her mom was satisfied with this. I looked back at Sarah and I watched as the hair that was against her face was moving like someone was slightly pushing it back away from her face. I was scared to move. Did anyone else see that? I evaluated each and every face in the room and no one seemed surprised or confused. Am I imagining things?

"Sarah, can you give me your arm?

Again I saw a movement, but this time it was like her arm was being lifted to rest on someone else's. I searched their faces again to see if they noticed that. Someone had to see that. It was obvious. I moved away from her. I felt sick; did I really see that?

"You know what? I really think she needs to rest. If you don't mind, I think everyone should go, and we should let her rest for an hour or two. Then, if you want, we can try again."

Her mom looked at me disgusted, "I think we should take her to the hospital."

I am sure she was distrustful because who in the hell am I to tell them anything. I probably look like a child to them too.

Clarissa spoke up, "Why don't we let her sleep for awhile, and we can go down stairs with Tony for a little bit. That way you're not leaving her here, but we can let her rest. If she is not better in a little bit we will take her in."

They seemed to agree with her. I volunteered for the first watch of course since that is the reason Clarissa has me here, for her, in the first place. She pulled me aside, "You are sure you can handle this?"

I wanted to hurry and get everyone out, "I will let you know if anything changes."

Everyone was filing out of the room. Jason and Kylie were last because they were sitting at the table. I walked everyone out but stopped at the top of the stairs, "Jason, do you have a minute?"

He stopped assuring Kylie he would be right there to wait for him at the bottom of the stairs.

I didn't know how to ask him about the things I saw in the room, "Um, when I was asking Sarah, to check her pulse this last time, did you see anything funny?"

"What do you mean?"

How do you explain that? "I don't really know. Is there anything I need to know?"

"About what? Sarah?"

"Sorry. I think I am tired too. I think we should call James, so she will wake up. I need to know if she is in pain."

"If you want to."

"How do we call him?"

"Use Sarah's phone."

I walked back in and started digging through her stuff to find her phone. I handed it to Jason after finding it.

He was messing with it and made a comment that didn't register right, "Eight phone numbers... hum."

I felt like I needed to explain my need for him to wake her, "I just need him to wake her up to make sure she is okay. Then I will let her sleep again."

He hit a button and waited.

"James?"

"Yeah, it's the same thing. Yeah, but I need you to talk to her. We need her to wake up a little."

"You got it."

He handed me the phone. I walked to the bed crawling closer to her and held the phone to her ear. I nodded for Jason to leave. He glared at me but left anyway.

"James." She grabbed the phone from me. I moved away from her quickly and backed up to the table and chairs.

"I'm fine James. I was only tired."

"Yeah, like last time."

She wasn't opening her eyes but she was talking to him, and she seemed perfectly healthy.

"No. I am good."

"I didn't. I didn't go water skiing."

"Nope, no basketball either."

I was only getting her side of the conversation, but he seemed concerned that she was doing too much.

"No volleyball."

"James, why are you angry with me?"

"I took a nap before the dance."

"NO! You're not. If you do, we won't make it forever."

"No James, it will wait."

"I feel fine. I don't get sick. I am just tired; that is all."

"Can't you just hold me 'till I fall asleep?"

"I felt you. I was almost sleeping."

What did she mean she felt him? Was that what I saw?

She was sitting up and hugging her knees, "No, why would Jason be here?"

"Oh, what time is it?"

"Oh shit. I am still in your room. I am going to be in so much trouble. I promised I would leave by 10 pm. Can you call me later?"

"I know. It's okay. Just finish please, James. Promise me!"

"I love you too."

"No, he's not here. Why are you asking that?"

"You didn't call me?"

"Oh, I must have been sleeping. I am better now. I need to get home."

She laid back down, "Okay, James, just once. My heart hurts too much for any more."

I could see her grab the blankets around her. Her breathing increased. What the hell was he doing? Or, how was he doing whatever he was doing?

"Oh, James, I love when you do that."

I was ashamed of watching her. I had to look away. I needed to leave this room. If she knew I was watching her… I took a quick glance to see if it was a good time to escape but noticed she was completely relaxed and rolled away from me to hug and curl into a pillow.

"If sharing your soul with me helps me fight this, I may need this every day."

"I know."

"I love you. I will be here when you get home."

"Yeah, I am getting up."

"It's only fifteen more days 'til I see you, my sweet, Cayuse."

"I love you too."

She hung up the phone and laid there holding the pillow. I was trying to sneak to the door, so I could at least pretend like I was only checking on her. I was trying to breath really slow as I moved, but the confusion was causing my pulse to race. I opened the door slowly. Oops, she was turning this way. I stepped into the room like I was walking in.

32. The Commitment

Sarah:

I rolled over looking at the door and Jake was walking in. "Um, you have to give me a minute."

"Okay," he backed out the door.

I noticed I wasn't wearing my clothes. I covered up in the blankets. "Jake, you can come in."

He came in and walked over to the bed putting his hand on my forehead, "You're not hot anymore?"

I looked up at him. He was so stern looking, almost angry, like the first day I met him.

"I feel really good. Why?"

He didn't look at me, "Let me feel your pulse, Sarah."

I put out my wrist. He took it placing his fingers a certain way and then was counting as he looked at his watch. I took a deep breath impatiently.

"It's good." He finally looked at me, but it was a weird look. "Do you have any idea what happened after dancing tonight?"

"Yeah, I got tired and came up to take a nap."

"That isn't exactly how that all happened, and there are a lot of very worried people down stairs."

"Why? What did I do now?" I covered my face. I was never going to see James again.

"While your face is under the covers, do you notice you are wearing different clothes?"

I pulled down the covers enough to see his face, "What did I do?"

His face softened and looked more concerned, "Nothing bad, but you were burning up and you fell asleep when you were eating Tony's steak. We couldn't wake you."

"Slow down. What happened?"

"Sarah, you fell asleep sitting at the bar. I carried you up here, but you had a temperature of 104. We had to get your temp down fast."

I was horrified that I didn't remember any of this. James was going to be angry with me. I had to know, "How did I get changed?"

"Um, Kylie did most of it, but we had to get cool rags on as much of you as possible and I didn't think you would appreciate a cool shower with me."

I was stunned and didn't know what to say.

"Clarissa, your mom, and your dad are down stairs right now trying to decide if we need to take you to the hospital."

"Oh shit. I feel fine now that I have slept. I can go home now. I don't need to go to the hospital." I got up and grabbed my clothes and went to the bathroom.

"Sarah, stop a minute."

I turned to look at him.

"You don't remember any of it?"

"Only that I was really tired, and I talked to James right before you came in."

"Do you want to stay here tonight?"

I could stay here in this bed, in James's room, but then I thought this was weird for him to ask, so I had to make sure, "What?" This was scaring me a little.

"I know you miss him, and everyone thinks you're already sleeping. I am supposed to check on you, so you could go back to sleep, and I could go down stairs and tell them you have made improvements and you just need to sleep. I will come back up and then leave. You could get a full nights rest and no one will be upset with you."

I could stay, he would leave, and no one would be mad at me. I smiled with satisfaction, "You would do that for me?"

He seemed gentler, "You let me join in on your fun, so I feel like I owe you."

"What's with all the doctor stuff?"

"I pay attention."

I gave him a grin, "So, how is this plan supposed to work out?"

"Well, I am sure that your mom and dad will want to come see for themselves that you are actually doing better. I will take your temp, so they can see that it has gone down. They will want to feel your head I am sure of that. You were only responding a little before, so maybe acknowledge them, but then lay back down like you need to sleep. Clarissa is here too, so I am sure your James will hear about this."

I grimaced at the thought, but if I was staying here I could explain it all to James, "You are really going to make it so I can stay here the whole night?" I fell back on the bed and spread my hands over the whole bed. He was making me so happy. Maybe I could get James to come to me tonight, so I could really enjoy his presence. I sat up and crawled off the bed and hugged Jake so tight, "Thank you, thank you, …thank you!"

He didn't hug me back. That is why I trusted him so much. It was refreshing to have someone that was nice to me without any ulterior motive.

Now I was excited, "So, when do we make this happen? I am still tired." I wanted to hurry up, so I could feel more of James. I think he was seeing past the sleeping in the bed because he looked at me suspiciously but didn't comment on my excitement. I smiled as innocently as I could with the biggest puppy dog eyes.

"Fine, crawl back in bed and I will go down and tell them that the fever broke." He walked to the door and took one last glance at me to see if I was ready.

I crawled in bed but still had questions, "Jake?"

He waited for me to ask.

"Did you help undress me?"

"Yes, but I didn't look, I swear."

"Really, not even a little?"

"No, Sarah, not even a little."

"Good. That would be weird."

I covered up and laid down closing my eyes. I felt so amazingly good lying in this bed. I would get to sleep in this great big bed, and I didn't have to run away to do it. I just wished James was here.

He took long enough that I was almost falling asleep again. The door was opening and I wondered if I was supposed to open my eyes yet. I should have made him go through the plan again. I would keep my eyes closed until I heard my name. I felt one then two people sit on the bed with me. Two hands touched my forehead.

"Sarah."

I opened my eyes and then closed them right away.

"Sarah, are you doing better?"

"What, I'm good, just sleepy." I opened my eyes again and looked at my mom. I could tell she was very upset. I smiled and closed my eyes again. I felt bad for deceiving her like this, but I needed some space and I wasn't going to get in trouble now.

I felt Clarissa's hand in mine, "Sarah, sweetheart?"

I opened my eyes again, and felt worse for deceiving her. She helps me to be with my James. I smiled at her and scooted down, "Sorry, I need to sleep now."

I felt Clarissa move first. I could hear her talking to Jake, "She is better, right?"

"She is doing better. Her pulse is strong and the fever is gone. I am going to give her some antibiotics to help fight the infection, but I am giving her a real general one, and I don't know if it will help much."

I felt my mother kiss my forehead, "She can sleep here. She does look a little better. Who will make sure she gets back okay?"

It was quiet for awhile and then I heard Jake, "Well if no one else will, I will make sure to get her home safely."

I wanted to smile so bad to let him know he was making me so happy but I didn't. I could hear everyone leaving the room. I rolled away from the door and closed my eyes. James, I love you so much, and you need to hurry to me. I need you to hold me so much. I took a deep breath and let the sleep come.

I heard the door again, but I didn't move. I didn't know who it was.

"Sarah."

It was Jake, so I rolled over, "Thank you. I will be fine now. I really do need to go back to sleep."

He didn't look at me, "Um. I had to promise I would keep an eye on you all night."

"Yeah, but I am fine now, and you know that. You can leave me here alone."

"I think I have to stay after last night. We almost took you to the hospital. You were really bad.

"It's okay, James gave me part of his soul, so I feel better. It lasts awhile and I won't get bad 'til I…" I was noticing he wasn't believing me. I knew I had to explain better, "I will only get that tired again if I over do it, so I will be fine until next weekend. I live a boring life when I am not here."

He stated matter of fact, "Sorry. I promised."

He pulled up a chair from the table and sat down at the foot of the bed putting his feet on the end of it. I was not happy. Now I couldn't entice my James to come to me tonight.

"Well, if you are going to stay you can't sleep in the chair." I got up taking the comforter off the bed and folded it once and laid it on the floor. I threw two pillows down, "There, now you can be a little more comfortable." I crawled back in bed and curled up with the sheet and blanket still on the bed. I curled up away from the side he would be on and hugged a pillow and closed my eyes. I grabbed my phone and put it to my mouth. I heard him get up and put the chair back by the table.

"How is your temperature?"

I felt my forehead and rolled over to look at him over the side of the bed, "I think I'm fine."

He put his hand up to touch my forehead, "Yes, it's still okay."

I smiled and rolled back over to sleep.

"Sarah?"

"Yeah?"

"What did you mean he gave you part of his soul?"

"I don't know how to explain it, but I get better for awhile when he does it."

"He makes you feel better?"

"Yep."

"Why won't you let him come home?"

"What?"

"They told me you won't let him come home to help you."

I rolled back over and looked at him, "You are going to think I am stupid."

"No. Really, I want to know."

"He wants me to marry him."

"Aren't you a little young for that?"

"Yeah, but I already said yes. We will wait 'til I am older, but I just feel that if he can't finish this one little thing, then…"

"Then what?"

"If he can't finish a commitment as small as this, then how can I expect him to finish living his *whole* life with me?"

"Wow."

I was still watching him to see his expression, but he had his eyes closed.

"What?"

"That's really deep."

"I told you. You think I am being stupid?"

"What does James think?"

"He wants to do whatever makes me happy. He is really torn over wanting to come home and take care of me, or stay, finish, and spend the rest of his life with me."

"Why are you making him choose between those two things?"

"I'm not giving him a choice. He has to stay and finish."

"But he wants to come home and take care of you."

I was happy as I thought about this, "But look how many people I have to take care of me. I will be fine 'til he gets here. Besides, his dad told me it would wait."

It was quiet now, so I rolled back over and closed my eyes.

My phone rang, "James."

"Sarah, can I please come home now?"

"No! You are so close to being done." I rolled over to see if Jake was sleeping.

"Sarah, you are getting worse."

"I only needed to sleep. I will be really careful this week. I won't play volleyball or anything; please James, just behave and finish."

"Sarah, you are driving me crazy."

"You're not here. I can't drive you crazy."

"Oh, you do. I couldn't feel anything wrong today. You didn't get sick, right?"

"No, James, I didn't throw up."

"Then what happened?"

"I just got really tired that's all. Everyone over reacted and freaked out."

"Sarah, my mom called me. She said you had a high temperature and she has someone there to watch over you."

"Really, who?"

"I don't know who it is."

I looked down at Jake on the floor. I tried not to think of anything because he would know someone was in the room with me. I rolled to the other side of the bed, so my conversation would be more private with my James.

"I love you and I can't wait for you to be here."

"Sarah, I am not going to let anything happen until you're better. I won't let it."

"You're not refusing me, are you?"

"No. I am asking you to wait until you are healthy."

"I will be healthy when you get home."

"No, I felt it and you know that."

"Yes, but after you shared your soul with me, my fever broke."

"How bad was it?"

"I think it was 104, but Kylie helped me change and then put cold towels on me to cool me off. I don't remember any of it. I was sleeping."

"Kylie helped you?"

"Yes. She is quite nice when she doesn't want to kill me."

"Kylie is helping you?"

"James, Jason was miserable helping me. It was better to involve her so he didn't have to help me so much. I told you he needed to be released from taking care of me."

"You're letting her help you? You need that much help?"

"James, I was sleeping."

"You passed out!"

"No! I wasn't passed out. I was very tired."

"Sarah, I have to come home. You need me."

"No. I do need you, but I will wait. You are not coming home 'til you're done and if you are going to argue with me, I'll…" I didn't want to say it.

"What Sarah, you'll what? Cut me off? Not kiss me? What, because nothing you threat will make me stay away?"

"James?" I started to cry. "I will have to give back your ring, and we'll just have to wait and see." My crying moved to sobbing.

"Sarah, please, don't do this to me. You are breaking my heart."

"My heart is breaking too James, but if you love me you need to finish." I could hardly breathe.

Jake was sitting up, so I got up and went into the bathroom and closed the door.

"Sarah, you know I love you and this training doesn't compare to how I feel about you."

"I know, but if you don't finish how can I expect you to last a life time with me?"

"Oh Sarah, please."

"Well, how am I supposed to feel, if you can't commit for six weeks to something?"

"You know it's not that. You know there are exceptions and you are my exception and you are sick. I need to be there."

"You will be when I need you the most. Please, James, stay and do your best. I will wear the ring no matter how hard it will be for my mom and dad. I love you."

"Why do you have to be so stubborn, little girl."

"That's why you love me. James, I am getting tired again."

"Feel your forehead, is your temperature going up?"

"Maybe, but I am upset. Why do you have to argue with me?"

"Because, I want to be with you."

"Soon, James, soon."

"I love you my sweet, Sarah."

"I love you my, Cayuse."

"Do you want me to stay 'til you sleep?"

"No, if I close my eyes I will be sleeping."

"I will call every day until I come home, okay?"

"Okay. James, you really do mean a lot to me."

"I love you more than you know, little girl."

I didn't want to hang up, but I had to go back to bed.

"Good night, James."

"Sarah, I don't want to let you go yet."

"I don't either."

"Okay, I will count to three and we'll hang up at the same time."

I giggled a little, "Okay."

"1, 2, 3."

I hung up. I had to; otherwise, I wouldn't have been able to let him go. I stood up and washed my face. I was upset. At least I didn't feel sick at all. I looked through stuff in the bathroom. I found a toothbrush and toothpaste. I loved to brush my teeth, it made me feel better. I washed my face again and took a deep breath. I went back to bed and curled up with a pillow. I was tired from arguing with James, and the tears were flowing. I couldn't hold them back as I drifted to sleep.

33. Doing Better

I woke to someone touching my forehead. I opened my eyes forgetting where I was. I saw Jake, and he was looking at me. "You are warm again. We need to take your temperature."

I opened my mouth waiting.

His eyes squinted as if he was suspicious, "You were crying in your sleep."

I wasn't expecting that, "What?"

"You were talking to James. After you fell asleep you were crying."

I was stunned. I didn't know what to say.

He was getting the thermometer ready, "You want him to come home, to not listen to you and come home, don't you?"

"No, I don't. I mean… yes, I want him to come home, but he really needs to finish this."

"You were really hard on him."

Again, I was speechless.

"You threatened to give back his ring. Don't you think that is a little harsh? He only wants to come home because you are sick."

I was feeling pretty guilty now, "I know, but I can't be his excuse for not finishing, or he will regret me latter."

"I don't believe that."

I was going to justify what I was thinking, "Look at all the failed marriages today. Most of them put the blame on each other. I don't want to be his excuse."

"He could always do it again after you are better."

"He's almost done. How about the temperature?"

He didn't seem happy with my explanation. He handed me the thermometer. Was he angry with me for my actions with James? I turned it on and put it in my mouth and closed my eyes to wait. It was still dark out, so I could sleep more. I heard it beep three times, and I took it out of my mouth and handed it to Jake. I rolled back over and curled up with a pillow.

"It's at 100 again."

I turned back to him, "What do you want me to do?"

He walked to the bathroom digging for something, then out to the kitchen area and looked in all the cupboards. He turned, but he was thinking about something, kind of out of it.

"What are you looking for?"

"Something that will take your temperature down."

"I have ibuprofen in my purse."

"That would help. I am going to run down stairs and get the antibiotics. I think we should give it a try and see if it helps with the infection."

I got up and started digging in my purse for the ibuprofen. Jake went out the door, and I found my pill bottle but didn't know how many to take. I usually just take two. I got up and got a glass of water and took two. What was taking Jake such a long time? I was getting really tired again. I set the glass of water by the bed and crawled back into bed. I curled up watching the door for Jake to return. I closed my eyes to rest until he came back in.

"Sarah."

I didn't want to open my eyes.

"Sarah!"

I slowly opened my eyes, but it was still dark out, and I was so tired, "How long did I sleep?"

"I was only gone for a little bit. I have something here. We'll try this, but I will need to watch you carefully to see if you have a reaction to it."

"Okay. I took a couple of ibuprofen; is that okay?"

"Yes."

He handed me two more pills. I didn't know much about Jake and he was giving me pills.

"Are you going to tell me what I am taking?"

"It's an antibiotic, and I will send the bottle with you. That way if anything happens, you will have the information with you. Do you want it in your purse?"

"Sure. Jake, I am feeling a little tired again. Do you mind if I…"

He sat on the bed taking my arm to feel for my pulse. I watched him, waiting for him to tell me I could sleep again.

"You can close your eyes, Sarah. You don't have to be awake for this."

I had no problem drifting off with him holding my arm.

Jake:

After she closed her eyes, I watched her as I counted. Oops, I had to start over and watch the clock. After I got a good count I stayed there and went through things in my head. She loves James and he loves her. Why was she so tempting for me? I could not have this precious beautiful girl. I propped a couple of pillows on the headboard and leaned back and put my hand on her forehead. She was still so warm. She curled into me. I knew I should push her away from me, but I knew this would be the only time I could have her this close to me ever again. I closed my eyes to enjoy her touch.

I woke and she was still sleeping. She was curled into me even more. I felt her forehead. It was working a little. I took her pulse and it hadn't changed at all. I scooted down a little to be more comfortable. I closed my eyes and held her while she slept. I tried to stay awake, so I could move away from her if she woke up, but the slumber was over powering me.

I woke again, but she had rolled away from me. I hope she didn't wake while she was curled into me. It would make it uncomfortable tomorrow. I got up and checked the door. I am glad no one checked on her while I was in bed with her. I would be the only one that knew. I locked the door and went back to the other side of the bed. I sat down and reached for her forehead. Her temperature didn't seem to change much, but it wasn't getting any worse. She grabbed my hand and kissed it. Then she pulled it to her cheek resting her face on it. I wanted to pull her to me to hold her so bad, but I couldn't let myself. I pulled my hand away from her. I must resist all the temptation to have feelings for her. I sat back and closed my eyes. I shook my head realizing I couldn't fight the temptation, and I opened my eyes to gaze at her. I carefully traced the hair away from her face, and her mouth turned into a grin. I moved a little closer scooting down again. I faced her just to watch her breathe. I closed my eyes trying to restrict myself from looking at her, but found myself opening them just to take that one last glimpse. I traced my fingers down her arm. When she reached out for me, I moved away. I stayed as far as I could from her on the bed, but watched her 'til the sleep came over me again.

Sarah:

I was waking up, but kept my eyes closed to stretch as I rolled over. It felt so good to stretch every inch of my body, "Uhm." I slowly opened my eyes looking out the window. I could only see a fraction, but I could see the sun rising. It was too early for day light, but maybe I could sleep some more. I stretched and rolled back over. Jake was there sleeping. He was so cute sleeping with the thermometer in one hand and his watch in the other. He must have been up most of the night checking on me. I closed my eyes to sleep a little longer, but I reached for his hand, wanting him to know I was thankful. His grip tightened, but he didn't open his eyes or say a word.

After lying there awhile, I realized I didn't need to sleep anymore. I grabbed my bathing suit, a clean pair of boxers, and James's dress shirt. I went to the bathroom to take a shower. It felt so good and I did keep it on the cool side. I wanted to get back to the trailer, so mom and dad could see I was better. I put all of the stuff I had worn in my bag for washing at home. I moved out of the bathroom and went to grab the pills Jake had given me. I read the label and it said to take them four times daily, so I took another one and sat down to write Jake a note. I looked at him still sleeping and he looked like a little boy laying there.

Dear Jake:

I hope you slept well. I had to get up, and I am feeling extremely better. I took another pill at 7:30 am. I am at the trailer with my mom and dad. I am leaving you a map, and you are welcome to join us for breakfast. If you don't get up till after 11 am, I will be at Sherburn's for water skiing and tubing. It is also on the map. Please come! If you need swimming trunks , James has a few pairs in the bottom drawer. I will be waiting for my check up.

Sincerely,
Sarah

I drew a map for him and marked the trailer and Sherburn's. I walked over to him and touched his face. He was so sweet for taking care of me, and I liked that he didn't hit on me at all. I pushed him over, so he wouldn't be sitting up anymore, and he didn't wake up at all. I shook my head. I was feeling so good that I felt like I could do anything I wanted today, for the first time in a long time. I went to leave and found the door locked. I looked back at Jake with the question on my mind, *why did he lock the door?* Maybe he doesn't feel safe here. That doesn't make any sense. I unlocked the door and walked out. I went down the stairs and into the kitchen. I found Tony and he looked like he hadn't slept all night. He was so excited to see me; he came over to me and hugged me. It was so tight I could hardly breathe.

"Sarah, are you okay?"

"Yes. I feel amazing. Jake gave me some pills and they really seemed to help, whatever they were." I kissed his cheek but noticed he looked at me a little funny, "Tony, what is it?"

"I tried to check on you last night. The door was locked."

"Yeah. I noticed that too when I left. Does Jake not feel safe here?"

Tony wasn't happy, "He stayed with you all night?"

"Yeah, I guess Clarissa asked him too." I giggled, "I found him with the thermometer in one hand and his watch in the other. I think he stayed up all night checking on me.

He was getting more upset, "He didn't try anything?"

"No, and that is exactly why I felt safe. He isn't like that at all. In fact he gave me a hard time for not letting James come home." I felt the lump as soon as I thought about James.

"Oh, Sarah, I have upset you?"

"No, you know how I feel about…" I slowly pulled the necklace out to show Tony how much James means to me. The tears were making it hard to see, "Tony, I said yes. We will be together forever once he gets home."

He came and hugged me, "I want to believe that, but…" He was remorseful, "…you have been so miserable without him."

"And I will continue to be miserable without him as long as he needs me to. I love him."

Tony kissed my forehead.

"Next weekend, okay?"

"Only if you are up to it."

"I wouldn't miss it unless I was in the hospital."

"Oh, please, don't say that."

"Tony, all I mean is that I love it here. I am so thankful for everything."

"Okay dear," he kissed my forehead again, "But please don't fall asleep like that again, you scared the crap out of me."

"I promise." I kissed his cheek and walked out. I went to my car and Jake came out of the upstairs room, "Wait."

"Did you read the note I left you?"

"What note?"

"It's on the table. See you in a little bit."

"Wait, Sarah."

"I have to go."

I got in my car and waved goodbye. I went to the trailer and walked in. Mom and Dad looked miserable. They both looked at me with amazement.

I needed to make them feel better, "See, I was just sleeping. I am okay now."

Mom walked to me and gave me the biggest hug; dad came over and put his arms around both of us, "So, you're feeling better?"

"Jake gave me something to fight the infection, and it must be working. Feel." I took both their hands and put them on my forehead, "See, no more fever. I am hungry though."

They finally let go of me so I asked, "What did you want for breakfast?"

Dad was not pleased, "Don't you think you should take it easy?"

"Are you kidding? I am so much better. Sit down; I am making breakfast."

I decided to make eggs, toast, and bacon. I knew how they liked their eggs, so I didn't have to ask. I got them theirs and sat down to eat mine. Jake didn't show, so I let it go. I cleaned up, did the dishes, and sat back down at the table with them.

"Mom, what time are we leaving?"

"I really didn't have a specific time. What are you thinking?"

"The boat is still down at Sherburn's so we have to go get it."

"*You* are *not* going skiing."

"I know that, but I could drive them for a little while, maybe only for a couple of hours... till like 1 pm.

Dad looked at mom. She shrugged her shoulders. I smiled because I knew the answer. I got up and hugged them both, "Why don't you both come down and watch; you will see I am fine."

Dad rolled his eyes at me.

I got up and moved to the front bedroom to get my stuff together. I took everything I had to wash out of my bag and put it in my suitcase to bring it home. I smelled them for James's scent because it still lingered on them. Oh, how I loved James. I grabbed a new towel and headed out.

"Are you guys coming?"

"Maybe in a little bit."

"I only want to stay for a little while, so don't take too long."

I walked into Sherburn's. Danelle was at the bar with her mom and they seemed really upset when they saw me. Danelle came running, "You are better?"

"Yep. Jake gave me something to help with the infection. I feel completely better."

Laura was holding back tears, "Can I get you something to eat, Sarah? You are so thin."

"I would love that, but I just ate with mom and dad. They will be down shortly, so you can ask them yourself."

"But, you are doing better?"

"Oh, I am so much better."

"Do me a favor and go talk to Brian. He has been upset all night."

"Okay, no problem."

I looked at Danelle for her to come with me. She got up and walked to the back with me.

She didn't believe my show for her mother, "Are you really *fine* Sarah or are you just putting on a good front?"

"Really, really, I am doing so much better."

"You better go talk to Brian."

"I don't really want to, but I suppose… Where is he?"

She looked up the stairs. I took a deep breath and walked up the stairs. He was on the couch looking pretty miserable. I walked around in front of him. He looked up at me, stood up, and hugged me. I could hardly breathe.

He started to kiss my cheek repeatedly, "I was so worried; are you okay?" He was still kissing my cheek, "What happened? Do you need to sit down?" The kissing was moving closer to my lips. He kissed me there in a passionless caring way.

"Brian." I was trying to talk in between the kisses, "Brian, stop."

He just kept going.

"Brian, I will have to leave."

He finally stopped and stared into my eyes.

"Brian, you can't have these feelings for me. You have to be okay with being friends."

He lowered his face from mine so that he was no longer looking at me, "Sarah, you are like the best friend I have. That is all. I don't want to lose you."

I lifted his chin, so he would have to look at me, "Brian, friends don't kiss friends like that."

"I just can't believe you are here and you're okay. What happened?"

"Remember Thursday when I was so tired?"

"Yeah."

"That's all it was."

"But they said you had a bad fever and your pulse was racing."

"Jake gave me some medicine to help fight the infection; I feel so much better. Let's go water skiing. Mom and dad said I could take you guys, and they are coming to watch. I did invite Jake since he helped me all night."

"What?"

"He stayed with me and took care of me. He was keeping my temperature down with cold towels and ibuprofen."

"He was in the room with you all night?!"

"Yeah, why are you upset? He's like a nurse or something at the hospital. He knew what to do."

"Sarah, one day with you and he will be infatuated with you. Don't you know how great you are?"

"Brian, you are over reacting... stop it. I am not that great, and everyone knows I love James."

"And look what that does for me. I still kiss you and want you; even though I know he could kill me with one blow."

"Brian, stop please, let's go have some fun. I need to do something to stay busy. Please, behave if he shows."

"Fine, but I am still in line before him."

I laughed, "Yes, you are. Let's go."

I walked away, but he stopped me and pulled me back in front of him. "You really don't feel anything when I kiss you?"

"Brian, I won't let myself. I love James."

"Can we try one for real, and then you can turn me down, please?"

I looked at him cautiously and pulled on my necklace until the ring came out.

He gasped, "Is that what I think it is?"

I glanced at him and then down to the ring with fulfillment, "Brian, I can't let anything happen with anyone other than James. I love him enough that *I said yes*."

He hugged me, "Oh, Sarah, are you sure? How can you decide something like that? I wouldn't be able to decide anything like that right now; how can you?"

"It's not like it's going to happen when he gets back. We are waiting two years."

"You have already discussed it?"

"Well, yeah, I have the ring. We have to talk about that stuff."

"You two haven't done it? How do you know he is the one?"

"I just know. Now, you have to quit kissing and hugging me or James will know."

"You wouldn't tell him?"

"No, but he feels everything I do, including the good and the bad."

"That's way too much info to handle."

"Good, let's forget about it and go water skiing. Can you call Mykala?"

"She wasn't happy with me. I was so upset about you."

"Call her and invite her. She will see you have feelings for her too."

"Um, I don't think so; I think I really blew it this time."

"Why do you say that?"

"She was coming on to me and I stopped her. I told her sometimes there are things more important."

"That might actually work to your favor. Call her, and I will meet you outside at the boat."

I went down the stairs and found Danelle, "Are you ready?"

"Am I ready for what?"

"Water-skiing, tubing, and swimming. I feel so good."

"You are kidding?"

"No, I'm not. Where is Tommy?"

"We got in an argument last night. I don't know if or when he will be back."

"So, you are all mine today?"

"Yeah, I guess so."

"Well, now I know how you felt when James was around, and I am so sorry."

She hugged me, "I am too."

34. A Little Fun

I went out while they were getting ready and walked down to the dock. I ran into Pat on my way down, "Do you want to go tubing with us?"

"Not really dressed for it."

"Oh, come on. Ask Brian if you can borrow something of his."

"Where is he?"

"Inside."

He headed up to see what he could do.

I sat down on the bench and waited. I heard footsteps, and I turned to see who was ready, but to my surprise it was Jake. He had James's swim shorts on and a t-shirt and he looked really uncomfortable. I stood up, "You decided to come?"

"I don't know about this." He was fidgeting, "The shorts are too big, and I feel like a dork."

"If you can dance the way you do, this is so much easier."

"First, things first." He walked over to me and put his hand on my head. I stood there looking at him impatiently, "Are you done yet?"

"No. We need to take your temperature."

"You are going to make a lot of people worry if you do that."

"Sarah, that is why I am here. To make sure you don't get any sicker."

"What do you actually do at the hospital?"

He only glanced up at me and was embarrassed, "I'm a…" he looked more directly at me, "…doctor." He waited for a reaction from me.

"Aren't you a little young for that?"

He was turning red, "I'm kind of a genius."

"Oh, how I wish I was."

He relaxed a little, "But you still have to let me take your pulse and temperature off and on."

"Fine, when am I supposed to take another pill?"

"About 12:30 pm."

"So, I have a little time." I sat down on the bench, and he came to sit with me and held up the thermometer. I took it and put it under my tongue. He took my wrist and was counting. Brian and Pat came down, and Brian looked worried.

I gave him the biggest grin I could, "Brian, he's just making sure I am okay to play."

Jake noticed them and then he looked at me. I smiled at him reassuringly.

Brian moved to the boat to check things to make sure everything was ready, "Yep, were good to go here. How is she doing?"

"She's okay, but not to go water-skiing or tubing." He was shaking his head no, so I gave him a little pout to beg. He leaned into me and said very quietly, "You just feel better; you still have a temp and your pulse is elevated. If you ask me, you should be laying down right now."

"Well, I guess it's a good thing you are here then." I jumped in the water. It was so cool and refreshing. If I had a temp the cool water would help. I came up and all three were ready to pull me out.

"Guys, I am okay, and I am not going to break. I was just cooling down a little."

Brian dove in over my head and Pat cannon balled into the lake. Jake sat down staring at me, "I don't like this. You need to take it easy."

"I won't go skiing or tubing myself, and you can stay by my side the whole time." I was trying to ease the moment, "It's okay for you to have a little fun while you are here."

He put his hand out to pull me out of the water. I took it and put my feet on the dock and pulled with all my might, but he didn't budge.

He chuckled, "See you don't even have enough strength."

"Fine, but you can have a little fun too."

I went to the ladder and climbed out and went to the boat. Danelle was walking down the dock. I noticed she was growing up so pretty. I saw a car pull up and a whole bunch of girls were piling out of the car. Another car pulled up and it was Katherine, Will, and Sam. I knew there were plenty of girls here, and the whole gang was here to watch over me.

I looked at Jake wondering how he was doing. As he watched more and more people show up the more nervous he was getting.

I stood next to Jake and I introduced all of them to him. I was explaining James's family to him. Sam walked over to me and got really close, "I heard it is a lot worse."

"Maybe, but I feel better. I don't get sick anymore."

"Can I feel?"

"Not now, maybe if we're in the boat alone."

"Fine, but you better make it happen."

"Fine."

"Fine."

He walked away from me, so I had to ask him, "Where is Amelia?"

He was grumpy towards me, "Guarded."

Jake turned so he was behind me and he laughed. I shook my head with disapproval.

I kept Jake by me the whole time. He sat in the passenger seat of the boat even though we still needed a spotter.

We finally got to Brian, but of course he wanted to ski. Danelle came with us as the spotter. She tried to make conversation with Jake, but he wasn't real responsive. He was more nervous than anything else. I gave Brian a few really good jumps, and then we headed in to go tubing. Jake took my pulse again and then my temperature while we were waiting for Brian to get the tube ready. He wasn't pleased with the results. I could tell by the look on his face. We took a few girls on the tube, but he wasn't paying attention to any of them.

We pulled in for a switch, and Jake did his little tests again. I was getting really irritated with him and his little tests. He moved closer, "You need to take the pill."

I grabbed my water and did what I was told and took the pill.

"Sarah, it is getting worse."

"Okay, just a half hour more please."

He did not approve, but I gave him a smile knowing I was winning, "So, we have tons of girls here. Don't you find any of them at least cute?"

"I wasn't looking. I am only here to watch over you."

"I told you, you could have a little fun too."

He shook his head and said sarcastically, "I am having a blast."

"You need to go on the tube."

"No. I don't."

"Have you ever been tubing?"

"No, and I don't care too."

"That's it." I turned to Brian, "I need the tube in the boat. I have to go do something really quick. Danelle, you need to come with me."

Brian looked worried and I gestured like I needed another test done. Brian didn't like it, but he put the tube in the boat.

Danelle got in the boat, "What do you need?"

"Your help for a little bit."

I looked at Brian pleasantly, "We'll be right back."

He was worried and Sam came running, "Sarah, is everything okay?"

"Yep. I will be right back."

I took off in the boat with Jake and Danelle. We went around the corner to a different bay where no one would see us. I pushed the tube out and looked at him, "I am not going to be done until you get on this for one ride."

Danelle was laughing, "You better because she will win."

He looked right at her angry but then his stiffness softened, "I really don't want to do this."

"I know, but you don't have a choice. Get on, or I am not listening to you."

He huffed and crawled onto the tube.

I decided if he never did this before he would need some instructions, "You have to hang on here and here, and lay on your stomach. I am going to push you out. When the line is all the way out give me thumbs up when you're ready." I pushed the tube and he was not happy at all.

I waited for the thumbs up.

Danelle was giggling, "Why are you doing this to him?"

"I don't think he has had much fun in his life, and he helped me to feel better. I want to see him smile. That's all."

"Sarah, you know he is going to like you too."

"No, I don't think so. He is here to doctor me up. Clarissa sent him."

"It looks like you're doing the doctoring."

I looked at her, "He has never gone tubing before, so watch him carefully please."

He finally gave thumbs up. I kicked it into gear. I took him around and around the bay. We went over waves and turns and I was whipping him all over. I slowed the boat and pulled him in, "Had enough?"

He rolled over on the tube and smiled, "I could stay out here all day."

I glanced over at Danelle and she shook her head, "Great, another one hooked."

"Danelle, stop that. He was having fun. Don't blow it for him."

I gave him my hand to pull him in the boat and he helped pull the tube in.

He walked over to Danelle, "You can't tell anyone I did that, okay?"

She gave him an odd look, but then he winked at her, "It's our little secret."

I was happy. He had fun and he winked at Danelle.

I took off heading for the dock, and when we got there Brian helped pulled the boat into the dock. I regretted to have to tell him but, "I guess I am done now. Can you drive for awhile?"

He came and grabbed my arm to help me out of the boat, "Are you okay?"

"Yes, but I am suppose to take it easy now. No more excitement for me.

Brian took the girls tubing while Danelle and I lay lazily on tubes in the water. Jake watched from shore. Sam came over to me and tipped me in the water. I saw Jake stand up. I shook my head no at him. Sam touched my stomach really quickly without my permission. He stopped and looked at me with fear in his eyes. He turned his head toward Danelle and smiled.

"Sam, what is this about?"

He didn't look at me but he said, "It's spreading more."

"Jake gave me something to fight the infection. I only started it last night Sam…SAM!"

He turned to me.

"You can check again next weekend okay. Don't tell James."

"I have to."

"No, you don't. Let it go another week and we'll see how it is. I will be better. Come on, Sam. I already feel better and now I am taking it easy."

Jake was walking into the water, "Sarah, is everything okay?"

I looked over at him smiling, "Yeah. It's fine."

Sam was disgusted, "How does James feel about that one looking after you?"

"I don't know, but right now he's helping me, so how mad do you really think he would be?"

He was looking at me disapproving. Jake was in the water to his waist. I gestured for Danelle to help. She moved to Jake and offered him her tube. She was a good distraction; he was actually playfully responding to her.

I looked back at Sam smiling, "See, it's not about me."

He hugged me and let me go, "We're going to go, but you are coming next weekend then?"

"Yes. Come see me at Tony's on Saturday."

"I will, but if you're not better, then I am calling James."

"It's a deal." I knew I would be better by then.

I waved at Will and Katherine. It was hard being nice to her knowing what she did to my James. Oh, how I wish he could be here right now.

I turned and noticed what everyone else was doing, but I realized I wasn't feeling great anymore. I made my way over to Jake and Danelle, "I think it's time."

"What, are you okay?" There was actually fear in Jake's eyes. I knew he understood. Danelle came under one arm and Jake under the other and we walked to the beach. I hoped mom and dad weren't watching now.

I sat down, and Jake took my arm and started to take my pulse while putting his other hand on my forehead. He looked at me and said, "Yes, you're done."

I eased up looking at him, "How bad is it?"

"Only 100, but your pulse is racing. What did James's brother say to you?"

"He feels things; he is special. He said whatever it was had spread from the last time he felt it."

I could hardly look at Jake. I was trying to catch my breath. I hated that I felt like this. I was getting pissed. Mom and dad walked down and over to me.

I looked up at them, "Dad you're going to have to bring the boat to the launch today. I am getting tired."

The fear was showing in his face.

"Dad, I am fine, just tired."

Danelle didn't believe me either.

"I am fine. I just need a nap. I will see you next Friday, okay?"

She nodded and hugged me. Brian came running down the dock. I looked at him and tried to calm him, "Brian, sorry the party is over. I will be fine, but I need to rest now."

Brian took over wrapping things up. Dad headed for the launch and mom took dad's truck to meet him there. Brian and Jake helped me to Jake's truck. I crawled in as Brian helped to guide me in.

I touched his face, "Brian, it's okay. Nothing a little rest won't help."

His eyes pleaded with me. He wanted to help me by doing something... anything. I gave him a sweet, soft, and yet tired smile, "We'll play basketball Friday; so be ready."

He nodded and closed the door for me. Jake turned the truck around and as soon as we were out of site I laid down putting my head on his thigh. He put his hand on my forehead and then traced back the hair from my face.

"It's okay."

He dug in his bag and pulled out a bottle of ibuprofen and handed me four.

I gave him a questioning look.

His slight grin was reassuring, "It's a little high."

Next he handed me a bottle of water. I took them and closed my eyes. We got to the trailer before mom and dad did.

I opened the door to get out.

"Hey, wait, what are you doing? Let me help you."

"Jake, I'm not that bad yet. I stopped before it got too bad; I really am okay."

I walked in and lay down on the couch.

He grabbed a chair from the kitchen, "No wonder you wanted to sleep in that bed."

I frowned at him, "Be nice. This is my second home."

He eased, "That's a good sign; you're still feisty."

I couldn't hold on anymore; I had to close my eyes.

He felt my head again, "I'm going to grab the thermometer. I'll be right back."

He came in with mom and dad. I looked around and then closed my eyes, but said out loud, "Don't worry; I stopped before it got bad. I need to sleep. What time do you want to leave?"

Jake felt my head again. I opened my eyes and gave him a dirty look to indicate he was being excessive.

Mom was so caring, "You take a nap. We'll see how you're feeling in a little bit."

"Yeah, but you might want to drive home, if that's okay?"

"Whatever you want, but you should sleep now."

I was so ready to fall asleep, but Jake felt my forehead again. Then he grabbed my wrist to feel my pulse, "If you keep poking at me I can't sleep."

He sighed, "I think she is alright for now."

35. The Ring

Jake:

Her parents looked so worried, and I should tell them she's okay, but I really can't do that at this time. I need to see what tests they have done. I need to find out what is wrong with her.

I whispered, "She's sleeping."

Her dad was upset with me and expressed it in his tone as he asked me, "What happened? Did she go skiing or tubing? What was she doing?"

I felt like I was being attacked, "She was only driving the boat. She seemed to know it was coming, and she even let Brian take over in the boat before she let us know she was getting tired. I don't know if she felt it coming, or if it came on that fast." I hesitated, "The antibiotic seems to be helping, but I would like to come down and go to the doctors with her on Monday."

Okay, that was being really forward, and the look on their faces was defensive, "Of course, I will have to check with Clarissa first, but if it's okay with you I will plan on it."

Her mom was uncertain of my intent, "Who are you again?"

"I am a friend of Clarissa's, and she called me in to keep an eye on your daughter."

"Why would she do that?"

"James."

"What do you mean James?"

"James loves her, and Clarissa doesn't want anything to happen to her."

"But what can you do?"

I could see their mixture of worry and disbelief.

"I am a doctor." I pulled out my I.D. and handed it to Sarah's mom.

"You're so young?"

I hated explaining this, "I'm a genius."

"Well, yes, if you can help her… anything."

I didn't want to push them too far, but this was my chance to spend more time with her and maybe figure out what I can do to help.

"If you want she can ride with me, I will follow you home, so I can monitor her the whole way."

Her mom was very distrustful, "Don't you live up here?"

"I am from the cities; I'll stay with my parents."

Finally, a sign of concession, and she smiled at me. I knew I was in. Just one more to get through and I was prepared to spend the next week finding out what was making her so sick.

"I'll have to make a couple of phone calls first; excuse me."

Okay. I need to leave this up to Clarissa, and whatever she decided I would have to live with. I opened my phone not knowing if I wanted the answer to this. I was afraid she would see through me, and that I was enjoying my time with her son's precious girlfriend.

"Jake, is everything okay?"

"No, actually; Sarah took off on me this morning. I must have dosed off, so I followed her to Sherburn's Resort where she was keeping herself so busy she wore herself out. She is sleeping now, running a slight temperature, and her pulse is racing. What would you like me to do?"

"What do you think we should do?"

"She has a doctor's appointment in the morning. I should be there to get her medical records to see what tests they have done. Maybe they are missing something."

Clarissa was being protective now but did not refuse my suggestion, "I was going to go down myself and take her to Dr. Johnson on Tuesday."

"Okay then. You have it handled, but you really don't want them to do all the same tests; they would take more blood, and that might not be good for her."

"Yes, you are right. You should go with her tomorrow. I will wait for your phone call."

"I will have to leave the hospital for a little while."

"I will take care of that for you. Plan on being back by Thursday. Will that be enough time?"

"I will study her records day and night if I need to. Clarissa, I will find out what it is."

"Would you like me to talk to her parents to explain?"

"I am sorry, but they were getting protective, and I had to tell them. Sarah also knows I am a doctor."

"She is getting to you?"

"No, she needed to know that the only reason I was following her was to help her medically."

"She loves James. Don't let her into your heart. You will get hurt."

"I have stayed numb for this many years; I can do this for you too."

"She is charming you without even knowing it. You had fun today with her."

"What do you mean?"

"My boys were there. They saw the way you watched her."

"I am here for her just medically. I don't care except for what you want me to do."

"If you are sure, but be careful because she is special."

"I will, and I will call you tomorrow."

"Thank you, Jake, and I will call your father."

"Thanks, goodbye."

"I will talk to you tomorrow."

I just stood there. Was I making a mistake? If I spend more time with her I would crave more. *I can do this.* I took a deep breath and went back inside.

"Clarissa has set it up for me to go to the cities with you. I will have to head back up here for work on Thursday, but I can help through Wednesday if you are okay with it."

Her mom walked up to me, "So, Clarissa sent you because James loves her?"

"Yes, that is right. I have to go get some things, but I will be back."

I walked over to Sarah and she wasn't as shallow as last night. I took her wrist and felt her pulse which had slowed. I grabbed the thermometer, "Sarah."

She didn't respond to me.

"Sarah, I need to take your temperature."

She rolled to me and opened her eyes; she was irritated with me, "I can't sleep if you keep bugging me."

"I am leaving for a little bit, but I need to make sure you are at least okay. Please, just open up."

I was waving the thermometer in front of her. She opened her mouth but closed her eyes. I put it under her tongue and waited. I looked over at her parents. First, I noticed her mom who was waiting impatiently and then secondly her dad who I couldn't figure out. He was either angry or extremely upset. It beeped and she opened her mouth. I took it out looking at it. I smiled, "She is okay right now. Her pulse is almost normal and her temp is just a little elevated. I believe letting her sleep is working."

I really think the medicine was helping too, "What time did you want to go?"

"Whenever you think she can go, and when you're ready."

"I will try to hurry, but if I am not back by 4:30 pm she will need another pill. They are in her bag. She took one at 12:30 pm."

Her mom walked over to grab her bag and pulled them out to look at it, but stopped and looked in the bag again. She put her hand in the bag and pulled out a necklace that was quite long. It had a big ring on the end of it. The tears came to her eyes as she turned to look at Sarah's father. He was instantly angry, and he stormed out of the trailer.

Sarah's mother looked at me to question me.

I shook my head, "I had no idea."

I knew there was a ring, but I thought it was the one she was wearing. I knew that this wasn't a good thing. I didn't want Sarah to be upset, so I spoke up, "I really am not trying to butt in, but I think questioning her about that might not be a good idea right now. I don't want to get her heart rate up. I think you should wait till she is better, maybe *all* better, before you say anything."

She nodded at me letting it fall back in her bag. She put her hand over her mouth and walked out. I couldn't help myself and went for a closer look. I pulled it out, and it was huge and beautiful, and yes, I would take that as an engagement ring. I slowly let it fall back in her bag and turned back to her with wonder. I was here because they were planning on getting married, and Clarissa knew she was going to be part of their family. Now I understand why she was so protective of her. I really needed to keep my distance now with no more hedging to be around her. I just needed to do my job. I just wondered how she could be so sure of something like marriage at such a young age.

I headed out of the trailer and walked up to her parents on my way to my truck, "It's obvious you didn't know about the ring, but please wait to talk to her until she is better. We really don't know what is causing her symptoms or making them worse."

They were reluctant, but agreed to not say anything.

"I am leaving to get my things, but someone should be with her at all times. Can one of you go back in, and hold your questions for later, please."

Her dad shook his head, "I can't go in there. I will shake the shit out of her to ask her what the hell she is doing."

Her mom walked in, but wasn't happy about it either. I didn't know what to say to her dad, but I had to try and calm him a little, "We really shouldn't upset her right now. I know this was a shock, but try to be patient on asking her about it. Please?"

He glared at me, "Did you know about this? Is that why Clarissa has sent you?"

I shook my head, "I didn't know about the ring. I just knew Clarissa cares about your daughter a lot, and it is because James loves her that I am here. So, you may be angry, but I assure you I wouldn't be here if it wasn't for them caring about your daughter. You might want to be thankful also because I am the best, and I will find out what is wrong with her."

The relief showed on his face and almost turned into a smile. I patted him on the shoulder and went to my truck.

"Hey, Jake is it?"

"Yes."

"Thank you."

I nodded and headed to Tony's

I went to fill Tony in on everything. He knew that I was a doctor and was sent to watch over Sarah. Clarissa had set that up, but to my surprise he knew about the engagement ring. I felt bad for leaving Tony alone at the bar, but he was going to have Jason help him if he needed it.

I went to get my things and headed back to Sarah. I did knock on the door when I got there, but walked in. I just couldn't wait to see her and that smile, but she was sleeping.

"Did she sleep the whole time?"

Her parents looked worried again that I said that, and her mom answered, "Yes, she hasn't moved an inch."

I walked over to her and felt her forehead, and it was the same as before I left, "Well, if she is going to sleep anyway, do you want to go?"

"That would be great. We could get her to her own bed."

I realized I would see where she lived. No, don't think of it that way. This was really going to take some self control.

They both agreed, so I picked her up to take her to my truck and I laid her down in the front seat.

She opened her eyes and there was that great smile.

"What are you doing?"

I didn't smile back... stay cold, "I am taking you home."

"Wait, what about my mom?"

"We are going to follow her; you need to sleep. Close your eyes and you will be home soon."

She actually listened and curled up on the seat. I looked at her parents, "Ready."

Her mom, Paula, got in the car and her dad didn't know what to say. I gave him a quick smile as I pulled out to follow her mother.

After about an hour and a half of riding, Paula pulled into a Dairy Queen. I followed and parked. She walked over to the truck, and I rolled down the window.

"Sarah and I always stop on our way home. Would you like something?"

"No, I'm good."

"Are you sure? You should wake her, and see if she wants something. I will go to the restroom, and I'll be back."

She walked away. I felt Sarah's head and she was still fine. I didn't know how to wake her without touching her.

"Sarah."

She didn't respond.

"Sarah."

Once again, there was no response. I traced my fingers on her face. She turned her face toward me and cuddled in more. Shit! Paula came back to my window.

"How is she?"

"She's still sleeping. I'm good; we'll wait here."

"I guess I don't need anything either. Well go."

I nodded waiting for her, but looked down at Sarah. I couldn't believe she was cuddled into me. I wanted to touch her face again. I waited for her mom to start again and I followed. I was tracing my fingers through her hair as we drove.

When we were close to the cities, I wanted to wake her to talk about the ring. She needed to know that they knew, "Sarah, can you wake up a little? Sarah?"

I traced her face and put my hand on her arm to shake her a little.

"What, more probing?"

I laughed with a sigh, "No, I need to talk to you a minute."

She opened her eyes looking up at me. I was completely melting. Those beautiful innocent green eyes with a dark ring around the color were so amazing. I totally forgot what I wanted to say.

"Jake, what did you want to talk to me about?"

She was sitting up. No, I didn't want this; yes, I did. I put both hands on the steering wheel.

"Um, you may get a little mad at me."

"Why?"

"Um… when I left earlier to get my things, I told your parents to give you a pill at 4:30 pm, and they were in your bag."

Sarah:

My heart dropped; I couldn't believe what he was saying, and I felt the tears coming.

He was panicking, "No, no Sarah, don't get upset. I just wanted to let you know. They aren't going to talk to you about it until you are better."

It hit me like a brick. I didn't read my poem today. My James, how could I forget my James? I was heartbroken. I lay back down and let the tears fall. I couldn't sleep again till I read my note. I was feeling so bad. I closed my eyes again as the tears dripped out. How could I be so horrible? How was I going to explain this to my sweet Cayuse?

"Sarah, why are you so upset? I told you that they wouldn't ask you about it until you were completely better."

"It's not that."

"What is it then?"

"You'll think I am stupid again," I covered my face and sat up putting my feet on the dashboard.

"Sarah?"

"He writes me love notes everyday, and I forgot to read the one for today." I peaked at him to see if he thought I was being stupid. His expression did not change.

"I really don't see what you are upset about; it's still today."

I was relieved; I could still read it because it was still today, "Where is my bag?"

He pointed at the car.

"Oh. I guess I will have to wait then." I realized I was in the truck with Jake and we were heading home, "Why are you going home with us?"

He laughed at me, "You really were in a deep sleep. You don't remember anything?"

"No. Is that funny?"

"I'm sorry, but I am going with you to the doctors tomorrow."

"I don't think so. I usually have a friend go with me."

"Well, I am too. I am getting your records to look at all the testing they have done. I might see something they are missing.

"Are you that good?"

He disapproved of my question, "Why else would I be here?"

Well then, you will need to lighten up and I am going to get him to have some fun. Maybe find him a girlfriend.

"Well, okay then."

We rode in silence, but we were getting close. I opened my phone to call Matt, "Hey, I'm back. No girl talk though."

"Why not?"

"I will explain later."

"So, how are you doing; still not getting sick?"

"No throwing up if that's what you mean."

"What else is there?"

"Just need a lot of sleep. Are you going with me tomorrow to the doctors?"

"Yeah, if you want me to go."

"Well, just to let you know, I have a new doctor that has been assigned to my case, and he will be going tomorrow. So, I was actually letting you off the hook."

"You don't want me to go?"

"No, it's not like that. If you want to go I will pick you up at 9 am."

"Yeah, I want to go."

"We'll be there."

"He's coming with you?"

"Yep."

"That is weird."

"I know, but its okay. I will see you tomorrow."

"Bye."

I hung up the phone and gave Jake a grin, "We have to pick up my friend at 9 am, so he can go with us."

"He?"

"James is okay with it. He didn't like me going through this alone."

Jake looked confused, but I ignored it. My James was special. I was more important than any insecurity he had. I closed my eyes and thought about his touch on my face and his sweet lips on mine. He better call me tonight, because I hate being away from him. We were pulling into my driveway. It was kind of long. When he stopped, I got out right away. I slept, so I was feeling much better again. Mom looked at me with worry.

"Mom." I hugged her, "I love you, and I will be fine. Jake will look at all the tests and find out why I am sick. He will make it all go away."

I smiled at her and grabbed my bag. I dug out my note and cupped it in my hand.

Jake gave me a funny grin and grabbed my bag first and then my mother's, "I'll just walk you in, and then I will go."

"Where are you going?"

"I'm going to my parents. They live here in town, and I am staying with them."

I was happy that this was working out so well. I held my note tight in my hands and walked in. I didn't have enough guts to pull my necklace out and put it on, even though I wanted to. It might stress out my mom.

He followed me though the house and I turned in front of mom's room, "Mom's bag in there."

He went in and set it down on her bed and then came back to me. I pointed into my room, "My bag in there."

He walked in and set it on my bed. He took one look around the room and came back out looking at me, "Small."

I liked that he didn't ask a lot of questions. I followed as he walked back to the living room, "I think you should take another antibiotic and some more ibuprofen. I will take your pulse and temperature, and then I will go."

I sat down on the couch and opened my mouth. He looked at me and shook his head. He pulled the thermometer out of his pocket and put it under my tongue. Mom sat in the chair across from the couch watching. He sat down and took my wrist. I looked at mom and smiled. She wasn't amused. The thermometer beeped when it was ready.

He took it from my mouth and read it. He shook his head with disbelief, "Sleeping helps and her heart rate is normal too."

I was giddy that I was fine now. I was still holding my note. I didn't want to forget about it.

"Well, I guess I am going to go. You're not doing anything tonight that I would have to stop back and check on you for?"

"Nope. I live a boring life in the city."

He smiled at me, "I will pick you up at 8 am, right?

"Yeah, that's fine. Did you want to eat with us?"

"No, I should really go see my family and if you are doing okay, it would be a good time to visit with them. The next few days I will be busy."

"Why, what are you doing?"

He raised his eyebrows at me like he couldn't believe I was asking, "I'm going to be reading medical records."

Oh did I feel stupid. I looked at mom, "I will walk him out if that's okay?"

She looked to Jake to see if it would be okay.

He grinned that fully little smile, "She's good right now."

She nodded to me, so I followed him out the back door and walked him to the truck, but stood away from the door.

He got in and looked at me, "You are feeling better; I could stay if you want me to."

That was very sweet but I was feeling better, "Nope, I have to read my note and go to bed early."

There was that grin again, "Do you want to read it to me?"

"No, it's personal."

He looked down, "He must really love you for them to go through all this to make you better."

"I hope so. I love him."

He was shaking his head, "See you tomorrow early."

I smiled at him and stepped further away from the truck, so he could pull out. I slowly walked inside and noticed my mom just sitting there. I wanted to bring up the ring but I didn't know how to explain it yet. I sat down on the couch because she wasn't looking at me or saying anything. She must be really angry with me.

"Sorry you had to drive home by yourself."

"Did he take your pulse and temperature on the way home?"

I really don't know. I slept most of the way, but I feel so much better now."

"So did you feel it coming on or did it just hit you?"

"It kind of comes out of the blue. I just get tired."

"You haven't gotten sick though?"

'No. That's what I can't figure out. Maybe the stress is gone so it's hitting me a different way. I do think the pills are helping me."

She smiled. I got up and went to the kitchen to find something to eat. I was hungry. She came out and helped me make some dinner. We sat down and ate and then retired to the living room. I sat on the couch and dozed watching a movie. Mom of course was reading, but when I started to doze off she shooed me to bed. I still had my note, and I crawled in bed to read it. Day 34:

You are as soft as the pillow I lay to rest my head on
You are as sweet as the honey dew I love to taste
You are my life, my desire, and my destiny
If you will still have me
I love you more than you know
James

The tears came to my eyes. I want to have him for the rest of my life. I did love him more than life itself. I closed my eyes with my phone in my hand waiting to hear from my Cayuse.

I answered my phone, "James." I sniffed a little.
"Sarah, what is wrong?"
"I miss you."
"Oh, how I miss you. Can I come home now?"
"Yes I don't want to be away from you anymore."
"Really?"
"Yes, James."
"Do you mean it?"
"Yes, James, I'm done and I need you."
"I am coming home."
"Thank you."
"For what?"
"For being the greatest love I could ever dream of."
"Oh, my sweet, Sarah. I can't wait for morning to come, so I can work my way home to you."
"I love you James."
"I love you more than you know."
"You keep saying that, but I have learned something while you have been away."
"What's that?"
"People have choices, James."

"Okay, what do you mean?"

"I choose you."

"Oh, Sarah, I want to hold you so bad right now."

"We might be heavily supervised."

"I don't care, but why do you think that?"

"They know about the ring."

"Good."

'No. It's not good. I guess they were pretty upset by it."

"You guess?"

"Yeah, I had the antibiotics in my bag and mom got them out and saw the ring."

"You had to deal with that on your own too?"

"No James, Jake told them they couldn't upset me, so they were not to talk to me until I was better."

"Jake... who's Jake?"

"He is the one your mother sent to watch over me. He's a doctor."

"So, you are spending a lot of time with him?"

"Yes, but he is distant with me. He takes my temperature and pulse."

"I am jealous of this Jake."

"James, your mom sent him. He is coming to my doctor's appointment with me tomorrow to get my file. He is going to see if they are missing something."

"What time is your appointment?"

"It's at 10 am in the morning."

"I should go."

"NO! Why?"

"Maybe I can get an early flight and come with you too."

"James?"

"What?"

"Can it wait? I need to hear you. You need to talk to me 'til I can sleep again. I have been in agony all weekend. I've been sleeping in your bed and... in your clothes. That was very hard to do without you there."

He talked sweet nothings in my ear until I slept. I was dreaming of him and all the wonderful things he makes me feel: I felt his hand tracing my face, and those big brown eyes melting me. I felt the kiss that I get lost in, and the desire to pull him as close to me as I could get him. I dreamt of the house, his arms wrapped around me, and the fog moving through the house. My dream moved to the fireplace laying on the rug and being as one and how perfect we were together.

36. Doctor Appointment

I woke to Day 35: I grabbed my note before doing anything else.

Our day will come soon enough
But soon enough for me I would not agree
Soon enough for you I don't think so
I will wait as long as you say
For it is you that makes me sway
I am strong but weak with you
You melt my heart and soul
I love you more than you know

James

I looked at the clock. Jake was going to be here in an hour. I got up and mom was already ready for work and was eating breakfast. I had a quick bowl of cereal. Mom offered to go to the doctor with me too, but I think I already had enough people going, and I didn't want to scare the doctor. I took a shower and got ready. I was supposed to get the results of the scan but I already knew the answer, so I really wasn't scared.

I texted James. *"Are you coming this morning?"*
>*"NO, couldn't get a flight. Still working on something."*
"What is that?"
>*"I'll tell you later."*
"K."

I was waiting patiently for Jake to show up. He was here five minutes early. Mom had already left, so I had to lock up the house. I had my necklace on and had it tucked in, and I felt it as I locked the door.

Jake was right behind me, "How far does this Matt live?"

"He's about fifteen minutes from here."

"We don't have to leave yet."

"Oh." I reopened the door and he walked in with me. He took my temperature and my pulse. I waited impatiently tapping my fingers.

"Are you nervous about something?"

'No, why?"

"You're antsy, and you're biting your bottom lip."

"Nope. I'm okay."

"Did you argue with James again?"

"Nope, he's coming home."

"What? When is he coming?"

"I don't know, but I thought about what you said and I decided he could come home. I am done fighting it."

"But I am here to take care of you until he gets back. Clarissa won't have me take care of you if he is here."

"That's good, right? You're off the hook."

He glanced up at me, "To tell you the truth I have only had three times in my life that were really fun and they were all with you. I was kind of enjoying it."

"You can still take care of me, and we can still have fun. James won't mind. He has a hard time controlling me, and he could use the help. I won't want to rest much if he is here."

He smiled but there was a change in him, "When is he coming?"

"I don't know. I just told him last night. He couldn't get a flight this morning so I am supposed to text him after the appointment. Maybe he will know then."

"We should go then."

He was distant and serious again. I think I hurt his feelings. I didn't want to do that because he was helping me. We got up and went out to his truck. I directed him to Matt's house. Matt was sitting on the steps waiting. He was early too. As he got in he looked at Jake with a glare, "Matt, this is Jake; Jake, this is Matt."

I leaned to Matt, "You better be nice."

He grimaced with a fake smile and put his hand out to shake Jake's. Jake returned the gesture.

"Are we still on for tomorrow? Can you still play?"

I was horrified. I had forgotten about the volleyball thing and I peaked at Jake through my eyelashes.

He wasn't happy already, "What now?"

"I play volleyball Tuesdays and Thursdays with Matt. Can we go?"

"He would go with us?" Matt asked with disgust.

I gave him a disciplined glare, "Matt, he has to watch over me all the time and if you don't like it then I can't play."

I turned forward very determined.

Jake was smiling, "You shouldn't go anyway; you would get tired out."

I really wanted to play. It makes me feel really good about myself. "Please, Jake, you can go with me; you can take my temperature and pulse the whole time. Pleeaassee?"

"I don't like it."

"You don't have plans tomorrow, do you? I mean you weren't planning on being down here anyway and you might have fun. There will be lots of girls." I turned to Matt encouraging, "Right, Matt?"

"Yeah, lots of babes in bikinis."

"How about we see how you are doing today. Did you take the antibiotic this morning?"

"Yes, I did and I feel so good. Please Jake?"

"I said we would have to see how today goes."

I looked at Matt remorsefully, "I am sorry, Matt."

Jake spoke up, "I didn't say no, but we'll have to see how it goes today."

Both Matt and I were grinning from ear to ear. It was pretty quiet after that. He knew how to get to the doctor's office that I was supposed to go to so I didn't have to give him directions. He pulled out the thermometer when we were getting close.

I complained, "Jake, we just did that before we left the house."

"Sarah, no arguments."

"Fine."

I looked at Matt. He smiled and nodded so I would follow doctor's orders. Jake grabbed my wrist and was counting as he looked at his watch. When the thermometer went off he looked at that. I tried to grab it but he wouldn't let me look, and I pouted. Matt grabbed my hands and shook his head no. I didn't understand why Matt was stopping me, but I quit bugging Jake for the thermometer.

Jake only told me that it was elevated.

"What was?"

"Your pulse is elevated. I think we really have to watch this carefully today. Grab a notebook out of my bag."

I did what he asked.

"Write down the time and write 100 degrees," and then he gave me the pulse numbers, which I didn't understand at all.

We walked into the doctor's office. I went to the counter looking back at Matt. I handed him my phone, "Do you want to put some stuff on it?"

He was playfully smiling, "Yeah." He took it from me and looked through it and then gave me a funny look and mouthed, "You only have eight numbers?"

I shrugged my shoulders and turned back to the counter and he went to sit and wait for us. Jake was grinning, almost insulting Matt with his look. I didn't want him to be smug, "Be nice. He is my friend."

"I didn't say anything."

"You didn't have to. For a non genius, he is the smartest person I know."

I turned to the person behind the counter, "I have an appointment at 10 am, and I will need a copy of my medical records."

"You will need to sign a release form." She pulled it out and put it on the counter for me. I signed it and pushed it back to her.

"Oh, you are only sixteen; you will need a parent or guardian's signature."

I turned to Jake. He pulled his wallet out and then his ID, handing both of them to her.

She looked at him smugly, "It has to be someone responsible for her."

He opened his phone and called someone, but smiled at me. When he started to talk he turned away from me, "Yes, we are having problems getting her records."

He turned back to me after hanging up, "It will be just a second or two."

It might have been a couple of minutes, and the phone rang behind the desk. She answered and said a lot of yeses and hung up the phone. Then she smiled the most pleasant smile, "I am sorry, Dr. Phallen. If you will follow me, we have a room for you right this way."

I pulled on Jakes arm and gestured to Matt.

"Yes, he can come with us."

I tried to get Matt's attention, "Matt, come here."

He got up, but he was still messing with my phone. I grabbed his arm so he wouldn't get lost. They brought us to a conference room. Jake held the door for me to walk in. I pulled Matt in and he sat in the first chair he came to looking up and then at me. I shrugged my shoulders. All this was making me very nervous. I moved closer to Jake wondering what was going on.

"You're fine, Sarah. Don't worry." He was pulling a chair out for me. I sat down and he sat in the chair next to me. My doctor, Dr. Justin, walked in. Jake stood up to shake her hand. She had my charts in her arms and sat it on the table in front of Jake, "Dr. Phallen, I didn't realize Sarah was getting a second opinion."

He was pleasant, "I 'm a friend of the Family."

He sat back down and opened the file. He was going through the file and asked, "Is this my copy or are you still working on it?"

"We're still working on it."

He started to read through things very quickly, and I was trying to follow what he was reading. Matt moved closer to me putting his hand on my arm. I was gripping the arms of the chair so hard my knuckles were completely white.

Jake leaned to Dr. Justin and pointed at something, "Is this something you were treating her with or personal?"

She looked at me, "Personal."

He didn't acknowledge me, but I had a feeling it was the birth control. He looked at her, "We need this… this…" and he ran his fingers down a little further, "…and this." He turned it to a new page. She was scribbling as fast as she could.

"This…this…" He turned to another page. "Yes, this…this…and this today. I want a phone call as soon as the results come in."

He looked at her sternly, "What I mean is, I don't want to wait until they all come in. I want the results of each test as each one comes in and we need to make this a priority."

"Yes, of course."

"NO! I mean immediately, she is getting worse, and she doesn't have time to wait any longer."

He was going through the papers again, and moving them so she could see what he was thinking about, "I want her off of this today, she's on an antibiotic so I wouldn't work anyway and it may be causing side effects that would hide what we are looking for."

I knew what he was talking about because the only thing I would be taking besides what he was giving me was the birth control.

She looked at me, "Sarah, are you ready?"

I stood up and she took me to a different room and had me change into a gown. We did all the tests he asked for and I was sitting there waiting by myself.

Jake walked in with Dr. Justin, "Sarah, I am going to show your doctor something. Can you lie down please?"

I lay down, but looked at him with fear in my eyes. I didn't want him to do anything and then I looked away.

He moved to touch my stomach, "Okay, come here."

He took her hand and put it where his was. They were right where James said it was. I was relieved a little because they were closer to it than before. She looked at him.

"See do you feel that?"

"Yes, but that's…she would be in pain."

He was trying to get me to look at him, "Sarah."

I turned to him.

"Does this hurt at all?"

"No."

"Even a little bit?"

'No."

He shook his head in disbelief and Dr. Justin looked at him, "You really think that is it?"

"Yes, but give me the results as they come in. We'll have to wait on these."

He pulled me to sit up. I looked at him pleading with him to say something to me, "Do you know what it is?"

"Not yet...not sure anyway, but we will know for sure with these results." He leaned into me a little and whispered, "If it's what I think it is; I can fix it. It may involve surgery, but let's just see. Get dressed, and I'll wait in the conference room."

I felt better as he walked out of the room.

Dr. Justin waited until he was gone, "Sarah, are you taking birth control?"

"Yes. I started them on Sunday."

"Well, you are going to have to restart them next month. You need to go off of them for now. Do you have a need for them yet?"

I was totally embarrassed, "No, not really."

"If you do anything you will need other protection, Sarah. She pulled out a small box and handed it to me. Then she went into another drawer and handed me another box. I looked at them and they said, 'Condoms' and the other said 'Foam'. Great, like I knew how to use either of them, "Sarah, if you really love this person, remember you are only sixteen and sometimes it's okay to wait."

Okay this is not fair. Here's another person telling me to wait.

I didn't know what to say, so I blurted out the truth, "Yeah, cuz I wouldn't know how to use these anyway."

She smiled at me, "Then it would probably be better to wait. You can get dressed."

"What does he think it is?"

"Let's just wait and see. It's very minor so don't worry yourself. I didn't realize you knew people that are very important. I would have worked faster."

"This is new to me; I didn't know either."

She was confused by my answer but gave me a quick smile and left the room. I got dressed and walked into the conference room. Matt looked at me and stood up. I put my hand up for him to not move to me and motioned for him to sit down. Jake was looking at some large scans on one wall. I walked over to him and stood there looking at what he was studying. He looked at me for a second, and then took his left hand to hold my right one and started to explain the different scans, and what each one covered. He got to the last one which was my stomach area.

"Sarah, there is no cancer anywhere. That is not a worry."

I looked at him and the tears were welling up in my eyes as he turned to look at me happily.

"Then what is it?"

He pulled me in front of him wrapping his arms around me lifting my right hand with his, "See this; right here?"

"Yeah." I felt so much more secure. He was treating me like a real person. "I think that is our culprit.

"What is it?"

"Your appendix, but I need the results to be sure. Usually people experience extreme pain and you have none. That's what makes me a little unsure."

He was pointing my hand over another area. "This..." he was sweeping our hands over another area, "...I can't explain, but we should know in a day or two. If it is, we'll just take it out, and you will be better."

I leaned into him a little for support. He turned me to him and put my face on his chest, "I will take care of this... of you."

I stayed there until my doctor walked back in. He took my hand and walked me back to a chair that was closer to Matt. Jake handed my hand to him. Matt took it as I sat down. I was feeling really weak again. This was too much for me to handle. I put my head on his chest. Jake noticed and came over to feel my forehead.

He directed Dr. Justin, "We need to get her home, and I need a shot for her now! She is burning up."

Matt felt my head and was scared.

I gave him a weak smile, "I'm okay. I just need to sleep. It will go away."

Matt didn't reply because he didn't know what to say.

Dr. Justin came back in with a shot and put it in my arm. I grimaced, and Jake went out of the room. I closed my eyes and rested on Matt.

When Jake came back in I could hear him, but I was so tired I couldn't open my eyes. I heard Jake, "We will take her out the back."

Dr. Justin replied, "Maybe she should go to the hospital until we know for sure."

"I will stay with her."

Jake picked me up so I curled into him, "Jake, it's okay; James is coming home. It will wait."

I felt Jake hand me over to Matt. I opened my eyes a little and we were in the truck. I tried to not fall asleep, but it was getting harder to stay awake.

Matt was moving away from me and I didn't want to move, "Wait. What...?"

"Sarah, it's okay. I'm at home. Call me later if you can?"

I opened my eyes a little.

"Sarah?"

He moved really close to whisper in my ear, "Tell me I am next in line after James. That you would be mine if he wasn't in the picture."

I put my hand on his face, "Yes, Matt, you are special to me too, but you know where my heart lays."

He smiled and kissed my cheek. He helped me lay down. I put my head on Jake's leg and didn't hear anything after that.

37. Relieving the Stress

I woke in my bed, and I was feeling better. I walked out to the living room looking around. I didn't think Jake would leave me alone. I continued to walk into the kitchen.

He was engulfed in papers, reading through my file, "You're feeling better?" He didn't look up at me.

I sat down at the table and looked at the pile of papers spread all over the table, "I thought you knew what it was?"

"Just making sure I'm not missing anything." He still didn't look at me.

I picked up one and attempted to read it. I finally gave up; the hand writing was horrible and really hard to read. He took it from me and set it back down. I leaned so my face was in front of him.

His mouth was growing to a grin, "What are you doing?"

"Nothing."

He was completely smiling now but shook his head.

"So teach me something?"

He was still reading, but turned to the next page.

"Maybe... how you read so fast."

He looked up confused, "What?"

"How do you read this so fast and then remember it?"

He grinned and scooted towards me. He put the sheet in front of us. "Look at all the small words that don't mean anything. I don't even see them anymore. I just read the big words and important information. If I need clarification, I go back and read more."

I turned to him, "That easy?"

"Yes, that easy. I had to do everything at three times the speed in order to get where I am today."

"How old were you when you graduated from High School?"

"Fourteen."

"Wow, you missed out on a lot of fun."

He was confused by my response.

I had to ask, "What have you done for fun?"

"Like what?"

"Have you been to Valleyfair?"

"No, I don't like rides."

"Really? When have you been on one?"

"Never."

"Well, I know you haven't gone water skiing or tubing. Have you ever played pool?"

"Why would I want to do that?"

"Have you ever gone swimming?"

"Yes, it's good exercise."

"You dance; where did that come from?"

"I had to entertain myself a lot and at college, so I watched and practiced by myself."

"What was the last movie you have seen?"

"Don't watch movies."

"Have you ever been to a movie theater?"

"No." He glared at me and looked angry with me, "Sarah, I do have to go through this material."

"Nope, you've done enough. It's time to wait for the results of the tests and for you to come help me." I was pulling him to the living room. I put a chair next to mine in front of the computer and pushed him to sit down. I pulled up YouTube and started playing videos, "I need to make up two dances for Saturday and you are going to help me."

"You can do this on the computer?"

I smiled and started showing him songs and videos. I asked which ones he liked and we must have spent two hours looking for two really good songs. We came up with him liking reggae. I was enjoying this. I showed him how we could make a medley of a few songs put together. He was getting excited about doing this. I watched him get up and suggest some moves for different parts of the songs. He wanted to put different parts of different songs together. We ended up putting four songs together for one of the dance lessons. I convinced him we would be in the country so we had to use one country song too. I made him listen to a few, and I finally got him to agree with one that was upbeat.

He sat back and took a deep breath. He looked at me sadly, "I really should have been looking at your files."

"You know what it is. You showed me and James said that was where it was coming from."

"He felt that?"

"Yeah. You were on the spot when you showed Dr. Justin.

"So you knew where it was coming from? Why didn't you tell them before this?"

"Yeah, my boyfriend feels everything I do and he says I am sick and it's coming from here…" I lifted my shirt to point to the spot, "And it's spreading across here." I traced my hand across my stomach.

Jake watched carefully as I moved my hand, and then he looked up at me very seriously, "He feels everything?"

I smiled, "Yes."

"So you two are connected in some way?"

"I think so."

He was looking depressed again, "I need to get back to work."

He got up and walked to the kitchen and started reading through the files again. I walked out slowly sitting down in the chair next to him, "Do you really think you can find out anything more by looking through those?"

He smiled without looking at me, "You need to rest if you are going to make up dances in a little bit."

I grinned, "You are going to stay and help me with the dances?"

He shook his head, "Yes."

"Fine, but we have a lot of work to do with that medley. I'll only take a little nap."

He stood up and put his hand on my forehead and fed me a pill. He took my temperature and checked my pulse, "You are still okay, but if you want to have energy later, you have to take a nap."

"Okay." I got up and went to my room.

I texted James.

"Are you coming yet?"

>*"NO."*

"Are you mad?"

>*"No."*

"Can you talk?"

>*"Nope."*

"I love you."

>*"I will call you later."*

"Please say you love me."

>*"More than you know, my sweet Sarah."*

I curled up with my pillow wishing he could be here to hold me. I love him so much.

Jake walked in and sat on the edge of my bed, "Are you okay?"

"Yep." I rolled over, so he could see my face. I wasn't crying.

"Is he on his way?"

"No." Then the tears started to well up and spilled over.

"Do you want me to sit with you?"

"Files."

"You're right they will wait." He moved to sit more on the bed with his back resting his back on the headboard. I lay on his lap with my head and chest facing away from him.

He ran his hand over my back, "I am sorry, Sarah."

I sniffled, "For what?"

"That you are missing him and that you're not well."

I cuddled in more.

"Did he say when?"

"Nope."

I closed my eyes and let the rest of the tears fall.

Jake:

I sat there just tracing my hand over her back. I wanted to know what she was thinking. How she was feeling? I leaned my head back. I did not want to care for her. She did really love him. I really enjoyed being around her so much. She makes me smile. The look on her face when she was scared made me want to comfort her. When she smiled at me from seeing me happy was very fulfilling. She was warming my heart. I didn't know that having someone in your life could bring you so much more satisfaction than doing what I have already done. Being a doctor wasn't filling my wants anymore. I wanted *her* to feel that way about me. I knew it was wrong and I will not let myself...I looked at her and touched her shoulder. I whispered, "Sarah?"

She didn't move. I rolled her over, so she could sleep. I placed her head on a pillow. I traced my hand along her face and she smiled. She liked when I touched her. No! She doesn't know it's me... or does she? I wanted to touch her more. I hesitated and looked at her. I didn't want to blow any chance I had to spend time with her. I got up and went back to my paperwork. I would wait till she was awake to get my fill.

Sarah:

I woke again but there was a lot of noise in the kitchen. I walked out and saw my mom and Jake cooking together. They were laughing and talking. I sat down at the table that was still filled with lots of papers. I saw his notebook with some notes on it. I tried to read it from the side, but it was hard to make it out, *'A Doctor's hand writing'*. They really didn't pay much attention to me, but Jake walked over and looked at me and closed his notebook, felt my forehead, and then smiled. He moved back to helping my mother without one word.

Mom looked at me, "Feeling better?"

"Ah, yeah."

"Would you please get out the TV trays so we can eat in the living room? Jake here has the table full."

They both laughed, but I didn't get the joke. So I went to get the TV trays out. I was still quite groggy. I was struggling with setting them up, and Jake came out to help me, "You must have been tired; you slept quite awhile."

I looked at him confused.

"Your mom has a second job that she has to go to, so I am staying awhile. Is that okay?"

I smiled because I really didn't want to be by myself, "Yeah, great."

It was hard to be excited when I wasn't really awake yet.

"Well, that didn't sound positive."

"NO, yeah, I mean I'm just not awake yet. I really don't want to be alone, so yeah I would like that."

He put his hands on both my arms and directed me to sit on the couch. "We'll get you a plate. I want you to rest."

I looked up into his eyes and got nothing, because he wasn't really looking at me. I sat down and leaned back closing my eyes.

They were walking in, and Jake was carrying two plates. He put one on the tray in front of me and the other next to me. Mom sat in her chair.

Jake had the remote and was clicking through the channels, "Do you realize there are over 200 channels on this thing? How do you ever decide what to watch?"

I held out my hand for the remote. I looked at him and then went through the movie channels and found a really old movie, 'Turner and Hooch'.

I looked at him and smiled, "Here, watch this movie; it's really funny."

I started eating and I had to chuckle because Jake was laughing right away.

Mom got up, "Sarah, I have to go. Will you be okay?"

"Yep, I got the dishes."

Jake was really into the movie. He didn't even see her get up because he was laughing. It was funny to watch. I got up and hugged her and started putting stuff away in the kitchen.

She looked at me, "Nick necklace."

I was stunned she brought it up but I knew what she was hinting at, "Thanks." I avoided looking at her.

"I'll be home at 11 pm."

"Yeah, I don't know if I'll be up. I am not really waking up. I could go back to bed right now."

"Then leave the dishes, I'll do them when I get home."

"No, I can do them. It's not going to kill me."

She looked at me angry.

I tried to lighten the mood by smiling really big at her saying, "Have a good night mom. I love you."

"You can tell me where you got the necklace later."

"Okay, anything you want."

It wasn't worth arguing about it with her. It was mine and I was keeping it, but only if James wanted me to. Oh James. I pulled my phone out and tried again.

"Can you talk now?"
>"Nope."
"K."
>"I love you."
"Thank you. I needed that."
>"Later."
"K."

I walked back in the living room. Jake was still into the movie. He was laughing and eating. I did fine it enjoyable watching him laugh. It was like sitting with a kid watching a movie for the first time. I walked over and sat down in the spot I was in before.

He glimpsed at me, "Have you seen this? It is so funny. I love that dog."

I shook my head and smiled, "Yeah, lots of time. It's an old movie."

He didn't look at me, "Really?"

"Yeah."

When he was done eating I brought his plate to the kitchen and started to wash the dishes. I could hear him laughing. It was making me laugh just listening to him. I almost felt bad that he missed out on so much stuff being a genius.

I decided to call Matt.

"Oh Sarah, are you okay?"

"Yeah. I slept and I am much better now."

"Who is laughing in the background?"

"Jake."

"He is still there?"

"Yeah, mom went to work, so he is staying 'til she gets home. They don't want to leave me alone."

"Sarah, you still love James, right?"

"Of course I do."

"You need to be careful. I saw the way he cared for you."

"It's not like that with him."

"Yeah, it is."

"No, he doesn't look at me that way. Let's just say like you do."

He laughed a little. "Okay, but he is going to like you, if he doesn't already."

"Whatever, Matt."

"Can you play volleyball tomorrow?"

"I think I can talk him into it. I am going to work tomorrow to drop off a Doctor's note so I won't have to work this week at all."

"Call me to let me know before noon. If you're not playing, I will have to find someone to fill in."

"Yeah, but I am planning on it."

"Okay, but be careful."

"Bye Matt."

38. Shorts

I hung up with Matt and went out to sit with Jake. I wanted to watch him watch the movie. The movie was almost over when he was interrupted by his phone. He stood up answering it and walked to the kitchen. The change in him was immediate, and he was back to his serious self. I stood up and followed to listen.

"No, I wasn't expecting that."
"Yes."
"Okay, and the other one?"
"Really?"
"No."
"Okay."
"Yes, whatever time they come in."

He hung up the phone and looked at the papers on the table and started to go through them looking for something. He pulled out the notebook and started writing stuff down. He crossed out two things on a list he had written before. He was so serious and it was intense. I sat down watching him. He stopped and ran his fingers through his hair.

I couldn't help myself, "What is it?"

He looked at me and pushed it all away from him. He was angry, "This sucks."

I got up and grabbed his hands, "Come with me. It's time for a break."

"No Sarah, I shouldn't have taken a break before. I am missing something. Just go. I need to look longer and harder."

I walked away. There was no competing with that. The movie was over now, so I turned the TV off. I went to the computer pulling up the music we had put together. I started it and turned it up. I was going through some steps and I heard him yell.

"Sarah, turn it down! I can't think!"

I turned it up. I didn't want to think about it. I needed to escape thinking about this and how I felt.

He yelled again, "SARAH!"

I closed my eyes and my ears to block him out. I needed to escape from this reality. I kept dancing with my eyes closed.

"Sarah?" His voice was softer.

I turned to see him walking into the room, "Shhhhh, I can't think like this."

I couldn't help but smirk at him. He walked over to the computer and turned it down. He stood there looking at me.

I felt obligated to justify my actions, "It's okay to not work all the time. You're still young, and you should have some fun too."

He walked up to me putting his hands on each side of my face just looking at me. *I needed James here. I needed to feel loved. Just don't kiss me. I can't return it. I love James. Please, do not kiss me.*

He didn't but he spoke, "Some things are more important, and you may not be there at all if we don't take care of this."

I looked at him melting. I was trying to convince myself, *I'll turn you down. Please, please, do not kiss me.* I closed my eyes losing my balance. His arms wrapped around me, and sat me down on the couch and then felt my forehead.

"Sarah?"

"Nope, I'm fine, really. I'll keep it down. I am sorry."

He knelt with one knee on the couch and hovered over me feeling my pulse by touching my neck, "Sarah, your pulse is racing."

"Yeah, I think I need to..., um..., go rest some more."

I took his hands and pushed them away gently and moved around him. I couldn't even look at him. I was so weak and I really needed to be held. I needed James here right now. I walked into my room closing the door behind me. He let me walk away without saying anything. Thank you god, please help me to be strong. I love my James.

My phone rang shortly after I went to my room. My heart leapt, "James!"

"My sweet Sarah, are you okay?"

"No."

"What is it? Did they find out...?"

"No, James, it's not that."

"Sarah?"

"I need your arms around me, James. I need you to hold me really bad right now."

"Where are you?"

"I'm in my room."

"Are you lying down?"

"No, but...I am now." I was lying on my side and I could feel him move next to me.

"James, I do need this, but I need to feel you for real."

"I know baby, not much longer." I could feel his hand trace my face. I needed this so bad.

"James, when are you coming?"

"I don't want to tell you. You will be disappointed in me."

"I am never disappointed in you. I just really, really need you right now."

I felt his kiss on my shoulder, then on my neck, and his arms wrapped tighter around me.

"James, I need this for real. I want to feel your warm lips on mine."

He was curling into me more, holding me with his whole body and then the rush came. He moved through me. I gasped. The feeling was amazing. It was like he touched every inch of my body at one time. I was completely relaxed.

I could hear his breath and he was crying. He was as miserable as I was."

"Sarah, I need you too."

"James, I was weak today."

"I know baby, I know." I could hear him; the sniffling gave him away.

"I only want you!"

"I know that too, my sweet Sarah. I am sorry."

"James, please come home. I am not strong enough to go another day without you."

"Sarah..." He was almost weeping, and I was crying too.

"Yes, my Cayuse."

"Please be strong enough to wait for me. I love you more than you know."

"How much longer, James?"

He gulped as if this hurt him more, "One more week baby, one more week. I'll be home on Monday."

I couldn't hold it in, and I was gasping for air because I couldn't breathe. My heart was breaking.

"No, Sarah, no. Don't feel that way. I am coming home, Sarah. Please wait."

"I will; I just hurt so badly without you here."

"Did Matt go with you today?"

"Yes, and so did Jake. He got a lot of special treatment. It was weird."

"Does he know what it is?"

"I'm not sure, maybe my appendix."

"That fits where I felt it."

"James, I need you here, so I can forget about this. I don't want this anymore. I want you. I need you to hold me and to help me forget. I need you to touch me and make me feel beautiful."

I felt the rush through my whole body again. I could hardly breathe, "Yes, James, I need you to make me feel loved."

"Oh Sarah, you will wait for me; I feel it. Just be strong a little longer. I will hold you 'til the end of time if you will have me?"

"James, I will and you are my forever." I curled into a pillow and listened to his breathing.

"Sarah?"

"I am just listening to you breathe. I miss you."

"Is there anything else I can do to help you wait for me?"

"Yes, come home."

"Sarah!"

"Why are you waiting another week?"

"I tried to quit, but they told me I was too valuable. They made me an offer that would allow me to finish; and Sarah...?"

I was sniffing, trying to hold the tears back, "Yeah?"

"It was you. You feel that if I don't finish this, that I can't commit to you for the rest of my life. I want you to see when I tell you I want you till the end of time that I really mean until the end of my life. It is you and only you, and that I can't live without you."

"I can wait for you. I am stronger now."

"Sarah." The sound of relief was in his voice.

"I needed to hear that; thank you, my sweet Cayuse, you bring me back to life. I cannot live without you either. That is why I am slowly dying here."

I could hear him, and he lost it. He was crying again, "Sarah, you are breaking my heart."

"But James, I will wait for you." I couldn't stop crying either.

We sat there not saying a word. Neither of us wanted to let go. It was so hard to breathe, and my heart was aching for him so bad.

"Sarah?"

"No, not yet, James. Not yet please."

"No, not yet; I love you."

The tears streamed down my face.

"James, my Cayuse. I don't only love you. I am totally in love with you."

I felt his hands on my face, so I closed my eyes, and his touch filled my heart. I felt his kiss, so soft and tender. The kiss came deeper. I felt his body on mine.

"James, no, I can't because my heart will hurt more."

I felt his hands trace over my body.

"James, can I dream about the house with you? Can you handle that?"

"Anything you need... tonight I am yours."

"Talk to me 'til I can sleep. I sleep better when you're here."

"I know my sweet Sarah, oh how I miss that."

"Tell me about this offer, and if I fall asleep it's so I can dream about you."

He took a deep breath, "When I went in to tell them I was quitting, I told them someone in my family was very sick and I needed to go home. They offered to let me take all the tests early. All the drills and procedures I have to do, they will help me late into the nights so I can finish. But to get it all done even early, it will still take a week."

He went on explaining in more detail, but I couldn't wait to dream about my Cayuse so I let the sleep come over me.

The dream was as beautiful as ever. The fog drifting in with James's arms around me, and our hands together tracing through it; A soft kiss on my shoulder and the tracing of my arms felt like he adored me; James sitting on the rug pulling me to him and fitting perfectly together; the desire in his eyes of wanting me as we moved together as one. The kissing; oh the deep passionate kissing was amazing. The dream went on forever.

I woke having to stretch to shake it off, and I felt amazingly better. There was no more weakness and no more being sick. The antibiotics must be working. I got up, but it wasn't quite morning yet. I went to the bathroom and wanted to go read some of Jakes notes on me.

Maybe I could steer him the right way some more. I needed to be good for next Monday, for my James's return. I didn't' want to be too tired for him. I wanted to be happy for his coming home to me. I went back to my room to read my note to start my Day 36:

I don't know how I live my days without you
When I am around you I see the best of me in your eyes
Sometimes I forget to breathe
And the thought of you
It makes me smile
I love you more than you know
James

I brought it to my chest and took a deep breath. I could handle one more week. I could wait forever; if I could just get rid of this sickness. I was determined to have a great day. I walked out with the kitchen table in mind, but Jake was on the couch. Why didn't he go home? I walked further towards the kitchen passing him as he slept. The light of the morning was just starting to come up. I sat down where the paperwork was still spread out. I opened his notebook and it looked like it was in French.

"Hum…hum."

I turned in my seat and looked at him with guilt over my face.

"I knew you were nosey."

"You wrote in a different language just to keep it private?"

"Yes." He was full of sarcasm.

"Why? It's about me anyway."

"Yes. But if you read the wrong thing you may worry and that would not be good for you." He smiled and walked over to me feeling my head and then took my wrist to feel for my pulse.

I sat in protest. He got me some ibuprofen and an antibiotic. I took the pills.

"So why are you up so early? You were supposed to take it easy."

"Yeah, well, I slept a lot yesterday and I really need to work on the dances." I rolled my eyes, "But I will keep it down."

He grinned, "You didn't sleep a lot last night."

I didn't know what he was talking about.

"I tried to check on you, but you were upset talking. I assumed it was with your James?"

"Yeah." I was going to avoid this conversation. I got up and got a bowl out for cereal. I poured myself a bowl and asked him, "Are you hungry?"

He smiled, "Yes, and you're avoiding this conversation. Okay, that's a new concept."

I gave him a glare to let him know I wasn't happy and then I gave him a bowl, a spoon, and a box of cereal. I poured milk in my bowl and then in his. I walked to the living room and curled up in mom's chair to eat. I turned on the computer and ate while it was booting up. He sat down on the couch and ate.

"So, you weren't hard on him last night by giving back the ring?"

"No." I looked towards mom's room and I could hear her moving to get up. "Shhhh."

I got started looking for moves on the computer. I wasn't paying attention to what Jake was doing.

After a little while I heard mom and Jake talking in the kitchen. My plan was to leave him alone until tonight so I could get him to let me play volleyball. I was going to win one way or another. Mom walked out and gave me a hug goodbye.

She stopped before moving away from me, "Do you want to tell me about the necklace and maybe what is on the end of it?"

I looked up at her. Jake was walking into the living room looking worried, "Mom, can we talk about it later?"

She smiled and kissed my forehead. Her gaze was full of love for me, and I didn't want to argue with her anymore. I loved her too.

"Yes, but can we talk about it before he comes home?"

I smiled as she walked away from me and out the door.

I went back to searching for moves for the dance. I tried to not think about Jake in the other room and I was avoiding talking to him. I was going to be a good girl and not bug him.

"Sarah, before you get too into that and I get busy with your file, we should go to your work."

I had already forgotten about that so I got up and headed to my room, "Yeah, I'll get ready."

"Don't try to look too good because they may not believe you."

I didn't put any makeup on, but I got changed and put my hair up. I put on sweat shorts and a tank top. I came out ready to go, "I am ready when you are."

He looked at me and then away, "I thought I told you to not look good."

I grinned. Well, that made me feel good, "What do you mean? I grubbed out."

He stood up and moved in front of me. His face was less than an inch from mine. This was going to be a really hard day. I needed to be strong because I loved my James. I just want him to be this close to me and kiss me and touch my face. I was going through withdrawals from James.

He looked into my eyes, "So you're doing better today?"

I put my hands on his arms and pushed him back a step, "Yes, I am fine today. I'm not tired at all."

"Then you are ready to go?"

I moved away and grabbed my bag, "Do you want me to drive?"

He looked at me puzzled, "You want me to ride with you?"

I was offended, "Yeah, do you have a problem riding with me or riding with a girl?"

"Neither, your car is small."

I was relieved and laughed, "Well, you will have to brave it today. Are you wearing that?"

"Why? What is wrong with what I am wearing?"

"Nothing, but do you have shorts?"

"Not with me."

I felt bad, "Okay."

I grabbed his arm and led him out of the house. I got in my car and watched him slowly get into the passenger side. He braced himself like I was already going to get in an accident. I shook my head and laughed, "You need to relax."

He braced himself, but pulled something from his briefcase and started to read. I just shook my head. He never stops for a break. We went to my work first. I walked in by myself and went to my boss's office.

He stood up right away. The window was facing my car, but I was still nervous about being alone in his office. He moved around his desk leaning on it but on the side where I was, "Sarah, how are you?"

I gave him the note, "They are doing more tests because it's getting worse, but it is not cancer."

He traced his hands down my arms so I took a step back.

"Well, whatever you need Sarah, we are all here for you." He stood up and hugged me.

The door opened.

"Sarah, are you okay?" I knew the voice and I smiled, and my boss let go of me.

"Who are you?"

I spoke up before Jake could reply, "This is my James."

Jake looked at me and he knew that I was uncomfortable."

He put his arm around me, "I think she needs to go now."

He turned me to guide me out of the room; he walked me to the car and opened my door for me, "He is creepy."

"Yeah, sorry I lied."

"Good reason, was he hitting on you?"

"I felt like he is, but I can't tell."

"I felt like punching his lights out."

I smiled, "Yeah, I do too, but I need my job."

"Not that bad."

He got in and we were off. He wasn't paying attention to where we were going, so I stopped at the mall.

He looked up shaking his head, "Sarah, you need to rest."

"Jake, shorts!"

"NO!"

"Yes, if you are going with me tonight you need shorts."

"Where do you think you're going?"

"Volleyball, where else?"

"No. You are not better."

"We are not going anywhere except into a store right now. We'll discuss that later." I got out and started to walk in.

He came running; he stood in front of me and stopped me, "You are going home. I am not like everyone else that gives into you, so you don't get upset." He was very angry with me.

"Jake, if you would just hurry and go with me we could be done in no time at all, and then it would be rest time." I took his hands and turned him to walk to the stores and started walking backwards, "Please?"

He was moving.

I was so winning this argument, "Please…?"

He took a few more steps, "You will hurry?"

"Yes." I let go of him and turned to walk with him. We went into the first store with guy shorts.

I looked up at him, "Your waist is 33 inches?"

He glared, "Yes?"

I grabbed nine pairs of shorts, only because I didn't know what he would like. I pulled him along as I grabbed more clothes, and he just rolled his eyes at me. He had his arms full when we got to the changing room.

"I am not trying on all of these."

"Nope, only the ones you like. I just didn't know what you would like." I smiled pushing him into a changing room.

"Do I have to show you them all?"

"Nope, whatever you like."

I walked over to the girl's section. I grabbed two new tank tops which were both loose. I also grabbed a pair of jeans, one size smaller, and a really cute skirt. Then I saw some shoes that would be great for dancing in. I went and paid for them and sat down outside the dressing rooms, "Jake, I thought you said fast."

He came out of the dressing room not looking too pleased, "I wouldn't have picked any of these. They are all baggy and big."

I looked at him with caring eyes, "If you had to pick one, which one would it be?"

"I guess... one of these three." He held them up looking for me to pick one. I smiled and grabbed all three and pulled him to another rack. I grabbed a muscle shirt and pulled him a little further. I grabbed a t-shirt and moved further, and then grabbed another t-shirt. I pulled him closer to the counter, "What size shoe do you wear?"

"What? No."

"Size?"

"Fine, 10 ½"

I grabbed flip flops, black because they go with everything. I pulled him to the counter, and he was pulling his wallet out, "You are nuts if you think I am going to wear any of this."

I gave the girl my card, "You are taking care of me so it's on me." I looked away, so he couldn't refuse.

He was smiling now, "I like the way you shop."

I handed him his bag, "You are kind of slow."

We headed to the car with our bags in our hands. He was smiling again. He had such a nice smile.

39. A Little Stubborn

When we were back in the car, he went back to reading my file right away. I decided he needed more fun so I started to drive to the speedway. I had a friend there. He didn't notice 'til we were almost there.

"Sarah, where are we going? You said you would rest."

I smirked a little because he was going to be in for it now. If he was scared before, this will be a total adrenaline rush. I pulled in and jumped out hugging my friend Terry, who was the manager there. He let us in, and I pulled on the track, up to the starting line.

"Sarah, what are you doing?"

"I like to drive very fast, and you might want to hold on now."

I floored it, and we went around the first curve kind of normal.

He was holding on now, "Sarah, stop."

I floored it more taking the second curve with the backend swinging out a little.

"What the hell are you doing?"

I smiled more and pushed it further. The third curve we went around completely sideways. As I pulled out of it, I slowed and stopped at the starting line where Terry was standing.

He was screaming, "Yeah, holly crap, Sarah, you can drive! I love to watch you. You are such a natural,"

I was jumping out of my car and hugging him, "Thanks Terry… I needed that." I looked back at Jake and he was slowly getting out of the car holding the door.

Terry asked, "So who's the guy?"

My eyes were gleaming, "A new friend Terry, so please be nice."

"He looks a little scared. He didn't know you were going to do that?"

"Nope." I turned to Jake. I felt guilty for surprising him like that.

"Jake, did you want to try?"

He was mad, "NO!"

"Terry, can I have a little more time on the track? I want to get him to give it a try."

Terry's smile was as wide as the Minnesota River, "Play nice Sarah."

"I'm always nice; you know that."

"Sarah?"

I smiled and walked over to Jake, "Your turn."

"I said No, Sarah."

"You liked tubing which was my idea and you didn't want to do it. You will like this too. It's safer than the road. Please?"

"I am not falling for *please* again. You are over doing it."

"Not if you're driving, come on, please?"

"If I do this you have to answer one question."

"It's a deal. What?"

"No, I will drive first, but I am not doing what you did."

"That's okay." I jumped in the passenger side. He slowly got in the driver's side.

He started going and he took it really easy the first time, but I was encouraging him to go faster, "Okay, now you feel it; go a little faster."

He was speeding up and then slowed at the curve.

"Come on, Jake. You can do better than that."

He gave me a disapproving look.

"Just a little faster. I know you can do it."

He pushed it a little faster and didn't let off the gas as the curve came, which resulted in the back end going out quite a bit.

"Easy, Jake, don't over turn; that's it… yes, that's it! Ha, you did it!"

He went around two more times pushing it a little more each time. Then Terry was waving the checkered flag at us.

"Jake that means we have to be done."

"No, I was just getting the hang of it."

I smiled as he pulled up to the starting line. I got out and hugged Terry, "Thank you so much. We'll see yah later."

I got back in the passenger side.

"Sarah, don't you want to drive home?"

"Nope, I got my fill." I leaned the seat back and closed my eyes.

He was totally grinning, "Hey, you can't go to sleep. You have to answer my question."

"Ask away."

It was silent. Why wasn't he asking? I said I would answer his question. I opened my eyes and looked at him, "The question…?"

"I just don't know how to ask."

"Just ask. I said I would answer."

"Last night…"

I opened my eyes and let the seat come up, so I was sitting up again. I knew where this was going; at least I think I knew.

"Did you want me to kiss you?"

I wanted to answer this very carefully. I didn't want him to think I liked him, but I didn't want to hurt his feelings either, "Jake, I was missing James so much last night. I really needed him badly, and I would have kissed you for the wrong reasons; so no I really didn't."

"Good."

I was relieved. He wasn't sad or upset by my answer. I pulled the lever again and put my seat back and closed my eyes.

"I wouldn't have known how."

Oh shit. He did want too. I pulled the lever again to sit back up, "What do you mean that you wouldn't have known how?"

"I have been a little busy and I have never done that before."

"Never?"

"No."

"My first kiss was a little over six months ago. I remember it was nice."

"I wouldn't know that either."

"I'm sorry."

"I'm not. Look what I have done."

I was thinking of all the things he missed out on and I felt bad. He really needed to have more fun. I picked up my phone.

Jake was irritated with me.

"Hello?"

"Hey... Matt."

"Are we good for tonight?"

"Yep... Can you invite a lot of friends?"

"Yeah, I usually do."

"I mean, friends like me."

"Girls?"

"Yep."

"Does this have to do with your doctor?"

"Yep."

"Does he know what you are asking me?"

"Nope."

"He's with you now?"

"Yep."

"How many?"

"A lot... I mean a lot."

"You got it."

"You want us to pick you up?"

"Yeah."

"See you about 4 pm."

"I'll be ready."

"Bye."

"Bye."

"Sarah, after today you really shouldn't go."

"I will have my doctor with me. I will be good and nothing will happen."

"I can't stop anything from happening, but it's my job to find the problem and fix it."

"So, right now, I am a job for you?"

It was silent for so long that I didn't think he wanted to answer me.

Finally he replied, "Taking care of you... no. Finding out what is wrong with you... yes."

"So, staying with me and taking care of me isn't because of Clarissa?"

"Of course it is, but that's not a job. I owe her my life, my education and everything. She sent me because I am the best and *her son, James, loves you.*"

"Is that a touch of sarcasm?"

"No, maybe... it's none of my business, and I wouldn't have met you if he didn't love you, so I am sorry I shouldn't have said it that way."

Okay we were to the *'me'* subject and I needed to distract him from me. I do love James and he loves me. It really isn't fair for anyone to even like me.

Here it goes with a distraction, "Did you like the driving?"

The smile on his face was like Christmas morning, "Yes, but it was still a distraction, which I shouldn't allow."

"You want to do it again, don't you?" He couldn't stop smiling. I was feeling good for making him smile.

"Of course I do. How often do you do that?"

"Not very often, maybe once in a two month time span. I go when my head is all cluttered and I don't want to think about anything. You have to concentrate too hard on driving. It wipes everything else out. Sometimes solutions come easier with a clear head."

"But sometimes, distractions aren't good, and now is not a good time for them."

"But if you work so hard; don't you deserve a break?"

His smile went away, "Not right now."

We were pulling into my driveway. There was enough time that I could still take a nap, "There is one more distraction... volleyball tonight."

"No, I can't."

"Okay, but I still have to go. It wouldn't be fair to Matt, and he has to show off for all the girls. You remember... *girls in bikinis.*" I was hoping this would get him excited, but he had no reaction.

Wow, he must really love his job.

We were getting out of the car and grabbing our bags. I shut the trunk, "Do you want to try on your clothes so I can see and help pick one out for tonight?"

"We're not going."

"Um, I am and either you can come with me or you can stay here. Your choice but I am going."

"You are infuriating."

At least I was getting a reaction now, "I am really good at that; you can ask anyone, but they also say I am irresistible. I don't feel it. How is that for you?"

"Not irresistible, maybe stubborn."

I smiled. Good, he can keep thinking that. It works for me. He set his bag down as soon as he saw the pile of papers on the table. He pulled the papers from his briefcase and put them on the table again. I pulled out a pair of shorts from his bag and a t-shirt. I was holding them up to picture what it would look like on him. Then I grabbed two more items from the bag.

"What are you doing?"

"Trying to see what would look best for tonight."

He rolled his eyes, "Fine, I will try them on for you, but I am still not going."

"Okay."

He grabbed the stuff from me and walked back towards the bathroom.

"You can use my room."

I turned on the music and started to go through the medley and deciding on a few steps. He walked out putting his hands on his hips in disgust. He was so cute. He looked like a surfer dude.

"Next."

He turned and closed my door. I was dancing again. It would be best if I were ready. He came out with a different outfit on. This was better, not so beach like, maybe good for a party or hanging out.

"Next."

He walked back in the room. I got through one song of the medley and I replayed it to go through the steps that I just worked out. He came out again. This was great for a warm summer night playing volleyball... and it was *hot*.

I smiled at him, "This one."

"Really?"

"Oh yeah, it's *HOT*! Girls are going to drool all over you."

"Is that a goal of yours?"

"Yep... I am going to take a nap now."

"Really?"

"Yeah, something about my doctor doesn't want me to over do it."

He grimaced at that one. I shut down the computer and went to my room. I folded his clothes that were in there and put them in a pile on my dresser. I crawled into the bed and curled up with a pillow and closed my eyes.

"Sarah?" He was walking in. I rolled over to sit up.

"Don't forget your pills." He was handing me an antibiotic, an ibuprofen, and a bottle of water. I handed him the bottle back when I was done, but he pulled out the thermometer and smiled.

I looked at him disappointed, "I feel fine."

He sat down on the side of my bed and leaned back towards me. "Sarah, please don't be stubborn about this."

Okay, I was melting. He was so cute. He looked so much younger with these clothes on. I opened my mouth. He felt my forehead but his touch was tender. I was getting uncomfortable. I held up my arm waving my wrist in his face, and he smiled and took it. The thermometer beeped, I took it out looking at it.

He grabbed it from me, "I am the one that is supposed to be the doctor."

"I don't even have a temp. See, I am fine." I was shoving it in his face to see.

"Sarah, your pulse is still racing a little."

"I was just dancing so go away, and I'll try to sleep. You'll see I am fine to play tonight."

"Maybe."

I rolled over and hugged a pillow and closed my eyes. He lay on the bed next to me.

Shit, now what? "Jake, what's up? I need to sleep so I can go tonight."

"Sarah."

I turned to look at him. *James, I love James.*

"I just wanted you to know… I did have fun today."

I relaxed with a grin and closed my eyes. I felt him move from the bed, but I didn't hear him leave the room so the sleep must have come swiftly.

The soft kiss of James's lips was tracing mine. I was looking into his beautiful deep brown eyes. I woke to the buzzing of the phone so I opened it.

>"Sarah, please not now."

I had forgotten but the dreaming came so swiftly that I didn't have time to direct it in a different direction.

"K."

>"Trying to study hard so I can come home soon."

"I know. I'm sorry."

>"Don't be sad."

"I'll try harder."

>"Later I'll call you."

"K."

>"1- 2- 3- breathe."

"I love you."

>"I love you more than you know." ☺

40. The Surge

I woke to my alarm and shut it off and stretched. I got up and got out my suit that I play volleyball in. I looked out the door and closed it all the way; he seems to come into my room pretty freely now. I put the chain on the door.

Yep, he was going to walk in, "Sarah?"

"I'm getting dressed."

"Oh, I'm sorry." He closed the door again.

I got my suit on, and I put shorts and a tank top on over it. I walked out to the kitchen with my bag in hand. I was ready to go. Jake was engulfed in the papers, and his hand was entangled in his hair.

"You came in wanting something?"

He didn't look at me, "Your alarm went off."

"Yep, I am ready to go."

"Okay."

"Are you coming with me?"

"Oh, yes… no. I need to keep looking."

I put my hand on his shoulder, "Jake?"

He ran his other hand through his hair. He was really frustrated.

He looked up at me, and I could tell he was upset. "Hey, how are you feeling?"

I gave him a slight grin, "I feel good."

He stood up and felt my forehead and then took my pulse, "Are you sure you really want to go?"

"Yep, I think you need a break too. You need to clear your head. Come with me."

"It's just weird; it keeps going back to the same thing every time, but the spreading just doesn't fit."

"Jake, forget it. Come with me please?"

"I can't; I only have one more day, and I have to leave and go back to work. I promised Clarissa that I would figure it out."

"Jake, remember you deserve a break too. Please, please come with me. You will have fun. It will get your mind off this and then when you come back you can get a clear look at it."

He looked at me not arguing, "I really shouldn't."

"Here," I messed his hair back in place. I grabbed his hand and pulled him to the door.

"Sarah, I shouldn't."

"I am feeling better, and you have to admit that I had no signs of weakness today. The antibiotic is working." I was still pulling him out of the house to the car. I opened the passenger door, "I am not taking 'no' for an answer…get in." I was very determined. He got in and I closed the door. I was hoping the girls in bikinis would get his mind off of things.

I got in and started to pull out of the driveway.

"Wait." He was changing his mind, shit.

"I need to bring some papers with me. I need to look at one more thing."

I pulled back up and gave him the keys to get back in the house. He went in and came out with his notebook and a few papers but no briefcase. I smiled. *He was making improvements.* He got back in and started to read through things. I started to head for Matt's house.

When I pulled up to his house, he came running out. He had to sit in the back seat. He did sit in the middle and scooted forward, so he could talk to us.

"Sarah, how are you feeling?"

"Good."

"So you can play, right?"

"Yep, did you invite some friends?"

"Yep, lots."

I was happy.

The three of us walked to the courts. I laid out my tanning mat. I pushed Jake to sit on it. I took off my tank top, and then my shorts, so I could get warmed up. Matt was already stretching and warming up waiting for me.

Jake was looking at me, "You do not play in that?"

"Yeah, actually I do. Why?"

"You're only wearing a..."

"Yeah, beach volleyball. This is what you wear when you play on the beach." I was laughing at his reaction.

I went on the court and we were hitting, setting, and spiking the ball to each other. More and more people were showing up because it was getting closer to starting time.

A group of four girls walked up, "Hey, Matt. We're here."

He smiled and ran to them hugging and kissing each of them on the cheek. I watched with a smile on my face as he did this. I still didn't understand how he even had any interest in me. These girls were the prettiest girls in school, and they were all over him. I walked over to Jake and he was watching Matt with the girls, and then he looked at me. The look on his face was confusing to me. It almost looked like he didn't understand why I wasn't angry. I gave him a reassuring grin.

Matt walked the girls over to Jake and introduced him to all of them. He said hi to each and every one of them and then looked at me glaring. Another group of girls walked up. There were six in this group, and they were hugging Matt now. He was introducing them each as he released them. Matt invited them to sit with Jake for the match.

Matt came out, so we were ready to play.

"What do you think? Did I do okay?"

"He's not really paying any attention to them."

"No, he's watching you."

"Maybe you could suggest to a couple of them to take him swimming."

"Good idea."

He ran over to one of the girls and said something in her ear. I could watch it spread like wildfire through the girls. Matt came out and we started the game. I wasn't doing great. Matt noticed. He walked by me, "Are you okay?"

"Yep."

"Are you nervous about him watching?"

"A little; I don't want him to think I'm over doing it."

"Sarah, you play better than this. Get to it."

I started to really put forth an effort to really play. We were behind, but we caught up in no time.

Matt was happy now, "That is what I am talking about. Keep it up girl."

I smiled, and we worked really hard and pulled it out and won the game. We had an hour before the next game.

Jake stood up as I walked over to him. He was glaring at me, "This was not nice, Sarah."

I didn't say a word. I grabbed my water bottle.

Matt came over next, "Who's up for swimming and cooling down?"

Matt was heading to the beach with a bunch of girls but yelled back to Jake, "Come on, man, we have to entertain."

The girls included him in the group that went to the lake to cool off. I sat down on the mat and watched for a little bit, but I was getting warm. I poured water over my head. I laid back and poured more water over my body trying to cool off. I couldn't let Matt down. I took a few breaths and was trying to concentrate on being ready for the next match. I quit watching them in the water and put the towel over my face. I poured water over it to try and cool down more because it didn't seem to be working.

"Sarah, what are you doing?" His voice was by my ear.

"Jake, you are supposed to be playing with the little girls."

"I don't have time to be playing; I told you that already." He pulled the towel off of my face and put his hand on my forehead.

"You are hot."

"And you need to stop fussing over me. You are a hot young guy right now, not a doctor. I am nothing to these people, and you shouldn't be paying *any* attention to me. All those girls are here for you to pay attention to. Please, go have fun; I am fine."

"We're going home right now!"

"NO, we're not. Quit paying attention to me. I am fine until later." I looked at him with tears in my eyes.

He moved closer to me, "Sarah, please let me take you home now?"

"Nope, but if you want to help me, go back and play with Matt. Distract him until I can catch my breath and cool down." I pushed him away, "Just go, Jake, just go."

He got up looking at me and walked away.

I pointed, "Just go."

I put the towel over my face again and lay back down. I poured more water over the towel.

"Sarah, let's go."

Jake was sitting next to me. His face was in his hands. I got up and put my hand on his head, "Jake, I am fine." I walked out and warmed up a little. We started the match, and I did really well at the beginning and we were way out ahead of the other team. Now all we had to do is hold on to the lead. That is exactly what we didn't do. Neither of us played very well, so we lost the match. Matt was upset, but I walked over to the mat. Jake was grabbing everything looking at me trying to hurry. He knew I really was almost done. I needed to sleep now.

He shielded me and handed me the thermometer, but I looked at him disapproving, "Jake, I know it's bad. Let's just go."

He wrapped his arm around my waist, and I wrapped my arm over his shoulder, as we headed for the car. He was watching me while I avoided his stare.

He yelled back to Matt, "Matt, we need to go."

"Yeah, hold up. We have to say goodbye to all these lovely girls. Jake, come here."

"Matt, we're leaving if you want a ride; it's right now."

We were away from everybody and almost to the car, and he picked me up, "Sarah, what are you feeling?"

Jake:

Shit she is bad. "Sarah, what are you feeling? Talk to me."

"I'm just tired, James. Let me sleep, please."

"Sarah, I'm Jake."

She was nuzzling into me; her lips were on my neck. This is not good. Matt was coming now.

"What happened? I thought she was fine. Is that why she wasn't playing very well?"

"Matt, can you driver her car?"

"Yeah, she has let me before."

"Her keys are in her bag."

He was digging and pulled out her phone; it was buzzing. He looked at me, "Do we answer it?"

"Yeah, but get the keys; I need to sit down with her."

He was still digging and pulled out the keys. As he opened the door for me he answered the phone, "Sarah's phone."

"Um, James?"

"Um, we were playing volleyball, and she's kind of out of it."

I got in the car while Matt was talking to James and trying to get in himself.

"Yeah, we didn't know."

"Yes."

Matt looked at me as he handed me the phone. I was going to be talking to this person that she loves, shit.

"James?"

"What happened?"

"She is exhausted, and now she is sleeping."

"You're supposed to be the doctor, so why did you let her play?"

"She didn't have a fever all day, she took a nap, and *she's very stubborn*."

He laughed, not exactly the response I was ready for, "That's my Sarah."

"Do you want to try and talk to her? She is still responding a little."

"What is wrong with her, Doc?"

"Everything points to appendix, but I can't figure out what the spreading is. It just doesn't fit. The antibiotic I am giving her is working. She didn't have a fever all day until now."

He was silent for a moment, and I didn't know what to say. I felt the same way, helpless.

"Would you like to try and talk to her? I could hold the phone to her ear."

I could hear him; he was…I think he was crying. He does love her. "Yes, please."

I held the phone to her ear. She wasn't saying anything. I looked at Matt, and he whispered to me, "Speaker..."

I pushed the button to speakerphone, "James, I couldn't tell if you were talking to her, so I put you on speaker."

"Sarah." She nuzzled into me more. I wanted to hug her more, but Matt was watching.

"Sarah!"

She heaved a huge breathe, "James, my sweet, Cayuse."

His voice softened, "Sarah, please talk to me."

I couldn't believe the reaction. She pushed to sit up and took her phone looking at me, "James, just a second, we need some privacy."

She moved off of my lap getting out of the car. She didn't go far, only to the side of the car and leaned against it.

Sarah:

"James, what is wrong?"

"You."

"No, my sweet. I just got tired."

"This is killing me. I can feel it. Sarah, promise me that you won't keep pushing yourself. If I can't be home until Monday you have to behave, please stop pushing."

"I was fine all day. I usually feel good playing volleyball. I feel bad for Matt. I didn't do well the second game."

"Don't worry about that, Sarah. You have something that is preventing you from doing your best. Just take a break for a week, and let me come home first…"

"James, I will take it easy, but can you call me later? I am really, really tired, and I can hardly stand here anymore."

"Sarah?" He was crying, and I felt so bad for making him miserable. "The doctor went to your volleyball game?"

"James, don't be mad. I made him, just in case..."

"OH, Sarah, when you say stuff like that you scare me."

"James, I don't know that I am going to make it through this; I really am having a hard time fighting this, and I am not as strong as I was before." I couldn't hold the tears back. Jake came out of the car, and I was losing my strength to stand. Jake lifted me in his arms.

"Sarah, I will find a way to come home. I don't know that you can wait either. If you don't ...I will die with you."

"James, don't say that. Just come home. I will be fine, your dad said…" I couldn't talk anymore and closed my eyes.

"Sleep my sweet, Sarah, I will call you later."

"I love you too, James."

Jake:

She closed her phone and held on to me. I got back in the car. I am not an emotional person, but tears were coming to my eyes. I shouldn't feel this way. I looked at Matt, and he looked the same as I felt. The tears were coming to his eyes also.

"Matt, we need to get her home. I need to get busy, very busy on looking at her file.

He nodded without a word. She was making noises in her sleep as he was driving us home. I pulled her closer because I didn't want Matt to hear her. I was finding it such a turn on even though I knew it was wrong. I glanced at him to see if he was noticing anything. He tried to look at me as we drove, but he was torn over watching the road or looking at her. My time was limited, and I needed to find out what this was before tomorrow night. I would have to call Clarissa if I don't have any answers by then. Her breathing was increasing, and I didn't know what to do. I looked over at Matt, and this time he was noticing. We were almost to his house from what I could remember. As he stopped, she heaved a huge breath and her whole body moved. Now she was completely relaxed in my arms as she spoke, "James."

I felt like I was violating her personal space. Matt looked at me and I didn't know what to say.

"That was weird."

I was looking at her, "You have no idea how weird that was. I could feel a... I don't know like a *surge* when she did that."

"What? Like electricity?"

"No, I don't know how to explain it."

He pulled to a stop in front of his house, "How are you going to drive?"

"Come take her and I will get out. I'll put the seat back, and you can lay her back down."

He came around the car quickly. I lifted her to his arms. He put his face by hers. I could tell he cared about her too. The agony came through on his face. I moved out of the seat and put the seat back. I ran around the car quickly. He had already put her in the seat but was leaning over her to talk in her ear, "Sarah, I love you too."

He kissed her cheek lightly looking at me with apology in his eyes, "She is so addictive that I can't help myself."

I glared at him with disapproval because that was ridiculous.

His face grew to a large grin, "You will love her too." He was moving away from her, but stopped and looked at me for a long moment. "...If you don't already." He smiled and closed the door.

I think maybe we should take her to the hospital, so there would be no more running around and staying busy for her. I could concentrate better and she would have someone else to look after her and not let her do things. I think maybe tomorrow, because I could take care of her one more day. I wasn't doing a very good job though, if she was still doing this to herself. No, she does this on her own. I looked at her and she was peaceful now with the smile on her face; I knew she wasn't in any pain.

Her breathing was increasing again, so I drove faster. I had to get her home. She was smiling and the breathing was getting even faster. She was speaking as I pulled into the driveway. Thank goodness her mom wasn't home yet. I got out and moved to get her out quickly. As I went to pick her up I heard her, "James, no. I'm tired; please, I need sleep."

Was she dreaming? I ran to the house and opened the door, so I could get her in. I was trying to hold her. As I pushed the door back she spoke again, "James, not now... too tired...no more."

I knew I had to get her to her room and leave her alone. I was walking through the house, and she started to hold on, "Sarah, you are home." I laid her on her bed. I couldn't put her head where it should be, because I was holding her backwards for that. I just grabbed some pillows and tucked one under her head. I touched her face lightly as I laid her head down. I was ready with the next one, so when I pulled away she could cuddle in, and I could slip this one into place. She always curled up the same way... hugging a pillow. Okay, here it goes. I went to pull my arm out and there was another surge from her. She gasped and her whole body tensed and relaxed at the same time. I pulled my arm quickly away, "No, don't go."

I was torn and looked at her with amazement. What the hell is going on? I felt her forehead and the fever was almost gone. She was smiling and the color was back in her face. That couldn't be part of the sickness, it was too... I just can't explain this.

Okay, let's go over this in my mind... James could feel her, maybe. He called at the weirdest times like when she was out of it and all hours of the night. She maybe feels him or dreams about him in ways that I just don't want to imagine. She is fine most of the time, but when it comes on she is just out. She is sometimes responsive, but has no strength.

I am so confused, and I am not even looking at the medical information. I went out and grabbed a lot of paperwork that I wanted to review. I walked back to her bedroom and went to the other side and put it on the bed. I was going through everything, but kept looking at her wondering what was wrong.

I heard the door; Sarah's mom must be home. I couldn't move, because I had to get through more material. I wrote a few things down like a review of what was going through my head. It just has to be... maybe two different things, and her body can't fight the infection because of the appendix. Her mom walked in looking at me for some answers. I probably looked like a mess. I was trying to go through things as fast as possible.

"Jake, did something happen?"

"She was playing volleyball, and she got really tired. She kind of scared me. I need to find out what it is. I didn't want to leave her alone either.

Her temp went up, and she was talking in her sleep. It really worried me." I was engulfed in the paper work.

"Why did you let her play volleyball?"

"I didn't. She is stubborn and would have gone without me."

"Should we lock her in her room? I kind of wanted to do that anyway, especially when James comes home in two weeks."

"She asked him to come home sooner." Shit, why did I tell her that? I really don't want her locked up in her room. She was still standing there looking at me.

"He is coming home now?"

"No, he is still trying to finish. Sarah just asked him to come home. She is weak and somehow she feels better if she knows he is coming."

"So, he's not on his way?"

"Not that I know of, but he did call right when she was getting really tired. It was weird, like he knew she was in bad shape. Both Matt and I talked to him."

"Did he! He calls all hours of the night and I don't like that either. It makes her more tired."

"Actually, she woke up enough to talk to him and then…" I remembered the surge in the car, then here. Her temperature broke after that.

"And then what?"

"It was like…" I looked at her, and she wouldn't believe me because I didn't believe it myself. "It was like he helps her calm down and then her fever broke."

"So, she does feel better after talking to him."

"She is really hard on him. She was making him stay away." I looked back up at her, "At least 'til now. She feels week, and maybe he protects her from things." I couldn't tell her he is protecting her from Jason, Brian, Matt, and maybe me. I was going through the papers again, but felt her standing there looking at me, "I hope this is okay. I just didn't want to leave her alone; I was just making sure she was okay. I only have one more night to figure this out, and then I have to go back."

"Yeah, I just don't really allow boys in her room."

I looked up at her pleading, "I just wanted to keep a close eye on her. The temperature has been up and down over the last two hours."

"Fine, but please sleep on the couch."

I put my face back in the papers as soon as I heard the word 'fine'. "I don't plan on sleeping. I need to find out the problem."

I heard her walk away.

41. Holding

Sarah:

I was stretching. I felt so good now that I could run a marathon. Well, not really, but I am so much better now after sleeping. I looked at the clock and it was 3 am. Jake was sitting on a chair on the side of my bed. Papers were spread over as much of the bed that I wasn't taking up. He was sleeping with his face plastered to the notebook in which he wrote his thoughts about my sickness. I gathered the papers and put them in a pile and moved them to the desk. I pushed him more on the bed and lifted his legs to the bed. He didn't move at all. He was really tired and heavier than I thought he would be. I smiled because I was taking care of him. I picked up my phone, and James had called at 2:56 am. That's probably why I woke up.

I called him hoping he wasn't upset.

"Sarah?" he was crying.

"Oh, my sweet, James. I didn't wake till 3:00 am, I am so sorry." The tears were welling up in my eyes. The sound of him made me upset just like he was. The aching in my heart was unbearable.

"Sarah, I was worried."

"I slept my, Cayuse. I am better now."

"Sarah, I can't live without you."

"You know I feel the same way."

"Then don't tell me you're not going to make it through this."

"I said that? James, I must have been really tired and weak. I am better now."

"So, now you're telling me you *can* make it through this?"

"Oh, yes, James. When you give me your soul I get better. As long as I have you; I will make it."

"Sarah, you shouldn't do that to me. I almost gave up myself."

"You have to finish whatever you agreed to and hurry home to me. We have to be together, and that's the end of it."

"I am so in love with you little girl."

"Still planning on Monday?"

"Yes, and I have my flight. I will be in at 10:00 am."

"Can I meet you?"

"I will take a cab to your house. I want you to be well rested when I get home. I want to touch your face, your lips, your arms, and your everything for a solid week."

"That sounds good to me."

"Can you go back to sleep?" He was concerned again.

"Yes, I could sleep some more."

"Time passes faster when you sleep. I need to study more, so I can stay on track for Monday."

"I love you, James."

"And I love you more than you know."

"James."

"What my sweet, Sarah?"

"What do you mean by that?"

"I will tell you when I get home."

"That is just mean. Tell me now. I love hearing your voice."

"This will give you more determination to make it 'til I get home."

"You are cruel."

"No, I want you to fight for something. I promise it will be something you wanted."

I smiled and shook my head, "I will be waiting for you."

"You better; I need you."
"I love you."
"Goodnight my love."
"Good night, James."

I hung up the phone and smiled laying back in complete bliss. I loved him so much. I heard Jake moving.
"Sarah."
I looked at him, "Yeah?"
"No, Sarah."
"Jake, what?"
He didn't say anything. I traced my fingers through his hair, and I found he was dreaming. I whispered to him, "Jake, I'm fine. I feel better now."
He wrapped his arm over me and pulled me close. I rolled away from him and curled up hugging a pillow and closed my eyes.

I woke to my mom touching my arm, "Sarah?"
I tried to sit up, but Jake was wrapped around me. We were both fully clothed and on top of the covers, so I knew she couldn't think anything of it. I looked up at her.
"Sarah, I told him the couch?"
"I didn't know; I was sleeping. I…" I was trying to move him away from me. He was heavier than I thought.
"Sarah, you might want to rethink that ring thing."
"Mom, it's not like that. I swear; I love James."
"Okay, but this is not right."
I closed my eyes because I knew she was right. He shouldn't be here if I love my James. She left the room, so I tried to move again but couldn't. I reached for my note for Day 37: I read it out loud to myself.

If I shall lie, I will die
If I shall cheat, I will lie
If I shall steal, I will cheat
I will not do any of these for in your eyes
I see myself better

You make me pure, truthful, and honest
You make me better than I am
Without you I will not live
For you are my existence.
I love you more than you know,
James

Now the desire was so much more of wanting James to hold me. I needed to feel him, to feel his touch. If James had been the one in bed with me, she would have kicked him out. I heard mom leave for work, and I missed this cuddling thing. He was sleeping, so what was the harm. I closed my eyes and wrapped my hands around his arm to sleep again. I have needed to be held so badly. I wanted my James here. It almost seemed like Jake knew what I was thinking, because he cuddled in more and held me tighter.

When we woke, I felt he was waking at the same time as me. I heard him whisper, "Sarah." It was so soft and in my ear.
"Yeah."
"You're awake?"
"Yeah."
"How do you feel?"
"Rested."
"What do you want to do?"
"Lay here."
"Really?" He sounded a little happy. He cuddled in more, "Okay."
I wanted this to last till James came home. I was totally using him, and I started to feel bad, but I couldn't let go. I felt protected and safe for the first time since he was here, and I needed this to help me get by. He reached with his hand to my forehead feeling it quickly, and then let his hand trace down my face to my neck. He rested it there, but I knew he was checking my pulse. I knew my heart wasn't racing. I could tell he was done checking when his hand relaxed, but left it resting there.

His breath came to my neck under my ear, and his muscles were flexing against my back. His legs were tightening next to mine. His whisper came again, "You are doing okay?"

"Yeah."

"I almost brought you to the hospital."

"Shhh, I'm better now."

He was tracing his face on my neck; I knew I could not react to him. James would know I was being weak again. I love James and only James, and I should not be allowing this. It was unfair to Jake. The whisper came again, "Sarah?"

"Yeah."

"I have the urge to…"

I stopped him immediately, "Shhhh Jake, you will have to leave."

His grip lessened, and he moved his arm back to my waist to rest there. I cupped his arm and pulled it around me. I didn't want him to stop holding me.

His whisper came to me again, "I will take anything you are willing to share with me."

My heart was breaking. I was leading him on, and I was going to hurt him. I knew it and couldn't help it. How could I be so cruel? The tears were welling up in my eyes; it was becoming more difficult to stay here. I closed my eyes, and the tears were spilling out tracing down my cheek. I reached up and tried to wipe them.

"Sarah, does this hurt you?"

"No, yes, I'm just sorry."

"It's okay. More than one person has warned me. I am here to make you feel better, and if this helps than I am okay with it. His face rested on my neck. His words hurt even more. I rolled more to hug the pillow. He released me enough to allow me to do this, but his hand traced my back. He moved close to me without laying on me. His fingers came to my face wiping the tears where he could see them. He moved down to my back again and rubbed it till I slept.

Jake:

I am a lost cause, no matter the warnings, no matter the cold heart. I am in love with her, and my heart was going to get hurt. She loves him. None of that matters right now, because she was allowing me to love her, to touch her, to feel feelings I have never felt in my life. The butterflies were going crazy in my stomach; my heart was racing, and I was making her feel better even though I couldn't fix her.

I whispered to her, "Sarah."

She moaned a little because she was almost sleeping again. I was helping her because this is what she needed more than anything else; she needed to sleep. I continued to touch and rub her back feeling every curve of her body next to mine. This feeling was so amazing and confusing at the same time. I should have kissed her, but I wanted her to kiss me to help me. I never did that before, and I don't want it to be horrible. I have heard that a kiss will determine everything, and I want her to want me, to want to kiss me, to touch those soft stubborn lips with mine. I moved closer to her; my body wanted to feel her next to me. I leaned over to trace my lips along her face and to my satisfaction she smiled. She likes this, and I was making her happy.

I tried again, "Sarah."

She was breathing so heavy; I knew she was sleeping. I didn't want to move away from this, but I will kiss her and if I did...that is not what she wanted. Why was I contemplating this? She loves him, and she would push me away. That doesn't matter, because I wanted to please her no matter what it did to me. I love her, so I laid there for as long as I could without advancing on her, but then it was too much. I had to move away from her. As I scooted away I heard her, "No, not yet. Please, James."

My heart was torn. That hurt more than I thought it would. I knew she wanted me to be him here with her, but a slight part of me really wanted her to want me here. I moved away some more.

"Jake?"

She said my name, so I stopped, "Sarah, you were sleeping."

She turned to me, and the scared lost look in her eyes was ripping me apart. I smiled to reassure her it was okay.

"Jake, I am so sorry." She closed her eyes and the tears were streaming down her face. I would want more if I go back to hold her, and yet I found myself moving to her to hold her again.

"Shhhh, it's okay, whatever you need."

"Jake, I am hurting you."

"Shhhh, Sarah, if I can't handle it, I would leave." I was lying. This was killing me. I wanted to kiss her so bad. The desire was growing so fast in me. I wanted her to touch me to hold me. This is not good. I closed my eyes and started to go over the files in my head, putting this touching out of my mind. I found myself kissing her shoulder and tracing my hand over her hips to her stomach, gliding my fingers over it. I wasn't even thinking about it, and I was pulling myself to her more. I had to stop myself now, and I pushed away from her, and she didn't' move to me. I laid back and tried to catch my breath trying to slow my heart that was pounding out of my chest. What was I thinking? I was torturing myself with her. I rolled away even more and just laid there. I was totally and completely a mess. I cannot believe all these people were right. I never let anyone into my life; how could she accomplish this in so little time? I was going through the thoughts in my head, and I came to a conclusion. I didn't want her to like me; it was a challenge that was all. I knew she wouldn't love me, so I was safe letting her get close to me. I could be free to open my heart. If she really did like me I wouldn't have shown her any feelings, and I would have pushed her away. I glanced back to her thinking *why did I want her so bad now?* I rolled off of the bed, and she didn't move or call to me. She was sleeping, and I was free to work on her files. I walked out looking at her one more time as I left the room. That was it!!! It was over, over right now. She loves someone else, and I had my work to go back to. There will be no more wanting. It almost felt like my heart was caving in like a big hole sucking the life from me. I will have to make a decision to not do that again…it hurt too much. If she feels this way about him, I can understand why she needed me to hold her.

42. Oh The Pain

Sarah:

I woke and my heart hurt more. Jake was gone, and I was missing my James more than ever. I had been very bad, and I didn't know how I was going to face him. I knew I had hurt him, but I would hurt James more. What the hell was I doing? I got up and went to the bathroom. I brushed my teeth and washed my face. Facing Jake was going to be very hard. What was he feeling? I wondered what he was feeling because I was being so unfair to him. I closed my eyes, and opened them to look at a *traitor*. I was betraying James's trust and I was betraying Jake's help, but I didn't want to do either. I heard a knock on the door. Shit! I'm not ready for this yet.

"Sarah?"

Shit, shit, this is sooner than I was ready for, "Yeah?"

"Are you okay?"

"Yep, just brushing my teeth."

"Okay, but I need to try something."

No, shit. He is going to kiss me. I couldn't let that happen. *Crap!* I opened the door, and he was standing there as cute as ever. He had changed clothes. He was wearing the clothes that would look good if he was hanging out at a party, but he had a dress shirt over the t-shirt. At least it wasn't buttoned up. I looked at him so worried that I was going to hurt him more.

"Are you sure you're okay?"

"Yeah, I kind of slept awhile."

He smiled, "Yes, you did."

He stood there looking at me, and I was feeling very uncomfortable. I felt the need to ask him if he was okay.

"Jake?"

He was looking nervous and excited as he smiled.

"Are you okay?" I couldn't look at him anymore because I was feeling so bad. "I mean I shouldn't have asked you to stay with me."

"Sarah, this has nothing to do with earlier, but I need to try something." He was pulling me to my room while I was refusing.

"No, Sarah, it's not what you are thinking. Please come here." He was leading me to my bed.

Did I push him too far? James said that if you push someone past that point it would be too hard to control.

"Lay down. I need to feel the spot again."

I looked at him scared and confused.

He was shaking his head, "It's not about earlier. Please sit, lay, and that's it."

I lay down on the bed looking at him.

He knelt beside me, "Okay, here is the spot where the appendix is." He pushed and moved his fingers around, "Does this hurt at all?"

I looked at him concerned and confused, "No."

He moved to the middle of my stomach and pushed not quit as hard, "Does this hurt?"

"Maybe a little nauseated, but no pain."

He looked at me with doubt in his face. He moved his hands over to the opposite side of my stomach. He pushed down and moved a little.

The pain was ghastly, and I was going to lose it. I sat up holding the other side and pushed him out of the way. I was going to be sick, I ran to the bathroom closing the door, so I could throw up in private. I really didn't have anything in my stomach, so it was more like dry heaves. It hurt so badly now that I fell to the floor. The pain was excruciating and I couldn't stand it.

He was trying to get in the door, "Sarah, you have to let me in. I have to help you!"

I tried to get him to wait in between the heaves, "Wait." I couldn't move to open the door.

"Sarah, let me in."

I tried to move out of the way, but it hurt and I couldn't move at all. He had the door open enough to climb over the toilet. He was picking me up and it hurt more, "Jake, stop! Just wait. It hurts more to move."

"I have to take you to the hospital now, Sarah."

"NO! Don't move me. It hurts. What the hell did you do to me?"

"I really didn't think it would do that. You didn't have any pain on the other side."

"Fuck! Jake, this hurts."

"I'm sorry, Sarah. It wasn't supposed to hurt there."

"So, what is it?"

"That's the problem, I'm not sure. It wasn't supposed to hurt when I pushed there. I still think it's your appendix, but that is on the other side."

"Well, you shouldn't have done that."

"But it helps me figure it out better. Sarah, we need to get you to the hospital."

"No! I am not moving. Can you get me a pillow? I need to lay down here till it quits hurting."

He was trying to lift me.

"Jake, no, leave me lay here. STOP it now. *Dam it, Jake.*"

"Sarah, this could be bad. We need to go now."

"NO. I was fine a minute ago. Just let me get through this fucking pain."

He was sitting down holding me, "Sarah, if it's your appendix it could burst and kill you."

"You said that was the opposite side. Just stop, and let me... *Fuck* this hurts."

"Sarah, please let me help you."

"Fine, then don't touch me and let me..." I was lying down with my head on his leg, "Just don't move me. Okay...it will go away. Just don't move me again."

"Sarah?" He was laughing, "You swear like a dirty old man."

I started to chuckle, "Oh shit, don't make me laugh; it hurts too much."

He rubbed my back gently, "Do you realize what this would look like if your mom came home right now?"

I was almost laughing again, "Jake, stop it... no laughing. It hurts."

We sat there quietly as he traced the hair away from my face. It was long enough for me to doze off a little.

Then he had to speak, "How is the pain now?"

"I don't know. I'm too scared to move."

"We can't stay like this forever."

"Um, I think I could. If I don't move, I don't feel that again. And by the way, you are not pushing on my stomach any more... *ever!*"

"I'm the doctor, and I might have to."

"Hell no! Never again! That was bad, Jake."

"Are you okay now?"

"I need to brush my teeth."

"Do you want to try and stand?"

"Nope, I'll just stay here like this. You can get me a couple more pillows and I will be fine."

I heard my phone, "Shit, that's James. He probably felt that."

"He really feels everything?"

"You still don't get it. Yes, he feels everything including the good with the bad."

"Is that why you won't respond to me? You won't let yourself have feelings for me?"

I looked at him, "We need to get to the phone. I need to answer him, or he will go crazy to get here. Do you want him on his way right now?"

The look on his face answered my question, "Okay, ready? We are getting up now." He was pushing me up to my feet as he lifted himself off the floor, "You okay?"

"Yep, no pain, but I'm not walking yet."

He ran out the door and grabbed my phone and answered it. I could hear him talking nicely to my James. It made me happy.

"James? Yes, just a second."

"Yes, I thought I figured it out, but I wasn't expecting it to hurt her."

"Yes, I'll bring the phone to her. Just a second; here she is."

He walked in and handed me the phone. I looked at him to give me some privacy, but he shook his head no and whispered, "You can't even standup."

I gave him a disapproving glare and then directed my attention to James, "James."

"Sarah, what happened?"

"Um, I don't really know."

"You are in pain?"

"Um… not if I don't move."

"Sarah, this isn't going to wait 'til Monday, is it?"

"Um, I don't know, James, it hurt pretty badly."

Jake was laughing and said out loud leaning to the phone, "James, she swears like a sailor when she is in pain."

I scolded him with my eyes.

"Can you ask him to leave, Sarah. I am just a little jealous."

"Um, James, I would love to do that, but I really can't walk right now."

"What?"

"The pain was extreme, and I really can't move right now."

"Go to the hospital."

"Jake was trying to make me go, but it hurts too bad to move. I just need to stand here a minute to let it pass first."

"I need to go. I need to come home now." I could hear him, and he was panting.

"James, what are you doing?"

"Running to the commander's office."

"James", I pushed myself to stand more. It didn't hurt so bad, "James, did you feel anything just now?"

"NO!"

"See, I'm doing better. I just straightened up. I am standing."

"Shit, Sarah, you are scaring the crap out of me."

"It's funny you said that, because I am in the bathroom."

He laughed and I was relieved that he was easing up, but I couldn't laugh with him because I was afraid it would hurt.

"Sarah, are you still in love with me?"

"Yes, James." I looked at Jake as I talked to James, "I am still in love with you from the bottom of my heart."

Jake walked away from me. I knew I hurt him now more than ever. I saw it in his eyes.

"Are you sure, Sarah?"

"Yes, James, I am so sure. I miss you terribly and want you to come home as soon as you can get here. I want to feel every little part of you touching me from your finger tips to your toes. I love everything about you and about us being together for the rest of our lives."

"Sarah, I feel your doubt too."

"James, it's not doubt. I have never doubted loving you. You should know that if you feel everything."

I know, but I also feel that you care about Jake, and it's driving me crazy."

"I do care about him, James. He is helping me, and you should be thankful too."

"It's hard to be thankful when he is the one there, and I am the one here. Sarah, I should have never listened to you. I should have stayed with you."

"James, I am waiting for you." I took a step, "*Fuck.*"

"What?"

"I was trying to walk and it hurts."

"What did he do?"

"He just pushed on my stomach."

"He put his hands on you?"

"James, he's a doctor, and he was checking a theory on a medical hunch."

"So, he was touching you, but he didn't know what he was feeling for, Sarah?"

"James, look here, MR, I love you and only you. I am not going to argue with you. I want you to come home, so will you please just hurry and get here. I don't care if you finish anymore. I mean I do want you to finish, so you don't hate me later, but James… I can't do this alone anymore. I need you, and if you can't be here then I need someone else's help. I am sorry that it is Jake, but please feel this in your heart, James. I love you!"

I was thinking very hard of our time in the house, being together as one, the pleasure and complete satisfaction of loving each other.

"Sarah, the night with the feather, I loved you."

"You don't love me now?" I started to cry.

"No, Sarah, that's not what I mean."

"James, say you still love me. I can't live without you."

"Oh Sarah, I love you so much it hurts."

"James, if it makes you feel better, he is leaving today."

"It does and I don't mean to be possessive, but Sarah he is giving you what you need and that makes me sad. I can't sleep anymore, and I am going crazy."

"I'm sorry, James. I will try harder." I was trying to walk to my bedroom and the pain was a little better.

"What are you doing?"

"I'm trying to walk to my bedroom."

"Is he there helping you?"

"Nope, he left when I said I loved you. He's giving me privacy with my Cayuse."

"Sarah."

"No James, please just love me enough to come home faster. I need you right now."

"Have him take you to the hospital."

"If I do he will stay."

"Why?"

"Your mom asked him to take care of me medically. If I am in the hospital, he will stay until we figure it out."

"Can you make it till Monday?"

"Truthfully, after today, I don't think so. That hurt so bad, but it was not near where you showed me."

"Why was he there?"

"James, please don't do that to yourself. He started on the spot you showed me. I told him what you felt."

"You did?"

"Yes, James, I told him you feel everything when it comes to me. He thinks we are soul mates."

"Every time you feel me move through you, I give you a part of my soul."

"Won't you run out if you keep sharing it with me? You have been giving me a lot lately."

He laughed.

"James, it's Wednesday. Only five more days and I will try to make it. I will be a good girl; I promise. Jake will go home tonight, and I will wait for you. Your dad said it would wait for you to come home and take care of me."

It was silent for so long that I thought we lost the connection. I sat down on my bed and lay back carefully. I gasped a little because I could still feel the pain, but it was definitely better.

"Sarah, are you okay?"

"Yep, I'm just lying down."

"You hurt that bad?"

"Yeah, actually it hurt a lot worse than this."

"Remember, he's the one that hurt you. I won't hurt you."

"James, I want to be with you and to make love to you when you come home."

"Sarah, nothing would make me happier. So, you are waiting for me."

"James, please, just hurry up,… will you already?"

He laughed, "You're not supposed to make me laugh when I am miserable."

"Yes, I am. We are forever. We're supposed to pick each other up. "

"But I am not there to help you."

"Yes, you are. You are in my heart and mind all the time."

"Sarah, I love you more than you know."

"James, that bothers me that you say that and won't explain it to me."

"I keep trying, but I will make sure you understand when I get home."

"Really, you could just tell me."

"Nope, want to see your face and maybe show you."

I took a deep breath with no pain. I sat up, "James, I think I am feeling better. Shouldn't you be busy right now? It's that middle of the day."

"Yes, I do need to go, but Sarah, you are more important than anything."

"I know you feel that way, and I love you more than you know."

"I know more than you."

"See, you are just difficult."

"Me? You are the one that is stubborn."

"James go, hurry and get done. I need you more than you know."

"Sarah, I know. I felt your need, but I wasn't the one to comfort you."

"Yes, you were. My mind was only on you. You should have felt that too."

"I do, but it still hurts, Sarah."

"I am sorry that I was weak. I will be stronger as long as you tell me you still love me."

"Sarah…I love you."

"I sighed with a smile, "Will you call me tonight?"

"Yes, whatever you need."

"I need you."

"Until then?"

"Until then my sweet, Cayuse."

He hung up the phone and I closed mine. I didn't know how to make this right for Jake. I did love my James more than life. I was very wrong to let Jake hold me.

43. Where Is The Pain

I got up very slowly; the pain was still there, but it was nothing compared to what it had been. I walked to the kitchen noticing Jake had both hands in his hair again, and he didn't look at me when I walked in. I wanted to put my arms around him to make him feel better, but that would be very wrong. I thought I would just see how this goes.

"Jake?"

"You're moving?"

"Jake, I am sorry."

"For what? I'm the one hurting you." He didn't even look at me; he just turned over another page, and he crossed something out in his notebook.

"Jake, I'm hurting you?"

"No. I knew you loved him the whole time. I am here only to help you and that is all."

"But Jake, I feel bad. I shouldn't have asked…let whatever it was…I just shouldn't have."

"Sarah, it wasn't like that." He looked me right in the eyes, "I am here to make you feel better, and that is it. You needed that to feel better, so that is what I did. That is it." He looked away.

"But when...you said?"

"That is it, and I am leaving tonight. The last time you will see me will be next week in the hospital. You won't have to deal with me poking and probing you anymore."

"What about Saturday?"

"Okay, maybe then."

"What about Friday for practice?"

"Okay, then too. But that's it."

"Next week; what is next week? Are you coming home with me again?"

"Kind of, *NO*. I scheduled surgery for Monday. I thought you would want him here.

"Can't it wait till Tuesday, and surgery...?"

"Sarah, we should be doing it today. This could be very bad if it bursts."

"You said that, but you said you weren't sure."

"I'm not, it will be an exploratory surgery."

"What does that mean?"

"We open you up and look around for it from the inside."

"I don't think so."

"I will talk to your mom tonight, and then I am leaving."

"It's Wednesday; she won't be back 'til 10 pm."

"Well, then you're stuck with me 'til then."

I walked out of the room finding it hard to breath. There was such a change in him. I didn't feel better. I felt maybe... like I deserved it though. But cutting me open seemed extreme for punishment for what I did. I went to the computer and put the head set in and turned on the music we put together for Saturday. I was trying to go through them in my mind, so I could forget about the rest of this. I put my head down on the desk resting my forehead on the edge. Everything was getting all crumpled in my mind. I was so confused, and I didn't know how to argue my point because I didn't know what point I wanted to make clear. I restarted the music without looking. I was going to be sick again. I grabbed the headset out of my ears, and quietly moved to the bathroom. I closed the door and tried to be really quiet. Great, here come *more* dry heaves, and it hurt so badly. The knock on the door startled me.

"May I come in?"

"No, I'm just...no."

"I brought pillows."

I smiled shaking my head. No, he was only trying to make me feel better. He didn't care about me; it was false. I had to keep him at a distance.

"I'll be right out."

I was brushing my teeth because I had to get rid of the taste in my mouth. He opened the door anyway.

"Jake, what if I wasn't decent?"

"I'm a doctor. I have seen everything, and you were getting sick."

"Not really...nothing left in my stomach."

"I upset you?"

"Nope, it's just all jumbled in my head. It's too much to handle at one time. I want you to feel that way. I will be okay."

I walked passed him and went back to the computer. I put the head set back on and started going through the music again. I didn't pay attention to what he was doing. He made it clear; he was only here to make me feel better. I really wasn't feeling better now, but I had to be strong. I didn't want to be strong, and I sure didn't feel strong anymore. I wanted to go to my room and weep, but I didn't want him to see me that way again.

I closed my eyes and listened to the music. I went through the songs so many times now that I knew the words by heart, but I didn't know what I was going to be up for on Saturday. I wanted something simple. I didn't know if Jake would do the Reggae medley with me anymore. I unplugged it, "Jake will this bother you?"

"No not anymore."

I smiled and got up to try and put some stuff together. He walked into the living room. It was small, and I could feel his eyes on me.

"You're not going to watch me are you?" I didn't bother turning around. I felt weird dancing in front of him now.

"You need energy, so I made you food."

I turned to him. He was holding a plate with a very large steak on it. I couldn't help myself, and I smiled, "You didn't have to do that, and I don't know how much I can eat."

"Grab a tray and try."

I walked over to get a tray and set it up. He put the plate on the tray and went to the computer.

"I was thinking we should make the medley, that I like, shorter."

I was desperate, "Why, don't you want to do it anymore?"

"Well, yeah, but Sarah, you are really weak and it might be too much."

I smiled, "Whatever you want. I will make sure I can do it."

"What are you thinking?"

"I'm not. I was looking at some moves. Do you want to see what I like?"

This was better because he was actually smiling at me again, "Yeah?"

I went over and pulled up one and then the side shows like 20 more. I clicked on the one I liked the most. "Watch this one…then this one…and this one," and I scrolled down, "and that one." I walked away and sat down. I took a couple of bits while he was watching the videos. He watched the next one and I took a couple more bites.

"How is it?"

"It's good."

"As good as Tony's?"

I smiled, "Yes."

"My dad is a really good cook. He taught me a few things."

"Is he a chef?"

"No, well some of the time. Let's just say he is good at everything."

"Where do they live?"

"Chaska."

"That's a little ways away."

"I live up north and that's even farther."

He was watching another one as I ate some more. I was half way through the steak, and I took a deep breath.

"Enough?"

"Yeah, I'm kind of full."

"Just sit and relax. Hopefully, it will stay down."

"Are you doing the surgery?"

He turned to me and his eyes were sad, "Do you really want to talk about it? You got so upset before."

"No, I guess not, but are you doing the surgery?"

"No. I will be there to supervise though."

"But I thought you were the best."

"Not at surgery. I will be there the whole time. I called in someone special, someone who is very good and will leave very little scaring."

"That's nice. Where is the scar going to be, and how big will it be?"

"Sarah. You are thinking about it. Let it go. You can't afford to get sick again, or we will end up with me doing it today. Are you finished eating?"

"Yeah, I guess so."

He got up and took my plate to the kitchen and put stuff away. He came back out and pulled me to my feet, "Do you want to try a little?"

I smiled, "Sure if it doesn't hurt."

He put on the medley that I had been working on. He played it through and started it over. I went through the first part I had put together, but he added some stuff.

"That's not going to be too hard for everyone to get?"

"If you can do it this sick then they should be able to do it feeling good."

I shook my head no, I couldn't believe it. I was feeling pretty good, and I didn't have any pain. We made it through the whole medley and he smiled, "Again?"

"Yep, gotta get it down."

We went through the dance six times and then I had to sit down. I was tired. I looked up at him and realized I was having fun.

"Do you think I can wait 'til Monday?"

"Are we back to this?"

"Yeah, I'm just wondering. I haven't gotten sick in a while or at least not like that, and I just feel so yucky."

"You don't feel good?"

"No, not really."

"Do you want me to call Clarissa and stay?"

"Yes…but yet no. Jake, I will want you to hold me and make me feel loved, and that is not fair to you. So, no you need to get back to your life."

He didn't get excited or anything. He didn't even crack a smile, "You would want me to hold you again?"

"Jake, you know what I mean."

"No, I don't. What do you mean?"

I took a deep breath. It was getting too deep.

"Will you help me with the other song?"

He smiled, "...avoiding answering me?"

I glared at him, "No, just buying time to think it through, so I can explain it better. It's all mixed up in my head, and I don't want to explain it the wrong way."

"You want more time; well then, I guess we could work on the next dance, but there are stipulations."

I was suspicious of him now. He could see the caution in my eyes.

"You have to let me take your temp and pulse." He smiled smugly.

"Fine."

"Fine."

He grabbed the thermometer and put it under my tongue as I held my arm out for him. He looked at me disapproving, "It's clearer here." He put his fingers on my neck. I stood there impatient. I was shifting my weight from leg to leg. The thermometer beeped. I took it out and looked at it. It was 99.8, so I shut it off.

"Why did you do that?"

"We have one more song to go through, and you are leaving tonight. I could really use the help."

He smiled, "I can turn it back on, and it goes to the last reading."

"Please, just help me get through this one, and then I will be done 'til Saturday."

"Not Monday."

"I am already having surgery, so what else is there?"

His eyebrows went up, "James is coming home."

"I will be in a hospital bed; he won't be able to hold me for awhile, right?"

"Well, kind of, but not really. Who gets to hold you on Saturday?"

"Nobody. That is for Tony; not me."

"Oh."

"Can you please just help me with this other song?"

"Yes, of course."

We worked on the song, and he wasn't as thrilled with this one because it was country, but once I got him going and showed him it could still be sexy he liked it. He had a lot more fun with it as we danced it a few more times.

I sat down, and he went through it again, "I could like this."

I smiled and watched him. It was after 7 pm when he finally looked at me, "You're really flushed."

"Yep, I am done for the day. You can keep dancing though, it helps me remember it."

He stopped and sat down next to me feeling my head, "I was going to leave, but I think I will stay till your mom gets home."

"I will have to be alone tomorrow and most of Friday. I will be okay. I am just going to bed anyway."

"Do you want me to hold you for awhile?"

"No, I will be okay."

"Do you want to explain what you meant before?"

"No."

"But I really need you to."

"Jake, I don't know how."

"I know you love James."

"Yes."

"But you like when I held you?"

"Yes."

"You don't love me."

"No, but I have gotten a little attached to you. You have been here so much; you help me; you make me laugh; I like when you smile, and it's just nice."

He smiled embarrassed, "Does it make you feel better?"

"Yes, but it's wrong; it's not fair to you, and it hurts James. He feels you are here with me and comforting me when he can't. It makes him sad."

"So, you don't want me to hold you?"

"Nope, I will have to tough this one out on my own. I will be okay... and Jake?"

He was looking distant again. I held his face to look at me in the eyes, "Thank you. I won't be as scared with you there on Monday."

He was still sad but got up and started to put his stuff together. I watched him go from room to room collecting his stuff. I got up and followed him. I didn't know what he was looking for, so I just followed like a puppy dog. We were finally walking out to his truck.

"You really need to go lay down, Sarah. No one is here to take care of you. You will have to be more careful."

"I will."

He gave me the biggest hug, "Saturday, we'll have fun dancing."

"Yeah."

He let me go and got in his truck; I was going to start to cry. Why did I want to cry? I love James. I told myself to stop it.

"Bye." He looked at me, and then started to back out of the driveway. I followed it down to the end of the driveway and watched as he drove off.

I walked back in the house, and I couldn't stop the tears anymore; I hurt so badly. I need James to come home and make this all go away. I lay down and curled up with my pillow. James always calls when I am upset; why wasn't he calling when I needed him? I need him now!!!

My phone rang just in time to save me from completely loosing it, but it was only a text.

>"Sorry."
"No, I'm sorry."
>"You okay?"
"Yeah, just miss you."
>"Are you sure?"
"Yep, it is you my love."
>"Taking test, call you later."
"K."

I closed my eyes. I heard the back door, so mom was home early. I didn't want her to see me like this, so I rolled to my side with my back to the door. She would think I was sleeping.

I was relieved to find out that it wasn't my mom. Jake was crawling in my bed with me, and I turned to put my face in his chest.

"And I was worried you would kick me out and push me away."

I laughed a little.

"I am only here 'til you are sleeping, or your mom comes home, okay?"

I couldn't say anything, so I just nodded.

"I know you love James, so no funny business."

I wiped my tears on his shirt.

"If you mess this shirt up, the girl that bought it for me will get mad at you."

I wiped my face more.

"Sarah, that's gross."

I looked up at him, and his eyes softened.

"I shouldn't have left you alone. I am sorry."

I covered his mouth with my hand, "You talk too much."

"Sarah," it came out muffled.

I lowered my hand to let him talk again.

He moved so his lips were close to tracing mine, "You have to turn away from me, because I will kiss you if you don't."

His breath traced my lips, and he grabbed a pillow for me to cuddle into. I turned away from him and hugged the pillow. He traced his fingers over my cheek and down my neck, and then moving them to my arm. He wrapped his arm around me to spoon his body to mine.

I whispered, "Thank you."

He traced his cheek against mine. I closed my eyes as his mouth moved so close to mine. I turned my face a little, and he was kissing me so close to my mouth. I turned my body to him a little, so I could look at him. He looked deep into my eyes, and then closed them as he traced his lips over mine taunting me to kiss him. He lightly wrapped his lips on my top lip and then moved to my bottom lip sucking for me to reply. He looked at me again.

I put both my hands on his face and moved my thumbs over his cheek bone. I closed my eyes, "Jake, I can't." I turned my face away from his.

He lowered his face to rest on my neck and continued to kiss my neck and shoulder. He didn't feel like he didn't know what he was doing. I was so relaxed and content in his arms. He did not advance, but he did stay there. I wanted to stretch to shake off the enjoyment, but I didn't move. I laid there and enjoyed every moment. If James could feel me…he was going to be hurt. I closed my eyes and let the dreams come. It was of the house; I was still with my James. The fog was rolling in, and our hands together swirling the fog in the candle light. I was delighted from the deepest part of my heart. James arms around me and I felt so safe. I knew it would be torture for James if I let it go any further, so I let myself enjoy that for as long as I could muster without getting hot with my love.

I felt a kiss and opened my eyes, "Jake, what are you doing?"

He was sitting on the side of the bed leaning over me, "I was kissing you goodbye, because your mom is home."

I smiled at him, "Thank you for giving me what I needed."

He smiled, "Come see me Friday. I want to check on you and we'll practice, okay?"

"Yes, I will see you Friday." I closed my eyes. I felt him get up, but he traced his hand over my face. I pushed harder to it, as he cupped it with his hand and then let go. He walked out, but I could hear him talking to her. He was telling her about Monday, but I didn't want to hear it, so I blocked it out and drifted to sleep.

44. The Magic of a Dream

I woke at 2 am. James hasn't called yet. He said he'd call every night until he came home. I was feeling really sad. I hoped he wasn't letting me go because of Jake. I wanted my James here more than anything in the world. I couldn't contain myself anymore because I needed him so badly. I rolled over to cuddle the pillow putting my lips to the phone. James, please, I need you. That was all it took and my phone rang.

"James, I needed you. I am sorry if you were busy."

I knew I hurt the person I love the most. I am so horrible, that they should let me die.

"Sarah, don't think that." He was crying.

It broke my heart to hear him this sad.

"I know you love me, but I shouldn't have left."

"Don't you dare put this on yourself; it's my weakness. I am so sorry."

"Sarah, I love you no matter what. Unless you tell me to leave you alone or you tell me it's over I will put up with whatever you feel. I was afraid to call you. After today I thought it would be over. I just love you so much."

I could hardly talk anymore; the lump in my throat was moving up.

I tried to swallow to keep it down. How could he be so understanding? I love him so much, "James, please come home now. I need you and I needed you today, and I will need you tomorrow. Please, please come home."

"Sarah, I can't, not 'til Monday."

"James?" Was all I could muster to say. I was desperately letting him know I still wanted him and only him.

"What do you want me to do?" He was torn into pieces; I could tell he was miserable, maybe more than me.

"Anything… something. I just need you so bad, and I am so weak without you here."

I felt the rush through my whole body. It calmed me immediately.

"James, I just need you."

"Sarah, I know. I feel your needs and your wants."

"I shouldn't live. I have been so unworthy of you and your love."

"Sarah, I have been bad also, and I don't know how to tell you something."

"Please, tell me it's not someone else. I deserve that, but please, James, tell me it's not that."

"No never. If I don't have you, I will not live."

"I can't handle that; please, don't say that. I don't deserve your love."

"Sarah, the night with the feather…"

"Yes, James."

"I loved you too much."

"James, what do you mean?"

"I just mean…I just mean I love you more than you know right now."

"James, tell me. I need to understand, and you have been holding this in long enough."

"Sarah, I need you to love me. I need you to live. Please, don't say you don't want to. I will die without you."

"I know, James. I am dying without you now."

I closed my eyes. My love for James was deeper than anything I could ever explain.

"I wish you wouldn't say that. My hands are tied right now, and I don't have any options on what to do."

"James."

There was silence. "James!" James, please, please answer me.

"Sarah."

I gasped at the sound of his voice. The hole in my heart was engulfing my insides.

"I'm sorry, James; it's okay. I'm the one that waited too long to ask you to come home. You just scared me cuz you didn't call."

"I was busy being miserable and *afraid*."

"James, that is my fault too." He didn't say anything, but it broke my heart that I hurt him this bad. How was I ever going to make it up to him? I can't!

"Sarah, there is always a choice."

"But James, I choose you."

He was silent again.

I couldn't help but beg him, "James, *if you will still have me?*"

"You know the answer to that."

"I hope I do."

I felt his touch against my face, "Oh James, I miss you."

I felt him trace my stomach, my chest, my neck, and then his lips traced mine. He was taking my breath away.

"James, anything you want. I am completely and wholly yours."

His body wrapped around mine. He wasn't pushing further. He was very tender tracing my body with his. The desire was growing in me. I wanted to feel him. I concentrated on touching his chest and tracing my finger tips on his face and his neck. I wanted to trace my mouth under his jaw line, to take in his scent.

"Oh, Sarah, I can feel you so good now. You haven't done that for awhile now."

I thought about wrapping myself around him and tracing my hands along his back to pull him closer to me.

"Little girl you are driving me crazy."

I could feel him next to my body so I concentrated on moving to him.

"Oooh, shit, Sarah."

"Shhh, James. I love you and I need to feel you." I taunted him more with moving my body to his until we were together.

"Sarah, I don't know if you want to do that; we still don't know how real this is."

I pushed him further until we were moving together in perfect sync. I squeezed as hard as I could. The pleasure I was causing was coming through with his noises. His breathing matched the rush I felt from him, but I continued wanting to feel him more.

"Sarah, stop."

I stopped on a dime. He didn't want this. He was going to push me away. *No, please, James. I need you more than ever.* "I'm sorry. You don't want this?" I was breathing so hard.

He moved and took over with being in control of the situation and was focused on making me feel so good. His moves complimented my body as our bodies moved so perfectly together. The tears came to my eyes because I didn't deserve this much pleasure from him. He was so good at bringing me the most pleasure that I could ever imagine. *How could I have ever...* the tingling started in my toes quickly rising up my body. As the pleasure grew, so did my moaning; it was too much, "James!" It came to me in a rush, first his and then mine.

"Shhh, Sarah, are you okay?"

"Oh, James, it was too perfect." I was exhausted and weak, "You made me feel so...wonderful."

"Can I stay here with you?"

"Yes, oh yes, James, but I am so tired."

"I know baby; it's okay, sleep. You will feel better tomorrow."

I was struggling to stay awake; I needed to feel him more. My desire to be with him was being satisfied and I didn't want it to end.

He reassured me, "I will hang up when you are sleeping."

"No, James...no sleeping. I need this so bad."

"Sarah, I will be home soon. I will not let you get away."

I started to doze off a little, but I didn't understand what he meant about not letting you get away. I wasn't going anywhere. I loved James. I want him and only him. I only let Jake hold me, because I was missing James. I wanted James's arms around me. I wanted James's mouth on mine. I want James.

"Oh baby. I needed you to feel that way so...bad."

"James, I am in love with you."

"I know, but it was just hard for me. I will give you whatever you want when I come home. I promise no more waiting if you are sure."

"I think you have already given me what I wanted a couple of times. It will just be nice to have you here for it."

He laughed a little, but then he traced his hands slowly down my arms. I felt his breath on my neck and a light kiss as he traced his mouth along my skin. The sleep was over whelming, and I could barely get out, "James, I'm sorry." The sleep came over me.

I was now in our dream. I could see his face and I could touch him. It was deeper and more erotic as he traced his hands over my skin adoring me. His eyes were soft and caring as his mouth traced over my face searching for those lips, and when he found them the kissing started. His mouth kissed my lips, down my chin to my neck, then to my chest, and still lower 'til he reached my stomach. I arched my back from the pleasure he was giving me, and he quickly came back to my face to look into my eyes to make sure I was enjoying him and not in pain. His body was tense and I felt him slowly move in me so carefully and delicately that my arousal came quickly. He hovered as he moved to me as to not hurt me, but the way that made him move to me was amazingly wonderful, and it caused an explosion of pleasure between the two of us. He pulled me close to him and rolled over, so I could lay with him. In my dreams I always had more strength and the desire overcame me and I moved to him more. A smile came to his face as he looked at me with disbelief that I wanted more from him. As I moved slowly to him he closed his eyes from the pleasure I was now giving him. I moved off of him just enough to slowly move back to him and he gasped and tilted his head back as his body was trying to meet mine. I smiled as he opened his eyes to look at me as we did this again.

"Oh my god, Sarah..."

He closed his eyes again as the pleasure grew. He was getting so he couldn't take the slowness and he pulled me to him so that he could hold me tight as our bodies moved together naturally. I needed to feel those lips and I got what I wanted. His mouth came to mine as our bodies moved together. It was so natural like we were meant to be together for eternity. When the eruption was coming the kissing stopped because neither of us could hardly breathe. Our eyes met and the rush came for both of us at the same time. The smile showed in his eyes with a glimmer. We stayed there looking at each other until my eyes wouldn't stay open anymore. He pulled my head to his neck as he rolled me over to rest. He stared at me as he traced his fingers along my face with adoration, "Sarah."

"Yes, my sweet, James." I closed my eyes.

"I am so in love with you."

I smiled, "And I you, my Cayuse."

I felt his fingers trace over my eyes, "Sleep baby. I will be home soon."

I woke to Day 38: I did feel better. Better than I have in quiet a few days. No sickness and no pain. Before I did anything for the day I needed to read my love note. I couldn't believe I was so miserable without him since it was only two weeks ago that I saw him. I wanted to see what my note would bring after last night. I took off my necklace and put the ring on my finger. That is where it should have been the whole time. I smiled to myself as I opened my note from James.

As I lay here with your whisper on my pillow
I can feel your breath on my face
Your scent fills the air as I wish you were here,
I wonder often how I can show you
But there is nothing that will compare
So just believe
I love you more than you know,
James

I looked at the clock. I had to call Matt and cancel. I needed to make it 'til Monday. I got up and my bed was a mess. Maybe it was a little more real than I thought it was. I pulled back the cover and there was stuff everywhere. Good thing mom wasn't home or she would think something was really wrong with me. I grabbed all my sheets and sat down with my phone. I really didn't know if I should bother him, but he might be happier if he knew.

"James, I think it was very real."
>"What?"
"Last night, was real."
>"Of course it was."
"No, I mean. Bed was a mess, real."

>"Really?"
"Yes."
>"We can't do that anymore."
"Why?"
>"Baby!"
"I don't care. I want to be with you."
>"You do care. I love you. Wait for me."

I thought about touching his chest, tracing my fingers down the front of him to the top of his pants.

>"Sarah, NO!"

I kissed his stomach, and sucked a little. I was smiling.

>"Not a good time for that, SARAH!"
"Sorry, just missing you."
>"Stop, please."
"K."
>"Later."
"I'll be waiting."
>"I'm frustrated now, thanks."

I giggled to myself and thought about biting his bottom lip.

>"You said you would behave."
"That is."
>"NO, it's not. Stop, or it will be a longer wait."
"Okay, okay. Later please."
>"Yes."

I love my James. I wanted it to be a full time something. There will be no more time apart; it didn't matter how, even if it involved a baby. I would get him all the time then.

I got up and brought my bedding down to the washer and I put in a load. I went back upstairs and had a bowl of cereal. I sat down to eat it while I called Matt.

"Sarah, how are you? I have been going nuts."

"Matt, I am better for now, but I can't play tonight."

"Why, does the doctor want to keep you to himself?"

"Matt! I am having surgery on Monday, but I have to make it till then or it could be bad. He has a specialist coming in to do it."

"What is wrong with you?"

"He thinks it is my appendix."

"That's not bad."

"He said it would be if it burst, and there is more that he doesn't understand, so they are doing an exploratory surgery."

"So, what does that mean?"

"They are going in to look around; it could be something else."

"I thought he was the best?"

"I am unique."

"You've got that right. Hey, can I come over or will the doctor get mad?"

"He's not here; he went home 'til Monday."

"You're kidding, right?"

"Nope, but Matt I really need to rest. I get really tired so easily, and I have to make it until Monday. So, coming over isn't a good idea. Plus, you have to find someone to play tonight."

"I don't want to play without you."

"Yes, you do; don't lie to me."

"Okay, I do, but it is the only time I get to be with you. How long will you be down?"

"He said three to six weeks, depending on how bad it is."

"School will be starting."

"I didn't think of that. I should try to get everything set up now in case it does take six weeks."

"Volleyball is over for you this year."

"Yeah, I guess so. You should try to get someone else, call me later to let me know who you got."

"Yeah, do you have to go?"

"Matt, I'm already tired."

"Okay, I'll call you later."

"Bye."

"Bye."

I took a deep breath and turned on the music for the dances and ate my bowl of cereal. I tried to remember all that Jake helped to make up, but I wasn't feeling my best when we did them. I finished my bowl and put it in the sink. I went through the dances which came back to me as soon as I started to dance them. I was going to be okay for Saturday.

I lay down and watched a movie. I opened my phone again and wanted to text James more. Jakes phone number was in my phone; I never put it in there. I decided to pester Jake.

"Working?"
>"Yes, how are you?"
"Better today."
>"Really?"
"Yep."
>"You're not playing volleyball?"
"Nope, told him already."
>"You're not dancing?"
"Just went through each one once. Nervous."
>"No more...rest. Have to go."
"K."
>"See you tomorrow."
"K."

That went okay. I did feel bad for using him, but that was not going to happen anymore. I loved James. Oh, James. I thought about tracing his face with mine. My phone buzzed.

>"NO, SARAH! Not a good time either."
"Sorry, bad habit."
>"No, good habit, bad timing. I love when you do this, but I am trying really hard to get done."
"Okay."

I thought about one long embrace, but not luring at all with only his lips on mine.

>"I do like when you do this to me."
"Do you want more?"
>"No, I'm already hot. Need a shower."

I laughed. I did love him so.
"Later..."
>"Yes, later, but if it's real?"
"Even better."
I smiled.
>"You are driving me crazy little girl."

"Good, sorry. I want you so bad right here and now."
>"Please, Sarah, don't."
"K."
>"I love you my sweet, Sarah."
"And I you."

I curled up and watched a movie. I slept off and on through the whole day. Mom came home around 6 pm. She came in looking at me.

"You didn't do anything today?"

"Nope, I need to make it 'til Monday."

She looked at me a little sad, "We shouldn't go up north this weekend."

"Jake is there, Mom. I will be okay."

"Do you promise to take it easy?"

"Yep, I have been good. It's just the sleeping thing gets in the way of me being on time."

"Well, yeah, and I don't want a repeat of last weekend."

I smiled at her reassuringly, "I am doing a lot better now."

She looked at me unsure, "Are you hungry?"

"Yeah, actually, I only had cereal today."

"Sarah, Jake left you a steak in the fridge. He made some extra. He said you needed more protein."

"Cool." I got up and went to the kitchen and pulled out the steak.

"Sarah, he left a noodle salad for you. He said something about you liking it a lot."

I was confused. We never had a noodle salad together. I looked and found a container with it in. I opened it. Was this Wilson's salad? How could he know about the salad? I took a fork and took a bite. Yep, this is Wilson's salad. I took two plates and heated up enough steak for both of us. I put some of the salad on both of our plates.

"Wait till you taste this. You are going to love this."

I walked out with two plates and handed her one.

"Sarah, you didn't have to do that. I could have gotten up."

"I haven't done anything all day. I can do this little bit."

She smiled at me. I watched her eat the salad. She didn't seem to like it as much as I did. Maybe it was who I was sharing it with before.

When I was done eating, I brought my plate to the kitchen. I walked back out and lay down to watch TV with mom. We watched until 9 pm. I got up, "Bed time for me."

"Are you tired?"

"No, not really, but I don't want it to get bad again. We have to go up north tomorrow, so I want to be rested."

She shook her head no, but smiled, "You are a very determined girl."

"Yep, thanks mom."

"You're wearing the ring?"

"Yes. I'm sorry. I just needed to feel loved."

"Sarah, we love you too, and you are too young."

"We both know that, mom. It won't happen for a few years. I just need to get used to the size of it. It's way too big. I will put it back on the necklace tomorrow to save it for later…a lot later in life."

She smiled because that made her happy.

I went to bed with my phone on my lips. I needed to rest for my time with James. My bed was already for tonight. I would hate to have to do laundry again tomorrow, but it would be worth it.

45. Desperate to Feel Better

I woke to my phone ringing, "James!"

"No, Jake."

"Sorry Jake. I was expecting James to call. What's up?"

"Are you doing okay?"

"Yeah, I am doing great. After I text you, I slept off and on all day."

"Have you been lonely?"

"Jake! Yes a little." I felt compelled to tell him how I was really feeling.

"You are still coming tomorrow?"

"Yes, but mom doesn't want me to. She is worried that the same thing will happen, so I have to be really good."

"So, no dancing?"

"That is the only thing I am being allowed to do."

"Good."

I smiled. I enjoyed that he liked to dance with me.

"Jake, how was your day, dear?" I was trying to be funny.

He did laughed, "You are weird, Sarah."

"How do you know that?"

"I was kidding."

"I am weird. Remember at the beach?"

"What?"

"When I told you I am nothing to those people?"

"Yes."

"Jake, I am the weird one at school. I am the dork, geek, or whatever they call us now."

"No way."

"Yes way."

"Matt doesn't feel that way."

"Matt only finds me interesting because I turned him down. He doesn't get turned down ever. I'm sure you could tell that."

"Sarah, when you were out of it, he kissed your cheek and said he loves you too."

"That was all show. He doesn't really. If we would have kissed at his house when I was there, he would have dropped me like a hot cake and moved on to the next girl. He doesn't really care about me. We just do homework together."

"Sarah, you really don't get what you do to people. You have a lot of people in love with you. You're like this person who is really good, and people just really love and care about you."

"Jake, were you treated weird when you were in school because you didn't fit in?"

"Yeah, but I was smarter than everyone."

"Well, I'm definitely not smarter than everyone, but people I am around most of the time think I am weird. They aren't nice to me."

"But you are so bodacious."

"That is only in the world where I feel good about myself. Up north I have more confidence in myself, and it was James who saw me as I was and loved me through the changes. Actually, it was his love for me that made me want to be better."

"Sarah, I already know you love him."

"Sorry. I just… nothing… I am not that great, Jake… that's all."

"Sarah, I tried to think that way. I had a wall up, a mile wide wall. People warned me. They told me you would warm my heart, and I didn't believe them. I hated you with a passion when I first met you. I wanted to prove everyone wrong."

"That's why you were mean to me. I kind of wondered about that."

"Sarah, your only goal was to soften me."

"It brought me back to my life at school. I was very uncomfortable with it."

"I'm sorry, and I wouldn't have tried so hard to be mean to you if I knew."

"Most people don't take the time to find things out, that's all. I found it very satisfying when you smiled."

"You like my smile?"

"Jake, I love James with all my heart, and I do not want to do anything that would hurt him. He loves me more than I deserve, but Jake…if there wasn't a James in my life… I *wouldn't* have turned you away yesterday. I wanted you to take advantage of the situation, but I am so *thankful* you didn't."

"So, I gave up my chance to steal you away?"

"No, Jake. I find you even more attractive because you respected what I wanted in my heart."

"So, what does that mean?"

"Jake, we will not have a chance to *ever* be together. I belong with James, but you made me want to be with you. There are very few people in my life that I wanted to be with. You just happen to be the one that I will always wonder about."

"That just doesn't help my case at all."

"Jake, you are great, and you will find someone as great as you someday. That's all."

"Sarah, why couldn't you tell me yesterday how you felt?"

"You would have kissed me."

"Yes, I would have."

"Jake, you have to promise me one thing if we are going to dance this weekend."

"What's that?"

"Promise me that you will not kiss me, or even try."

"What?"

"Promise me!"

"Why?"

"Because… that will win my respect more than anything. I was truthful with you, so you have to do this for me."

"I can't promise that."

"Then I will not see you 'til Saturday."

"What?"

"Jake, if you can't promise me, than I can't be around you."

"But what if you need to be held?"

"Jake, this weekend isn't about me. It is for Tony and that is it."

"You are being hard on me."

"No, I'm not. I just don't want to hurt James and use you to fill my needs knowing that it was not meant to be."

"Fine, I promise. But if you kiss me, I will not turn you away no matter who it hurts."

"That's a deal. Jake, I need to sleep a little, or I'm not going to be able to practice tomorrow."

"Okay, okay... and I suppose James will get upset if he can't get through."

"He will be okay. He's better at being understanding than I am."

"Sarah. I…"

"No Jake…you don't. Trust me. I am not that great."

"Goodnight, Sarah."

"Goodnight, Jake, I will see you tomorrow."

We both hung up. I think that went well. Now, he will just *have to* keep his promise to me. Okay, James, if you called me already, please call me again. James, please can you call me now? I looked at the clock, and it was only 11:45 pm. He usually calls later, so maybe he was still busy.

My phone buzzed, so I opened it.

>"Sorry baby, busy."

"K."

>"It will be 2 am, is that okay?"

"I will be waiting."

>"1- 2- 3- breathe."

I smiled because he knew just how to make me feel better. I closed my eyes, curled up with a pillow, and cuddled up to it pretending it was my James. Sleep came over me quickly. I told myself *no dreaming, and it's not allowed.*

The dreaming started anyway. He was moving in under my leg and arm. I curled into him. I was kissing his neck moving under his ear and traced my hand over his chest. My phone rang, so it woke me. "James?"

"I like when you do that."

"Do what?"

"Let me come to you."

"So, it wasn't a dream?"

"No baby. Can you feel this?" He was tracing my leg pulling it more over him and messaged it. He wrapped his other arm around me to hold me close to him. I rolled to him more and went for the ear. I sucked on it and breathed in it. I could feel his body tense.

"Sarah, you should be resting."

"James, you should be here." I was being playful and took a deep breath in his ear. He gave me the reaction I wanted as he pulled me on top of him. He traced his hands slowly down my back, "I miss this so much, Sarah. I needed for you to want me this way."

His kiss was hot. He sucked my top lip luring me in for more, and then he moved to my bottom lip using his tongue to pull it into his mouth. Our mouths moved together breathing heavily as our lips complimented each other. The gentle touch of his hands to my back and the perfect kiss was arousing me. He rolled me to my side as his hand slowly traced down my side from top to bottom, and his legs were moving in between mine as they entangled together. I liked the way he touched me, and I tried to pull him to me more, but he lessened and traced my face with his hand.

"James, you're not in the mood to be with me?"

"Yes, always, but I was missing this so much, that I want to cherish every moment of this."

He rolled me to my back and took my hand in his bringing it to his mouth. He kissed each finger tip slowly. When he had kissed each finger he turned my hand over to kiss my palm, moving slowly upward to my wrist and then made his way up my arm to my neck. He kissed under my chin as I tilted my head back to allow him to suck and kiss me there. I felt his hand lightly cup my breast, "What do you like most?" He moved down to trace my nipple with his tongue.

I couldn't clear my head because he was so intoxicating, but stuttered as I said, "Um…it's all… um… so good… love your touch in every way." I was entangling my fingers in his hair to hold him gently to me as I looked down at him. His eyes were full of desire, but had a touch of concern in them that he wasn't making me happy. He traced his hand down my side to my thigh which he pulled up more. He moved down and kissed the inside of my thigh very lightly and then moved his open mouth against it, and then he kissed it over and over again. I could hardly breathe as my chest heaved with desire. He sat back on his knees looking at me and my complete bliss over his seduction of me. He traced his hands up my stomach as he moved to hover over me. I traced my legs along his sides, because I wanted him to come to me.

"Sarah, do you want this? He traced himself against my stomach as he watched my face.

I closed my eyes, because I really did want to feel him inside me, "James, are you teasing me?"

He traced himself against me again, but moved further down so he slightly glided against me and then moved back up to look at me. I looked directly into his eyes pleading for him to come to me. His look was curious, "Are you scared to touch me?"

I was scared. I didn't know how to touch him, "Is that what you want me to do, James?"

The kiss came under my chin, and he kissed my neck so luring and very seductive as I heard him whisper, "Yes."

I lightly moved my hands down his chest and stomach until I reached him, but he guided my hands to show me how to touch him in an incredibly amazing way. He pushed my fingers against him and moved it down further, "Ohhhh, Sarah." He closed his eyes as he showed me what he liked. I moved him to trace against me because I wanted to feel him too. He looked at me as his hand guided me more, and I pulled him to touch me again. He closed his eyes to enjoy the touch. He let go of my hands and moved to look at me as I did it again.

"Ohhh, Sarah, I need you now."

"Yes, James." I put him where I was, and he pushed into me.

I gasped with the feeling of satisfaction.

"Sarah, you have never touched me like this."

I was breathing so hard I couldn't talk, and then he was moving to me. I had moved my hands to his waist but kept moving them to his butt to pull him to me harder. My desire was far more than I could imagine, and his movement was getting faster and faster as he moaned with pleasure until I felt his rush in me, "Oh god, Sarah. I am sorry. You made me so I couldn't slow down." His face was in my shoulder.

I turned to his ear, "James?" He turned to look into my eyes and he could see my misery, because I was still full of desire. His face came to mine to look me in the eye and his movement started again, but very slowly and complimented the pleasure in me. I shuddered and moaned with every movement into me. A smile grew on his face because he knew I was so close to feeling complete pleasure. I tightened on him as he moved to me, and the buildup was intense. I couldn't contain the sounds of my pleasure as he continued to touch me in a way that was extremely erotic. I let go of him to grab the blankets beneath me because I could feel it coming. I couldn't control my body anymore and then the rush came like I have never felt before as he pushed hard to me and moaned with pleasure pulling me tight to him as he held me there. My whole body was trembling, and I couldn't move without shaking. He looked into my eyes, "Are you okay?"

I nodded, but I didn't' know how to tell him that what he did to me was beyond amazing. The tears came to my eyes as I said, "I think so."

"We shouldn't be doing this. It could hurt you."

"James, shhhh. Let me have this. Surgery is on Monday, so we will have to wait for awhile. We can't do this tomorrow, because I will be at the trailer."

"You're going to be at the trailer this weekend?"

"Yes, I'm going to dance at Tony's, but that's all James. I will wait for you to come home."

"That changes things a little."

"What changes?"

"Oh nothing. Sarah?"

"Yes."

"I love you."

"I love you too. Do you want more?"

"No, can we lie here, and can I stay 'til you sleep?"

I felt better after being with him, and I wasn't weak anymore. I moved over top of him and kissed his chest. It didn't take much coaxing for him to respond to me. His touch was still gentle and tender as we made love again. I didn't understand how this was possible, but I felt better than I had in a long time.

"This is as good as…" His kisses came harder to my face in search of my lips.

I moved to kiss him, but asked, "Good as what?"

His kisses traced my lips and my face, "Just wait; it feels better; trust me, I know."

"You have felt this good with…?"

"Only you baby; only you. I will explain when I get home." He pulled me to lay with him, and I curled up next to him.

I held his arm and kissed his shoulder, "James?"

"No, Sarah, no more today. I can't stay awake."

"It feels better than this?"

"Yes."

I felt him kiss my forehead. He pulled me more to him, so I could rest my head on his chest. "I have a surprise for you."

"What?"

"It wouldn't be a surprise if I told you."

"So, you are teasing me?"

"Yes."

"That's not nice, James."

"Sarah, sleep. Monday will come soon enough."

"I am having surgery that day. I am sorry."

"You will have it before then."

"Don't tease me."

I nuzzled in and laid there holding on to him. I was afraid to let go, but sleep came swiftly again. I don't remember what we were talking about, but I was in heaven.

46. Getting Weaker

Day 39: What a glorious day. I was feeling like I wasn't sick at all. Mom already left for work. I pulled the sheets back to see how bad it was. It wasn't as bad as the day before, but I still needed to wash the sheets. Now for my love note from James.

Far apart feel the distance
This amazing feeling I am holding on
My breath stops as if I can't
You take it from me with just a thought
My heart weakens without you
But a touch would bring it back
For it is you I cannot live without
I love you more than you know,

James

I am sorry about tonight James; I love you. I imagined the biggest hug and my phone buzzed.

"1- 2- 3- breathe. I love you."

I smiled because I did love him so much. I got up and put the laundry in right away, and then I went up to eat. There was steak left, so I finished it and then the salad. I was full and everything felt great.

I ran through the dances a couple of time each. I put my laundry in the dryer and packed my stuff away. I didn't know if I wanted to wear skinny jeans or not. I decided to go shopping for boots to wear with the skinny jeans if that was what I was going to wear.

I took a shower and fluffed my hair with spritz. I looked okay, but not great. I put my skinny jeans on, so I could see how it would look with boots as I shopped.

At the Mall I roamed the stores for an hour or so and finally found the pair I was looking for. They were a little more than I wanted to spend, but they looked good. I also bought a pair of jeans that fit a little loose that would go over the boots. I was feeling flaunty and with the bigger pants I could wear a shorter shirt, something to show off the stomach. I was a little proud of how thin I was. I went home and changed into regular clothes and lay down 'til mom came home.

I did fall asleep, but woke refreshed. Mom was going to drive because we couldn't have me get warn out. I hated being babied, except *by James*. I slept off and on the whole way up to the trailer. She didn't stop anywhere. We walked into the trailer, and I still had the ring on, so I turned it so dad wouldn't notice. I put my stuff in the bedroom, and put together a small bag with both pairs of jeans, the boots, one shorter tank top, and one loose shirt in the bag. I didn't know how I would feel tomorrow, so I was planning on taking a shower in James's room before the dance. They wouldn't be able to refuse me if James wasn't here. I went out of the room, and lay down on the couch. Dad looked at me worried, but mom filled him in.

"Do you want to go to Sherburn's with us?"

I didn't want to push any subject too hard, but… "Dad, if it's alright with you two, can I please go to Tony's for a short while? I want to go through the two songs to make sure I am ready for tomorrow. Then I will come to Sherburn's to check in, and I will make it a short stay and then come back here to rest more."

He smiled looking at my mom, "She's growing up."

I protested, "No, I just get tired easy."

"Okay, but only a couple of times."

I was still lying down and pushed for more. "Brian is going to want to go skiing tomorrow, so if I go get him to bring the boat down, can I go and supervise? I won't do anything but lay around, please."

"Sarah, that might be too much."

"I know, but I won't do any driving, and I will only go for an hour or so. Then I will rest for a good four hours before Tony's."

"Let's just see how you feel in the morning."

"That's fair."

He was happy that I gave in so easily. I went to the room and grabbed my bag for tomorrow. They both looked at me as I walked out, "These are just clothes for tomorrow. I'll take a shower in James's room." I could see they were not happy, "It's okay; he isn't there, so I will be alone."

Mom was interjecting, "Jake will be there."

"But he is there to look after me and my illness. He's not the one you are worried about. You know... I am in love James."

I realized that was the first time I said that out loud in front of them. I knew they were not happy, so I smiled at them both, "And he's not here."

They did lighten up a little. I sat down on the couch to catch my breath, so dad came over to me concerned. I returned an apprehensive look, because I knew they didn't want to upset me. I was totally taking advantage of that.

"It will be a very short stay. I promise." He smiled weakly, and I got up and hugged him, "Thank you."

I went to my car to head towards Tony's. I wanted to stop at Sherburn's, but I had to practice before I got too tired again. As I drove I realized that I hated being here without James. I pulled into the back of Tony's place. I didn't see Jake's truck, and I was a little relieved. I went up the stairs and went into James's room. I put my bag on the table and looked around the room. It was going to be awhile before I would see this place again after the surgery, but James was going to love it. I went out and locked the door, but as I turned to walk down the stairs I noticed Jake was sitting at the bottom of the steps. I went down the stairs and sat on the step behind him.

"Jake, what are you doing? Are you okay?"

"Waiting, I didn't know if you needed privacy."

"Nope, came to practice that's all."

"What were you doing in the room?"

"I was putting my clothes for tomorrow in there. I was planning on a shower."

He stood up happily, "So, you're not sad?"

"Nope, I am good."

"How are you feeling?"

"I think okay, but I'm really tired all the time. I slept the last two days almost all the time."

"Your body is trying to heal itself, Sarah. Do you want to rest before you dance?"

"I am all rested out."

"Are you sure?"

I gave him a distrustful look, "I am sure."

I got up and we came down the last stairs together. As we started to walk towards the kitchen, he put his arm around my shoulder, and put his hand on my forehead, "No temp."

"No, I have been good. I told you that."

He released me when we walked into the kitchen. Tony was there and rushed to me, "Sarah, oh Sarah. How are you?"

"Okay, I guess." I gave Jake a scolding look, "You told him?"

"I had to. You need to be really careful; if more people know about it, we can all watch over you to make sure you are okay and not overdoing it."

I was angry with him, "Fine."

I turned back to Tony and hugged him, "Tony, he's over exaggerating how sick I am. I really feel good today." I leaned into him, "James is coming home on Monday."

He gave me a grin and kissed my cheek, "If tomorrow is too much, Sarah, just say the word. You are more important than any of that."

"Tony, you know I love to dance."

"Well, go practice then."

I walked into the bar and to the stage. I put the music on and started it, and then went out to dance. Jake didn't come to help me with the country song, but I made it through twice. I put the other one in and started it. Jake came out to the floor and started to dance to it. I sat and watched as he moved to the music. He was so good at this. He put up his finger to motion for me to come out and dance with him. I restarted it, and went to the dance floor to go through it with him two more times. I went to restart it again, and I set it up to replay 'til I stopped it. This time he was adding moves and was dancing facing me. He was very close, but we were still going through the dance. He moved behind me and helped me to move more. We went through it a few more times.

"Jake, stop. It has to be simple enough for everyone. Just do it without touching, okay."

"How do you think I am going to coax girls to come to the dance floor if I don't do it facing them?"

I was smiling. He was really good at this, and I let myself enjoy the dancing. It started again and he danced the same way as we had worked on, but after a little he began to move to me again. It was getting a little hot.

I tried to remind him, "You're just doing this to coax other girls, right?"

"Why? Does this bother you?"

"No, I love to dance and I just…want it to be easy for everyone. Not a dance for us to get hot with."

He grinned and moved closer, "You're *hot*?"

He was so close I could feel the heat from him, "You're dancing really sexy with me."

He moved so his leg was between mine, and his arm wrapped around my waist, "You are turned on by me?"

I heard Tony yell from the bar, "Jake, we have work to do. I think you've got it down."

Jake stopped and gazed into my eyes. He wanted to kiss me and I knew it, but to my relief he just smiled a little saying, "Tomorrow."

I shook my head smiling because he did make me feel better.

He was backing away from me, "Call me if you need me tonight, anytime. You can let me know if you're weak or need someone to take your temp."

I shook my head no, but I giggled at the suggestion. I hated that I could not return the feelings. I did love my James. If James touched me like that, I would have pulled him up stairs to take advantage of the hotness.

I went to turn off the music, and Jake went back to the bar. I slowly walked to the bar and sat down because I was already tired.

Tony came to sit by me, "Jake thawed a large steak for you."

"Tony, it will have to wait till tomorrow. I promised I would behave, so I have to go."

"Sarah, you never listen."

"I need to this time; I'm sorry."

"James is going to be angry with me."

"Under the circumstances he will understand, or he will have to deal with me." I hugged him so tightly, "I will see you tomorrow."

Jake insisted on walking me out. Tony wasn't pleased, but I reassured him, "Its okay. Jake just wants to take my temp and pulse."

I looked at Jake so that he was reminded that he was there to make sure I am okay. He followed me to my car, and he did feel my forehead as we walked to the car. Then he turned to put his fingers on my neck for the pulse. I tried to be careful, so I took his hand and placed my wrist in his hand. He smiled as he took the pulse there, but glanced up at me as he was counting. He finally let go moving his eyes back up to meet mine, "You're still okay."

I huffed with satisfaction, "Yep. I will go rest now, and I will take it easy 'til tomorrow."

"Can we have more time tomorrow?"

"Maybe, we'll have to see, but I am yours on Monday." I smiled slightly at him as he opened my car door.

"I will be waiting for tomorrow then, unless you call me." He had a mischievous grin on his face as he bent down to hug me. As he let go of me he lingered with a thought.

"Jake, I won't be able to come back tomorrow."

"Fine, but Sarah, you said…"

"I know, Jake, but I can't." I was pleading with him to not even think about kissing me.

He slowly moved away and closed my door for me, but looked sad from my reaction.

My heart was breaking for hurting him. I drove to Sherburn's and went in. Mom and Dad weren't there yet. They probably needed time alone. I was trying to be chipper as I walked in, but I was getting really tired.

Laura gave me a huge hug, "So, there is something wrong with you. I knew you were *wasting away*." She kissed my cheek as she directed me, "The kids are in the house; go ahead. Do you need to rest?"

I gave her a thankful smile and headed to the back door. I walked in without knocking and went through the kitchen. I could hear them all in the living area, so I peeked around the corner at them. Danelle jumped up and hugged me. I hugged her back, "You missed me?"

"We heard."

"What did you hear?"

"You are having surgery on Monday, and that we are all not allowed to let you do anything."

"Like what?"

"No basketball, no volleyball, and especially no water skiing."

"We'll just have to see about that."

"Sarah, you will get us in trouble."

"I wouldn't do that, only if they let me. I am still hosting the dance tomorrow at Tony's, so they can't be that worried."

"It wasn't your parents that came and talked to us."

"Who was it?"

"Your doctor," she leaned into me, "He is so cute."

I looked at her suspiciously so she tried to explain, "He is so nice to me and doesn't pick on me like everyone else."

"You like him?"

"I wouldn't say that, but he is…" She could see by the look on my face that I was enjoying this.

"Danelle." I was so grinning at her. I loved that she liked him. My mind started working it all out. Her birthday was in a month, so she was going to be 16 and he was 18. When is his birthday? Um? This could work; he was innocent enough to wait for her. She was very pretty and would get even better with age. I just wonder if he had any realization of her. I will have to work on that. I get to play matchmaker again. I liked when I got to make other people happy. Now, how was I going to get her to come with me tomorrow?

She pulled me toward the couch, and I noticed Brian and Mykala sitting there. Brian didn't look at me at all, but he did scoot closer to her to make room for Danelle and me. I smiled at Mykala as I sat down. She wasn't as friendly as normal. She seemed almost mad, so I just continued to make my way on the couch between Brian and Danelle. We were just watching a movie, but with how tired I was I knew that if I didn't do something I would fall asleep. I continued to blink and yawn.

"Are you okay?" Danelle was looking at me.

"Yeah, I'm just getting tired. I should probably go."

"Actually, you are supposed to stay 'til your mom and dad get here."

I looked at her not understanding what she was saying. Between her vague look and my head getting foggy I was confused.

"We're supposed to watch over you until they show up. They said something about needing to discuss how they are going to take care of you once you're home."

"If they would ask, I am sure James would come take care of me."

"He's not supposed to come home for another week or so, right?"

"Monday."

"That's a bummer; he's coming home the day you have surgery."

I grimaced.

"That sucks for you."

I laughed a little, "Yes, it does."

I felt Brian's hand move to mine just resting it on top of mine. I smiled because he wanted to show me he cared, but didn't want Mykala to know. I turned my hand over to let him know I understood, and he continued to trace his fingers over mine.

"Well if you are stuck with me for awhile," I squeezed his hand and let go crossing my arms and scooting back.

"Sorry, Mykala and Brian." I watched as he turned to look at her.

She was not happy and said, 'I think I better go?"

I leaned forward to look at her, "Mykala, please stay. I am leaving as soon as my mom and dad get here. I am really tired."

She gave me a little smile. I leaned back and closed my eyes again, "Danelle, can you keep checking for me? I need to rest here for a little bit."

"Yeah, sure." I didn't remember anything after that.

47. A Little Pain

"Sarah…Sarah…you wanted me to wake you when your mom and dad got here."

I opened my eyes. I was curled up in Brian's arms, but Danelle was the one waking me. I blinked a couple of times trying to sit up. Brian was trying to hold me back to stay in his arms. I pushed a little harder to sit up. I needed to go to the trailer to sleep, "Do they know I was sleeping?"

"Yeah, I wasn't supposed to tell them?"

"No, they will just worry more." I tried to push myself up.

Brian moved closer to help me stand, "Sarah, I think I should drive you home."

I was out of it and stood there looking at him. I knew I wasn't driving, so I just nodded, "Did Mykala go home?"

"Yeah, your parents weren't showing up, and you were kind of cuddling into me. She wasn't happy."

"I'm sorry, Brian."

He took my face in his hands lifting my face to look at him in the eyes, "It's okay. Are you okay?" He gave me a gentle smile.

I could hardly keep my eyes open, and I blinked as they stayed shut a little longer than a normal blink, "Yep, just get tired real easily. Jake says my body is working so hard to fight whatever it is, and that I'm going to get more and more tired 'til we get rid of it."

Brian released my face, and I opened my eyes.

Danelle was standing next to me with worry on her face, "He's on his way."

"What? Why?"

"Sarah, you are burning up."

"Oh." I sat back down. I didn't like feeling this weak. Brian was helping me, moving really close to me. Danelle moved to my other side.

"Guys, I am really okay. I was just tired. I am okay now because I slept. I am ready for basketball; does anyone want to play?"

They both were very disgusted with me. I was relieved to see some reinforcements when Laura walked in, but Jake was on her tail.

He looked at me shaking his head, "I thought you were only going to stop for a little bit?"

"I took a nap, Jake. I am okay now. Brian said he would drive me home."

I glared at him to not over react. I think he got it, but still walked over to me and put his hand on my forehead. He raised his eyebrows as he looked at me, and then his eyes softened, "If it's alright with you, Brian, I will follow you and bring you home after we get her settled in."

"Yeah, no problem."

Laura walked over to me, "You are making all of us worry." She kissed my cheek lightly, and I smiled for her.

"I will be better on Monday, right Jake?"

He didn't look at me, and hesitated on answering me.

"Jake! Right?"

"Yeah, let's get you home." Jake leaned down to pick me up, and I shook my head no at him. I pushed myself up and wobbled a little, so both Brian and Jake moved to my sides to help me out the door.

I was protesting, "Guys stop. I was just sleeping. I am fine to walk on my own. Quit babying me." I pushed them both away.

Jake was irritated with me, "Do you have to be so stubborn?" Okay, maybe he was angry.

I didn't care, because I was fine now. I got in my car on the passenger side. I looked at them both and closed the door.

Brian came around my car and got in, "I am getting to drive your car. Do you want to go for a spin?"

I laughed, "Yeah, but I would get you in trouble, so no thanks. I needed to laugh."

He looked at me, "You do feel better?"

"Yes, I just get tired that's all. Sorry about Mykala."

"That's okay. I give her so much attention now it's almost sickening. I think we do it every day now."

"That's more info that I wanted to know."

He chuckled a little shaking his head as we started to drive. I looked back, and Jake's eyes were on me. I was going to have to do this fast.

"Brian, I am talking dad into getting the boat tomorrow. I really, really need to have some fun. I have been in bed for two days, and I can't stand it anymore. I asked dad if I could come get you, so you could drive the boat down to your place, but Brian…will you please let me ski?"

He looked at me, and then back at the road, "I can't do that. If something happened to you, I would never forgive myself."

"Brian, just a couple of little circles close to the dock." I looked at him with the deepest puppy look I could come up with, "Pleeaassee."

"If I agree to it, who would spot us? No one will allow you to go."

"Talk to Danelle; tell her I am going crazy. I really, really need to do this. I am tired of feeling helpless."

"Sarah, I can't agree to this."

"Brian…I will…"

"What are you saying?! You are that desperate that you would…?"

"I don't know. I just really need to do this. I get the feeling that Jake isn't telling me everything, and if something happens on Monday…I just need to do this."

"That is exactly why I can't agree to this, Sarah, if it is really bad…I can't."

"Brian…You can and you will. I am going to pick you up at 9 am. You need to be up. I just want to go a couple of times around, and you are going to help me."

"I am not. You have to wait till you are better."

"Brian, Jake said I could be down for six weeks. The season will be over. Pleeaassee?"

We were pulling into the driveway. He stopped and looked at me in a very stern way, "I can't."

"I will see you at 9 am. You will not refuse to help me, will you?"

He smiled, and I knew I had won. I got out of the car, and started to walk in. It was already dark, so I hurried in and turned on an outside light as Jake pulled in. I hurried to the first room and got changed into sleeping shorts and a t-shirt. I grabbed a light blanket and wrapped it around me as I walked back out. They were talking in the kitchen, and I was happy they were getting along. I sat down on the couch and fluffed a pillow to lay back.

"See, Jake. I am *behaving*."

Jake walked over to me with the thermometer and held it out for me. I took it and put it under my tongue. I was being impatient with it. I was tapping my fingers on the couch waiting. He put out his hand. I gave him mine with my wrist up. He took it, and sat down counting and looking at his watch.

"*Sarah*!" He was trying to get me to stop being impatient.

The thermometer beeped. I took it out and handed it to him. The look on his face showed me he was worried. He was still counting. He finally let go when he was done.

"Brian, you can take my truck because I am staying." He didn't look at me. Shit, this wasn't a good sign.

Brian asked, "She's that bad?"

He turned to Brian, "No not that bad; I just want to wait till her temperature goes down."

He got up to get me some ibuprofen, and some water in the kitchen. I hated that they were talking about me like I was out of it. I am still *fully* aware of everything. I was getting more and more irritated.

I was going to try again with Brian, "Brian?"

He came over to me sitting on the couch. I looked at him very serious, "You can take my car. I won't need it." I leaned to him trying to whisper, "That way Jake can leave when my temp goes down."

He moved back a little looking at me in shock, "Sarah?"

"Brian, promise you will come here at 10 am, and you can take my car."

"You don't want to be alone with him here? Or, do you?"

"Brian, I just want to go skiing tomorrow, and if he knows he won't let me. He needs to go when I am better, so I can go with you tomorrow."

He was still suspicious of what I was asking him.

Jake walked back over to us, "What is she planning?" He was handing me the glass of water and the ibuprofen.

I looked up at him and smiled, "Nothing for my doctor to hear." I was trying to be playful, but Jake was not amused.

"Brian, don't let her talk you into anything. She is very convincing."

"Jake, don't talk about me like I'm not here."

"Sarah, I know how convincing you can be, and I think Brian is smart enough to see through your plotting."

He turned to Brian, "Right?"

Brian looked at me squinting his eyes, "Yeah, she is good at that."

Jake was not going to let me win, any way I looked at it. I sat there quietly and took the ibuprofen with a little huff handing the glass back to Jake. He walked back into the kitchen.

I was going to try again, "Brian, I don't want him to stay. Take my car, so he can have his truck to leave. Meet me at 10 am here, and I won't water ski, but you still get to use my car for the night."

Jake turned and looked at me. I was watching, and waiting for Brian to answer me. He wasn't giving in either. Shit, I don't like this. I always get my way. *Why wasn't this working?* I closed my eyes, and leaned back.

I was going to change the subject a little, "So, do mom and dad think I'm all broke down and weak now?" They weren't answering me. "I actually feel fine, I'm just tired."

I opened my eyes, and they both were gone, *What the hell was going on?* I didn't hear the door. "Jake…Brian…?"

I heard nothing. Did I fall asleep? I got up, and walked to the door to see both vehicles still here. Mom and dad weren't back yet. I didn't fall asleep, so where did they go? Now I was getting mad. They were talking, and I am sure they were talking about me. That is not what I wanted.

I sat down in the chair trying to think of where they could possibly be, "Brian…Jake…?"

Then I heard them in the front bedroom. I got up, and walked quietly down the hallway. They were whispering, so I tried to listen, but I couldn't hear anything. I turned the corner to show them I was there. "What are you two doing?" I smiled to show them they didn't have anything over on me.

"Sarah, what are *you* doing up?" Jake was being very firm with me.

"I feel fine, Jake."

"And your temperature won't go down 'til you rest. Go lay down. We'll be out in a minute."

I stormed out, and grabbed my keys. I didn't want to be here anymore. I rushed out the door. Amazingly their conversation ended very quickly at that point. I got in my car and turned it on. Jake and Brian both came running out. Jake pushed Brian in front of my car so I couldn't pull out.

Jake opened my door, "What the hell do you think you're doing?" He grabbed my arm, "Sarah, I am not playing; get your butt back inside now, and lay down or I will take you to the hospital right now."

He was pulling me from the car; it was still running. He was hanging onto my arm. I looked at Brian confused, and scared, because Jake was really upset and forceful. Brian was shaking his head to let me know not to protest Jake's demand. Jake reached in my car, and grabbed my keys from the ignition throwing them to Brian. "You are not going anywhere, and I can't believe you would act this way. Sarah, this is just…stupid." He let go of me staring into my eyes with fury in his, like he was waiting for me to answer him.

I couldn't answer him because I felt a lump in my throat.

"What, Sarah?"

The tears started to well up. I didn't know what to think, or how to feel other than upset with him. He was being so forceful. It must be worse than what he was telling me.

"Don't try to get out of this by crying. Get back inside and lay down. I am not playing around."

Brian walked to me putting his arm around my shoulders, "Come on Sarah. Let's get you back inside." Brian was guiding me into the trailer.

I looked back at Jake. He wasn't looking at me anymore. He had his hands resting on the top of the car, and his head was down. I kept my eyes on Jake until I was in the trailer. I was looking for anything from him. That really scared me.

Brian was guiding me to the couch, but he was being really careful.

"Brian, what did he tell you?"

"Sarah, I don't think the boat idea will work tomorrow. He said he really didn't know how bad it was, but he made the mistake of not taking you to the hospital on Wednesday. He is so worried that something is going to happen. He feels responsible for letting you hurt yourself. Just for once, Sarah, take it easy till you get this taken care of."

"Fine, I will behave for the night…but at least take me boating tomorrow, even if I can't go stupid water skiing."

"I think he would agree to that, but I wouldn't bring it up to him tonight. He is really upset with himself, and you pushing yourself make him feel worse."

"Thanks Brian." I crawled on the couch and lay down.

He sat beside me and felt my head, "You are really hot."

"It doesn't help when I get upset, Brian. I will be okay. A little sleep will make that better. Are you leaving now?"

"I don't know for sure, because I don't know what he is thinking. Just close your eyes, and I will see you at 10:30 am."

"I said 10 am."

"Sarah, 10:30 am… no earlier."

I laughed slightly. He was trying to be firm with me too.

"Okay."

I rolled to the back of the couch and closed my eyes. He traced his hand over my cheek, "Brian, I really do feel fine right now."

"I know, just try to do what he tells you for the night."

"Night, Brian." I turned to look at him, "Are you taking my car?"

"If you're still okay with it?"

"Yeah, that's fine. I will see you tomorrow."

I turned to the back of couch, and he traced his hand down my back as he got up and walked outside. I heard the car start, and then he drove away. I didn't move; I was trying to get the sleep to come swiftly, so that I wouldn't be tempted to let Jake hold me.

It wasn't quick enough; I heard him come in. I didn't say anything to him. He came and sat down on the couch next to me.

"Sarah?"

"What?"

"I'm sorry, but you just don't know when to stop pushing."

"Sorry."

He traced his hand down the side of me, "Sarah."

No, Jake, no please don't touch me. "What?"

"I should have taken you to the hospital on Wednesday; I was being selfish."

I didn't know what to say. I felt him lay down next to me wrapping his arm around me, and he lifted my face to look at him.

"I wanted more time like this. I liked the way this feels, and I didn't want it to end."

I turned to him, and put my face to his chest. It was too hard to look at him as he was explaining to me about how he felt.

"If I fixed you... I wouldn't get to spend any more time with you. I am sooo sorry, Sarah. You are very sick, and I shouldn't have kept you like this."

He scooted down, and traced my neck with his mouth. I could feel his breath, and I felt comforted. It was so nice to feel someone real next to me, to hold me when I was so confused about my illness, but he wasn't James. I was caring about Jake so much, that I did not want to hurt him. I didn't want to turn him away, but this would crush my sweet amazing man I loved. I held on tight to Jake, and closed my eyes repeating in my head. James I love you so much, please come home now. I have no fight in me anymore, and I need you. I love you and only you. I need this to be you.

Jake traced his face along mine and then his lips touched my cheek lightly; he continued to move over my face with those soft lips, taunting me with his light tender touch. The pain in my heart for hurting James was unbearable as the tears trickled down my face. I couldn't say anything to Jake; I didn't know how or what to say. I didn't want to hurt him, but my heart belonged to James 100%.

I heard Jake whisper, "Sarah, turn around, so I don't kiss you."

I turned around, and closed my eyes as his arms wrapped around me to hold me.

"Jake?"

His mouth moved over my neck to my ear, "Yes."

I swallowed, and tried to say something. I hated that I was allowing this. Please James; know I love you, and I need this to be you holding me here.

Jake's whisper came again, "It's okay Sarah. I know."

I was thankful when I heard mom and dad's truck pull up. Jake was moving away from me, and I turned grabbing his hand in desperation. I wanted to tell him I am sorry. He smiled at me just slightly as he leaned down to kiss my cheek. I turned into his kiss so that my mouth was there for him. I wanted him to kiss me as bad as I didn't.

He hesitated, "You don't want this, and I know that…I know you shouldn't, but please come dance with me tomorrow. I will let you go after that. Not because I want to, but because I have to." He continued to move to me, but only kissed my cheek, and then he walked away from me out of the trailer. My heart was sad, but also rejoicing. I love James and only James with all of my heart.

I heard mom and dad walk in the trailer. Mom came to check on me. She felt my forehead, and I turned to her.

"How are you feeling?"

Other than my heart breaking right now, "Really, I feel good. I was just tired. I will be fine now."

She caressed my cheek, "Goodnight then."

"Night, mom."

I turned to the back of the couch curling up in a ball. I hated being here without James to hold me. I imagined his arms around me with his fingers tracing along my skin on my stomach and the sweet whisper in my ear, "*Baby, I am coming home.*" Sleep came easily with the feel of comfort that I would see James in a few days. I whispered back, "*I am forever yours.*"

48. The Surprise

One more day of my misery down. Brian better be here by 10:30 am. I didn't want dad to have any time to say no. I lay on the couch as long as my body would let me. I finally got up when I heard dad moving around. I went to the first bedroom and closed the door. I got my suit on and took out my note for Day 40:

I worry that this is coming to an end
And this pain is killing me
But it's not over because I will not let you go
I give you all that I have
For my heart is in your hands
Please take care of it for I only have one to share
Your heart aches and I weep
But baby if you will still have me
I am coming home!
I love you more than you know,

James.

I put it to my heart. I knew he was going to be home in two days. I couldn't wait to wrap my arms around him. I kissed the note and smiled. I opened the door and went out to have breakfast with Dad.

He smiled at me as I walked out, "Are you feeling better?"

"Yep, I slept. I am ready for my last dance for awhile."

"What do you want for breakfast?"

"I don't care, anything. I will be good with a bowl of cereal, if you don't feel like cooking."

"You are so easy. We should keep you sick all the time."

"Hey, that's not nice."

"Well, you definitely have enough people looking after you. We know where you are all the time, even if you don't tell us. I am kind of enjoying this."

"Dad, be nice."

"So, you let Brian take your car last night?"

"Yeah, Jake stayed with me for awhile. I think 'til you got home."

"See Sarah, boys should go home at night, and not stay here with you all night, like James does."

"Dad, don't start."

"I see you are wearing the ring."

"Yep, but it will go back on the necklace when he gets home. I have needed some comforting over the last few days, and it makes me feel like he is here to protect me, like it was before he left."

"Well, just to let you know. I don't approve of it at all."

"Great, dad, I didn't need to hear that today."

"So, still planning on going on the boat today?"

"Yes, if it's okay with you."

He was smiling again, "I really like you this way."

"What way?"

"You're asking instead of demanding."

"So, is that a yes or a no?"

"When are you going?"

"Brian is going to be here at 10:30 am. I want to go early, so I can rest for tonight."

"How long will you be?"

"Well, by the time we get down to the dock it will be 11 am, so I really don't want to be down there for more than an hour. Is that okay with you?"

He laughed, "You are doing it again."

"What?"

"Asking."

I shook my head in disbelief.

"Yes, fine."

"Can I sleep in James's room before the dance? He's not here, and I could sleep in a real bed. I didn't sleep great last night."

"Yes, but call me when you get there, and I want Tony to check on you."

I smile; this was going easier than I thought. I didn't do my hair or makeup. I just pulled it back into a pony tail, and lay back down 'til I heard my car.

"Dad, will you please bring the boat to the launch?"

"I am really enjoying this. Remember this when you are better."

I rolled my eyes again and went out the door to greet Brian. Mykala was with him. I walked over and hugged her first and then Brian, "I see you got stuck with Sarah duty too."

She chuckled and smiled at me.

We followed dad to the launch. I let Brian drive, and I sat in the back seat. It was only fitting for Mykala to have the front seat, being with Brian and everything. We got the boat off the trailer. Mykala was getting in the boat with Brian.

"Mykala, I'm not supposed to wear myself out, so would you mind riding with me and actually driving me?"

"What?"

"I could use the help."

I needed to apologize to her about last night. She smiled and came back to me. I gave her my keys. She ran out into the water, and said something to Brian. He kissed her ever so lightly, and then looked at me. I turned away to let them have a private moment. I got in the passenger side as I watched dad drive off waving at me. I waved back.

"Mykala jumped in my car, "I can't believe you are letting me drive your car."

"Mykala, that wasn't the real reason I asked you to drive me."

"Why, what's up?"

"I wanted to say I was sorry about last night. I didn't mean to interrupt you."

"That's okay. We do it every day, so one day without it isn't going to kill me."

I know it was killing me to not have James. Did she really love him? I felt bad that they might be together and not be in love. That would not be a good situation. She drove us down to Sherburn's. We didn't talk 'til she put it in park.

"Thanks for thinking about me enough to say you were sorry. Most people wouldn't care enough to do that."

"Mykala, I am happy you are with Brian. He is really great once you spend a little time with him."

"Yeah, but if you feel that way, why aren't you with him?"

"Because... I have James; I *love* James."

She was really beaming now. I think she understood.

We got out of the car, and Mykala went down to the dock while I went in to get Danelle. I found Paul at the bar. He directed me to the house, so I went up the stairs to find Danelle still sleeping. I sat down on the couch and touched her arm, "Danelle, I only have an hour. Are you coming down?"

She opened her eyes, "You're supposed to be resting."

I smiled at her, "That is why I only have an hour."

I was pulling her up. At least there were four of us, and I wouldn't be the third wheel. She was crawling to get up. Now I was happy.

I went down to the dock. Brian and Mykala where cuddling in the boat waiting for us. I definitely was the third wheel.

I tried to make light conversation, "So, who's first?"

Brian didn't look at me, "Since you can't drive or water ski, neither of us gets to go."

"Brian, if you want to water ski, right now is the best time. I feel the best in the morning, and I haven't done anything that would wear me out yet."

He looked at me with doubt. He whispered something in Mykala's ear and then released her. I sat in the driver's seat looking at him. He sat down in the seat across from me, "Jake told me you would do this."

"Do what?"

"You are trying to do stuff you really shouldn't be doing."

"Do you want to go or not?"

He looked at me as a smile came over his face, "You really feel fine?"

I smiled because I knew I had won. Put a mark under Sarah for another point for me. I got up and went to help get everything out.

He stopped me and sat me back down, "Sarah, you're not supposed to do anything that will wear you out. I will get it ready."

I was halfway there to getting my way. I think he had Mykala here, so that it wouldn't be so easy for him to give into me, but so far I was getting my way.

Danelle came down, "What are you doing, Brian? You know that..." she glanced at me, so I smiled at her.

"I feel really good right now, and we won't get to do this the rest of the summer. Besides, I forced him." I looked at Brian and he was smiling like this was the best news yet.

She got in the boat and sat across from me.

"Danelle, do you want to drive?"

"NO!"

"But, I can sit behind you and tell you how to do everything."

"I don't think so."

"I'll get him up, and you can take over."

She was thinking I was plotting, but I really wasn't. I was thinking more that I wouldn't be doing what I promised not to."

Brian was ready and gave me thumbs up. I gunned it and took it around once and looked at Danelle. She shook her head at me. I brought him by the dock, and he dropped a ski. Now was the fun part. I took it back out and made waves with the boat and gave him a really good jump. It was great. He really knew how to get air with the jumps. I went around again and gave him another jump.

Mykala turned to me, "I didn't know he could do that?"

I laughed and turned to do it again, and he did two jumps one right after the other. He was really smiling now.

"Last time you weren't watching him. He is so good at this."

I turned the boat to make another wave and then another jump. I was thinking, *Brian you owe me.* He waved me in. I brought him by the dock. He let go and rode the ski all the way to the beach. I have never been able to do that.

I turned to bring the boat back to the dock, and he helped pull us in. I got up and grabbed my wet suit and started putting it on.

Danelle came over to me, "You are not going."

"Okay."

"Then why are you putting the wet suit on?"

"…because, I *am* going… just two little circles, nothing crazy, no jumps. I will stay on two skis and …and…Danelle, please. I just need a little to get me through. I haven't gone in a long time, and the rest of the summer is out for me."

"It's not up to me. You will have to get him to drive you."

I looked at Mykala, "Please help me. Make him say *yes*, please."

She was smiling, "You think I could talk him into letting you do this?"

"I know you can."

"I am not asking him; he will get mad at me."

I squinted my eyes at her, and yep I had to do it, "You will have to forgive me then."

I got out of the boat, and grabbed the ski's bringing them to the end of the dock. I looked at Brian.

"No way, Sarah, I have already let you get by with driving. I am not doing it."

"Brian, you owe me. I just gave you a great ride, and you know it."

"No." He looked over at Mykala to help him, "I can't, Sarah."

I moved closer to him, and put my arms around his waist looking into his face. I was talking to him very quietly, "Brian, two little circles right in front of the dock." I stood on my tippy toes, "Pleeaassee?"

"Fine, but only two little circles."

"You know it's my own fault. I will admit to everyone I didn't give you a choice."

"I didn't think you would resort to this." He looked down at me holding him.

I smiled, "You didn't give me any other options." I let go of him, sitting down on the end of the dock putting on the skis, "You're pulling me from the dock. I'll use less energy if I don't have to balance myself in the water."

"Sarah, I can't do this."

"Brian, get in the boat. Hurry up; I am almost out of time."

"You're getting tired?"

"No, Brian. I promised I would go rest at noon."

He got in the boat and started moving it to get it ready to take off. I gave him thumbs up. He took off and went straight out. He was turning the boat to start the circle. I was in heaven with no pain and no sickness. I had the thrill of adrenaline. Oh, how I missed this. He was keeping it close to shore, and we circled to take our first pass by the dock.

I noticed there was someone walking down the dock. My heart dropped at the same time as it leapt from my chest. He was walking down the dock taking his shirt off and laid it on the bench.

Is that…? Shit. We were making the pass about 100 yards from the end of the dock. I let go. He dove off the dock. I let the water rush into me. I was struggling to get the skis off and tucked them under my arms. How was I going to explain this? Shit…shit…I was trying to swim to him quickly, but I was shaking so badly. I couldn't control the emotions. The tears were coming so fast, and they started spilling right away. Oh, I was going to pay for this.

He finally got to me, grabbing the skis from me, tucking them under his arms and trying to hold me at the same time. I could hardly breathe, and I didn't know what to say. I just stared at him desperately wondering what I was supposed to do. He touched my face, so I leaned into his touch and closed my eyes. He wiped the tears with his thumbs. He pulled me to him wrapping his arm around my waist. He was taking my breath completely away just looking at me that way. I couldn't take my eyes off of him. I was looking to him to see what was next. I wrapped my legs around his waist and arms around his neck and pulled as close to him as I could. Our lips were almost touching. I was staring into his eyes and melting. The trembling was over whelming.

"Sarah."

I closed my eyes because the feelings were too much. I couldn't handle this.

"Sarah, please look at me."

I opened my eyes, and I was completely gone. The tears were streaming down my cheeks. He kissed me softly at first, but then the passion took over. I kissed him with everything I had left in me. I wrapped my hands in his hair to hold him to me to never let him go. I wanted him right here and now, and nothing else mattered.

"James?" I mouthed to him.

"I know. I love you too."

He was trying to hold on to the skis, but yet hold me and touch me all at the same time. I had to let go to keep from going under with him.

He smiled slightly, "Surprise!"

I was all over him again, kissing every inch of his face until I found his lips again. Oh, the kissing; I was so lost. I could stay here for the rest of my life.

"Sarah…you have to…*stop*… can't breathe."

I stopped and looked at him with surprise. He smiled and then went back to passionately kissing me more. My breath was lost. I was gasping for air, but I wanted it to never stop. He quit kissing me to pull me to his body, so he could hold me tightly. I was trembling so badly, but I wrapped my arms around him and held on for dear life. I didn't want to let him go ever again.

My left hand was near his face. I didn't plan it that way, but he glanced over at it as his mouth turned up in delight, "You are wearing my ring?

I released him enough to gaze into his eyes.

"You are mine?" The tears were streaming down his face.

"Yes, James. *I'm forever yours.*"

His kiss came deeper and more passionately than I could ever imagine.

I knew at this very moment that I was in love; I knew I was going to be okay, and that my James was home to take care of me…

Characters

Sarah Sullivan	
Paula Sullivan	Mom
Tucker Sullivan	Dad
James Swanson	Sarah's Boyfriend
Carl Swanson	James Dad
Clarissa Swanson	James Mom
Will Swanson	James Brother 2nd oldest
Sam Swanson	James Brother 3rd
Tamara	James Sister youngest
Katherine	James Betrothed
Amelia	Sam's Betrothed
Jake Phallen	Doctor Friend of Clarissa's
Wilson Phallen	Clarissa's Houseman
Josie Phallen	Wilson's Wife/ Jake's Mom
Danelle Turner	Sarah's Best Friend
Laura Turner	Danelle's Mom
Paul Turner	Danelle's Dad
Brian Turner	Danelle's Older Brother
Jason Gasser	Tucker's 2nd Employee
Kylie	Jason's Girlfriend
Karla	James's so called Girlfriend
Tony	Tavern Owner
Sandi & Kate	Sarah's Dance Helpers
Dr. Justin	Sarah's First female Doctor
Mykala	Brian's Girlfriend
Pat Hanson	Friend of Brian's
Matt Erickson	Friend of Sarah's
Tommy	Brian's Friend
Allen Kreaton	Sarah's boss at the dealership

Upcoming Sequel- Growing Tears

1. Surprise

Where do we go from here? I wanted him for the rest of my life and I knew, at least I thought I knew, he wanted me for the rest of his life. The look in his eyes was still so sad. I love him. I hoped he saw that in mine. I put one of my hands on his face. He was thinner, but felt real. I was still wrapped around him, but couldn't stop looking at him.

Today wasn't Monday, it was Saturday and he came home to me because I needed him. The kissing resumed, the deepest kiss we could have without being in each others skin.

"Hey, guys!" Shit, Brian why are you interrupting this. I have wanted this so bad; why can't you just leave us alone? James broke the kiss to look up at Brian.

"You might not want to keep her in the water very long."

James looked at me and smiled, "Why?"

"Um, she gets really weak and you wouldn't want her to fall asleep in the water."

His gaze turned to sadness as I watched his face change.

I couldn't take my eyes off of him, even though the sadness was not what I wanted to see, "Brian, James is here now. I will be okay."

My James smiled at me. I was in heaven.

"No, James. I'm not kidding; we need to get her out of the water."

He took his eyes off of me, no I didn't want that. Come back to me here.

"Brian, here I will lift her to you." He was pushing me out of the water.

I didn't want to let go of him.

"Sarah, I will be right there. Its okay, let go. I will be right with you. Just get in the boat."

I let go of him, but I did not want to. Brian took my hands and pulled me to the boat sitting on the side of it. He was pulling me in, Mykala wrapped a towel around me, and Danelle put her arm around my shoulder. I didn't take my eyes off of James. He handed a ski to Brian, and then the other one. I went back to pull the rope in. He came up to the side of the boat with one swift movement pulling him self in. He moved to the front with Brian and they were talking. I didn't want anyone else to have my James; he was mine. Well, at least he was looking at me. I didn't want the girls fussing with me.

James:

I couldn't take my eyes off of her, but wanted to know why they were being so protective of her. I new she had gotten weaker. She did look so thin, but she looked good to me. I wanted to touch her and kiss her till there was no tomorrow. I was standing in the front with Brian.

"So, why was she water skiing?" I wasn't looking at him at all.

"She is very persuasive."

I smiled. She did have that way about her.

"You tried to kiss her. So, I guess I am supposed to punch you now?" I was completely smiling at my sweet Sarah. I had no intentions of hitting him. I just wanted to scare him a little.

"I wasn't the only one and I don't know how you do it?"

He caught my attention so I looked at him, "What do you mean?"

He looked very uneasy, but was trying to find his words, "If I was alone with her I wouldn't…"

I couldn't help remembering touching her face softly and then… "I take a lot of cold showers and she lets me do this."

I was smiling at my sweet Sarah and went to her to hold her. She was so beautiful, I didn't know if I could keep my hands off of her. Danelle and this other girl were wiping her off. Was she really this weak? She didn't feel weak; she had strength to hold on to me. I liked when she was aggressive and I am totally turned on. I shoed them away, so I could put my arms around her.

"Do you want help with the wet suit?" I started to unzip it.

She looked at me like she wanted me to take over taking care of her. Her hands traced my arms. I slowly unzipped the suit to help her out of it. She slipped it off her arms. I was so hurt to see her there was nothing left. She was so thin and frail. I felt so bad that she had gotten this bad in the little time that I had not seen her. She started putting it back on. She knew I wasn't pleased.

"Sarah, its okay, I am here now"

I helped her take it off the rest of the way. I wrapped the towel around her. Danelle was up by Brian and the other girl. I noticed how cute she was. She was angry with me as I looked at her. I was afraid she was pissed, but that is what I liked about her. She didn't put up with any bull shit. I turned my sweet Sarah away from me and put my arms around her, and sat down on the back seat to hold her. I looked at Danelle, she was so angry I couldn't help but feel I had to say something. She came back by us and helped cover Sarah more. I put my hand on the top of her head. "Its okay now, I will take care of her."

I looked at my sweet Sarah, and she was just staring at me. I wanted to kiss her more. I touched her face, and she closed her eyes pushing her face to my hand. I wanted to take her away from everything and just make her better.

Brian drove the boat in to the dock. I looked around, but I could tell the only thing she was thinking was the shock of me coming home. I was so happy to fill the need. I wanted this so bad for so many days. I held her closer to me and kissed her cheek. Then I brought her hand with my ring on it to my mouth. She had made me so happy. She wanted to be with me. I kissed every finger looking at her as I did this. She smiled that precious sweet smile that I couldn't resist. I turned her hand over to kiss her palm. She traced her thumb over my face as I did this. She was happy. I loved to see the passion in her eyes. The engine was cut and the boat glided toward the dock.

I had to push her away to help.

"No, James."

I looked at her. The devastation in her eyes saddened me.

"Its okay Sarah, I'm not leaving just helping. You are leaving with me. I will not go with out you."

She seemed to ease a little, but the tears in her eyes were welling up. I had a hard time letting her go. I kissed her forehead and sat her back down. I grabbed for the dock. I jumped out and secured it to the dock. Danelle and Mykala were helping her stand up and step on the seat and then on the side.

I grabbed her from them, "Do you want to get dressed?"

She wasn't saying a whole lot. It was making me nervous. Danelle got out and took Sarah to the beach and get her things out.

I turned on Brian, "She is that bad?"

He looked at me surprised that I didn't know. He looked away, "Let's see. She has been with us about an hour and a half, but she went skiing so you might have about a half hour and she will need to sleep."

My heart was breaking, "Two hours?"

"Yeah, that's about all she can do, and then the sleeping, the deep sleeping. No response, nothing, so I would get her to where you're going pretty quickly."

I felt horrible. I couldn't believe that my dreams were so off. I had no idea. We stay awake longer than that on the phone. They just didn't know my Sarah. She couldn't be that bad. Danelle was helping her dress as I looked at her. She was looking at me, maybe to make sure I wasn't leaving without her.

Brian spoke to me again, "James, get going. She will need to rest. She has the dance tonight and she will need to sleep at least 3 hours or she won't be able to get through the night."

"Then she won't do it." I was angry. If she needed to rest then I wasn't going to let her dance.

"James, that is how she got by without you here. She has a commitment and she will want to do it. She is very persuasive."

I smiled because he was right. She was *very* persuasive. I looked at her as I walked to her.

I took her bag keeping my eyes locked on hers, "Are you ready?"

She smiled. Oh how I loved that smile. I started walking up the hill with my arm around her. She seemed so okay. She was smiling and walking with me. She even had an upbeat in her step, but she was so thin. Every rib showed and her hipbones did stick out a little.

I turned to Brian and Danelle, "Thank you. She will see you tonight."

I turned back to look at my Sarah, but said to them, "She's mine now."

The smile on her face melted every inch of me.

Sarah:

I couldn't stop looking at my James. He was so much my protector and he was here to take care of me now. I would follow him to the end of the world if that is what he asked me to do right now. We walked out to his bike. I panicked as I stared at him. I was scared to ride. I was getting tired.

"Can you ride to Tony's with me?"

I knew I couldn't drive, because I was getting tired. I looked at him and then at my car.

"Sarah, if you can't ride we can take your car."

I loved to ride. I told myself I can do this.

I smiled, "Yeah, I'm fine."

I wasn't really fine. I needed to sleep, but James was here and I wanted to be with him.

"Do we need to go to the trailer?"

I smiled with guilt on my face, "Nope."

"Don't you need to get your stuff and check in?" He looked so worried, but I couldn't have planned this any better.

"I do have to check in, but I brought my stuff to your place yesterday. I was going to sleep really good in your room and take a shower for tonight."

The smile on his face was amazing, "Did you know?"

"Know what?"

"Know I was coming home? I wanted it to be a surprise."

"It was, I didn't know." I smiled.

He got on the bike, but I was hesitant. I could make it to Tony's because I have my James. I could do this. I got on the back and put my arms around his waist, "OH, how I missed this." He pulled my arms tighter turning a little and kissed my lips softly. He let my lips go, but looked at me, "Are you sure your okay to ride?"

I smiled, "Just to Tony's okay?"

"Yes."

He started to drive. I was kissing his back and holding him so tight. We turned off the lake drive onto the highway. I moved my hands under his shirt tracing his stomach and his chest, and I was still kissing his back. I was getting tired so I closed my eyes. I moved my hands to his thighs and squeezed them and moved them closer to him. He was pulling over and stopped.

"Come here little girl. You have got me so hot." He was pulling me from behind him to the front of him so I was facing him. My legs laid over his, and the kiss came so deep so passionate. He held my face in his hands, but he was standing now, "Are you sure you're okay?"

I looked at him, and the desire was building in me. I wanted to feel every inch of him next to me so I just nodded.

He tilted me back to lie across the tank and traced his hands up the front of me. I closed my eyes because his touch was what I desired. My heart was beating so hard and my chest was heaving to breath. His mouth came to my chest and he kissed it so luring. He was getting worked up and the heat was building. He pulled me to him and wrapped one hand around my waist to my back and pulled me to him to feel his desire for me. I gasped when I felt him hard and ready. The kiss was so deep, and I was getting so lost. I needed to sleep right now. I released the kiss and put my face to his chest.

"Sarah, you are not okay."

I shook my head no. I couldn't look at him. I wanted to feel him so bad, but the sleep was coming and I couldn't keep going.

He lifted my face, "Sarah?"

I opened my eyes and looked at him, but I was done.

"Shit, they weren't kidding."

I closed my eyes and wrapped my arms around his chest and put my head down on him. I felt him just holding me.

His chest seemed to be hurting, "Okay, baby, it's okay. I will get you to Tony's."

I held on, but felt him holding me in front of him. I couldn't move behind him because I wouldn't be able to hold on.

We pulled into Tony's. He stopped and pulled my face up so he could see me, "Sarah?"

I opened my eyes and smiled at him, "Its okay James, I took a nap."

He was breathing so hard, "You scared the crap out of me, what the hell was that?"

"James, I just get tired."

His face was so sad because it hurt him letting him see me like this. But I was going to be better now that he was home. I smiled at him to show him I was doing better. He rested his forehead on mine. I heard someone walking out of Tony's, but I didn't have the strength to look.

James move to look, "So, you must be Jake?"

I looked at Jake and smiled, "Jake, this is my James; James, this is my Jake. I mean my doc, Jake."

James looked at me, "Sarah, are you okay to get up?"

I smiled at him and he pulled me off the bike, but still holding me. He was moving to Jake, "Nice to finally meet the man who was taking care of all of my Sarah's needs."

He was extending his hand, but I didn't like what he said. I let go of James, "James, be nice. He was and is still taking care of me and you best be nice Mr. or...."

He turned to me and kissed my forehead, "I'm sorry, and you'll what? I don't think you can do anything; not in your condition."

He was still extending his hand to Jake. Jake shook it as James leaned into him, "Sorry man, just a little jealous. I really do appreciate all you have done for..." He turned to kiss my forehead again, "...my sweet Sarah." He looked at me and took my face in his hands, lifting me to look at him, "Are you okay? I'll go up stairs and take a shower...." He whispered in my ear, "cold shower" and then he was louder again, "So you can have a minute to talk to Jake."

I smiled at him, "Yeah, I'm okay."

James kissed my lips, but soft and light and grabbed a bag from his bike and ran up the stairs.

I looked at Jake, but I was in need if sitting down. I started to walk to the steps. Jake was looking at me and I could tell by the look on his face that he knew what was coming, "Suppose our dancing is off?"

"No, Jake, the dance is not off. I still want to dance with you." I was trying to sit down on the step, "I just need to sleep first."

"But, he is here."

"Jake, he is very understanding. He knows you held me, and he knows you gave me what I needed. Like he said… he was jealous, but he understands you have been there for me and he respects that."

Jake smiled at me. He walked over to where I was sitting and he bent down and kissed me right on the lips, "Sarah, just wait. Don't go up there. Don't be with him, just wait. Please."

"Jake, I am not going up there to be with him. We're supposed to wait till I am 18. I just need to lie down." I was leaning my head on the post at the bottom of the steps.

Jake felt my forehead, "Sarah, you are burning up?"

I looked at him. I was almost completely gone.

"Sarah, you are not okay?"

I shook my head no.

He picked me up and started walking up the stairs to James.

James came out the door in a towel, "What happen?"

"What were you two doing? She shouldn't be doing anything?"

"When I found her she was water skiing."

Jake:

"She promised me she wouldn't do any activities. James get out of the way. Shit what the hell. She new it was absolutely a no for her."

I laid her on the bed she was burning up. I looked at him, "James, I can't give her ibuprofen when she's sleeping she needs to cool down now. Couldn't you tell she was burning up?"

"Yeah… no... I don't know... I was just happy to..."

I couldn't even look at him. I went to the bathroom and turned on the water. I made it semi warm, but maybe a little cooler. James was carrying her into the bathroom. He walked into the shower with her. He was crying so I couldn't watch.

"James, just till she is awake enough to take the pill."

He sat down holding her. I had to leave. I stood out of the bathroom just listening for them to need me. He was pleading with her to wake up; the tears in my eyes were coming. I wanted to be there to hold her to make her feel better and I couldn't it was him that she wanted.

He sounded a little excited, "Sarah, that's it baby come back to me. Sarah, Sarah, open your eyes and look at me now. That's it Sarah, I will have to leave. Sarah, Jake needs you to take something. Keep those eyes open or I am leaving. Jake come get her."

I moved around the corner as soon as he said my name. I picked her up from his arms and carried her back to the bed.

"Jake, its okay. James is home to take care of me now. You don't have to worry anymore."

"Sarah, Stay awake. James said he'll leave again. Don't you dare. Sarah! Fight this; you need to take these."

I was putting them in her mouth and giving her a sip of water, "Sarah you have to swallow or these wont help."

His strong voice came from behind me, "Sarah, I will have to leave."

She opened her eyes again and swallowed them. I laid her back down. She curled into me and I backed away.

I couldn't look at him, "James, she will be better in a little bit, but you need to be here to hold her. It helps her fight what ever this crap is. Just…"

I grabbed the glass of water and sat it on the sink.

"You love her."

I couldn't believe he was saying or asking me that.

"I know you do. I felt it. I feel what she feels."

"Yeah, and you do some shit that is out there. You could help her." I turned to look at him. He looked as bad as I felt. "She says you give her your soul. That helps the most."

"She told you?"

"James, I was holding her… in this state once. When you did it."

He just stared at me. I don't think he knew what to say.

"James, if you can. Please do that; it helps her the most."

I couldn't stay to watch; I had to leave. I went out and went down to Tony's. I would check in a half hour to see if she was better.

James:

I wanted to know what it looked like when I did that. He saw what I did to my sweet Sarah, but I have never seen it. I hovered over her looking at her. I usually closed my eyes to concentrate on passing through her, but this time I just wanted to watch her. I was thinking very hard on doing this. I was trying very hard to make this happen. I have never been this close to her when I did this. I stared at her harder, and she gasped as her body arched for only a couple seconds, and then she relaxed. Oh shit, that wasn't what I was expecting. Jake saw that? I moved away from her. She moved to curl into me. I was so happy. She was responding. I touched her face she pushed to my hand.

I kissed her hand she smiled, "Sarah, I love you."

"James... I love this, but I need you for real."

"Sarah, open your eyes."

She looked at me, "James. You seem so real. I love you, but I am so tired right now." She closed her eyes.

I couldn't handle this. It is tearing me apart. I moved closer to her and lifted her to me to hold her. I kissed her forehead, traced my hands down her arms, and touched the lower of her back. I had no idea she had gotten this bad. She should have gone in a long time ago. No wonder my... Clarissa sent someone to watch over her. She was amazing to look at so peaceful. I scooted down to be closer to her. I kissed her lips, and she was kissing me back. I released her lips to let her sleep. I closed my eyes to sleep with her.

I heard a knock on the door. I tried not to move her, so she would still sleep. I went to the door. It was Jake again. I opened the door for him to go to her to check her.

He felt her forehead and glanced at me, "Did you do what I asked you to do?"

Shit it didn't help, "Yes, I did, why what's wrong?"

"Come here and feel her. She is getting better again."

I walked over and felt her forehead and looked at him. He took her wrist and was watching his watch. I couldn't take my eyes from him, because I knew he was here to help her, but I hated him with a passion. He wanted my Sarah and she cared for him. This was not going to be easy.

"You know she loves you?"

I was happy he knew this, "I kind of hope so."

"When I held her she didn't look at me. She wanted it to be you."

The tears were coming to me. I love her so much. I needed to hear that. I wanted to break down and fall apart.

"We used you to get her to respond to us. We threatened her with you, but it kept her fighting harder. I am afraid she won't fight as hard with you here. She thinks everything is going to be okay, because you being here is going to fix everything."

I closed my eyes, was he telling me she would be better if I left.

"James, all I am saying is you have to keep a close eye on her until Monday. We will find out what it is and get rid of it."

I kept my eyes on her, but asked, "It is her appendix then?"

"Well, I am pretty sure it is, but she said you felt the spreading, and that's the part I don't understand. I won't know for sure until I open her up and look what is going on inside."

I moved around the bed and laid down so my face was near her stomach. I looked up at him, "Do you want to know exactly where it is?"

He was torn. Like he didn't know if he could watch what I was going to do.

He sat down on the other side of Sarah, on the bed.

"You can really tell me that?"

"I feel what she feels, but it's more than what she feels. I am tuned into it, so I can pin point it."

I laid my face on her stomach.

Jake pulled her back to lay on her back so she wasn't curled up.

I moved over her a little more and touched her stomach to feel it. I lifted my face and looked at him, "It's coming from there."

I kept my hand on the spot.

He put his hands were mine were and I moved away from touching her.

He put both hands; finger tips to the spot and felt around, "It has to be her appendix's feel this."

I put my hands where his were, but he pushed my fingers down and I could feel a hard lump.

"See, it's really enlarged." He let go of pushing my fingers into her stomach.

I looked at him, "What is all this then?"

He looked at me confused, "What?"

I traced my hand, "It's spreading, and it's worse than it has ever been. I feel it here." I moved to show him everywhere where I felt it, "All of this area."

"That is the part I don't get."

He looked at me, and I could tell he wasn't happy that he didn't understand. I took her hand and put it to my face and kissed it.

"I will let her sleep longer. She is pretty determined to dance tonight. She will wake up in about and hour looking and acting fine. Don't be alarmed by it. Just keep a close eye on her, okay."

"Where are you going?"

"I will be there tonight. I kind of took your place bartending. It's yours when you want it back, but keep a close eye on her."

"Of course, but she shouldn't dance tonight?"

"Well, I guess that's up to you and her, but she will win."

"Why are you so sure?"

"UM, just a hunch. Do you want me to check her before she goes down?"

"Yes, of course."

"I will be back by 4:00 pm. Try to keep her resting until then."

"You got it, and Jake... I maybe jealous of your time with her, but I really am thankful. I do love her and would do anything for her."

"I get it."

He turned to walk out. I gazed at my Sarah and curled up to her to hold her. I rested my face to hers and closed my eyes.

Forever Yours	**Book 1**
Wasting Away	**Book 2**
Growing Tears	**Book 3**
A New Beginning	**Book 4**

Melissa M. Marlow
Web Pages- or leave a comment.
http://home.comcast.net/~mmmarlow/site/
Book email is: mmmarlow@comcast.net